D0994423

By Kate Ellis

KATE ELLIS

Playing with Bones

PIATKUS

PIATKUS

First published in Great Britain in 2009 by Piatkus
This paperback edition published in 2023 by Piatkus

1 3 5 7 9 10 8 6 4 2

A CIP catalogue record for this book
is available from the British Library.

ISBN 978-0-349-43491-9

Typeset in Baskerville by M Rules
Printed and bound in Great Britain by Clays Ltd, Elcograf S.p.A

Papers used by Piatkus are from well-managed forests
and other responsible sources.

MIX
Paper from
responsible sources
FSC® C104740

Piatkus
An imprint of
Little, Brown Book Group
Carmelite House
50 Victoria Embankment
London EC4Y 0DZ

An Hachette UK Company
www.hachette.co.uk

www.littlebrown.co.uk

For Olly

Chapter 1

The girl raised her hands in a feeble attempt to save her life.

Everything was fading now and the old gas lamp loomed in and out of focus as she tried in vain to push away the thing that was gripping her throat.

Unexpected thoughts ran through her mind as she struggled: that her expensive new shoes would be ruined by scraping against the hard pavement; that her attacker smelled of cheap aftershave. The important events in the girl's short life didn't flash before her as she'd expected. Only the irrelevancies. The small details.

She felt herself losing the fight and, as the cathedral clock struck two, she sank to her knees, her fluttering fingers plucking at the soft silk tightening around her neck.

Once she'd slumped to the ground like a discarded toy, the killer went to work with the knife, leaving the wound on her small, bare foot glistening like raw meat in the glow of the street lamp. Then slowly, almost lovingly, he placed the doll beside her body, like a parent placing a favourite plaything in a sleeping child's bed.

He raised his head to look around the silent close and when he spotted a child's pale face staring down at him from the upstairs window, her eyes meeting his in silent accusation, his body began to shake.

Joe Plantagenet had had a restless night and at six in the morning, with the light peeping through the blinds, he'd decided to get up and have an early breakfast of croissants and coffee. He had bought the croissants as a treat for himself because Maddy was away. But somehow they didn't make him feel any better.

Suddenly the telephone on the sideboard shattered the drowsy silence. Joe picked it up and fumbled for the button that would stop its insistent noise. A glance at the clock told him it was six forty-five and he knew there was only one reason why someone would ring him so early. It was the hour for bad news.

He heard DS Sunny Porter's voice on the other end of the line, annoyingly alert. Perhaps he was a naturally early riser, Joe thought as he drained his coffee cup.

It was too early in the day for pleasantries and he was grateful when Sunny came straight to the point. 'Body's been found in Singmass Close off Gallowgate, sir. Young woman. Milkman found her lying on the pavement – shock made him drop two bottles of semi-skimmed. Doc says it looks like strangulation but she won't commit herself till the post-mortem.'

Joe suddenly felt wide awake. 'She never does. Any ID?'

'Yeah. Her handbag was found under her body so we can rule out a mugging gone wrong. According to a young person's ID card she's a Karen Strange . . . address in Bacombe.'

Joe sighed and closed his eyes. His shoulder had begun to ache. The site of the gunshot wound he'd sustained in Liverpool nine years before – when, as a new DC, he'd been summoned with his sergeant, Kevin Hennessy, to a routine job which turned out to be anything but – still gave him trouble, especially at times of stress. Kevin had been fatally wounded but Joe had survived feeling a confusing mix of guilt and gratitude. 'How old is . . . was . . .'

'Nowt but a lass . . . about eighteen or thereabouts. Terrible,' Sunny added quietly. There were many in CID who thought Sunny Porter was as hard as nails. But, after working with him for five years, Joe knew otherwise.

Joe glanced at the empty kitchen stool by his side. Maddy was down in London. But she hadn't stayed overnight at his flat for the past fortnight – not since the night she had bared her soul to him, offered the ultimate commitment. The night he'd taken her hands in his and told her as gently as he could that he didn't feel ready for marriage. After all, they'd been together for less than a year, having met when Joe had saved the life of her colleague at the Archaeology Centre. Although Joe had great affection for Maddy, there were times when he'd felt that wasn't enough – that the spark that had been there with his wife Kaitlin who'd died so soon after their marriage, was missing. At the age of twenty-two Joe had given up his calling to the priesthood for Kaitlin; and he'd have given his life for her. Perhaps he'd always known in his heart that Maddy couldn't take her place.

A few days after Joe had let her down gently, Maddy had dropped her bombshell – the irresistible job in London, too good an opportunity to miss. She had travelled down by train yesterday for the interview and was staying with old university friends for a few days. When he'd seen her off at the station, he had been careful not to offer an opinion on her possible move. It was her decision, after all. But he'd found her departure unsettling and the thought of it nagged away in the back of his mind like a dull headache. Perhaps the old song was right – you don't know what you've got till it's gone.

He heard Sunny's voice again. 'You still there, sir?'

Joe scratched his head. 'Sorry, Sunny. I suppose I'm needed at the crime scene,' he said. He still wasn't dressed but perhaps a shower would wake him up.

Sunny's reply was predictable. Detective Inspector Plantagenet was needed ASAP. It was obviously murder and the wheels had already been set in motion. Madam – as Sunny habitually called DCI Emily Thwaite behind her back – had issued her orders. And Emily wasn't a woman who took no for an answer.

Joe slid off the stool, ready to make for the bathroom. But just as he was about to put the phone down, Sunny spoke again.

'It's a strange one, this. Really weird.'

Something in Sunny's voice made Joe's heart beat a little faster. 'How do you mean?'

'Well, there was this doll beside the body and . . .'

'And what?' Joe wished he'd get to the point.

'You'll have to see for yourself, boss. But it isn't nice.'

Joe had never expected that a murder would be. He hurried to the bathroom, impatient to discover what Sunny meant.

The unhappy milkman had reported his gruesome find at six that morning and DCI Emily Thwaite felt as though she'd been on the phone ever since, the receiver surgically attached to her ear.

The last thing she needed was a high-profile murder on her patch. The previous afternoon the child killer, Gordon Pledge, had escaped from a prison van while he was being transferred from Wakefield prison to Full Sutton and the hunt for him was on. Top priority. And now this. A dead girl in the middle of Eborby. What else could go wrong?

She sipped the tea her husband, Jeff, had made and tried to consume a slice of toast in between briefing her colleagues and making sure Daniel, her youngest, had

4

everything he needed for his Saturday morning swimming lesson. After a short-lived crisis concerning a pair of missing swimming trunks, Emily looked at her watch. The SOCOs were over in Singmass Close going about their business. However, as senior investigating officer, she knew that she should be there on the scene, keeping her eye on things.

She'd already dispatched someone to visit the dead girl's address but she wanted to speak to the people who knew Karen Strange as a matter of urgency. She needed to get to know the victim. She needed to know her habits, her thoughts, her loves and her hates. And she needed to know who had hated – or loved – Karen enough to kill her: Emily knew from experience that twisted love could lead to murder, just as loathing could.

Emily looked at Jeff. Although he was starting to show the inevitable signs of age – the thickening of the waist and the deepening lines – he was tall, fair and still good-looking enough to be the object of the occasional teenage crush amongst his female pupils at the high school where he taught history. She didn't have to issue him with his orders. He was used to the routine by now. When the call had come in he'd taken charge of the children and, as it was Saturday, he knew he had to drop Sarah at ballet after taking the boys to the swimming baths.

She knew that she should be thankful that Jeff supported her in her career. A lot of men she knew wouldn't be so understanding. It was a source of regret that she never seemed to have the time these days to find the right words to tell him how much she appreciated him, and most nights she arrived home exhausted, her brain buzzing with the day's frantic business. But one day, when she had a moment, they'd have some quality time – how she hated that expression – together. But not yet. She had a murderer to take off the streets. And from the sound of it, this was no domestic or a fight at closing time. This one sounded odd.

She checked her reflection in the hall mirror and ran a brush through her unruly fair curls. She had a pretty, freckled face with a slightly turned-up nose and, if it wasn't for her little weight problem – brought about by too much snacking on the move – she reckoned that she wouldn't be bad for her age. But dieting was for those with time on their hands.

Her thoughts were interrupted by a small voice. 'Mummy.'

Emily looked round. Her daughter, Sarah, was standing at the bottom of the stairs in her Forever Friends pyjamas. At six years old, Sarah had always been as boisterous as her two brothers, but over the past couple of weeks she'd seemed quiet, preoccupied.

'What is it, love?' she asked as she picked up her brief-case.

'Grizelda wants to know where you're going.'

'Tell her I've got to go to work. I've got to catch some naughty people and lock them up. Have a good time at ballet, won't you, love.' She bent down to give the little girl a kiss.

'Kiss Grizelda,' Sarah ordered imperiously.

Emily kissed the air a couple of feet from Sarah's face. The imaginary friend phase probably wouldn't last long and in the meantime, there was no harm in going along with it. It probably meant that Sarah was imaginative, she thought with a passing frisson of maternal pride.

But she knew she couldn't linger. She blew Sarah a kiss and hurried out to the car. First stop the crime scene. Second, the victim's family. She wasn't particularly looking forward to either.

It was too early for heavy traffic so the journey into the city centre only took ten minutes. When Emily arrived at the insignificant-looking archway leading from Gallowgate onto Singmass Close, she saw blue-striped crime scene tape festooned across the entrance. Two elderly women with shopping trolleys were standing there, craning their necks to see what was going on. Emily could have told them not to bother – the body would already be screened off. Ignoring the double yellow lines, she parked up on the pavement behind a patrol car.

Singmass Close itself lay behind a small arch, little more than a gap between an Italian restaurant and a charity shop, opening onto a wide alley with medieval stone walls to the right. To the left stood a plain Georgian building swathed in scaffolding – once a ragged school for an orphanage, it was in the process of being converted into offices fit for twenty-first-century business. Beyond this was a close of tasteful modern townhouses constructed around a central courtyard, built in the 1980s on the site of a maze of dank and crumbling slums. Until the area's phoenix-like renaissance, Singmass Close and its surrounding maze of streets and alleyways had been a place of darkness, tucked away like a shameful secret at the rear of Eborby's magnificent cathedral. Now a blanket of gentility had been flung across the Close. It had shed its dark past and changed beyond recognition.

She gave the uniformed constable on guard a brisk smile as he lifted the tape to allow her through. As she struggled into the set of paper overalls she'd been handed, her eyes searched the close for a familiar face.

Eventually she spotted Joe Plantagenet standing by the yellow-and-white tent that concealed the body. Like her, he wore a disposable suit but she was sure that it looked better on him than it did on her. He was an inch or so shorter than her husband, Jeff, with longish dark hair, freckles, a nose that was perhaps a little too big and bright-blue eyes which looked as though they could see into your soul. His expression was serious. Joe was never one for the gallows humour that helped some of their colleagues get through the day.

She walked over to join him – he looked up and gave her a sad smile. 'Hi, boss.' His voice was deep with a trace of a Liverpool accent.

'So what is this place?' Emily asked. As she'd only transferred to Eborby from Leeds less than a year before, she was still getting to know the city.

'It's called Singmass Close because the Vicars Choral who lived here used to sing mass at the cathedral when the canons couldn't be bothered.'

'Oh aye?' she said, trying to sound interested. She could have done without the history lesson but she knew Joe was into that sort of thing. His girlfriend, Maddy, worked at the Archaeology Centre so the interest had probably rubbed off.

'So what have we got? I take it you've had a look?'

'Only a quick peep. The doc's in there doing her bit. It's a strange one.'

Emily saw a flicker of uncertainty in his eyes. Something about this murder had disturbed him. Like any police officer, Joe was used to violent death and she wondered what was so different about this one.

'Has the doc given her verdict yet?'

'Probably strangulation – some kind of ligature – but there's no sign of the murder weapon so, presumably, the killer took it away with him.' Joe shifted from foot to foot as though he wanted the business over and done with.

'Time of death?'

'Two o'clock in the morning, give or take an hour. Dr Sharpe won't commit herself before . . .'

'The post mortem. Why is that woman always so bloody cautious? You OK, Joe? You look tired.'

Joe gave his boss a small smile. 'Didn't sleep too well, that's all.'

'You and me both.'

'No news of Gordon Pledge?'

Emily shook her head. 'He can't have got far. All patrols are on the lookout for him and uniform are checking out his known haunts.' She hesitated for a moment. 'I suppose we'd better have a look at this body,' she said with determination. She'd found from bitter experience that professional detachment was the only way to deal with such things.

She began to walk towards the tent, some of the SOCOs acknowledging her with a nod as she made her regal progress. She turned her head and saw that Joe was following a few paces behind like a mourner in a solemn procession and she heard his words echoing in her head. 'It's a strange one.'

In a matter of seconds, she'd see for herself what he meant.

At Eborby's busy railway station, Michele Carden examined the contents of her purse. Fifty-five quid. There was no way she'd get as far as London. That had been the plan, of course, but Michele's plans had a habit of crashing to the ground . . . like the time she'd tried to get to the Leeds Festival and the tickets she'd bought from a lad at school had turned out to be fakes.

She put her purse back in her pocket, cursing the price of rail travel and settled back on the uncomfortable plastic seat in the bustling station café, her rucksack by her feet, looking round as though she was waiting for someone. The last thing she wanted was for anyone to approach her and start asking questions.

She'd arrived on the Thirsk train half an hour ago and ordered a diet Coke, which she drunk slowly, knowing she had to make it last. It would never do for anyone to guess that she hadn't a clue what her next move was going to be.

Michele had dressed with care as usual. At five foot eleven with glossy dark hair and a clear skin which was the envy of her classmates, she knew she looked good in the clothes she had collected during her Saturday trips to Eborby when she would patrol the racks of Top Shop in search of the latest look. She wished she had a magazine to read but she hadn't thought to bring one and buying one from the station bookstall would eat into her precious escape fund.

She took another look in her purse as though she hoped the notes would have bred and multiplied since it had last been opened. But no matter how often she counted, the sum was still the same. The plan had been London but now necessity made her toy with other options. Leeds was a possibility. But Leeds was a bit too close for comfort.

She took her mobile from her pocket. A text had just come in from Laura. WHERE RU? She was about to reply but then she had second thoughts. Laura might talk. And careless talk cost freedom.

She switched the phone off. If she was really serious about making her bid for freedom, she'd have to break with the past – break with her boring, oppressive school and her sad family and friends with their small-town minds. She was aiming higher. Sod Leeds . . . Plan A was back in operation. She was going to London and she was going to make it big.

If the train was too expensive, there were alternatives. Eborby's coach station wasn't far away. And there was always the cheapest form of transport of all . . . hitching.

She had just finished her Coke, draining the can of every last drop to get her money's worth, and she needed the loo. Then she'd make for the coach station to see how often the London coaches ran. As she picked up her rucksack and rose from her seat, she heard a voice.

'Excuse me.'

10

Michele looked round. A middle-aged woman was standing by the table. Michelle had noticed her arriving ten minutes before, sipping a latte at a table at the far side of the café. She was probably ten years older than Michele's own mother but she was dressed far more expensively. The little suit with the carefully arranged scarf suggested Paris, as did the perfume and the immaculate make-up. Chanel . . . that pink tweed suit was definitely Chanel. The woman was slim with jet-black hair cut in a glossy bob. Her mouth turned down slightly at the corners and she didn't look particularly friendly . . . but the well-dressed and immaculately groomed rarely do.

Michele hugged her rucksack close, suddenly wary. This woman could represent authority. She could be someone who would bring her dreams to a sharp halt there and then. But as she edged away, the woman smiled – a businesslike smile rather than a warm one.

'I hope you don't mind my approaching you like this but my name is Sylvia Palmer. I run a model agency in Leeds. Perhaps you've heard of it . . . Palmer's Models.'

All Michele's wariness suddenly disappeared. Had she heard of Palmer's Models? Should she have heard of Palmer's Models? Perhaps she should have done – after all, wasn't modelling her life's ambition? Somehow she had taken it for granted that everything glamorous went on in London. But maybe she could get what she wanted nearer home. Her heart was beating fast as Sylvia Palmer looked her up and down and offered her a manicured hand, which Michele shook limply.

'Do say if you're not interested but I really think you're the type of girl we're looking for. Have you ever done any modelling?'

Michele flicked her hair off her face self-consciously. This was a dream come true. 'Er, no . . . but I've always wanted to . . . I mean . . .'

11

'You'll need a portfolio of photographs, but my agency can arrange all that . . . free of charge, of course. We take our commission when you get work.'

'Er . . . yeah. Great.' Michele shifted from foot to foot. What do you say when somebody comes up out of the blue in a station café and offers you all the riches of the world?

Sylvia Palmer looked at her watch. 'Look, have you any plans for this afternoon? Only one of our top photographers is doing a shoot at a place out in the country in a couple of days' time and I need someone to help get everything ready. So if you're free . . .'

Had Michele any plans? Silly question. The only plan Michele had that day was the pursuit of fame and fortune. And it looked as if those two elusive things had just come right up to her and said hello. 'Yeah great,' she said, lost for anything more eloquent.

'My car's outside. We'll go out the back way, shall we? I'll lead the way.'

Michele Carden didn't need asking twice. As the woman hurried ahead, she swung her rucksack onto her back and followed several yards behind.

Joe thanked the sergeant who lifted the flap of the tent to let them in, making a note of their arrival on his clipboard. His face was serious. Joe thought he looked like a man who'd had a shock.

Inside the tent, a small young woman with dark-brown curly hair was kneeling on the ground, bent over the corpse. She looked up and gave him a shy smile, her eyes flicking towards Emily who was standing by his side. Joe felt a little embarrassed as he always did when he recalled Dr Sally Sharpe's drunken confidences at the CID party last Christmas. She had kissed him with alcohol-fuelled passion and told him she fancied him. Then she'd offered to take him back to her flat but he'd declined her offer tactfully, assuming that it was the wine talking. Sally probably didn't remember. At least he hoped she didn't.

'Hi Sal,' he said casually. 'What can you tell us?'

Sally placed a swab carefully in a screw-top jar and sat back on her heels. 'Like I told you before, I reckon she died in the early hours of the morning between one and three but I might be able to tell you more when I get her on the slab. And she was strangled . . . some sort of ligature.'

'Any sign of sexual assault?' he asked, glancing at Emily who was staring down at the body, her plump, pretty face solemn.

'Not that I can see.'

Joe looked down at the dead girl. Her pale blonde hair was tugged back into a pony tail and her freckles were half veiled by a layer of foundation. Her eye shadow was heavily applied and she still retained a trace of scarlet on her lips. All this and the skimpy mini skirt and plunging neckline told him that she'd been for a night on the town. And in Eborby there were only a handful of places where you could paint the town red. It shouldn't be difficult to find out which of these Karen Strange had been to. Unless he was wrong . . . unless the skimpy clothing was being worn for professional reasons.

'Any chance she was on the game?' Emily asked quietly, as though she'd read his thoughts.

It was something Joe hadn't liked to consider – but he supposed the question had to be asked. 'I had a word with Jamilla before,' he said. 'She's been to break the news to the family. The victim lived at the address with her parents so I wouldn't have said so. All girls seem to dress like that for a night out, don't they?'

Emily nodded sadly. She was a mother and Joe guessed that the thought of any daughter of hers flaunting her assets like that was making her uncomfortable.

13

Sally shifted a little so they could get a better view. 'There's something else you should see.' She lifted the dead girl's left foot gently. It was bare and stained with dried blood. 'The big toe's missing. Freshly severed with some sort of sharp knife I'd say. There's not that much blood around so I'm sure it was done post mortem.'

'I understand her handbag was found with her,' said Joe.

Sally nodded towards a large plastic evidence bag containing a small, new-looking jewelled handbag with a chain strap. 'It was underneath the body so she probably fell on it. Her purse and her mobile haven't been touched and apart from her make-up, there's a packet of condoms and her ID card.'

She passed the bag to Joe who peered through the shroud of plastic at the young persons' ID card. The fuzzy, washed-out photo of the blonde girl looked quite unlike the corpse on the ground. But he knew from experience that people can look quite different once the spirit that makes them who they are has departed. He'd once seen a picture of the dead Marilyn Monroe taken in the morgue which bore little resemblance to the vibrant woman on the cinema screen.

Sally's voice interrupted his musings on mortality. 'Have you seen this?' She pointed to another bag.

He edged his way round the body slowly and picked it up. As a stared at it, a pair of eyes stared back. Glass eyes, cold, multifaceted blue, in a pale, painted face. Porcelain with rosebud lips, pink-tinted cheeks and sandy curls. He moved the doll and the staring eyes closed as if the thing was dead. Then as he turned it upright it snapped back to life again, studying him through thick lashes.

He handed the bag to Emily.

'It was found beside the body,' said Sally. 'Weird. Unless she was a doll collector and she was taking it home. But . . .'

14

He watched as Emily studied the doll. It was about two feet tall with a face that was at the same time both sweet and malevolent. It was dressed in a white smock, yellowed with age, and Emily fumbled with the plastic until she had a clear view of the left foot. As she stared, it took her a few seconds to realise the significance of what she was seeing. 'The toes have been hacked off,' she said, puzzled.

'And it looks like a fresh break,' said Sally. She hesitated. 'If someone's tried to mutilate the doll like the corpse, whoever it is must be seriously weird.' She studied the doll again. 'This looks like an antique,' she said after a few moments. 'Not something you'd just leave lying around in the street.'

Joe looked at Emily. She was listening intently. 'Where exactly was it found?' she asked.

Sally pointed to the spot. 'It looks as though it was put there deliberately. Maybe part of the killer's ritual.' She frowned. 'What do you think it means?'

Joe gave an apologetic shrug. 'No idea.'

Emily shook her head. Like Joe, it seemed, she hadn't a clue. Yet. But Joe knew from his months of working with her that she was an optimist by nature and her mind was probably beginning to plan all the possible lines of enquiry. It was just a matter of where to start.

As Sally began to put her things away in her case, Joe knelt on the ground by the dead girl and looked at her closely before closing his eyes and whispering a small, unobtrusive prayer for the dead. He thought that someone should treat the poor girl lying dead on the paving stones as a human being and put in a good word for her soul. When he'd finished, he looked up. Sally was preoccupied but he saw that Emily was watching him. She gave him a brief, flickering smile before averting her eyes.

'What about house to house?' Emily asked as they left the confines of the tent.

'Sunny's organising that.' Joe took a deep breath. There were some things – unpleasant things – that you can only put off for so long before they had to be faced. 'We'd better go and have a word with the parents. You'll come with me?'

Emily answered in the affirmative and they began to walk. There was drizzle in the air but it wasn't cold for late October. As they were about to leave the close, Joe took a last look around. Several of the little houses, he noticed, had windows overlooking the scene of Karen Strange's death. If the residents were members of Neighbourhood Watch who suffered from insomnia they could have the case wrapped up within twenty-four hours. But things were rarely that straightforward.

He was about to follow Emily to Gallowgate when he glanced up at the end house and saw something that made him catch his breath. Sitting there in a small upstairs window, watching the scene below, was a doll with a pale porcelain face and smirking rosebud lips.

The Doll Strangler reached over to switch off the radio. The switch was sticky – marmalade probably, hardened over several days. He licked it off his finger.

The body of a female had been found early that morning in Singmass Close. The police were going to release more details later. The name of the place brought it all back. It was fifty years ago but the memory was just as vivid as if it had happened that morning.

When he closed his eyes tight he could almost hear the sound of her heels on the cobbles. Click click click. She was getting nearer.

Click click click. How fast she walked. She would have been nervous walking at night though a place like Singmass Close with its huddled houses and its dark shadows.

Click click click. Here she was. Come on, he thought as

he clenched his fist, reliving every moment, every emotion. Come closer. He felt the soft silk of the stocking in his hand. And the knife was there – the knife that would stop the dancing.

He'd carried the doll in the holdall. The doll he had mutilated, imagining what he would do to the woman coming towards him. With his eyes closed he could see her now in the yellow-grey mist sent up by forty thousand smoking chimneys. She was turning the corner and he could see her under the dim street light, tottering across the cobbles on her high heels. He recalled how he'd stepped back into the shadows and pressed his body against the wall, his heart thumping, almost feeling faint with anticipation. Click click click. The timing had to be right.

She hadn't been able to see him but he could see her. He had almost smelt her fear beneath the waft of cheap scent. So near now.

This was it. With his eyes still shut, he stretched out his stiff arms, imagining the softness of the silk stocking between his hands. But then the arms dropped to his side. Something was wrong. The ragged child was there again watching, mocking. Spoiling his fantasy. He wished he could kill her. He wished he could stop the giggles and the taunts.

But he wasn't sure how you went about killing a ghost.

Chapter 2

Karen Strange's parents lived in a sprawling Victorian villa in the tree-lined suburb of Bacombe. The house stood on the main road just a mile from the city centre. If you continued west, you would reach the city walls and if you continued east, you'd soon meet open country.

Joe loved Eborby's rich history. His late father's family had lived in Eborby for generations and Joe had grown up with tales of how he was descended from an illegitimate child of Richard III, who'd been Eborby's local hero back in the late fifteenth century. Joe had no idea whether this was true or not but his father had believed it, even though he'd allowed himself to be lured from his native city by Joe's Liverpudlian mother. As a result, Joe had been Liverpudlian born and bred and, after his abortive year at the seminary, he had joined Merseyside police, still with the fire of idealism in his eyes, thinking he could make the world a better place. But after Kevin's death he had needed to escape the bad memories, so he had transferred to Eborby because he had roots there – and in Eborby, roots ran deep.

He studied Emily's face as they got out of the car. She looked serious and the fine lines around her eyes seemed deeply etched beneath a layer of make-up. She hadn't said much during the journey. But then he hadn't felt much like talking either.

'This is it,' she said. 'Nice place.'

Joe made noises of agreement. The Stranges' house had a glossy black front door, pristine white paintwork, expensive curtains at the windows and colourful tubs of flowers flanking the entrance. The young girl in her tawdry clubbing clothes didn't seem to belong in these elegant surroundings. But perhaps that was the point she'd been making.

'Here goes.' Emily took a deep breath and rang the doorbell.

Jamilla had arranged for a policewoman to stay with the Stranges – family liaison – and it was she who opened the door. She was a well built young woman with straight dark hair and an expression of studied sympathy that Joe usually associated with funeral directors. As she admitted them she didn't smile. There was little to smile about.

'Mr and Mrs Strange are called Vince and Barbara,' she whispered. 'They're in the lounge. They seem to be taking it quite well,'

Joe found this hard to believe. It was more likely that they were too stunned to speak or that they were adept at hiding their emotions in front of strangers.

Emily nudged his arm. He knew that she would leave him to do most of the talking. She reckoned he was good at that sort of thing. He himself wasn't so sure.

They followed the young policewoman into an elegant lounge with beige furnishings of expensive simplicity and an impressive original fireplace. There was money here, Joe thought to himself. And taste – in his experience, the two things didn't always go together.

Vince and Barbara Strange sat on separate armchairs, avoiding each other's eyes. Vince was a big man, handsome in a rugged sort of way, and his wife was a stick-thin blonde in tight jeans. It was only the lines on her face that betrayed her age. Seen from behind she could have passed for a teenager.

Joe arranged his features into a mask of sympathy. 'I'm DI Joe Plantagenet and this is DCI Emily Thwaite. We realise it's a very painful time for you . . .'

'You want us to identify her, is that it?' It was Barbara Strange who spoke. Her voice was unemotional but Joe assumed that if she let the mask crack, she'd probably break down completely.

Joe was tempted to tell the woman to let go; to have a good cry if she wanted. But that would hardly help the investigation so he returned to the matter in hand. 'I'm afraid we will need a formal identification,' he said quietly. 'I'm sorry. And we have to ask you some questions.' He looked at Vince who seemed stunned, like a wild creature caught in car headlights.

'Are you feeling up to talking, Mr Strange?' Emily asked.

Vince Strange looked up at her. 'We'd better get it over with. And if it helps you catch the bastard who killed her . . .' The words were said half-heartedly, without vehemence. As though he was just going through the motions.

Joe asked their permission to sit and Barbara answered with a vague wave of her hand. They could do what the hell they liked. Karen was dead and nothing mattered any more.

'Have you any other children?' Joe asked, dreading the answer. If Karen was the only one . . . the thought was almost unbearable.

'Our son's at the university here.'

'Does he live at home?' Emily asked.

Barbara shook her head. 'He shares a house with some other students.' She looked at her husband, her eyes wide with panic. 'We'll have to tell him. Oh God, he doesn't know . . . we'll have to . . .'

'We'll need to speak to him,' said Emily. 'And everyone Karen knew. Did she keep an address book here or . . .?'

The answer was an absent-minded nod from Barbara. She stood up but Joe shook his head. 'It's all right, Mrs Strange. It can wait a few minutes. If you're feeling up to it we'd like you to tell us all you can about Karen.' Or the version she'd let her parents know, he thought to himself. Working in CID, he was only too aware that parents often don't know half of what goes on in a teenage girl's life. 'Is that OK?'

The couple both nodded meekly.

'What did Karen do?' he began.

'She's in the sixth form. She's applying to university. She wants to study English.'

Joe noted the use of the present tense but they made no attempt to correct it. The realisation that Karen wouldn't be taking up any university place would sink in soon enough.

It was Emily who asked the next question. 'Which school's she at?'

'Hicklethorpe Manor.'

'And where was she going last night? Did she tell you?'

'Of course she told me. She tells me everything. She was going to The Devil's Playground with her friend from school – Natalie. She didn't have school next day so I said it'd be all right,' Barbara said defensively, as though this plump, motherly woman in the big, comfortable raincoat was questioning her maternal capabilities.

'So you know who she was with?' Joe caught Emily's eye. This sounded hopeful. If her friend saw her with her killer this one might be easier than they'd expected.

'Do you think we let her just wander the streets?' Vince said impatiently. 'We always know who she's with and where she's going.'

Joe looked into Vince's eyes. 'But you didn't report her missing when she failed to arrive home last night?'

21

The dead girl's father opened and closed his mouth as though he couldn't think of an explanation. His wife, however, was quick to supply one. 'She told us she was going to stay the night with Natalie. That's why we weren't worried.'

It seemed that their trust in Natalie was misplaced. And she had just become number one on their list of people to interview.

'Was your daughter interested in dolls at all?' Emily asked. 'Victorian dolls . . . did she collect them or . . .'

The Stranges looked at each other and both shook their heads, puzzled. 'She used to like dolls when she was little,' she said. 'But . . . Why do you ask?'

'It's just that an antique doll was found near . . .' Somehow Joe couldn't bring himself to say the words 'near her body'. It seemed too brutal. The couple looked as though they still expected their dead daughter to walk in any moment.

'Do you have a recent photograph of your daughter?' Emily asked.

Barbara Strange stood up and walked over to the chest of drawers. She took out a school photograph and handed it to Emily who studied it for a few moments and then passed it to Joe. It seemed to bear little resemblance to their corpse, apart from the general build and colouring. But then they'd not really studied the dead girl very closely. That would come later at the post-mortem.

Joe saw Emily sling her capacious handbag onto her shoulder and rise from her seat. 'If we can have Natalie's details . . . And it would help us if we could have a look through Karen's things.'

Vince looked flustered. 'Yes, of course. Er . . .' He looked at his wife. Joe thought he looked like a helpless child searching for a responsible adult.

'Look, Natalie's Karen's friend,' said Barbara. 'She'd never just leave her like that. I know she wouldn't.'

Joe could have told her that he'd dealt with cases where teenage girls did lots of things they shouldn't do when their parents' backs are turned. But he didn't.

Once the Stranges had provided Natalie's address and phone number, Joe told them that the family liaison officer would take them to the hospital as soon as they felt ready to conduct the formal identification of their daughter. The words sounded cold and he felt cruel. But they had to be said.

It was time to have a look at Karen's room. Joe knew they'd have to search their way through her possessions. They'd have to dig away until they knew Karen almost as well as her family did.

Vince and Barbara had just led them out into the hall, their hands touching for support, when all of a sudden the silent hallway was filled with the sound of a key turning in the front-door lock. Joe and Emily exchanged looks. This was probably the student son, Chris, home on a Saturday to dump his washing in the parental machine. Joe saw that the Stranges had frozen like the victims of some fairy tale curse and all eyes were focussed on the front door as it opened slowly.

As the girl stepped over the threshold, Barbara Strange uttered a strangled cry.

But Vince hurried forward, barging Emily out of the way. 'Karen,' he said, taking the shocked girl in his arms. He held her there as she began to push him away. Barbara, tears streaming down her face leaving black trails of mascara, grabbed at her daughter's arm, holding it tightly, unwilling to let go.

Joe watched them, feeling their relief, almost rejoicing with them inside but careful to keep up a mask of professional neutrality. He looked at Emily and saw a smile playing on her lips.

But there was an expression of strong distaste on

23

Karen's face as she slipped from her father's grasp with a roughly whispered 'Give over. Can't you fucking leave me alone?' She scowled at Emily and Joe. 'What the fuck's going on?' she asked, suddenly on her guard.

'We thought you were dead,' Barbara sobbed accusingly, clawing at her daughter's sleeve, trying to hold onto her child but being denied that basic need.

'I think we need a word, Karen,' said Emily in her best headmistress voice.

Joe should have known that nothing is ever straightforward.

The car was flash. Black BMW four by four. Just what you'd expect from the head of a modelling agency. The only trouble was that, sitting in the plump leather back seat, Michele Carden couldn't see out of the heavily tinted windows and the feeling of having no idea where she was going was rather disconcerting . . . like being abducted in a particularly sumptuous van.

Ms Palmer had become quite friendly, chatting about the agency and the assignments her girls had done. But she made it absolutely clear that she expected hard work and dedication. And punctuality. Never mind all the stories about supermodels turning up when they felt like it, the reality was quite different. And you started at the bottom, doing the menial tasks and learning the job. The work was tough and often unglamorous but there were rewards for those who saw it as a career rather than an opportunity to have a good time. Ms Palmer didn't tolerate slackness. Professionalism led to success.

This all sounded fine to Michele. When she was a top model she'd go back home and gloat over all her sad friends in their sad little lives and their university courses that led to boring jobs. Michele Carden was going places.

As they drove Michele caught tantalising glimpses of

the passing landscape through the front window and they seemed to be out in the middle of the country. They were on their way to the scene of the photo shoot. The very words held glamour. Photo shoot.

Suddenly the car swung off the narrow road and onto a rough track. Michele could see a building ahead through the front windscreen. A house surrounded by high trees and green fields.

'Is this it?' she asked. It didn't exactly look like the scene of a photo shoot but, from the pictures she'd seen in magazines, she knew they used some strange and unglamorous places.

Sylvia Palmer kept her eyes on the track as the BMW rocked this way and that. 'This is it. Nobody's here yet but Barry will be coming up soon. He's the photographer. I expect you'd fancy some coffee?'

'Yes. That would be nice. Thank you,' Michele replied, remembering her manners. This woman held her future in her well-manicured hands.

The back door was opened and Michele climbed out, looking around. She was indeed in the middle of nowhere, not another house to be seen in any direction amongst the rolling dales. Only sheep – lots of them. The scenery was breathtaking but Michele preferred the shops any day. Scenery was boring. She followed Sylvia Palmer up the drive towards the house.

It wasn't the sort of place she would have associated with a woman like Sylvia. It obviously used to be a farmhouse but the farmer and his family had probably moved to pastures new long since. The double-fronted building looked rather dilapidated with flaking green paintwork and a drooping gutter.

Sylvia turned to her. 'Bit of a dump, isn't it? The story the client wants is edgy rural chic.'

Michele nodded earnestly.

Sylvia unlocked the door and stood aside to let Michele enter first. Then she ushered her through a narrow hallway into a square room that generations gone by would have called the front parlour. Michele took in her new surroundings. The furnishings had seen better days and everything seemed to be covered in a thin layer of dust. But she said nothing. It wasn't any of her business.

Sylvia told her to make herself at home while she arranged for the coffee to be brought. She flopped down on the sofa. It was surprisingly comfortable and for the first time, Michele realised that she felt tired.

After a few minutes, Sylvia Palmer returned with two mugs of steaming coffee. Michele was hungry and she'd hoped for biscuits. But then if she was serious about a modelling career, she was going to have to learn strict dietary discipline. Biscuits would be out from now on.

'Sorry,' said Sylvia. 'I'll have to get my laptop out of the car. I'm expecting an important e-mail from New York. A contract for one of my girls,' she added casually.

Michele nodded, impressed. Maybe one day she'd be in New York. Her heart lifted as the world of fashion beckoned. Sylvia told her to drink up and watched her as she took the first few sips. The coffee tasted bitter but Michele didn't care. This was the start of the rest of her life.

Even when her head began to spin just like it had when she'd smoked a joint at her mate's house, her only thought was that she hoped she wouldn't spoil her chances by being ill.

And when she finally lost consciousness, she was unaware of being lifted off the sofa and carried upstairs.

Karen Strange sat on the sofa scowling at nobody in particular. Emily had asked the Stranges if they could speak to their daughter in private for a few minutes. They hadn't looked happy but they'd agreed.

If Karen was worried by a visit from the police, she was hiding it well.

Emily had brought the small bag found by the body with her in a plastic evidence bag. She pulled it out of her own large handbag and handed it to the girl. 'Can you confirm that this bag belongs to you?'

Karen examined it briefly and nodded. 'Yeah. Why?'

'It was found by the body of a young woman. She was murdered in Singmass Close last night. Strangled. Do you know how your bag came to be there?'

Karen took a deep breath. 'Nat picked it up from where we'd been sitting . . . she must have thought it was hers. We found we'd bought identical ones in Topshop and we'd both brought them out last night.' She rolled her eyes. 'I was pissed off cause she's always copying me . . . asking me where I got things and turning up in the same thing a couple of days later. She was always doing it.'

'Are you talking about your friend, Natalie Parkes?'

'Yeah, that's right.' The girl looked wary.

'Tell me what happened last night,' said Emily. 'When did you find out you had the wrong bag?'

Karen glanced towards the door as though this was something she didn't want her parents to hear. 'When I got to Jon's room I opened the bag and saw all Nat's stuff in there. I was going to ring her this morning . . . get my bag back. Look, it can't be Nat, can it? Someone must have pinched my bag from her.'

'Who's Jon?' Joe asked.

'Jon Firman. I met him last night. I went back to his place. He's doing his PhD at the uni.'

'You spent the night there?'

She looked at Joe defiantly. 'Yeah. At one of the halls of residence on the campus. He won't want to get involved. He's engaged.'

Joe leaned forward. 'We need to talk to him – he might

27

have seen something.' He saw the girl scowl. 'We can be discreet if that's what you're worried about.'

Karen pouted and looked away, as if he and Emily were a pair of tiresome relatives out to spoil her fun, and Joe wondered whether the seriousness of the situation had sunk in yet. Her friend was probably dead. Murdered. But it seemed that Karen Strange was adopting the strategy of the ostrich and burying her head in the sands of her own self-absorption.

'Have you got a photo of Natalie?'

Karen hesitated for a moment before getting up and walking to the bureau in the corner of the room. She opened a drawer and took out a class photograph – the type taken at every school in the land. 'That's her,' she said, pointing to a pretty blond girl in the back row. 'That's Nat.'

Joe caught Emily's eye. It was the dead girl. There was no mistaking it this time.

'Tell us about Natalie,' Joe said gently. 'What's she like?'

Karen shrugged her shoulders. 'Cool. Clever. She went through some heavy stuff when her dad buggered off but . . .'

'Any brothers or sisters?'

'One brother. Will. But she never talked about him much. He's quite a bit older and . . . He kept trying to order her about . . . kept asking her where she was going and all that. She told him to piss off and lighten up.'

'He's probably concerned for her,' said Joe, mentally adding the words 'someone had to be.'

'He gets on her nerves,' was Karen's reply.

Joe gave the girl what he thought was an understanding smile. 'So tell me exactly what happened last night.'

Karen looked at him uncertainly before launching into her account. 'We met outside The Devil's Playground at nine-thirty,' she began.

Joe nodded. He knew of The Devil's Playground, a club in the basement of a Victorian office building not far from the castle, popular with Eborby's student population and not as grim as its name might suggest.

Karen continued. They'd done the usual, taken advantage of the cheap drink offers and had a laugh. Then Karen had been chatted up by Jon and she had only caught glimpses of her friend for the rest of the evening.

'Anyone else there you knew?'

She shrugged again. 'A few people. I saw Nat talking to Brett Bluit at one time.'

'Who's Brett Bluit?'

'Boy from school.'

'Boyfriend?'

She shook her head. 'Just a friend.'

'Did you see her with anyone else?'

'A few people. Blokes. But I couldn't describe them. I had better things to do than watch Nat all night.'

'Did you see her leave?'

'Yeah. She passed me and said she was off.'

Emily shifted in her seat. 'Was she on her own when she left?'

'Yeah. I think so.'

'Not with this Brett?'

Karen gave a snort of derision. 'Do me a favour. No way.'

'You weren't worried about her going off on her own?'

Karen didn't answer. She'd probably been too pre-occupied with her new pick-up to think of such things. And now she must be feeling bad . . . even though she was being careful not to show it.

Emily looked the girl in the eye. 'If Brett was talking to her, he might have noticed her leave.'

Karen looked away. 'You'll have to ask him. But I saw

him there after she'd gone. He started chatting to me while Jon was getting me a drink – had to tell him to fuck off. Three's a crowd and all that.'

'We'll need Brett's contact details,' said Emily.

The girl hesitated. 'His number's in my mobile.'

'Got his address?'

Karen stood up. 'It's upstairs. I'll get it.' Suddenly she looked worried, as though the gravity of the situation had just hit her. She hurried out of the room.

'What do you think?' Joe asked as soon as Karen was out of earshot.

'I think we need to speak to Brett and anyone else who was at the club last night,' Emily replied. 'And while we're about it, we need to discover all Lady Natalie's little secrets.'

Joe couldn't argue with that.

'So Karen Strange came back from the dead did she, ma'am?'

Joe saw Emily give Sunny Porter a businesslike smile. The short, wiry Sunny – who had been rather ambitiously baptised Samson – looked rather pleased with himself. But then it was his birthday and he'd just been distributing cream cakes amongst his colleagues. Even Emily, who always claimed to be watching her waistline, had accepted; but then it would have been churlish to refuse his largesse.

'She gave us a bit of a surprise,' said Joe who'd been standing behind the DCI, deep in thought. 'I suppose we should have known from the photos if we'd been paying attention, but the two girls are rather alike.'

'Hope they don't decide to sue for distress caused,' said Sunny, ever the pessimist. 'Cost a lot nowadays do hurt feelings.'

Joe sighed. Sunny might have a point if the Stranges

turned out to be the litigious type. But it was something he preferred not to think about just at that moment.

'So what did she have to say for herself, this supposedly dead girl? How come some other girl had her bag? Was it nicked or what?'

'Apparently her friend Natalie had an identical one and they must have got mixed up. When Karen looked in her bag she found she'd picked Natalie's up by mistake.'

'She'd kept her front door key with her though.'

'She always keeps it in her jacket pocket, apparently,' said Emily. 'Any luck at Natalie's address?'

Joe shook his head. 'No reply and the neighbours claimed the family keep themselves to themselves. It's just mum and the two kids. Older brother in his mid twenties and Natalie. No husband about.'

'Posh address,' said Emily. 'If the mother's divorced she must have got a bloody big settlement. Big house and kid at private school. So there was no sign of the doting mummy? Mind you, the girl's eighteen. Doting mummies aren't exactly appreciated at that age. Anything else come in, Sunny?'

'Nothing yet, ma'am. Let's just hope we get something from the house to house.'

'Any sign of Gordon Pledge yet?' Joe asked.

'Bloody private security firms,' Sunny muttered. 'Couldn't trust 'em to organise a prayer meeting in a nunnery. Man kills a little lass and they allow him out of the prison van 'cause he says he feels a bit sick.'

The killer of twelve-year-old Francesca Putney had escaped across fields and the men paid to guard him had been too idle or unfit to pursue him so they'd called in the police. As yet there'd been no sign of Pledge but Joe was certain he'd turn up sooner or later. Besides, that was really uniform's problem.

'So it looks like Natalie Parkes is our dead girl,' Sunny said before taking a bite of cake.

'We saw a photograph,' said Joe, remembering the image of the attractive young woman, so full of life. 'It's her all right. I wondered whether to ask Karen to do the identification . . .'

Sunny nodded with approval. 'Why not?'

'I don't like the idea of getting a teenage girl to look at something like that,' said Joe quickly.

'If you ask me, Karen Strange is a hard little bitch.' Joe saw Emily press her lips together with disapproval.

Joe said nothing. Emily could well be right but he had a sneaking suspicion that Karen's toughness was a shell hiding the vulnerability beneath. The officer sent to Natalie's address had put a note through the door asking the family to contact the police urgently so it was possible that the mother would arrive home and contact them before the dilemma arose.

'What do you make of the doll?' Joe asked. He noticed Sunny staring at him, suddenly interested.

'God knows,' said Emily.

Joe looked round the incident room. It was buzzing like a bee hive with officers making phone calls and typing into computers. He raised his voice. 'Have any of the search teams found the girl's missing toe yet?'

There was a mass shaking of heads. The missing toe hadn't turned up anywhere near the body. Which probably meant the worst. The killer had taken it as some sort of macabre trophy.

'I'll try Natalie's home number again,' said Joe, taking his mobile phone from his pocket. But there was still no answer. However, as soon as he'd given up, the phone on Sunny's desk rang.

After a brief conversation, Sunny looked up at Joe. 'There's someone down at the front desk. Says his name's Will Parkes. Says he's Natalie's brother and he's got your note.'

Joe began to make for the door and Emily followed. Perhaps this time they'd get somewhere.

DC Jamilla Dal looked up at the window. The doll was still there, staring down at her. After what they'd found down there in the close below, it gave her the creeps. All ten of the little houses round the close had been visited and the residents they'd spoken to had all been helpful, expressing appropriate shock.

However, there were still some blanks on Jamilla's list. The young couple at number two were away on holiday and the man at number ten was abroad on business. And when Jamilla had called at number six there'd been no answer, even though she had the impression that someone was at home.

She tried the house again but there was still no reply. But as she gave up and walked away, she had a strong feeling that she was being watched so she swung round quickly, a thrill of fear running through her body. And as she turned, she caught a movement out of the corner of her eye, a slight shift of light behind one of number six's net curtains. Someone was playing games. Or avoiding talking to the police, which was worse.

She tried the doorbell again, keeping her finger pressed on it, long and insistent, but there was still no answer. There was nothing for it: she'd have to give up for now. But she'd be back.

Michele Carden's head was still spinning. She was lying on a bed. A narrow single bed with an iron frame and a lumpy mattress. When she shifted she could hear the springs groaning beneath her.

She was in a small bedroom with old-fashioned floral wallpaper and a sloping ceiling. And her head ached. She opened her mouth and tried to shout but no sound came out. Perhaps it was because her mouth was dry, parched. When she attempted to sit up she flopped back down again and felt tears welling in her eyes.

There was no sign of Sylvia Palmer. She was alone.

Chapter 3

Joe reckoned Will Parkes needed a sympathetic shoulder to cry on after identifying the body of his only sister but no members of his immediate family seemed willing or able to provide one. He had an uncle a London barrister – who made the right sort of noises when Will called to break the news but he said he was far too busy to come up to Yorkshire and offer his nephew any support. This, as far as Joe could see, seemed to be a recurring theme in Will Parkes's life – and probably that of his sister.

Will had cried when he'd identified his sister in the mortuary and Joe couldn't help feeling sorry for the young man. His own family might not have had much in the way of money but at least they would have been there for each other in a time of crisis.

Will had provided him with nuggets of information about Natalie's life. When their parents had divorced five years ago their father had taken himself off to the States to run the New York office of a major British bank. He kept enough money flowing to provide them with a fairly lavish lifestyle but, apart from that, he had chosen to sever all contact with his ex-wife and children. Their mother, he said, was somewhere in the South of France with a fashion photographer called Thierry.

Will told Joe sadly that, as he was five years older than Natalie, they had never been close and she'd never confided in him about her private life. But she was still his sister . . . his own flesh and blood.

While Joe questioned him gently, Emily sat silently by his side, listening for lies and inconsistencies. But as far as he could see, there were none. Will Parkes knew nothing of his sister's death, Joe was sure of that, and he had the impression that Natalie had ensured that her big brother had known very little about her life. They'd lived in the same house but in different worlds.

There was no mention of dolls and severed toes during the interview. There were some things the police liked to keep to themselves so that any false confessions could be filtered out. And besides, Joe thought the information might distress Will unnecessarily while the shock of Natalie's death was still raw. Emily agreed and as soon as they returned to the incident room, she ordered the team to dig out any recent cases anywhere in the country that showed any similarities, however tenuous.

If the killer of Natalie Parkes had struck before, they needed to know.

A fine birthday it was turning out to be for DS Sunny Porter. It was Saturday and his wife, Pauline, had booked a table for that evening at the local Indian – near enough to walk so the birthday boy could enjoy a drink or two. But with the murder, a celebration was out of the question. He'd be working late and some things couldn't be helped. That was just how it was and Pauline rarely complained.

Sunny glanced at his watch. With this silly girl – he could tell she was silly by the sort of clothes she was wearing – getting herself murdered, he could be here all night if madam had her way.

He looked at the pile of witness statements on his desk and sighed. It seemed that the residents of Singmass Close had all been fast asleep in their beds at the time the girl died, which was hardly surprising considering that the doctor had estimated the time of death to be around two in the morning. She might as well have died in the middle of nowhere rather than in the centre of a city, he thought as he opened his desk drawer in search of a pen that worked.

When the drawer was open he saw a parcel lying there, inexpertly wrapped in orange paper decorated with green bottles . . . his elder son Craig's little joke. It had been shoved into his hand that morning with a gruff 'Happy birthday, Dad. I saw this and thought of you.' And with everything that had gone on that day he'd forgotten about it till now.

He reached into the drawer and felt the package. Definitely a book. Sunny had never really been the reading type so he wondered why Craig had considered the gift so appropriate. Curious, he looked round. Nobody was watching so he began to tear at the wrapping. And as the title of the book was revealed, he smiled to himself. *Foul Murders and Dark Deeds in Eborby*. It didn't occur to Sunny that the present might be a pointed reminder that he spent more time on Eborby's dark deeds than he did on his family. Sunny was just pleased that his lad had chosen something fitting.

After another furtive check to make sure that he wasn't being observed, he began to flick through the pages until one chapter heading caught his attention. 'The Doll Strangler of Singmass Close'.

Sunny fetched himself a tea from the machine and settled down to read. After all, he deserved a break.

Michele had tried the door but it was locked.

Sometimes she'd hear footsteps outside the room,

footsteps that approached, stopped, then retreated again. And distant, muffled voices, like faint sounds heard through water. She didn't know whether not being alone frightened her more than abandonment. Where was Sylvia, the woman who'd brought her here? Had it been a trick? She'd read about the Wests . . . seen films like *The Silence of the Lambs*. And her imagination supplied any number of horrific scenarios.

Michele needed the toilet. She had aspired to the highest echelons of the fashion industry, to a life of pristine glamour, and the last thing she wanted was to wet herself. The indignity would be too much to bear on top of everything else.

She began to cry. Heart-rending sobs. She wanted to be back home. She wanted her mother.

The footsteps were approaching again, getting nearer. She wiped her eyes with her sleeve and cowered against the iron headboard as the door opened with a loud creak.

Emily looked at her watch. Four o'clock and not a chance of getting home in the foreseeable future. Jeff didn't seem to mind being landed with the kids on a Saturday . . . although she sometimes feared that one day his tolerance would snap. She hoped he wasn't encouraging Sarah's obsession with this imaginary friend of hers. But she told herself it was nothing to worry about – just a phase like so many others. She yawned suddenly, overwhelmed by tiredness. But as Joe entered her office after giving a token perfunctory knock, she straightened her back and assumed an alert expression.

'You OK?' he asked. She saw that he was looking into her eyes and she suddenly felt self-conscious.

'Course I am.' Joe was a hard man to fool and she wasn't sure that she could manage it. 'Any word on that Gordon Pledge yet?'

Joe shook his head. Emily knew that Pledge could be miles away by now so he turned her thoughts to more pressing matters, leaving uniform to get on with their job. 'Any luck with the contents of Natalie Parkes's bag?'

'Not yet.'

Apart from a tiny pink mobile phone all Natalie's bag had contained was her student ID card, a purse containing a ten-pound note and some loose change, a hairbrush and a well-stuffed make-up bag. The phone was now with one of the team and, with any luck it would tell them everyone the victim was in contact with. And, if fortune was really smiling on them, her killer's name might be there on the list.

'I've sent someone over to bring Brett Bluit in for a chat,' said Emily. 'I just hope he hasn't got awkward parents. I've suggested he's taken to the interview room as soon as he's brought in. And then we can leave him for around twenty minutes to stew. Soften him up nicely.'

She saw that Joe was about to say something when he put his hand up to his shoulder. She could tell that he was in pain but he was trying hard to conceal it.

'Playing up again?'

He managed a brave smile. 'It sometimes happens when it's going to rain. I could make a fortune forecasting the weather. Who needs the Met Office, eh?' Emily could tell that his smile was forced as he slumped down in the seat opposite her.

There was a knock on the door, a bold rap. Emily shouted 'come in' and the door burst open. Sunny Porter was standing there waving a thin paperback book around in an excited manner, an eager look on his weather-beaten face.

'Ma'am, have a look at this.' He almost ran over to Emily's desk and deposited the book open in front of her. Emily saw the chapter heading – 'The Doll Strangler of

Singmass Close' – and gave Joe a glance before she began to read. She turned the page, a feeling of triumph welling up inside her: the feeling of an explorer who had just spotted the shore of a new and undiscovered country.

When she had finished, she pushed the book over to Joe who bent over it in intense concentration. From the expression on his face, she suspected that Sunny's discovery had made him forget the pain in his shoulder.

After a few moments of silence, Joe spoke. 'So let's get this straight. Natalie Parkes's murder seems to be identical to the deaths of four young women back in the nineteen fifties.'

'Looks like someone's playing games,' said Emily quietly. 'They've heard about these murders and thought . . .'

'Could it be the same bloke?' said Sunny.

Emily considered the question, wondering if the idea was as stupid as it sounded. Whoever killed those four unfortunate women back in post-war Eborby would be drawing his pension by now . . . probably past murdering anyone, never mind a fit, healthy young woman like Natalie Parkes.

'This original killer would be more likely to batter them to death with his Zimmer frame,' she observed. 'Anyway, the murders stopped suddenly in nineteen fifty-seven so he either left the area or . . .'

'He kicked the bucket himself.' Joe picked up the book and examined the front page. 'This was only published this year.'

'So our killer could have got hold of a copy and . . .'

Joe nodded. 'It seems more likely than the murderous pensioner theory and there must be other books about famous Eborby murders. This sort of thing sells like hot cakes.'

'Or maybe he heard about the murders from an elderly relative. Let's face it, Joe,' Emily said with a sigh. 'The possibilities are endless.' She looked at her watch. 'Probably time to stroll down and stick a few electrodes on this Brett Bluit's testicles.'

She saw Sunny grin dutifully at her joke but Joe seemed preoccupied, deep in thought.

'You ready?' Emily asked.

Joe took a deep breath and gave his injured shoulder a surreptitious massage. 'As I'll ever be.'

Brett Bluit was a good three inches taller than Joe but he was thin, lanky and a martyr to acne. Joe was hardly surprised that the attractive, mini-skirted Natalie had spurned a liaison with such a specimen. He didn't even look as if he had a particularly sparkling personality.

It had already been agreed that Joe would do most of the talking because Emily considered that the man-to-man approach would go down well.

'I believe you liked Natalie,' he began, an expression of studied sympathy on his face.

The boy blushed behind his acne. 'Yeah.'

'You asked her out?'

Brett shrugged his shoulders. 'Might have done.'

Joe leaned forward confidentially. Man to man. 'I knew a girl once when I was your age. Gorgeous she was but she gave me the elbow. I took it so bad I signed up for a seminary and started training to be a priest.'

Brett raised his head, suddenly interested. Joe's approach seemed to be working.

'Tell us what happened at The Devil's Playground last night.' Joe sneaked a surreptitious glance at the clock on the wall. It was five-thirty and his stomach was beginning to rumble.

Brett began to drum his fingers on the table top, a nervous gesture. 'Nothing much to tell. I had a few drinks and talked to Karen for a bit. Then she picked up this bloke and I went home.'

41

'And you talked to Natalie.'

The boy looked up, uneasy.

'No need to be nervous, Brett. We just need to know everything that happened last night. Did you see Natalie with anyone?' Joe said, assuming his best father confessor voice.

'Yeah.' He hesitated as though he was making a decision. 'I went outside for a smoke and I saw her walking off down the street. This car drew up and she sort of bent down to speak to the driver.'

Joe and Emily looked at each other. If the boy was telling the truth – and it was always possible he was lying through his teeth – this might be an important development. 'Did you see the driver?'

Brett shook his head. 'No, but I reckon it was someone she knew.'

'Could the driver have been someone she met in the club?'

'Don't know.'

'Did she get into the car?'

'Didn't see. I'd finished my fag so I went back inside.'

Joe leaned forward. He could smell the faint aroma of cigarette smoke on Brett's clothes, which seemed to support his story. 'What make of car was it? What colour?'

'It was a Toyota . . . sporty model. I couldn't tell what colour it was in the street lights but I think it was darkish.'

'Don't suppose you noticed the number?' Joe knew from his days at the seminary that miracles occasionally happen.

'I saw part of it. It was 2007 reg and I think it had a P in it . . . but I can't be sure.'

'Well done,' said Emily. 'You're absolutely sure you didn't see her get into the car?'

He shook his head. 'No. Like I said, I went back into the club. Then not long after that I went home.'

'Alone?'

'Yeah. Nobody else lives down my way.'

Joe gave the boy an encouraging smile. Then he felt another sudden twinge in his shoulder and shifted in his chair, trying to get comfortable and failing. 'What kind of girl was Natalie?' he asked.

Brett thought for a few moments. 'She liked adventure. Wanted to go round the world before uni.' He hesitated. 'She said she liked danger. She liked to take risks.'

The three fell silent for a few moments. Natalie had taken one risk too many.

There was one last question Joe couldn't resist throwing in, just to see the reaction. 'Ever heard of the Doll Strangler of Singmass Close? He killed four women back in the nineteen fifties.'

Brett Bluit frowned, puzzled, and shook his head vigorously.

Emily stood up and gave the boy a businesslike smile. 'Thank you, Brett. We might want to speak to you again so don't leave the country, will you?'

He looked at her, uncertain whether she was joking or not, and mumbled his thanks before making a quick getaway.

'What do you think?' Joe asked when the constable had led him from the room.

Emily thought for a moment. 'I reckon the poor lad worshipped Natalie from afar but he didn't stand a cat in hell's chance. It wouldn't surprise me if he didn't follow her out of the club deliberately, hoping for a chance to talk to her alone.'

Joe looked at his watch. Almost six and no chance of getting home in the foreseeable future. Not that he was in any hurry to return to an empty flat. 'I'll get someone to check out that Toyota.' Suddenly he realised the rumbles in his stomach were getting louder. 'We'd better send out for a takeaway. Do you fancy Indian or Chinese?'

Emily started comparing the relative calorie counts in her head. But it wasn't long before she gave up and opted for a Chinese. With prawn crackers.

Michele blinked at Sylvia Palmer who was looming over her, holding a tray.

'How are you feeling?' the woman asked, her face impassive, devoid of emotion.

'What happened?'

'You fainted.'

'Why is the door locked?'

'It wasn't locked. It's just stiff, that's all.'

Sylvia placed the tray on the bed beside Michele and then stepped away. Suddenly Michele felt a little silly. There had been no reason to panic and she hoped, prayed, that she hadn't made a fool of herself. She looked down at the tray and saw a round of toast and a cup of weak tea. But then she had to watch her weight for her new career so she'd expected nothing more.

'Are you feeling up to coming downstairs now? There's lots to do. We need to get the place ready for the shoot.' As she said the words her gaze was focussed on the window, as though she was avoiding Michele's eyes. 'I'll be back to collect your tray,' she said, making for the door.

Michele sat on the bed staring at the tea and toast, which suddenly seemed as desirable as a cordon bleu banquet as she sat alone in the fading light. Then, as the door closed, she heard a click. As though somebody had turned a key in the lock.

The Doll Strangler endured the ersatz pop music on the radio and the mindless chatter of the morning DJ, waiting for the news. And when it started he turned up the volume. He had to know if it was real. He had to know if it was happening again.

'Police are investigating the murder of a young woman in Singmass Close,' the newsreader said in a voice that was verging on the cheerful. Singmass Close where he had made those women suffer all those years ago. There was no mention of a doll. And no mention of how she'd died. But the police took their time revealing that sort of thing. He knew that from experience.

He could never understand why they'd called him the Doll Strangler. He hadn't strangled dolls. He'd strangled women. Live flesh and blood women. He'd left the dolls there because the children told him to. They liked dolls . . . and he wanted to please them.

He remembered the women's names and he whispered them to himself like a mumbled prayer. Marion Grant, Valerie Seddon, Vera Jones, Doris Cray. And Alice of course.

But Alice had been different. Alice had lived.

Chapter 4

Joe woke at six the next morning; as he opened his eyes and remembered he was alone, a feeling of emptiness overwhelmed him. When he'd arrived back at the flat the previous night, after trying without success to contact Natalie Parkes's errant mother in the South of France, he'd found a message from Maddy on the answering machine. When he'd called her back at eleven-fifteen, she'd been in a bar with her friend. The interview had gone well and they'd told her they might want to speak to her again within the next few days. Joe had tried to feign enthusiasm. But he knew he wasn't a good actor.

When his call to Maddy had finished he'd put music on loud to drown the silence – Deep Purple to remind him of his mad teenage days when he'd played drums in a heavy metal band playing uninspired cover versions. But when the accountant next door had called round to complain, he'd turned it off. He didn't like the man but, on the other hand, he didn't particularly want to fall out with the neighbours. After all that excitement he hadn't slept well.

At seven he showered, dressed, dragged a comb through his hair and grabbed a quick breakfast of toast and coffee before leaving the flat. As he walked towards the city he considered his priorities for the day ahead. He needed to follow up Brett Bluit's statement about the car and he'd send someone to gather up all the available CCTV footage – it was possible that the killer's image was captured for posterity somewhere. And he needed to find out everything he could about the crimes of the Doll Strangler back in the 1950s.

The sky was glowering grey – real autumn weather – and it looked like rain but he was well prepared in his waterproof jacket. He had lived in the north all his life and being ready for all weathers was second nature. When he reached the grey stone mass of the city walls he stopped for a while trying to come to a decision. He knew he was expected at the incident room but he felt a sudden desire to see Singmass Close again now that the circus of the crime scene investigation had departed.

He walked under Canons Bar, catching a strong whiff of urine, and looked upwards at the wooden teeth of the ancient portcullis poking out of their stone slit like the fangs of some sleeping animal – a reminder of Eborby's warlike past. When he emerged from the shadows he saw the cathedral's golden towers looming above the crazy maze of narrow medieval streets and the sight reminded him that he hadn't seen George Merryweather for a while.

George was one of the cathedral's canons, responsible for exorcism in the diocese, along with any other problems thrown up by the occult or the supernatural. The disorganised, rather jovial George seemed like the last person anyone would pit against the powers of darkness. But George, like his ultimate boss, moved in mysterious ways. Joe had often thought that he lulled the forces of evil into a false sense of security and caught them off their guard.

The two men had met shortly after Joe's arrival in Eborby, when he had investigated a burglary at the clergyman's home. They had talked and talked back then, often into the early hours, Joe returning time and time again to unburden his soul. George had understood Joe's grief at

losing Kaitlin in a tragic accident six months after their
wedding and his guilt and confusion about Kevin's violent
death some two years later. He had helped him to come to
terms with what he'd lost and what still remained. Joe
made a mental note to get in touch with George sooner
rather than later. But in the meantime he had a murder to
investigate.

He continued down Gallowgate until he reached
Singmass Close and stood in the archway for a few
moments, staring at the crime scene tape and the small
heap of cellophane-wrapped flowers that marked the spot
where Natalie Parkes's body had been found. A pair of
elderly ladies, early risers like many of their generation,
were chatting to the young uniformed constable guarding
the scene. They looked as if they were enjoying the excitement, fussing over the young man like a pair of
grandmother hens.

As he marched towards the constable and his admirers
the larger of the two ladies shot him a suspicious look. 'We
don't know nothing, love. You can ask all you like but we
can't tell you nowt.' She sounded as if she'd said those
words many times before and was getting sick of repeating
herself.

Joe smiled and held out his warrant card. 'DI
Plantagenet. Had a lot of trouble with reporters, have
you?'

The woman's expression changed, like a dark cloud lift-
ing. 'You could say that, love. Won't take no for an answer
some of 'em. Mind you, Tony here's seen them off,
haven't you, love?' She gave the young constable a fond
look and he blushed crimson beneath his helmet.

Joe gave young Tony an encouraging smile, wondering
how long it would be before the press cottoned on to the
fact that four women had been murdered in exactly the
same location fifty years ago. The details of the doll found

by the body hadn't yet been released but once it was made public there were several tabloid editors who would think all their birthdays had come at once. Joe could just imagine the headlines. 'Has Singmass Close Doll Strangler struck again?' It was a question he was asking himself.

'Poor lass,' the woman continued. 'You're not safe anywhere nowadays, are you?'

'You're right there, love. It's not like it used to be in the old days,' said Joe, giving Tony a barely discernible wink. 'I take it you live here then?'

'Oh aye. Number five just over yonder.'

'Nice little houses.'

'Oh aye. Very handy they are.'

Joe noticed her shiver slightly. It seemed colder here than it had been on Gallowgate . . . but that might have been his imagination.

'You remember what it was like round here in the old days . . . before these houses were built?'

'It were right scruffy round here. Nowt much more than slums, so I'm told. Not that I was here. I lived in Ripon . . . only moved here to be nearer my daughter.'

Joe looked at the other woman enquiringly. 'And I've moved from out near Pickering.'

Joe tried hard not to show his disappointment. Just his luck to find a couple of Singmass Close residents who hadn't been around there in the 1950s. However, there must be hundreds – if not thousands – of Eborby residents who could give him chapter and verse on the Doll Strangler murders. There had already been a couple of calls to the incident room before he left the previous night, helpfully drawing the police's attention to the murders in those same streets many years before. And once the press office released the details of the doll, all hell would break loose.

Joe was relieved to leave the confines of Singmass

Close. It was as though a weight had been lifted; as though he was no longer being watched by unseen eyes. He hurried on down Gallowgate and saw the cathedral looming to his right.

It was a drizzly Sunday and too early for the tourists to begin prowling the streets or for the bells of the great cathedral to disturb the Sabbath silence. As Joe passed the soaring church, people were drifting into the south door for morning communion and he experienced a fleeting desire to join them, to sit there in the shadowy tranquillity of the huge nave listening to the familiar, comforting words that would help him make sense of life, death and suffering. He wavered for a few seconds, staring at the great oak door. But he knew he had to be at the station for Emily's morning briefing. And then there was the post-mortem. Another reminder of mortality.

As he walked on through the morning streets he could smell the rich aroma of chocolate in the air, drifting across the city from the chocolate factory on the northern edge. He crossed the bridge over the grey, swollen river and when he arrived at the incident room he found most of the team were already there. Only Emily Thwaite herself seemed to be absent, but it wasn't long before she bustled in looking harassed and shouting to the assembled officers that her briefing would take place in ten minutes.

Joe followed her into her office. 'Everything OK, boss?'

She turned round and gave him a feeble smile. There were dark rings under her eyes and she looked tired. 'I was up half the night with our Sarah.' She picked up a file off the desk and slumped down on her leather swivel chair. 'Did you ever have an imaginary friend when you were little, Joe?'

Joe shook his head. 'Don't think so. Why?'

'Sarah's got one . . . name of Grizelda. We thought it was quite cute when it started but now it's become like an obsession. We've got to put meals out for bloody Grizelda and leave a space in the car and . . . Last night she kept coming in saying Grizelda was crying. After the fifth time, I'm afraid I lost it a bit and told her not to be so bloody stupid.' She gave Joe a guilty smile. 'Jeff said I've probably scarred her for life.'

'I'm sure she'll get over it,' Joe said as he sat down. 'I believe nobody's been able to contact Natalie Parkes's mother.'

'The South of France is a big place.' She paused. 'I finally got hold of the father in New York before I went home last night. He took it remarkably calmly.'

Joe raised his eyebrows. No father he'd ever known would have taken the news of a daughter's murder calmly. 'I take it he's coming over.'

Emily shook her head. 'Said there was no point till the funeral.'

'Surely there's his son . . .'

'Don't tell me, Joe, tell him.' She looked at her watch. 'Time to rally the troops. PM's booked at nine-thirty.'

Joe walked out into the incident room where pictures of the dead girl in life and death had been pinned to a large noticeboard, the contrast so shocking that it almost took his breath away.

Next to the noticeboard was a white board on which Emily had scrawled various observations. Everyone who was at The Devil's Playground on Friday night had to be traced, interviewed and eliminated, and the car Brett Bluit had seen draw up beside Natalie had to be found as a matter of priority. And someone had to drag the original files on the Doll Strangler murders in the 1950s out of the archives to see whether there was a genuine link with the case from the past or whether reading about it had just given some sick killer a gruesome idea to copy.

When Emily asked about the house-to-house interviews it seemed they had drawn a blank. Only Jamilla Dal had anything of interest to contribute. She had tried to call at number six Singmass Close on several occasions but nobody had answered the door, even though the neighbours had claimed there should be someone in. And the doll in the window staring down at the murder scene had made her uneasy. It reminded her of the doll found with the body, she said with a shudder. Joe told her to try again. Jamilla, the only Asian officer in CID, was a level-headed young woman, not one to let her imagination run away with her. If Jamilla felt there was something wrong, Joe knew it was worth investigating.

He sat beside Emily and listened while she announced that first thing on Monday morning Natalie's friends at Hicklethorpe Manor School would be interviewed. They needed all the information they could get about the dead girl. And all the gossip.

Once the briefing was over, Joe drove to the hospital with Emily sitting beside him. She said nothing as he steered through the traffic, cursing the tourists who were circling like vultures in search of a precious parking space. It wasn't like Emily to be silent, but he knew she was psyching herself up for the post-mortem. Joe felt the same. He still hated the intrusion into the privacy of the dead.

Dr Sally Sharpe looked remarkably cheerful when they arrived . . . almost as if she didn't mind her weekends being disturbed by the necessities of work. But for a pathologist, Joe supposed it came with the territory.

Sally gave him a coy smile, ignoring Emily for the moment. 'Ready?'

He breathed deeply and smiled, ignoring the hint of promise in her eyes.

Natalie Parkes was waiting for them on the stainless steel table. She looked as though she was asleep and Joe hesitated before accepting Sally's invitation to draw nearer so he could get a better view of the proceedings.

Sally began her minute examination of the naked corpse, noting every mark and scar and observing that there were marks around the neck consistent with strangulation by a ligature – something soft like a scarf or a tie . . . or a stocking.

Sally spoke matter of factly into a microphone suspended above the table, nodding to her assistant when she wanted something photographed for posterity. She continued her examination, ending with the conclusion that the big toe on the victim's left foot had been severed cleanly by some sort of sharp blade.

Joe watched as Sally ran her gloved fingers over the dead girl's torso before making a Y-shaped incision in the chest. He almost expected Natalie to cry out as the flesh was sliced open but all he could hear was Sally's voice keeping up a running commentary. As he watched her going about her work, he was torn between marvelling at the wonderful creation that is the human body and feeling slightly queasy at the sight of the girl being violated in the name of science. When he glanced at Emily he saw that she was staring at the microphone, her lips set in a determined line.

'She'd had a fair bit to drink,' Sally observed as she emptied the stomach contents into a bowl. 'If she'd kept it up at that rate, she'd have been on this slab in a few years without the help of a strangler.'

Emily wrinkled her nose at the smell. 'She was young,' she mumbled. 'Everyone's entitled to do daft things when they're young.'

Joe caught her eye and gave her a weak smile, wondering whether she was remembering her own misspent youth before her wings had been clipped by marriage, kids and a career in CID. She'd never talked about her early days much but he imagined that she would have been a bubbly and attractive teenager.

He was glad when it was over, when all the samples had been taken and the body sewn back up again, respectable for the relatives.

'So what do you think? Anything we should know?' Emily asked as they walked to Sally's office.

Sally didn't speak for a while. It wasn't until she'd sat down at her desk with the two police officers opposite her, eyes wide, awaiting her opinion, that she finally delivered the verdict.

'There's nothing too unexpected. The cause of death was strangulation, there's no sign of sexual interference and the toe's been cut off after death with a sharp blade – a knife or scalpel. It's a fairly neat job . . . but I don't think our friend cut up bodies for a living.'

Emily leaned forward. 'Not someone with medical training then?'

Sally gave an enigmatic smile. 'Not a butcher either . . . or an abattoir worker. But one thing I am sure about is that she died where she was found. There's no indication that the body was moved.'

'What about that doll beside her?' said Joe. 'Could there be some sort of ritual element to the killing?'

Sally gave him an apologetic smile. 'I can only give you the facts. Interpreting them is your job.'

'Do you think the same knife was used to cut off the girl's toe and mutilate the doll?'

'I don't do post-mortems on dolls,' Sally replied quickly. Then she spoke again, more co-operative this time as though she regretted her abruptness. 'Maybe,' she said. 'But the hands and feet are porcelain, aren't they, so it'd be easy to break the toe off.' She looked at Joe. 'Have you discovered anything about the doll? Is it an antique or . . .?'

It was Emily who answered. 'We think it is but we're going to get an expert to confirm it. If we can find out where it came from . . .'

'We'll be halfway there,' said Joe, suddenly aware that he'd finished Emily's sentence for her . . . something he'd only associated with long-married couples. He looked at her and grinned and she gave him a tentative half smile in return.

'Have you heard that there were four similar murders in the nineteen fifties?' Joe asked.

Sally's eyes widened in surprise. 'It's not been mentioned on the news.'

'We're keeping it under wraps till we know more about the original crimes. But the press is sure to make the connection soon.'

Sally rolled her eyes. 'Matter of hours, I should think. They'll be like pigs in muck. Was this fifties killer ever caught?'

'Afraid not.'

As they took their leave of Sally, Joe, like Emily, was only too glad to get out of that place of death. They both needed some fresh air and a strong coffee.

'I reckon she fancies you,' Emily said bluntly as Joe unlocked the car doors.

Joe looked at her, curious. 'Who does?'

'Little Miss Frankenstein. Sally. All the time she was cutting up that body, she was giving you the come on.'

'I wasn't looking.' Joe wondered if she knew about the incident at the Christmas party. There wasn't much that escaped the DCI's notice, if rumour was to be believed.

'Let's get back to the station. I need a coffee to wake me up.'

Joe glanced at Emily sitting in the passenger seat. She had her handbag on her knee and she stared ahead, frowning slightly, like a woman with a lot on her mind.

Michele was hungry. Sylvia had taken her downstairs the previous night and watched while she dusted and polished the furniture in the living room. It was necessary, she said. The place had to be immaculate for the coming photo shoot.

After she'd cleaned Michele had looked for the little canvas bag containing her mobile phone but Sylvia had told her it had been left in the car and she'd get it for her later. But she'd never kept that promise.

Then Michele had had to cook. Four meals – for herself and Sylvia and for two unseen people whom Sylvia had said were photographic technicians staying in another part of the house. Michele did it without question, just as she'd cleaned and polished. Perhaps every model went through this. Perhaps it was some sort of apprenticeship. But sausage and beans seemed very mundane sustenance for people involved in the glamorous world of fashion – somehow she'd expected sushi or Thai. But she was too excited by the promise of involvement in the photo shoot to ask too many questions.

Sylvia had ordered her to have an early night and she had slept like the dead in that plain little attic room. When she awoke in the morning her head was aching. And the door was stuck again.

Michele sneaked a look at her watch. It was nine twenty-five. She'd slept in late and she hoped it wouldn't go against her. But as the bedroom door opened to reveal Sylvia standing there, looking *soignée* as ever with a fixed smile on her face, she knew she'd got away with it.

'I'm afraid the kitchen floor needs cleaning,' Sylvia said apologetically. 'And I take it you can cook a Sunday dinner. Chicken?'

Michele looked at her in panic.

'You see that photographer I mentioned is arriving soon and he'll expect to be fed.'

'I'll try,' said Michele desperately. 'The door's stuck again. I need the loo.'

Sylvia smiled. 'Of course, dear. Such a nuisance. I'll try and get it seen to.'

Michele clambered off the bed, still wearing the T-shirt she'd taken from her rucksack. 'My other bag . . . did you find it?'

'Sorry. Not had a moment to look. Later,' Sylvia said quickly. 'You'd better get dressed. There's a lot to do. I'll get you a change of clothes. Wash the ones you've been wearing and hang them to dry in the kitchen. Not outside. Never outside. And there's more washing to do as well. You can do it when you've cooked the dinner.'

Michele nodded. She had to show willing. She'd never have thought that models' clothes needed washing – but she was learning.

Sylvia returned a few minutes later with a carrier bag containing clean clothes.

Clothes that were fashionable but too big. Clothes that seemed to be designed for another girl altogether.

Sunny Porter had shared the story of the Singmass Close Doll Strangler with the entire office, reading aloud from the book he'd received for his birthday, thinking it would save precious time. Emily had requested the 1950s case files from the archives in the basement and seven more calls had come in from elderly people who thought they were being good citizens by pointing out that four women had once died in Singmass Close.

The more Joe learned about the old case and the murder of Natalie Parkes, the more he realised that the similarities were no coincidence. Either the original killer had decided to resume his old hobby in his dotage or someone had read about the old case and decided to emulate a murderer who had disappeared into the night over fifty years before and had never been caught.

Sunny's book, however, made absolutely no mention of

severed toes, which either meant that the original killer hadn't mutilated his victims – and the dolls found with them – or that the police hadn't revealed it to the press at the time. Joe knew that the original files would tell him for certain, but in the meantime, he sat at his desk and closed his eyes, going over what they had so far and getting things straight in his mind.

His musings were interrupted by a young DC who stumbled into the incident room, laden down with a pile of dusty box files. As soon as Joe realised that he was making for his desk, he hurriedly cleared a space on the cluttered surface.

When the DC relieved himself of his burden, a cloud of dust flew up, making everyone in the vicinity cough and splutter. 'Thanks Mark,' said Joe, with a hint of sarcasm as a fine layer of dust began to settle on his desk and computer screen.

Joe called Jamilla over. He'd need someone to go through this lot with him . . . someone he could rely on to sort the useful from the irrelevant.

Once he'd explained what he wanted, Jamilla opened the first file and began work. And it wasn't long before she'd discovered that the bodies of the Singmass Close victims back in the 1950s had indeed been mutilated, as had the dolls found beside them. But this fact had never been revealed to the public at the time.

Now all they had to do was discover whether the information had been released at a later date . . . and whether it was contained in any of the true crime books that proliferated on the shelves of most of Eborby's bookshops . . . or even on the Internet somewhere.

It was nine-thirty in the evening before Joe had a chance to leave the office and head for home. His head was aching and if he was to be any use the next day, he needed an early night. Since Maddy had left for London there was nothing in prospect but early nights with a couple of bottles of Black Sheep or Sam Smiths for company, and he was almost glad to have the inquiry to take his mind off the potentially seismic shift in his domestic fortunes.

The thought of Maddy's interview nagged at the back of his mind as he made his way home. There had been several women since Kaitlin's death but Maddy was the only one he'd felt close to. She had become part of his life over the past months and he couldn't help wondering whether this reluctance to make their relationship more permanent wasn't a mistake. He suspected that the job application had been some sort of test. If it was, he was afraid he'd failed miserably. He hadn't been able to take her hand and tell her that he needed her because the wounds of the past were still too raw and painful. Even when he thought they had healed, that he could start again, the memories always seemed to be there, nestling in the recesses of his mind like sleeping monsters.

Everywhere seemed quiet as he walked on through Vicars Green. Eborby was the sort of place visitors came to England to see – picture-postcard quaint with narrow medieval streets and crooked overhanging buildings – and there were times when you could hardly move there for Japanese and Americans wielding expensive cameras. But today the autumnal chill had put off the tourists.

He made his way down Gallowgate towards Canons Bar and stopped at the entrance to Singmass Close. Then he wandered through the archway, past the stone chapel and the old Ragged School with its skips and scaffolding, onto the paved square. Natalie Parkes's body had been dumped at the far end, where Singmass Close led out to Andrewgate.

The police tape was still there, swamped now by a growing heap of cellophane-wrapped flowers, arranged by someone into an impromptu shrine to Natalie Parkes. Some of the flowers had been left by her school friends but Joe knew that most of the tributes were from people who'd never known her in life – people who'd felt moved for some reason to mark her death. A teenage girl bound for university with all her life before her. It was sad however you looked at it.

As he stared at the spot, he suddenly felt that he was being watched. But when he swung round he noticed a sheet of blue plastic hanging from the scaffolding around the old Ragged School flapping gently in a non-existent breeze and he smiled to himself. He was getting jumpy. It was then he spotted the pale porcelain doll again, sitting in the upstairs front window of number six. The thing seemed to be watching him with great interest and he felt a small thrill of fear. But he told himself not to be so stupid. It was a doll, nothing more. A child's plaything. But there seemed to be something vaguely malevolent about that expressionless porcelain face.

He remembered Jamilla saying that number six was the only house that hadn't been visited; that either there'd been nobody in, or the occupants weren't answering the door. He saw a light glowing behind the frosted glass of the front door, a spot of brightness in the evening gloom, and he felt in his coat pocket for his warrant card. If the residents of number six had been avoiding the police, they weren't going to escape this time.

He rang the bell and shivered. It had suddenly turned colder. Inside the house he could hear approaching footsteps, shoes tapping on a wooden floor. Then the door opened a few inches and a woman peeped out cautiously. But with a murder in the neighbourhood, caution was hardly surprising.

'I'm Detective Inspector Plantagenet, Eborby CID. I know it's late but I wonder if I might have a quick word.'

The door opened a little wider to reveal a slim woman

in her early thirties with short brown hair. Her large hazel eyes were outlined in kohl and she was dressed from head to toe in black: tight black jeans and black sweatshirt like a scene shifter in some modern theatre. And she had a stark, striking beauty that made Joe catch his breath. He knew her and yet he also knew that he'd never seen her in his life before. Kaitlin. She was the image of Kaitlin and he felt his stomach lurch.

'I can't help you. I didn't see anything.' Her voice was accentless and slightly husky and he could sense anxiety behind her words.

'You were out when my colleagues called.' These words were the first that came into his head and he was just glad that they sounded fairly sensible.

'Yes,' she answered.

'Does anyone else live here?'

She hesitated. 'Only my daughter, Daisy. She's five.'

'I don't suppose she saw anything . . . if she couldn't sleep . . . Has she mentioned . . . ?'

'Daisy wasn't here that night. She was staying at a friend's. I was here on my own.'

'I noticed a doll in the window. Does that belong to Daisy?'

The woman nodded.

'If you remember anything, will you call me?' Joe felt in his pocket for his card and when he handed it to her he could feel his hands trembling slightly. 'Anything at all, however trivial.'

Her eyes met his and she gave him a wary half-smile. Almost Kaitlin's smile but not quite.

'I'll send one of my colleagues to take a statement. Just routine.'

'Won't you call yourself?' It might have been wishful thinking but he thought he detected a hint of disappointment in the woman's voice.

'If I get the chance.' He wavered for a moment. 'You, er . . . didn't tell me your name.'

'Polly . . . Polly Myers.'

'Thank you, Ms Myers,' he said formally, turning to go. He needed to be out of there.

He retraced his steps through Singmass Close with an uncomfortable feeling that he was being watched. Perhaps Polly was still at the door, he thought. But when he turned to look he saw that she wasn't there.

As he hurried on through the archway back onto Gallowgate he could hear that the Royal Oak's karaoke evening was in full swing and an out-of-tune baritone was pleading with someone to please release him.

'Gladly,' Joe murmured as he made for home.

They'd released her name. Natalie.

The Doll Strangler read the report again, rocking to and fro, mumbling the name Natalie . . . remembering ever sensation. He recalled every sound in that silent close fifty years ago – their gasps and the gurgling and choking as they died – and he felt a tingling in his loins as their death agonies ran like a video through his head – the bulging eyes then the dreadful stillness broken by the giggles of those children like wind rustling through leaves.

He knew the dolls were still sitting up there in the loft, staring with their cold glass eyes. He hadn't seen them for so long but he knew they were waiting for him up there.

He needed to feel the life flowing once more into his cold, stiff limbs so he poured himself a tot of whisky with shaking hands.

'To Natalie,' he whispered. 'And to the next one.' Then he raised the glass to the empty air before swallowing the warm, golden water of life.

Chapter 5

It was nine o'clock on Monday morning and Sunny Porter was ploughing his way through a pile of musty files. DI Plantagenet had said it was important to trace anyone involved in the case back in the 1950s who might still be around. In Sunny's opinion they'd be better off grilling some of those kids from The Devil's Playground again. They had all pleaded ignorance but one of them must have got hold of a copy of *Foul Murders and Dark Deeds in Eborby* and decided to commit a copycat killing. Sunny would have staked a week's pay on it. But a quiet voice interrupted his thoughts.

'There's a girl just been reported missing, Sarge. Name of Michele Carden. Lives in Easton . . . village on the way to Thirsk. She was last seen boarding the train to Eborby at her local station.'

Sunny Porter looked up at DC Jenny Ripon, who didn't look more than eighteen – the age of Natalie Parkes – and was, in Sunny's opinion, still wet behind the ears. 'Oh aye?'

'With this murder of a young girl, I just thought we should be keeping a look out for anyone of a similar age who's been reported missing, that's all,' she said, defensively. Killers like that didn't usually stop at one victim. 'And that other girl . . . Leanne Williams. She's still not been found.'

Sunny Porter scratched his crotch and Jenny looked away, embarrassed. 'Aye, you're right, love,' he said. 'But you've got to remember that lasses go walkabout every day. Row at home . . . my parents don't understand me. This Michelle'll probably be back within twenty-four hours. Nowt to worry about, if you ask me.'

'The mother's contacted all her friends and nobody's seen her. One of them said she'd talked about going off to London to find a modelling job.'

'There you are then,' Sunny replied, slightly relieved. They had enough on their plate with the Singmass Close murder without worrying about some silly lass seeking fame and fortune.

'But she only had about fifty quid with her.'

Sunny sighed, surveying the pile of paper on his desk. 'So she might have been daft enough to hitch. It's not our problem. Let the Met sort it out.'

'I can at least see if she was caught on CCTV at the station. We might be able to find out if she picked up the London train.'

'You do that, love, if it makes you happy. The rest of us are busy sorting out this murder. And we've got to do it before he decides to have another go. There were four back in the nineteen fifties. He could be out to break the record.'

'The mother's downstairs in reception. Shall I . . .?'

'Aye love, give her the usual spiel. They usually turn up within twenty-four hours, etcetera etcetera.'

'It's been forty-eight hours already.'

'She can't be too worried if she's only just reporting it, then. Off you go and have a word with her if you must.'

Sunny saw Jenny Ripon shoot him a contemptuous glance. She was young, he thought. She'd learn.

When Jenny reached reception she saw a woman sitting on the upholstered bench near the front desk, playing with a mobile phone, flipping it open and staring at the screen as though she was expecting a call or text. She looked impatient rather than anxious, as though the girl's disappearance was a nuisance rather than a life-shattering event. She was a middle-aged glossy blonde in a businesslike black suit – rather like DCI Thwaite's but better cut.

She looked up as Jenny approached and her expression was more one of irritation than worry.

'Mrs Carden.'

The woman gave a cautious half nod. 'The name's Pugh actually – Caroline Pugh. Carden's Michele's father's name . . . my first husband. Look, can we get this over with? I've got to be at a meeting in an hour.'

'You want to report your daughter missing, I understand? Michele, isn't it?' Jenny sat down on the bench beside the woman and caught a whiff of her perfume – Gucci Envy. She'd been given some herself last Christmas.

'I didn't want to bother, if the truth be told, but my younger daughter said we should and I was in Eborby today for a meeting so . . .'

Jenny watched her and caught a brief glimpse of anxiety behind the cool exterior. Perhaps this woman was more worried than she was letting on. 'When did Michele go missing?'

'She stormed out on Saturday . . . took some things with her. We left it till yesterday then I phoned round all her friends from school but they said they didn't know anything.'

'Did you suspect any of them were lying . . . covering for her?'

The woman shrugged. 'Who knows?'

'What school does she go to?'

'Hicklethorpe Manor. She's doing her GCSEs this year. She gets the train into Eborby every day so she's used to finding her way around.'

Jenny made the connection. Natalie Parkes had been in the sixth form at Hicklethorpe Manor and DCI Thwaite was going to have a word with her classmates later that morning. Perhaps there was a link. Showing a bit of initiative in front of Emily Thwaite would do her career no harm whatsoever, she thought to herself as she gave the woman a sympathetic smile.

'Have you got a photograph of Michele?' she asked hopefully.

She was rather surprised when one was produced from the Prada handbag. She took it and looked at the girl pouting at her from beneath a curtain of shiny dark hair. Michele Carden was stunning all right. Definitely model material – tall, slim and photogenic, three things Jenny herself knew she could never be.

'I'd better take down all the details.'

Michele Carden's mother glanced at her watch. 'You'll have to be quick,' she said.

As Jenny began to write, Caroline Pugh tapped her fingers impatiently. Almost as if she had more important things to do than to find her missing daughter.

There had been a special assembly at Hicklethorpe Manor School. A ritual to remember, and in some cases to pray for, the family of Natalie. A girl who had everything to live for. A life cut tragically short.

The school itself was housed in a fine Georgian building, once home to Eborby's mayor, not far from the city centre. When the elegant building had become a school, an array of ugly extensions – sports halls and science laboratories – had sprouted like unsightly growths on a beautiful face.

It was the headmaster himself, Mr Benjamin Cassidy, who greeted Joe and Emily. His face was grave and he was wearing a black tie, as though he was already in mourning.

The tall, dapper Mr Cassidy reminded Joe of a man he'd once arrested in Liverpool; an immaculately dressed solicitor who'd murdered his wife, cut up her body and scattered the pieces around Delamere Forest. As he received Mr Cassidy's appropriately firm handshake, he tried to put this resemblance out of his mind.

'Terrible business,' the headmaster said once they were seated in his study. 'I thought the assembly might help our students come to terms with the tragedy. A public act of mourning is always cathartic, don't you think. And we're bringing in counsellors of course.'

'Really?' said Emily, tight-lipped. Joe knew she had no time for anything she considered to be psycho-babble. The Emily he'd come to know was of the 'get on with it and what doesn't kill you makes you stronger' school of thought. And she was no stranger to problems, he thought, especially when Jeff, her husband, had been falsely accused of sexually assaulting a pupil back in Leeds. That had been Emily's nightmare time – just as the deaths of Kaitlin and Kevin had been his.

One look at Emily's sceptical expression told him that he had to do the talking. 'I'm sure you'll do all you can,' he said smoothly. 'In the meantime, we'd like a word with Natalie's classmates. We need to find out all we can about Natalie and the people she mixed with.'

It might have been Joe's imagination, but for a split second, Cassidy's guard slipped and he looked frightened. 'It was a maniac, surely. A maniac attacked her on her way home.' The words came out in a rush. 'I really don't see how talking to my students would . . .' His words trailed off and Joe had the uncomfortable feeling that there was more behind his objections than a concern for the finer feelings of his pupils. Something personal maybe.

'I'm afraid it's necessary or we wouldn't ask.' Joe wasn't going to be messed around. Teenagers kept each other's secrets and he needed to know whether Natalie had any. He glanced at Emily and she gave a slight nod. It was time to cast their bait and watch the reaction. 'I don't know if you're aware that another of your pupils has been reported missing.'

'Students. We call them students,' the headmaster corrected.

Cassidy was beginning to get up Joe's nose but he tried not to let it show. 'You do know about it, then?'

Cassidy hesitated, arching his fingers beneath his chin in a gesture of consideration. 'I don't actually. You'll appreciate that other staff deal with day-to-day absences so I wouldn't necessarily be informed right away. Who is it and when did he or she go missing?'

'Her name's Michele Carden . . . she's in her GCSE year.'

'Really.'

Joe glanced at Emily again and saw that she was tapping her fingers on her knee impatiently.

'You must know what year she's in,' she snapped, looking the man in the eye.

'There are six hundred students here. Unless one of them stands out for some reason, it takes a while to put a face to the name, as I'm sure you'll understand,' he said smoothly.

'Well Michele would stand out. She's tall and stunning. Wants to be a model.'

There was a flicker of something in Cassidy's eye that Joe thought could be lust, there for a split second then swiftly suppressed. 'Yes, I think I can place her now.'

'Did Natalie and Michele mix with each other at all?' Emily asked.

Cassidy turned to Joe as though he'd judged him to be the most sympathetic of the pair. 'You know what teenagers are like, Inspector. Particularly the female of the species.'

He gave Emily an apologetic smile and she scowled back. 'I'm afraid I can't tell you whether Michele and Natalie had anything to do with each other outside school. Perhaps some of the other students might be able to help you. Although I feel I can't allow them to be interviewed without their parents' consent,' he added smugly, looking like a chess player who'd just made rather a clever move.

'Most of Natalie's friends are in the sixth form, surely. And most of them will be over eighteen,' said Emily. 'And for those that aren't, I'm sure you or one of the teachers wouldn't mind being present as an appropriate adult.' Her mouth formed a charming smile, which disappeared as swiftly as it had appeared.

Check mate, thought Joe to himself.

'Where were you on Friday night, Mr Cassidy – around one-thirty in the morning?' Emily asked.

'Why? Surely I'm not a suspect.' Cassidy sounded quite indignant. 'If you must know I was at home.'

'Can anyone verify that?'

Cassidy swallowed hard. 'I live alone, Chief Inspector. You'll have to take my word for it.'

'I take it there's a room we can use?' Joe asked.

'Of course.' Cassidy stood up. He didn't look pleased but he knew when he was defeated.

Once provided with a room – a classroom with posters of kings and queens and assorted historical events ranged around the walls – Natalie Parkes's classmates streamed in one by one. They'd already spoken to Karen Strange and Brett Bluit, and they didn't elaborate on the information they'd already given. However, they seemed more relaxed this time, as though they were old hands at dealing with police questioning. With their new-found confidence, Joe hoped they'd be able to catch them off their guard. But he was to be disappointed. Both Karen and Brett were word perfect. Almost as though they'd been rehearsing.

The others all told the same story. Natalie was either amazing or great. She was mature and sophisticated and she seemed to have been everyone's friend. However, few people claimed to know much about her life outside school and some even said she seemed rather aloof and secretive. But every one of her classmates seemed to have reached the same conclusion. Natalie had walked home alone and had met a killer who was out looking for a young woman – any young woman. Natalie had been in the wrong place at the wrong time.

Nobody seemed to think that Natalie would be stupid enough to accept a lift from a stranger. But then Natalie had been attracted to adventure. There had been an aura of glamour and mystery around Natalie. Maybe – although it was never actually said – a whiff of danger and sex.

The consensus of opinion was that Natalie wasn't really into drugs, even though she, like many others, enjoyed the odd spliff from time to time. By the time the interviews were finished, Joe and Emily were coming round to the popular theory. Natalie's murder had been a random act of violence. A killer had learned the details of the Doll Strangler murders in the 1950s and had decided to emulate them. Natalie Parkes had just been unlucky.

While they were there Emily thought it would do no harm to have a word with Michele Carden's friends and they found them only too willing to talk. Michele and Natalie had had little, if anything, to do with each other. They were in different academic years and Michele, in spite of being fairly bright, had developed an aversion to academic life in recent months. According to her self-appointed best friends Camilla and Laura, she'd become obsessed by the idea of becoming a model and she was convinced that she could make it big in London, given half the chance. And they reckoned she had a better chance than most. She was tall, slim and gorgeous with exquisite taste in clothes. However, her potentially charmed life was hampered by a bitch of a mother who did her very best to thwart the girl's dreams and force her into some godforsaken university or other.

Michele had talked to her friends about running away . . . just disappearing down to London and trying to make it in the world of fashion. Camilla and Laura were sure she'd be all right. Michele could take care of herself, they said with brittle confidence.

'So what do you think?' Joe asked Emily as they made for the car park at the side of the school building.

'Some of those little madams deserve a good slap,' was Emily's verdict. 'Or a spell living on the Drifton Estate. Daddy buying them posh cars for their eighteenth. I had to wait till I was twenty-five and working.'

'I'm sure it was good for your soul,' Joe said with a grin.

'And you'd know all about that,' she said sharply. She never seemed to forget Joe's brief stint training for the priesthood and he sometimes wondered why it was so important to her.

'Actually the sixth formers have been to the Drifton Estate,' he said. 'Didn't you see those posters in the entrance hall about the community projects the school's involved with? At the end of the lower sixth, they send the kids to the Drifton Estate to do decorating for pensioners or they help out in a day nursery or an old people's centre. According to Cassidy's blurb on the posters, it fosters a sense of social responsibility.'

'Social responsibility my backside,' Emily snorted. 'Gives them a chance to sneer at the peasants.' She began to march towards the car.

'You've really got it in for this sort of place, haven't you, Emily? Any particular reason?'

She didn't answer for a few moments, as though she

was considering her reply carefully. 'They give certain kids an unfair advantage.'

'Is that all?' Joe sensed there was something more, something personal perhaps. Emily hesitated, as though she was about to make a revelation. But she thought better of it.

'And I didn't like that Cassidy character,' she continued. 'Slimy as a slug's prick, that one.'

'You do have a lovely turn of phrase at times, boss.'

'Hangover from my time in Leeds,' she said with a wink. 'Eborby's far more genteel.'

'Just be thankful you didn't transfer to Harrogate. You reckon Cassidy's in the frame?'

'I'm keeping an open mind.'

As Emily started the car, Joe's mobile rang. After a brief conversation, he ended the call. Just as Emily turned onto the main road, she glanced over at him.

'Well?'

'That was the station. A 2007 red Toyota sports model was captured on the CCTV camera of a pub just down the road from The Devil's Playground around one o'clock on the night of the murder. The registration number's been traced.' She paused for effect. 'It's owned by Karen Strange's mother.'

Emily flicked on the indicator. 'We'd better have a word. But I've got to see the super first. He thinks we should do a TV appeal for witnesses.' She hesitated. 'You don't fancy having fifteen minutes of fame do you, Joe?' she asked tentatively. 'Your chance to be a celebrity?'

Joe didn't reply.

Michele sat on the bed and listened for any slight sound, straining, sniffing the air like an animal trying to catch the scent of a predator. Yesterday she'd cooked, cleaned and washed but there was still no sign of any models and she hadn't met the promised photographer.

The door to her room was still stuck, although Sylvia had promised to do something about it. She'd used a chamber pot last night and it still had to be emptied. Perhaps modelling assignments were always like this, she tried to tell herself. All models said it was tough and perhaps this was what they meant.

But since yesterday a tiny voice had been nagging inside her, saying something wasn't quite right. She'd done her best to ignore it but after two nights in that little room and all the work she'd had to do, that voice was growing louder and more insistent.

She heard footsteps outside on the landing. Sylvia's footsteps; the tread of her stilettos on the linoleum. Then came the metallic sound again, like a key being turned in a lock, and the door opened.

Sylvia always looked smart and fashionable and today she wore a fitted white shirt and black linen trousers. A green silk scarf was expertly knotted around her throat and her make-up was impeccable as usual.

'Good. You're dressed,' she said with a beaming smile as Michele scrambled to her feet, clumsy as a new-born giraffe.

'Can I have my mobile? I want to let my mum know I'm OK.'

Sylvia looked apologetic. 'I'm so sorry, dear. I looked but I couldn't find it. And besides, there's no signal out here in the back of beyond. And the land line's out of order. Terrible nuisance. So sorry.' She smiled again. 'You're going to meet Barry today.' The way she said it made the promised encounter sound exciting. 'He's one of the country's top fashion photographers.' She paused, looking Michele in the eye. 'Then I'm afraid there'll be more work to do.'

Michele said nothing as her emotions swung between suspicion and hope. Some of the clothes she'd washed yesterday had been more like an old lady's nightclothes and those sheets had definitely had a whiff of urine about them. But at that moment she didn't like to ask questions. It was possible that her future career might be in the balance.

She followed Sylvia down the stairs and allowed herself to be led towards the open living-room door, her heart beating fast. Suddenly she caught sight of her reflection in the mirror. Her once glossy hair needed a good wash and the short skirt and T-shirt she was wearing hung off her tall, slender frame. She looked like a scarecrow, she thought to herself . . . or a refugee in borrowed clothes.

'I look a sight,' she said to Sylvia.

The woman turned with a cold smile. 'Don't worry, dear, you'll look fine once you've been in make-up and we've done something with your hair. Perhaps Barry might take some snaps for your portfolio if we ask him nicely.'

Sylvia propelled her forward and as she entered the living room, she saw a man sitting in the armchair next to the empty tiled fireplace. He was thin and bespectacled, half bald with a fringe of mousy hair around the base of his pale, shiny scalp. He studied Michele and the intensity of his gaze made her take an involuntary step back.

'This is Michele,' said Sylvia as though she were showing off some prize specimen.

'I'm sure she'll do,' the man said with a forced smile.

A look passed between them; a look Michele couldn't read. She stood there awkwardly. If this was Barry, he looked nothing like a top photographer.

'I'd like to watch the shoot if that's OK. I'm really keen to learn,' Michele heard herself saying, anxious to please.

Sylvia turned to face her and her cold eyes bored into

hers. Something was about to happen. And she suddenly felt a flutter of nerves in her stomach.

'They're shooting out in the countryside today. Barry's joining them later, aren't you, Barry?'

The man nodded.

'Anyway, there's lots to do here.' Michele saw her eyes meet Barry's. 'In fact I think it's time you were introduced to Alice.'

Sylvia took her elbow firmly and steered her towards the door. And she was too taken aback to utter the question she most wanted to ask. Who was Alice?

Chapter 6

With most of the team out pursuing enquiries, the incident room was virtually empty. Which was just how Joe liked it. It gave him a chance to think.

He needed to talk to Vince and Barbara Strange about the whereabouts of their Toyota on the night of Natalie's death. But they wouldn't be home till later so he seized the opportunity to study the files on the Doll Strangler murders in the 1950s.

The papers were yellowed with faint, uneven typing, but as Joe read through the statements and the post-mortem reports he became lost in another world . . . in an Eborby that had existed long before he was born. A monochrome city of grime, of smoky chimneys, bomb damage and post-war austerity, largely undiscovered by the tourist masses. In the days before Eborby had been prettied up and polished to a sparkle there had still been dirt and grubby industry around the city centre. And there'd been grim slums, nests of festering deprivation and ugliness which had since been planned out of sight and banished to the likes of the Drifton Estate, well hidden from tourists' camera lenses.

In 1954 when the first body was found, things like sex and death were only spoken of in euphemisms and hushed voices. Back then Singmass Close had been a dilapidated cluster of workmen's cottages, crowded around the medieval chapel and a crumbling Georgian building known as the Ragged School, which had been used for the education and care of destitute children and orphans back in the early nineteenth century.

By the 1950s the children were long gone; at the time of the murders, the upper floors of the Ragged School were used for storage and the ground floor was a dolls' hospital, where toys were brought for repair. Because of the dolls found with the bodies, the dolls' hospital had been investigated but the proprietor, a man called Albert Jervis, had been ruled out as a suspect. According to the records, Jervis had solid alibis for three of the murders. Too solid perhaps. If Joe had been in charge of the case, maybe he would have checked them out more thoroughly.

The first victim was a nineteen-year-old shop assistant called Marion Grant. She had walked home alone from the cinema and her strangled body was found next morning down a narrow alley near the old Ragged School, a doll lying by her side. Marion's big toe had been severed, just as Natalie Parkes's had been. And the doll beside her had borne the same mutilation. Marion had argued with her boyfriend Peter Crawthwaite, a couple of days before but an unbreakable alibi meant he'd been eliminated from enquiries.

Several memos amongst the musty-smelling papers emphasised the importance of keeping the details of the mutilation confidential, certainly until a conviction had been secured. As the culprit had never been caught, those details had never been leaked. The chief investigating officer in those days – a man called Frazer – had obviously run a tight ship and, as far as Joe could see, nobody had broken the rules. The mutilations had never been made public.

The second victim was a typist called Valerie Seddon. A

few weeks after the first murder she had been visiting her invalid aunt one evening, leaving just as darkness fell. She never arrived home and was found in a back snicket behind a row of houses in Singmass Close, again with a doll lying beside her. The big toe of her left foot had been neatly severed, as had the doll's. Again the dolls' hospital was investigated but nothing suspicious was ever found. Albert Jervis had claimed that the dolls hadn't come from his premises but this had never been proved one way or the other.

Two more murders followed. Both victims had been strangled with a ligature just like the first two, something soft like a scarf or a stocking. And both had been mutilated. The third victim, Vera Jones, was a young barmaid coming home from her shift and the fourth, Doris Cray, was an assistant at a local bakery, walking home from a friend's house. The police assumed that the killer had carried out the mutilations to obtain gruesome souvenirs of the crimes. But the purpose of the dolls, mutilated in exactly the same manner, had always remained a mystery.

Joe reread the papers and sat staring at the type until it swam before his eyes. Four deaths then the killings stopped suddenly. Perhaps because the Doll Strangler – as the press had come to call him – had moved from the area . . . or died. The sudden cessation had baffled the police back then. And as Joe read the files, it baffled him too.

'Joe. A word when you've got a moment.'

He looked up and saw Emily disappearing into her office. She had just been to see the super and she didn't look happy. He tidied the files on his desk and followed her into her office.

As he entered, she slumped down in her chair and looked up at him, attempting a smile which turned out more like a grimace of pain.

'I'm making a public appeal tonight with Natalie's

brother. The super thinks it might jog memories but I think it'll just bring all the weirdos in Yorkshire crawling out of the woodwork. Once some bright spark from the *Eborby Argus* latched onto the connection with the nineteen fifties murders, all hell broke loose in the press office.'

Joe sat down in the seat at the other side of her desk. 'It's just the kind of thing the press love to make a meal of. Doll Strangler resurrected from the grave.'

'I don't suppose anything new has come in while I've been out?'

'Not yet. But I've been going through the nineteen-fifties files.'

'I've had a quick glance at them myself. If our friend's intending to follow the pattern, we've got a lot to look forward to. I've asked uniform to increase patrols in the Singmass Close area.' She gave a deep sigh. 'Bloody hell, Joe, I could do with a drink.'

'You've got to go on TV exuding authority, boss.'

'So maybe a bit of Dutch courage wouldn't go amiss.' She looked Joe in the eye and grinned. 'But if that's out of the question, it might help to go over what we've got so far.'

She scrabbled for a sheet of paper and a pen to jot down their thoughts. When she was ready, Joe began. 'Natalie Parkes goes for an evening out with her friend, Karen Strange, to The Devil's Playground. Nothing particularly bad known about the place apart from a few class B and C drugs being available on the premises. Natalie accidentally walks off with her friend's handbag and Brett Bluit sees her talking to someone in a car belonging to Karen Strange's mother. Karen herself spends the night with a bloke and she arrives home in blissful ignorance the next morning. Brett Bluit claims to have gone back into the club after seeing Natalie at the car and he says he went home soon after that – story confirmed by his doting mother who conveniently lay awake listening for him to come in.'

'That figures.'

'You reckon? He's eighteen.'

Emily smirked. 'It's obvious you haven't got kids, Joe. I'll be waiting up for mine till they're in their forties.' She stopped suddenly and Joe could tell she'd just remembered that Kaitlin had died before they'd had a chance to have children and she was cursing her tactlessness. He gave her a small, reassuring smile: the last thing he wanted was for her to feel that she had to tread on eggshells whenever they talked.

She moved on quickly. 'Natalie's body's found in Singmass Close, near where the victims were found in the nineteen fifties. Identical MO . . . the ligature, the doll and the mutilations. Where the hell did that doll come from? That's what I want to know.'

Joe shook his head. 'They never discovered the source of the dolls in the old murders. But reading the reports from the time, I started to wonder whether Albert Jervis who ran the dolls' hospital in the old Ragged School was lying when he said he couldn't tell whether any of his dolls were missing. But he had alibis for all the murders.'

'Anyone else in the frame?'

'Jervis had an assistant called Caleb Selly – bit of a loner but he had an unbreakable alibi for the first murder victim, Marion Grant. Caleb was visiting the house of Marion's boyfriend, Peter Crawthwaite. They played in the local cricket team together. Crawthwaite's dad was a magistrate. Selly stayed for a drink or two.'

'I take it the magistrate was there?'

'He was out at a function. It was just the son, Peter, who provided the alibi.'

'Any other suspects.'

'A few possibles but no probables. It was as if the killer disappeared into thin air. Nobody heard or saw anything.'

Emily looked up. 'Sounds a bit like Jack the Ripper.'

'Only this one wasn't kind enough to send the body parts to the police or leave writing on a wall near the scene of the crime. In fact he left no clues whatsoever. Even the dolls couldn't be traced.'

'He was playing games with the police by the sound of it.'

'The question is, is this latest one doing the same?'

'We'll get him,' Emily said confidently. 'Our main problem is doing it before he has a chance to kill again.'

'Want to come with me to see the Stranges?' he asked, hoping the answer would be yes. She had a good ear for a lie.

'Sorry, Joe, I've got this TV thing. Not that it'll do much good.'

Joe smiled. 'Stardom beckons then.'

The Doll Strangler was learning more about Natalie Parkes. It was in the paper. It was on the TV and radio. Natalie Parkes. The schoolgirl. The innocent victim. How they loved that image of violated purity.

But he'd also heard more worrying words: 'Police are investigating the possibility that Natalie's murder might be connected to a spate of killings back in the nineteen fifties and they would urge anyone with information to come forward.'

The police had remembered after all this time. But they didn't know about him and they didn't know about the children – the ones in his head who had tormented him and egged him on, poking and scratching at him if he prevaricated. Whispering in corners. Scratching with their long fingernails at the skirting boards.

81

There were still secrets they could never discover. The secrets of the grave.

As Joe sat down opposite Karen Strange's father, Vince, he noticed that the man looked uneasy. Which was just as Joe had hoped.

'Your wife told the officer who phoned earlier that you borrowed her Toyota on Friday night,' Joe said, watching the man's face carefully.

Vince nodded. 'I went to the golf club. I was there all evening until around eleven. Ask anybody.'

'We will, sir. If you can just tell me who you were with. Names and addresses if possible.' Joe smiled and Vince edged back on his seat a few inches, backing away even though he had nowhere to go.

'Did you know Natalie Parkes well?' Joe asked after the names had been provided.

'I hardly knew her at all. She was one of Karen's friends, that's all.'

'What kind of a girl was she?'

Vince looked down at his hands. 'Like I said, she was just Karen's friend. She never talked to me apart from to say hello. What do you expect me to say?'

It was as if he was already being interrogated in the interview room. Guilt was sweating from every pore. Or was it guilt? Perhaps, Joe thought, it could be something else.

'What about after that? Did you or your wife go out again in the Toyota after you'd returned from the golf club?'

'No. We had a drink then we went to bed.'

'Did you sleep well?'

'Not particularly. It's always hard when they're out . . . waiting to hear the key in the lock and all that.'

'But Karen was supposed to be staying with Natalie. You didn't think she was coming back.'

The man looked flustered. 'No, of course not. I forgot . . . sorry.'

'Your car was caught on CCTV on the night of Natalie's murder. And we have a witness who saw her talking to the driver.'

This time there was no mistaking it. Vince Strange looked scared.

'Well, I wasn't driving and neither was Barbara. Like I said, we were in bed. There must be some mistake.'

Joe stood up. 'We'll need to speak to you again, sir. And we'll need to send someone over to examine the car,' he said.

'You won't find anything,' Strange said. For the first time during the interview he actually looked sure of himself.

'We'll be in touch,' said Joe.

Michele could hear her footsteps echoing on the bare, splintery wood of the narrow staircase. Sylvia walked in front of her and the man was behind. She could hear his laboured breathing as though the effort of climbing the stairs was getting to him.

Her feeling of unease was growing again and she was starting to ask the questions she'd been crushing in her head as soon as they'd popped up. Why was there no sign of any models, clothes or make-up people? And why was it that she couldn't quite envisage Barry wielding a camera?

They reached the landing – an enclosed space lined with closed doors, claustrophobic with its heavy brown wallpaper and dark varnished woodwork, and Michele felt a sudden desire to escape. But her way was blocked. There was no way out.

She could hear Barry wheezing behind her in the expectant silence as Sylvia began to lead the way again past the attic staircase and down a dim, narrow corridor. There was a single door at the end, well apart from the other upstairs rooms. Sylvia reached in her pocket for the key and when she had unlocked the door she turned the polished brass knob slowly and pushed it open.

Michele felt the blood pounding in her ears as Sylvia's hand grabbed her elbow tightly. Then she was steered firmly towards the open door and all the illusions she had been nurturing began to fall away. Why had she been so stupid, so desperate? Why hadn't she known right away that there would be no photo shoot, no modelling career? It was just a run-down house in the middle of nowhere and she'd been too blinkered to see the truth she didn't want to see. And now she was trapped there like a frightened animal.

'Alice.' Sylvia's tone was cajoling, as though she were talking to a child. 'Alice, this is Michele. Say hello to Michele.'

Sylvia propelled her forward . . . forcing her to take a step into the unknown.

Chapter 7

They had Natalie Parkes's phone and, according to common wisdom, a teenage girl's mobile phone would give them everything they needed to know about her secret life. The numbers of all the people she didn't want her family to know she was in the habit of calling would be entered into that phone. And one of those people could be her killer.

Once Joe had requested a detailed examination of the Stranges' Toyota, he noticed the young DC, a lad who had shaved his head to hide the fact that his hair was thinning prematurely, studying the tiny pink phone and noting down names and numbers.

He perched on edge of the DC's desk. 'Any luck?' he asked, nodding at the phone.

'Most of them are just school friends but there's one I haven't managed to contact yet. It's listed as "Stallion" and Natalie rung it on the night she died. The bad news is that it's a pay-as-you-go phone so it's untraceable.'

'Keep trying the number,' Joe said as he gave the young man's back a token pat. A bit of encouragement in the face of adversity sometimes worked wonders . . . but it couldn't make Stallion answer his phone and identify himself. That would take persistence and a bit of luck.

Emily was still out of her office. Sunny had told him

that she'd gone off to the press conference, hair brushed and face freshly made up. She would be there now, sitting behind a desk with the press officer on one side and Will Parkes, the token grieving relative, on the other.

Joe was making for his desk, ready to go through the reports of the Singmass Close doll murders in the 1950s for the umpteenth time when he heard an excited voice calling, 'Sir, he answered.'

Joe looked round. The shaven-headed DC was standing up now, his eyes aglow with triumph. 'Who did?'

'Stallion.'

'Well?'

The triumphant look suddenly vanished. 'He . . . er . . . said hello and when I said who I was, he rang off. I've tried since but the phone just goes onto voicemail. I've left a message to call me,' he added with almost pathetic optimism.

Joe tried to muster a sympathetic smile but failed. He was young. He'd soon learn that not everyone relishes a cosy chat with a police officer.

Especially when, like Stallion, they probably had something to hide.

'Keep trying,' he said, glancing at his watch, wondering what time he'd be able to get home that night.

It took a few seconds for Michele's eyes to adjust to the dim light. The faded cotton curtains, heavily lined with blackout material, were drawn across so that only a few chinks of outside light escaped from the top where the rail met the wall. The only other light was provided by a dim 40-watt lamp on a cluttered table by the bed.

As she became accustomed to the gloom, she could make out a figure lying in the bed beneath an old-fashioned quilt. She stared at the head resting on the pillow; the toothless mouth gaping open and a cloud of grey hair spread out around the face like a halo. An old lady – hardly the monster conjured by her imagination.

She turned her head and saw that her captors were gazing down at the old woman with saccharin smiles fixed to their lips and the sight of them made her feel slightly sick. The woman in the bed looked completely helpless. Her body had given up and so, probably, had her mind. The only spark of life was in the watery grey eyes that watched her as she took a step further into the room.

Michele took in her surroundings. On the shelves that lined the far wall sat a dozen antique dolls with watchful eyes. Cold blue glass set in dainty porcelain faces of malevolent sweetness. They were mostly dressed in white – the picture of innocence – and their hair hung in ringlets around chubby pink-cheeked faces. They stared as Michele took another step into the room, their rosebud lips smirking as if to say that she was their prisoner. And there would be no escape. Ever.

Sylvia broke the silence. 'This is Alice. You will make sure she's clean and fed and you will change the bed as soon as it is wet or soiled. Do you understand?'

At first Michele didn't realise that Sylvia was talking to her. But then she realised that the woman's eyes were fixed on her, as though daring her to utter a word of defiance. It all made sense now: the nightclothes; the urine-scented sheets; the meals for four – Sylvia, Barry, Alice and herself. Nobody else. No photographers or lighting staff.

'When you've dealt with Alice, you can make sure the house is clean. And you'll cook all the meals. You've done well so far,' Sylvia added.

Michele knew she'd done well: she'd been trying so hard to impress; to show she was willing to work hard for a step on the ladder of fame. But now she was afraid and her mind started to ponder the question of how she could make her escape.

She looked at Alice, wondering whether to say something to her, to try and strike up some sort of relationship like she had with her own grandmother who had died five years back. But Alice stared ahead, her eyes as blank as those of the dolls lined up on the shelves.

Vacant but with a hint of fear.

At ten o'clock Joe Plantagenet made for home, taking the route past the cathedral. And as he walked down Gallowgate he stopped at the entrance to Singmass Close again. The place was beginning to assert a magnetic attraction, something he didn't feel inclined to resist as yet. The answer to his puzzle lay in that close, he was certain of it. And so did Polly Myers.

He stood in the archway, staring at the little enclave of houses. There were lights in some of the windows: the residents had to continue their lives at the murder scene as best they could . . . just as their predecessors had had to do over fifty years before.

He looked across at number six – the home of Polly Myers – suppressing an impulse to knock on her door. It was far too late. Besides, she'd said she'd seen nothing on the night of Natalie's murder.

He turned away. It wouldn't do. Even though the resemblance was uncanny, she wasn't Kaitlin and he mustn't carry on like this.

Suddenly he caught a movement out of the corner of his eye but when he turned his head he saw it was only that sheet of blue plastic flapping against the scaffolding surrounding the old Ragged School again. Nothing to worry about.

He left the close and once he'd passed under Canons Bar, he could see his flat ahead, nestling against the grey city walls.

The flat he called home was in a small modern block,

built low and unobtrusive to blend with its historic surroundings. Inside the flat was plain and soulless but he liked the view of the city walls from the living room window because they reminded him of his insignificant place in history . . . and he sometimes found that comforting. It brought his troubles into perspective.

When he unlocked the door he was struck by the brooding silence and he suddenly longed to see Maddy emerging from the living room to greet him, telling him about her day at the Archaeology Centre. About the awkward school parties and the tourists' foibles.

He stood there for a few moments in the heavy quiet, feeling an emptiness almost akin to physical pain. Then he saw the red light was flashing on the answer phone so he listened to the message. It was Maddy. Could he call her?

But first he bent down and picked up the post lying on the door mat. Two bills and an interesting-looking packet, a brown padded envelope addressed to DI Plantagenet with no sender's address on the reverse. Curious, he chucked the bills onto the hall table and tore the package open.

He had guessed it was a book of some kind but the title surprised him. *The Children of Singmass Close*. There was no accompanying note so he picked up the ripped envelope and examined it, finding no clue to the sender's identity. He carried the book and the telephone handset through to the living room and slumped down on the sofa.

He called Maddy's mobile number and she answered after three rings.

'Hi, how are you?' She sounded glad to hear from him.

'OK. Busy with this case.'

'It's been on the news down here. Weird.'

There was a pause. 'Heard any more about the interview?' Joe asked, trying to sound casual.

'Yes. They rang me. I've been called for a second interview tomorrow. More of a chat, they said. Sounds promising.'

'Great,' said Joe. He closed his eyes. He needed a drink.

'Miss you,' she said, a note of desperation in her voice.

'You too.' Another pause.

'I'd better go,' she said.

'Speak to you tomorrow.' He heard the dialling tone and felt a sudden pang of desolate loneliness. Then he picked up the book. He needed a distraction.

It was a thin glossy volume with a picture of modern Singmass Close on the front cover. The transparent figure of a little girl in Victorian dress was playing with a hoop on the flagstones. A ghost. Intrigued, Joe began to flick through the pages.

The first chapter contained a potted history of Singmass Close and the surrounding streets. How it had started out as the site of the College of the cathedral's Vicars Choral in medieval times. After the Reformation the buildings were used to accommodate the old and infirm. Then, when most of these medieval buildings had crumbled, small houses were built in their place along with a Ragged School erected by public subscription to house and educate orphans.

Joe fetched himself a bottle of Black Sheep from the kitchen before picking the book up again. Maybe a long soak in the bath later would ease the aching muscles in his shoulder, he thought. In the meantime, he returned to *The Children of Singmass Close* and scanned it quickly, picking up the salient points.

The houses had disintegrated into disreputable slums while the Ragged School descended into a sort of junior workhouse with a cruel and avaricious master called Beamish who sent his unfortunate charges out to work as skivvies or chimney sweeps, keeping the money they earned for himself. When a child died he avoided paying for the burial by putting it about that they'd gone away to work. But in reality, he hid the bodies under floorboards and in cupboards; when the Ragged School was closed and converted into light industrial units at the end of the nineteenth century, a number of little skeletons and mummified bodies were discovered and given a Christian burial.

Joe read on. Beamish had finally gone mad, claiming that children were after revenge . . . that they followed him, hungry and unstoppable, with their pale, dirty faces and their long, ragged, filthy fingernails that would claw at his eyes. He'd ended up in Eborby Asylum, blind and screaming with terror after scratching his own eyes out. The ghostly children, it was said, still played and whispered in the shadows of Singmass Close. Over the years they had been heard there – and occasionally seen. And Singmass Close was a place that dogs refused to enter at night.

He finished his beer and sat staring at the page.

Who would have gone to the trouble of sending him the book? The author maybe – a Mr, Mrs, Miss or Ms P. H. Derby. For some reason someone had felt that he should know about the crime scene's dark past. And as he opened another bottle of Black Sheep, he wondered what that reason was.

Chapter 8

Dolls. As a child Jamilla Dal had a vast collection of them. But over the intervening years, she hadn't really given them much thought, and she was rather surprised to find that the antique dealers she was visiting that Tuesday morning regarded them as such desirable collectors' items.

She traipsed from antique shop to antique shop in the company of Sunny Porter, carrying a plastic evidence bag containing the mutilated doll found by Natalie Parkes's body.

All the shops they visited came up with the same negative answer but several identified it as a French model manufactured in the late nineteenth century and commented on its fairly good condition – failing to notice the mutilated foot through the thick film of plastic. However, nobody would admit to selling it . . . or to ever having seen it before.

After the ninth shop, Jamilla could tell that Sunny was growing impatient. He kept taking a cigarette packet from his jacket pocket, examining the contents, then putting it back.

'Trying to give up?' Jamilla said hopefully. Whenever she went near Sunny, the stench of tobacco smoke that clung to his clothes, caught in her throat and made her want to cough.

Sunny's reply was an ungracious grunt as he consulted the list in his hand. 'Next stop's a place called "Bridget's Bygones".'

'I take it you want me to do the talking?'

'You better had.' Sunny didn't exactly feel at home amongst the doll-collecting community.

They walked down Boargate and branched off onto a narrow street lined with Georgian buildings. Some had been converted into offices, but the majority were small shops. An exclusive shoe shop, a tiny shop that sold herbal toiletries, a sandwich shop of the superior variety and, at the end of the street, Bridget's Bygones.

The window of Bridget's Bygones was full of dolls. Dolls in all shapes and sizes, some gigantic, almost toddler-sized, others tiny enough to inhabit a dolls' house.

'In you go, then,' Sunny said impatiently. He wanted to get this over with and get back to the incident room for a decent cup of tea.

The mousy girl behind the counter looked up eagerly as they entered, as though she'd been bored and was glad of a bit of human contact. There were more dolls inside the shop, sitting on shelves staring down at Jamilla and Sunny as they showed their warrant cards.

'Are you the owner?' Jamilla asked, careful to keep the plastic bag containing the murder doll concealed behind her back.

The girl had lost her keen expression and now she looked nervous. 'No, Bridget's not here. I'm Simone. I just help out.'

It was time to produce the doll. Jamilla placed it on top of an overturned dolly tub with a flourish. 'Do you recognise this doll? We're trying to find out where it came from. Was it bought from this shop?'

Simone picked up the bag and examined it closely. 'No,

93

it's damaged. Look at the foot. Bridget only sells perfect stuff.'

'You have sales records, I take it,' said Sunny. 'We want to be sure.'

The girl looked up at him as if he'd just threatened her with violence.

'It would be very helpful if we could see them,' said Jamilla gently, trying to retrieve the situation.

'Like I said, I just help out.'

'Where can we find Bridget?' Jamilla tried hard not to sound impatient.

The girl suddenly looked uneasy. 'I don't know. When I got here yesterday I just found a note saying she'd be away for a while. It's a good job I've got a key.'

Jamilla saw a panic in the girl's eyes that set an alarm ringing in her head. All was not as it should be. 'Any idea where she is?' she asked gently.

The answer was a shake of the head. 'I tried to ring her home number but . . . Can you tell me what all this is about?'

'It concerns the murder of a young woman in Singmass Close. You'll have heard about it on the news, I take it?'

The girl's eyes widened with horror and she nodded.

'What about those sales records, love? Why don't you have a look for them. It'll save us a lot of time,' Sunny said with a smile that was in danger of becoming a threatening leer.

Simone gave him a nervous look before disappearing into the back of the shop. Sunny and Jamilla waited, looking around, avoiding the glazed stare of the dolls watching them from their vantage points around the walls.

'The sales book's not here,' Simone announced in a whisper when she returned. 'Bridget must have got it with her. Perhaps she was doing the accounts or something, I don't know.'

Sunny and Jamilla looked at each other. 'We'll need Bridget's address,' said Jamilla.

As the girl recited the address, Sunny wrote it down in his notebook.

'Can I keep the shop open? I don't want to let Bridget down. She's been very good to me and . . .'

'I see no reason why not,' Jamilla said with a reassuring smile.

'We might want another word, love,' was Sunny's ominous parting shot.

Jamilla glanced back at the girl. If they wanted to get at the truth, they needed to talk to Bridget. Wherever she was.

It was almost lunchtime and Joe decided to grab himself some fresh air and a change of scene. The Stranges' car had been taken to the police garage for a thorough examination but he knew he'd have to be patient. These things were never done quickly. In the meantime he needed to discover who had sent him the book. It was doubtful whether he'd be given P. H. Derby's address over the phone so a personal visit to the offices of Eborby House Publications was probably his only option. He could have sent an underling, of course, but they were all busy pursuing enquiries. Besides, the book had been sent to him so it could almost be categorised as personal.

Eborby House Publications published books about local history, from archaeology to the supernatural, but it occupied surprisingly modern premises on the first floor of a small office building off Eborby's main shopping street where the national chain stores congregated together like a gang of bullies. Once Joe had introduced himself, saying that he wanted to contact the author of *The Children of Singmass Close*, a secretary of terrifying efficiency provided him with a name and address. Philip Derby, she told him, lived above an antiquarian bookshop near the cathedral. You couldn't miss it.

Joe started to walk back through the city, wondering why Derby had posted the book to his home address instead of handing it in at the police station. But, as he was one of the few Plantagenets in the phone book, his address wouldn't be hard to find. He'd tried to make his number ex-directory on a few occasions but he'd been defeated by the Byzantine workings of the telephone company. Perhaps he'd try again – a little harder next time.

The dark grey skies overhead threatened rain, but it held off as he pushed his way through the streets, weaving between the sightseers who roamed slowly like curious cattle, and just before he reached the cathedral square, he came across the tall medieval building which housed Eborby Old Books.

As he stepped inside the dimly lit shop with its uneven floors and mysterious crooked staircases leading upwards to more delights, he felt a thrill of anticipation – the thrill of the hunt. And when he asked the bespectacled lady behind the counter whether Mr Derby was at home she directed him outside where he saw a grubby, half hidden doorbell he hadn't noticed on the way in. He pressed it and waited. Then when nothing happened, he pressed it again.

He was about to give up when he heard a voice from above. But this was no angelic summons. 'Piss off,' the voice drawled by way of discouragement.

Joe took a step back and looked up. A hostile face was looking down at him from a small leaded window in the overhanging upper storey that had been flung open.

Joe took out his warrant card and held it up. 'Mr Derby? DI Plantagenet. If I could have a word . . .' He looked round to find he'd attracted a little audience of Japanese sightseers who clearly thought this was a quaint local custom, like morris dancing.

The man's manner suddenly changed. 'Come on up, dear boy,' he called as his head disappeared from sight.

Joe had to climb a succession of steep staircases to reach the top of the building, each narrower than the last and some lined with books of varying vintages. When he got to the top he found the door open. A good sign. At least he was welcome.

Philip Derby was younger than he'd expected. He couldn't have been more than forty but he had the dishevelled look of an actor playing an eccentric academic in an amateur dramatic production. The baggy corduroy trousers and tweed tie didn't seem quite right and his thinning fair hair, flecked with grey, was rather too well cut. Joe noticed a tweed jacket with leather patches on the elbows hanging up in the narrow hallway which could have been selected by a wardrobe mistress fond of clichés.

Derby led the way into the flat and Joe noticed the eclectic variety of objects that cluttered every surface. A large, dusty ammonite lay in the empty hearth and the walls were crammed with old prints and watercolours, many verging on the erotic. It was the study of a Victorian eccentric bachelor. A cabinet of curiosities. As Joe sat, a cloud of dust ascended from the old horsehair sofa.

'I've come to thank you for the book.' Joe began. 'It was you who sent it?'

'Yes. Look, sorry about . . . I've had trouble with . . . financial troubles, you understand. Some people won't take no for an answer . . . they keep calling and . . .'

This explained the hostile reception. Joe didn't know whether to be insulted or amused at being mistaken for a debt collector. 'What made you send me the book?' he asked, noticing a slight uncertainty in Derby's eyes as he considered his reply.

'Thought it might come in useful.'

'Why?'

'Singmass Close. The dead girl was found there, wasn't she? A man I know walks his dog past there every night. The animal barks every time it reaches the bloody place and there's no way he can get it to go in. He tried to take a short cut down there one night because he wanted to be home early. Bloody creature wouldn't budge. And people have felt that they're being watched. Unquiet spirits, Inspector. And then they built new houses there: any form of disturbance on a site like that brings them out . . . like turning over a stone in the garden. And they've started renovating that old Ragged School . . . making it into offices. I wouldn't be surprised if that's got them going again.'

Joe sat in silence for a few moments. 'When you were writing the book, did you check out the facts? Did these things really happen? Beamish and the children?'

Derby nodded vigorously. 'The records are in the city archives. Beamish was admitted to Eborby Asylum in eighteen fifty-five. Died there three years later, raving about the children coming to get him. Said they were clawing at his eyes. He scratched his own eyes out . . . ended up blind and insane.'

Joe shifted in his seat. With the murder investigation he knew he really didn't have time for all this. But on the other hand he was intrigued.

'Have you caught your murderer yet?' Derby asked the question casually, like someone making polite conversation.

'The inquiry's still ongoing.' He hesitated for a moment. 'What made you think knowing about the children of Singmass Close might help us?'

Derby gave a theatrical shrug. 'I heard a doll was left at the scene. Dolls. Children. That particular place. It seemed to make perfect sense at the time.' He scratched his head. 'Not sure it does now. I've always suffered from an overactive imagination, Inspector. Perhaps that's why I chose to be a writer.'

'Of fact, not fiction.'

'Which is which? Sometimes it's so hard to tell.'

'You didn't send a note with the book. Why was that?'

'Didn't really think it was necessary.' He grinned, showing a row of crooked teeth. 'I thought a spot of anonymity might be more intriguing. And I was right. It's brought you here to my little nest.'

Joe tried to hide his irritation. But something about Derby made him curious. He'd sent the book out of the blue, drawing attention to himself during a murder inquiry. He'd known killers do that – almost as if they couldn't help themselves. And he'd cultivated this slightly old-fashioned, eccentric persona, which somehow seemed a little artificial, as though he was playing a part.

'Do you do anything other than writing?' Joe asked.

'I have a part share in the bookshop downstairs . . . not that it makes me a fortune. And I do some teaching. It allows me time for my writing.'

'Ever worked at Hicklethorpe Manor?'

The answer was a vigorous shake of the head.

'Did you ever meet Natalie Parkes, the girl who was murdered?'

There was a split second of hesitation before Derby shook his head again.

'You know there were four similar murders in Singmass Close in the nineteen fifties?'

Derby didn't answer.

'It's been in all the papers – that there might be some sort of link. Copycat killing and all that. Four young women were killed in Singmass Close back then . . . and dolls were left by their bodies.'

'If it's the same man he'll be getting on a bit.'

'We're following a number of leads, sir,' said Joe stiffly.

His instincts told him that he should keep his distance from this man. 'I'm surprised you didn't make the connection with the fifties murders, being interested in local history.'

'Post-war Eborby is hardly my cup of tea, Inspector. My interests lie much earlier.' He looked Joe in the eye. 'From your accent, you're not from round these parts yourself. The banks of the River Mersey, at a guess. Am I right?'

Joe nodded but said nothing. This man already had his address – he wasn't going to share details of his private life with him as well.

'Incidentally, why did you send the book to me? Why not DCI Thwaite? She's the chief investigating officer.'

'I saw your name in the local paper. A DI Plantagenet told our reporter and all that.' He leaned forward, a sly smile on his face. 'I rather liked the name.' Derby gave Joe an apologetic half smile and moistened his lips. 'Look, maybe you'd like to meet for a drink some time. We could meet some friends of mine . . . see if we share any interests in common.'

Joe stood up, wondering what was behind the invitation. Not simple friendship, he was certain of that – or a sexual proposition. 'I've got to get back to the incident room. Thanks for your time,' he said with stiff formality.

Derby looked away.

'And thanks for the book,' Joe said before hurrying down the staircase into the shop, aware of Derby watching his disappearing back.

When he neared the cathedral he saw Emily Thwaite in the distance, striding ahead towards Singmass Close in her businesslike suit. Joe was surprised to see her walking. But then she had mentioned she was thinking of enrolling at Weightwatchers before Natalie Parkes had got herself murdered and forced her to change her plans.

Joe broke into a run and eventually caught up with her. She looked pleased to see him.

'Anything new?' she asked. 'I've been in a bloody meeting. Useless waste of time. Did you see me on the news last night?' she added shyly.

'Yeah. I caught the late bulletin. Good performance, boss.'

Their eyes met and she smiled. 'Thanks. I wanted another look at the crime scene to remind myself of the lie of the land.'

'I'll come with you.' Joe fell into step beside her. 'Did you know that the area's supposed to be haunted? I was sent a book. *The Children of Singmass Close*. I've just been to see the author.'

Emily stopped. 'And?'

'He asked me to go for a drink with him.'

Emily grinned. 'Was he after your gorgeous body or just lonely?'

Joe thought for a few moments. 'I know it might sound that way but I think he might have had another agenda.'

'Like what?'

Joe found himself wondering, recalling Derby's words and gestures. There was something about Derby he couldn't quite pinpoint. 'To be honest, I'm not quite sure.'

'Did he have anything interesting to say?'

'He hinted that the murders could be connected with these Victorian kids who died in the Ragged School – the building with all the scaffolding. They're supposed to haunt the site. Think about it, Emily. Children. Dolls. Dolls left at the murder scene. Could there be some connection?'

'We're looking for a nutter, not a ghost.'

'You're right, boss. But he's a nutter who knows the story.'

He saw Emily nod. She had to give him that one.

They'd just passed the National Trust shop on the corner and the entrance to Singmass Close was in sight.

'Wonder if anything's come in from the TV appeal yet,' said Joe, trying to sound optimistic.

Emily said nothing and marched on ahead.

Michele sat there on the bed spooning the thin soup between Alice's trembling lips, experiencing a small thrill of satisfaction every time the old woman swallowed a few drops.

At first she hadn't spoken to the old woman. But now she found herself keeping up a narrative, finding comfort in talking to another human being, even one who didn't respond.

The collection of antique dolls on the shelf gave her the creeps. She hated the way they stared at her, as if they were watching her performance and judging. She would have liked to throw them out of the window, to get rid of their smug rosebud simpers and their hard glass eyes. But the window was barred, like a nursery or a prison. Whether those bars were for her or for Alice, she didn't know. But she suspected they served to imprison them both.

She took another spoonful of soup and blew on it carefully as Sylvia had instructed. She had the uneasy feeling that, should she disobey Sylvia's orders, there might be unpleasant consequences and she didn't like the man Sylvia addressed as Barry. When Sylvia's gaze was elsewhere, he had stared at her small breasts in a way that made her feel uncomfortable.

Last night she'd been locked up in the attic room again with the chamber pot and this time Sylvia didn't even try to pretend the door was stuck. She suspected that she'd been given something to ensure that she slept – something that left her head fuzzy and her mouth dry in the mornings.

The subject of modelling and photo shoots had suddenly been dropped. It had been the bait and now that Michele had fallen into the trap, there was no longer any need for pretence and lies. She was there as a prisoner. She was there to work. And no matter how hard she looked for an escape route, she couldn't see one. The place was isolated and she was either locked in or watched by Sylvia or Barry.

Last night, before she'd fallen into her deep, chemical sleep, she was sure she'd heard another male voice, lower pitched than Barry's, but it could have been her imagination. And as she'd lain on the narrow bed that morning, she'd found herself listening for any sound in the country silence that might bring hope of escape. But she'd heard nothing.

She put the spoon up to Alice's lips but the old woman shut them tightly like a stubborn toddler and the soup dribbled down the front of her flannelette nightdress. Michele swore softly.

She placed the soup bowl on the bedside table and crossed the room to the chest of drawers under the dolls' malevolent gaze. But as she reached out to open the drawer where the clean linen was kept, the sound of raised voices in the distance made her freeze.

She could just make out snatches of conversation. A man and a woman.

'Can't take the risk.'

'He mustn't know.'

'Who's he going to tell?'

'In the freezer . . . won't see.'

She recognised Barry and Sylvia's voices and she wondered who they were talking about. Who was the 'he' and what mustn't he know?

As Michele stood there, quite still, listening for any words that would provide hope of escape, a door slammed

103

somewhere in the distance followed by a still, heavy silence.

The Doll Strangler had seen her on the TV last night with her smug professional concern as she appealed for witnesses. She had had the doll with her and she had shown it to the world. In his day women like DCI Emily Thwaite would have known their place, he thought with mounting anger . . . something akin to the anger that had led him to put the silk stocking around the throats of those women and squeeze until the life had left their bodies. He'd have liked to do that to Emily Thwaite . . . to silence her arrogant tongue for ever.

It wouldn't be long before another one died. Once tasted, the power over life and death was irresistible.

Chapter 9

Natalie Parkes had been seen on the night of her death by no less than twelve people who were prepared to swear that she had been sitting on a bench on platform nine of Eborby railway station, that she had been walking down Boargate arm in arm with an older Asian man, that she had been hanging around Scarborough bus station in the early hours of the morning, and that she had been walking by the river with a small dog. All these alleged sightings would be checked out of course but Joe and Emily both knew they would lead to dead ends.

'Anything new?' Joe asked as Emily shuffled into her office. He noticed that she looked tired. But then they'd been keeping long hours.

'We're still waiting for the verdict on Vince Strange's car. But his golf club story checks out. He was there all right. So was the Deputy Chief Constable. They both left around eleven. But even so, we only have his wife's word for it that Vince was home safely tucked up in bed at the time Natalie left The Devil's Playground. You got anything else?'

Joe took his notebook from his jacket pocket. There was so much information coming in that he needed a reminder. 'Karen Strange spent the night with a bloke called Jon Firman who confirms her story.' Joe hesitated.

'I've been wondering about this "Stallion" on Natalie's mobile phone. Could she have been leading some kind of double life?'

'We've spoken to all Natalie's friends and there's been no mention of any Stallion. I thought it could be the nickname of someone in her social circle but nobody seems to recognise it. And apparently Natalie was unusually secretive when it came to her sex life.' She thought for a few seconds. 'It's always possible that she went for older men and kept quiet about her conquests.'

'Perhaps. Any leads on this missing girl yet – Michele Carden?' Joe asked.

'She was caught on CCTV in the railway station but she seemed to be alone. Trouble is, the cameras don't cover everywhere. If she'd caught a train . . . or gone out of the back entrance . . . The Met's missing persons unit's on the lookout for her. I bet that's where she's gone.'

'Don't know what these kids expect to find in London when they arrive there at King's Cross without a penny apart from exploitation by pimps and sleeping rough.'

He saw Emily raise her eyebrows, probably surprised at the vehemence of his words. The subject of London had touched a nerve and this rather surprised him.

'Look, I want another word with a woman who lives in Singmass Close. Number six. Her window directly overlooks the crime scene and I'm sure she knows something. I told her I'd go round and take a statement.' He tried to make the words sound casual.

'Can't do any harm to put the pressure on,' she said with what looked to Joe like a knowing wink.

As Joe left the incident room a young constable handed him a sheet of paper – an urgent message from Forensic. A necklace with gold letters spelling the name Natalie had been found underneath the passenger seat of Barbara

Strange's red Toyota and this juicy morsel of news made his heart beat a little faster. But his initial excitement vanished rapidly as he realised that Natalie could have been in her friend's mother's car quite legitimately at any time during her time at Hicklethorpe Manor. If Natalie had lost the necklace some time ago, someone might remember. But what if she had been wearing it on the night she disappeared?

He told the constable to report the find to DCI Thwaite and noted the apprehensive expression that suddenly appeared on the young man's face. There were some who considered Emily as fearsome as a man-eating tiger. But Joe knew she had her soft spots even though she didn't always reveal them to everyone at work.

Joe needed an opportunity to think so he decided to walk. As he passed the railway station where Michele Carden was last seen, he began to wonder what had happened to her – and Leanne Williams, the girl who'd disappeared some weeks earlier. The two girls were somewhere out there, alone and vulnerable. But in the arrogance of youth, they probably weren't aware of the danger they might be in. He felt exasperated at their foolhardy stupidity. But when he'd been their age he too considered himself invincible.

The sight of the cathedral brought George Merryweather to mind again. Although George spent a good deal of time exorcising unquiet spirits, the man always managed to cheer him up if life was ever getting him down. And with the news of Maddy's second interview, he felt unsettled. Or perhaps it wasn't Maddy. Perhaps it was meeting Polly Myers – almost like seeing Kaitlin raised from the dead.

He contemplated paying George a visit on the pretext of asking him about the ghostly children of Singmass Close. But when he looked at his watch he knew there wasn't time. The investigation was moving too fast. And he needed to see Polly again.

Passing through the archway into Singmass Close, he caught a whiff of garlic and herbs from the Italian restaurant nearby. But as soon as he stepped into the Close itself the restaurant's Mediterranean liveliness suddenly seemed a world away. Here the buildings blocked out the bustle of the shops and the traffic noise, and left the place in brooding silence.

The doll was still sitting in the window of number six, staring out with unseeing eyes as Polly Myers opened the door and greeted him with a nervous smile.

He smiled to put her at her ease. 'I'm here to take that statement. Just routine. All right if I come in?'

She led him into the living room with a bare wood floor and walls painted in rich shades of terracotta and aubergine, which seemed to suck the air and light from the room. As she invited him to sit she kept glancing at the staircase in the corner of the room. There was no sound from upstairs. If there was a child in the house, she was being remarkably quiet.

'I need to ask you about last Friday, the night Natalie Parkes was murdered. Did you go out at all?'

She shook her head. At a certain angle her resemblance to Kaitlin was heart-rending but at other times it was hardly there at all.

'You told me that your daughter was staying at a friend's that night. You didn't take advantage of the situation and . . .?'

'No. I told you. I was in all night.' Polly looked away. There was something she was hiding and Joe couldn't make out what it was.

'Did you see anyone on the close that night? Anyone behaving suspiciously?'

She shook her head.

'Has anyone been hanging around? Anyone you didn't recognise?'

'Only the builders working on the Ragged School. But they all go home at five on the dot.'

'And you've not seen any of them coming back after dark?'

'No.'

The builders had already been interviewed and eliminated. But it was a question worth asking – just in case. 'Where's your daughter now?' Joe asked gently.

'At the childminder's. I was at work this morning.'

'Where do you work?' Suddenly he was anxious to learn more about her.

'Ethnic Arts. It's on Boargate.'

Joe nodded. He knew Ethnic Arts. Maddy admired the jewellery in there on a regular basis.

He glanced down at Polly's left hand and saw there was no wedding ring on the third finger. 'What about Daisy's father?' He knew the question was probably tactless but he needed to know.

He saw a flash of panic in Polly's eyes. 'He's not around,' she said quickly.

There was a sound from upstairs, a muffled thud like something falling onto a thickly carpeted floor. Then the sound of soft footsteps above their heads.

'Is someone upstairs?'

'It's probably noise from next door. The walls are so thin in these houses.'

He looked into her eyes. A darker shade than Kaitlin's. 'Is something bothering you?'

She shook her head and said she was fine. Then her lips parted and she looked uncertain, as though she'd had second thoughts and decided to confide in him after all. But after a split second the indecision vanished. 'You wanted me to make a statement. There's really nothing much to say but . . .'

109

Joe took her statement, writing slowly, somehow reluctant to bring the encounter to an end. But eventually he couldn't put off his departure any longer. 'Look, if you ever want to talk about anything . . . discuss any problems,' he said. 'I'll give you my number.' He handed her his card and she looked at it closely before putting it in the pocket of her long black cardigan.

As she shut the front door behind him he glanced upwards. It could have been his imagination but he could have sworn the doll had moved. It had shifted a foot to one side and its arm was raised, as if in farewell. Joe's heart began to beat a little faster. Perhaps someone had been upstairs after all. Someone Polly Myers didn't want him to see.

He turned back and he was about to ring the doorbell again when he heard his mobile's tinny ring tone. It was Emily.

A witness had seen Natalie wearing the necklace found in the Stranges' car on the night she died and Vince and Barbara Strange were being brought in for questioning.

Emily wanted him there.

Polly Myers stood at the foot of the stairs, gulping in deep breaths of air in an effort to calm herself. Perhaps it had been a mistake not to answer the door to the police during those first days. She had drawn attention to herself . . . and to Daisy. And that was the last thing she wanted.

She had lied to the police. She'd kept Daisy at home because she hadn't wanted to let her out of her sight . . . not since she'd learned he was out there. But she'd told Joe Plantagenet that Daisy was at the childminder's because she hadn't wanted to risk her being questioned. She'd been through enough already in her short life.

'Mummy,' a little voice called from upstairs. 'Mary says she's hungry. Can I give her something to eat?'

Polly looked down at her hands. They'd started to shake. Perhaps she should take Daisy to stay with Yolanda again. She was getting used to staying there – she'd been there on the night the girl was murdered in the close. At least she'd be safe with Yolanda.

And maybe that way she could get her away from Mary's influence once and for all.

'I've got an uneasy feeling about that Polly Myers,' Joe said to Emily as they walked side by side to the interview room.

'Oh aye? Why?'

'She said she was alone but I'm sure there was someone upstairs.'

'So she's up to a bit of hanky panky and she doesn't want to share it with the police. Hardly surprising.'

Joe said nothing. Emily could well be right. But Polly Myers hadn't seemed like an embarrassed woman caught in the act. It had been more than that. She'd been frightened of something.

'I just wondered if we should question her again. Her house overlooks the murder scene and . . .'

Emily sighed. 'Maybe another time. Our first priority is to see the Stranges. Then you can buy me a pint afterwards. Sam Smiths for preference.' She hesitated. 'On second thoughts I'd better get straight home tonight and read through those files again – see if there's anything we've been missing. Jeff and the kids see little enough of me as it is so at least that way I'll be there in body if not in spirit. Polly whatever her name is can wait till tomorrow. If she's got a kid in tow, it's unlikely she'll do a moonlight flit.' Joe could see she was frowning, deep in thought.

'That Bridget . . . the one who owns the doll shop Sunny and Jamilla visited – Bridget's Bygones. There's still no answer from her home address and the girl who helps her in the shop has no idea where she's gone. It just seems odd to me that she sells antique dolls and she's chosen this moment to do a vanishing act.'

'I've got a couple of DCs trying to track her down.' She looked up at him as though she'd just remembered something. 'You never said before how your Maddy was getting on in the Smoke. How's she doing?'

He didn't answer for a few moments. The question was unexpected. But he should have known that Emily never forgot to follow up an unanswered question. That's why she was good at her job. 'She called last night to say she'd been called for a second interview.'

He saw Emily raise her eyebrows, as though she sensed his lack of enthusiasm. 'You'd rather she didn't get this job?'

He considered the question for a few seconds. 'It's a once-in-a-lifetime chance. Too good to pass up.'

Emily looked him in the eye. He knew that after all her years in CID, she could spot evasion and half truth when she heard it. 'That's the authorised version. What do you really think?'

What did he think? He wasn't sure. 'Like I said, if it's what she wants.'

'As long as I don't lose you to the dubious charms of the Met,' she said with an uncharacteristically shy smile.

Joe didn't answer. He checked the time again. Five-fifteen – the time when most people would be contemplating their journey home.

'Let's have a word with the Stranges,' said Emily. 'I'd be very interested to hear his explanation of how Natalie Parkes's necklace came to be under the passenger seat of his wife's Toyota.'

'Are we seeing them separately or together?'

Emily considered the question for a few moments. 'Together at first, I think. I want to see the body language – how they react with each other.'

Joe couldn't argue with that. They'd both be watching for the unspoken signals. The little glances.

When they reached the interview room Joe noticed that Barbara Strange looked anxious and the fine lines that formed a spider's web around her eyes and upper lip seemed deeper today. Perhaps it was the harsh light from the fluorescent strips above . . . or perhaps it was because she was feeling the strain.

Vince Strange sat beside his wife. He looked up as they entered the room and his expression gave nothing.

'Thank you for coming in,' Emily said politely as she sat down opposite the couple.

Joe saw Vince Strange glance at the uniformed constable sitting by the door. 'I had to miss a meeting. It's very inconvenient.'

'What exactly do you do, Mr Strange?' Joe asked, more out of curiosity than anything else.

'I'm a partner in Kirby's . . . the Chartered Accountants.'

Joe nodded and looked at Barbara. 'What about you, Mrs Strange?'

'I'm a physiotherapist. I work part time at a private clinic,' she replied, her mind clearly elsewhere.

Emily opened her handbag and took out the plastic evidence bag that contained Natalie Parkes's necklace. She handed it to Strange who shot his wife a wary glance.

'Ever seen this necklace before? It belonged to Natalie Parkes.'

It was Barbara Strange who answered. 'I think I've seen her wearing it but . . .'

'What about you, Mr Strange?'

Joe watched him carefully as he made a pretence of trying to remember, frowning and holding the bag up to the light. 'I can't remember,' was the final answer. 'I can't say I notice things like that. I mean, you don't, do you?'

Joe saw him glance at his wife, as if for reassurance.

'So you can't explain how it came to be under the passenger seat of your wife's car.'

There was a flicker of panic in the man's eyes, swiftly suppressed. 'She must have dropped it sometime when Barbara was giving the girls a lift somewhere. Isn't that right, love?'

His wife nodded nervously, as though she anticipated disaster.

'We have witnesses who saw Natalie wearing this necklace on the night she died,' said Emily quietly. 'Your daughter being one of them.'

Barbara looked as though she'd been punched. But perhaps betrayal was worse. 'She must be mistaken. Or perhaps Natalie had two necklaces like that.' She was clutching at every available straw now. 'Look, Vince was at the golf club then he was home with me. He didn't go out again. I swear.'

Joe suddenly had an idea. 'What about you, Mrs Strange? Did you go out in your car that night?'

Barbara Strange shook her head vigorously.

'You might have been worried about Karen. You might have gone to offer her a lift home,' said Emily. 'We're always worried sick about our kids, aren't we?' she continued. Joe had to admire the way she was playing the mum card but omitting to mention that her children were as yet too young for unaccompanied nights out. 'It's the sort of thing I'd do, offer them a lift home even when it's not particularly wanted . . . just for my own peace of mind. You can never go to sleep until they get in anyway so you might as well . . .'

'I didn't go out. I'm telling the truth. Neither of us went out after Vince got back from the golf club. We thought Karen was staying at Natalie's so we weren't worrying about her.'

'But she didn't stay at Natalie's, did she?' Joe said sharply. 'She went off with a man and left Natalie to get herself murdered.'

He saw Barbara flinch at the brutality of his words but he knew he wouldn't get to the truth by tiptoeing about.

Barbara swiftly regained her composure. 'Karen feels terrible about letting Natalie down and I think that's punishment enough, don't you, Inspector?'

Joe didn't reply. Karen Strange hadn't seemed particularly repentant when they'd spoken to her, but perhaps then the true horror of the situation hadn't sunk in.

Emily had a determined look on her face. Joe knew she wasn't going to give up until she found out the truth.

'Is there any chance that anybody else borrowed the car? Your son's at university here, I believe.'

Neither of them answered.

Joe caught Emily's eye. They were onto something here. 'He has borrowed your car in the past, I take it?'

He noticed a furtive look passing between the Stranges, over so swiftly that if he hadn't been looking out for it, he'd have missed it.

'Yes.'

'You told us he doesn't live at home.'

'He shares with some other students in Hasledon.'

'But he was home on Friday night?'

Barbara's eyes widened and Joe could tell that she was torn between lying to the police and defending her young.

'Well?' Emily prompted.

Barbara hesitated. 'OK. He was at home that night. But we never heard him going out.'

'You're sure about that?'

Barbara nodded vigorously.

'We'd like to have a word with your son. Where can we find him?'

The Stranges hesitated, as though saying no was an

option. In the end it was Vince who recited an address in Hasledon as his wife watched him, her lips pressed together with what looked like pent-up fury.

It was Vince who spoke next. 'When can we have the car back? It's very inconvenient for my wife. She . . .'

'You can pick it up from the police garage,' said Emily. 'Just report to the front desk and they'll tell you where to go.' She stood up.

'What do you reckon?' Emily asked once they were back in the incident room.

'We need to speak to the son as soon as possible.'

'I've just sent a patrol car round to pick him up.' Emily scratched her head. 'Is it Vince . . . or Barbara? Or is it the son? Want to place bets?'

'No,' said Joe. 'But Sunny Porter will. He usually runs a sweepstake on most major cases.'

Emily raised her eyebrows. 'You are joking? What about my predecessor – your old DCI? Did he know about all this?'

'Know about it? He usually won,' Joe said with studied innocence.

'What about you? What do you think of betting on the outcome of a murder inquiry?'

He shrugged. 'Things get tense in the incident room. It helps people let off steam. And I haven't come across anyone manufacturing evidence so that they can win a few quid.'

'Well I see no reason to change the status quo. I might even have a little flutter myself.'

Joe checked the time and found that it was flying too quickly as usual. 'We need to have a word with Christopher Strange. He could easily have borrowed his mum's car and picked up Natalie Parkes.' The words 'and killed her' were left unsaid.

DC Jenny Ripon knocked at the door. The news she

brought wasn't exactly bad. More frustrating. Chris Strange wasn't at home or at the university and his house mates didn't expect him back until the early hours because it was someone's birthday.

'OK,' said Joe, resigned. 'We'll call on Chris Strange first thing in the morning. He's a student – and probably a student with a hangover – so there's only one place he'll be.'

'Under the nearest duvet?'

'Got it in one.'

Michele had looked out through the small, barred window of Alice's room while she was changing her incontinence pad but had seen nothing but clouds, sheep and fields. There was no help out there. At first she had found dealing with Alice's most personal needs disgusting but now it was becoming routine. If someone had told her that she'd be able to do something like that a week ago, she'd have laughed in their faces and said no way.

Now that she was clean Alice seemed calm and Michele knew that it would soon be time for her to do the afternoon cleaning. All the pretence about entertaining people from the fashion industry had now been abandoned and Michele knew that she was being kept there as an unpaid domestic servant, to look after Alice so that the immaculately groomed Sylvia didn't have to soil her beautifully manicured hands.

But there was a nagging worry in the back of her mind that there might be a more sinister reason behind her imprisonment. Something connected with the second male voice she'd thought she'd heard – the voice of the stranger. She'd read stories in the paper about people being kept as sex slaves and forced into prostitution, and her enforced solitude was feeding her imagination.

She heard the key turn in Alice's door as it was

unlocked to release her for her next task. She walked out past Sylvia meekly, head bowed. She knew what was expected of her now and somehow obedience was easier. And probably safer until she could find a way out of there.

She made for the kitchen and Sylvia followed behind, issuing terse orders, all charm gone. When Michele had summoned the courage to ask about the modelling the previous day, Sylvia hadn't answered. She hadn't even laughed.

Like any prisoner, she felt herself growing used to the routine of her day . . . drifting into an unquestioning acceptance. Once the floors were cleaned, the brasses polished, she retired to the kitchen to deal with the washing – mainly Alice's bedding and clothing. When the washing machine was on, she began to search the cupboards. Sylvia had ordered shepherd's pie.

But when she couldn't find the potatoes Michele began to panic as she imagined the possible consequences of failure. She began to search more frantically, tears pricking her eyes, willing the vegetables to appear by magic.

Then she looked through the lean-to window and saw the sack of potatoes in the corner, which meant that she had a problem. Sylvia had told her quite clearly that she wasn't allowed in the little lean-to off the kitchen with its cupboards and its big chest freezer. The door to that particular room was kept locked at all times and only Sylvia had the key.

She had not learned yet whether disobedience had consequences. But it was a risk she didn't care to take. However, she reasoned that any punishment might be more severe if the dinner wasn't on the table.

The sight of a key left in the lean-to door seemed like providence. Sylvia was usually so careful about things like that and Michele wondered whether she was meant for once to use her initiative and find the potatoes for herself.

And there they were, sitting on the floor like forbidden treasure.

Michele turned the key and entered the lean-to with its roof of dusty glass and mouldy wood. Her heart lifted as she squatted to take the potatoes out of the sack, wrinkling her nose at the smell of the earth caked around them. She took an armful back into the kitchen and dropped them on the table before returning to lock the door.

But she hovered in the doorway, key in hand, wondering why this unimpressive little annexe was forbidden territory. There was a big chest freezer standing at the far end like some pagan altar and she approached it with a mixture of curiosity and fear. And when she lifted the heavy lid it opened with a complaining groan.

Then Michele looked down, expecting to see brightly coloured packets of frozen vegetables and plastic shrouded chunks of vacuum-packed meat.

The food was there all right, arranged around the edges of the thing that lay the length of the freezer. The naked young woman looked like a mannequin, the stiff frozen flesh lying pale amongst the brightly packaged food, staring upwards with sightless eyes.

Michele guessed that she was around her own age. And she was definitely dead.

Chapter 10

Michele shut the freezer quietly and dashed out, locking the lean-to door behind her, her heart beating fast. She had covered her tracks so there was no reason for Sylvia or Barry to know she'd been anywhere near that freezer. No reason at all for them to suspect that she knew what was in there.

She sat down at the kitchen table, staring at the potatoes, her heart racing, paralysed with fear. If they had killed one girl, what was to stop them killing twice? She had to stay alive. And the only way she could think of to do that was to bide her time and do as she was told until she had a chance to escape.

She jumped when the kitchen door opened. But she breathed deeply, trying to hide the terror she felt as Sylvia walked in and stood there looking down at her, a frown on her face.

'Haven't you finished yet?'

'Almost.'

'When you've done the dinner take up Alice's tray. Then she'll need changing and you can give her a new nightdress while you're at it.'

'Yes.'

Michele lowered her eyes meekly and Sylvia gave a nod of satisfaction before moving to leave. When she reached the door she turned back. 'And you'll have to do more potatoes. We've got a visitor.'

Michele opened her mouth to say something but thought better of it. And as she peeled the potatoes, tears began to stream down her face and into the pan.

Joe reached Gallowgate, trudging home through the night-time streets after another frustrating day. He'd wanted to question Christopher Strange and judge for himself whether he could be capable of Natalie's murder. Surely nobody could do something like that and appear like a normal human being. But Joe knew from experience that it sometimes happened. People weren't always what they seemed.

Suddenly the ringing of his mobile phone interrupted his thoughts.

'Hi. Not still at work are you?' he heard Maddy say.

His heart sank. He'd forgotten to ring her as he'd promised. But before he could pour out his apologies and excuses, she began to speak. 'That murder's been on the news down here again. They mentioned something about him copying some serial killer in the nineteen fifties. Is that right?' She sounded concerned – or perhaps just intrigued.

'It looks that way.' Joe wasn't really in the mood to talk about the case. He'd had enough. 'How did the second interview go?' he asked.

'Really well.' She sounded excited, full of it, and he tried to make enthusiastic noises, hiding his sinking spirits. He wasn't surprised that it had gone well – Maddy was capable and eloquent, just the sort who'd make a good impression – but he was rather surprised that some little demon deep inside him, barely acknowledged, had been hoping for disaster.

'When will they let you know?' He tried to sound

positive, cheerful and he wondered if she could see through the act.

'Soon. Better go. Speak to you tomorrow.'

He heard the dialling tone and stood there in the darkness as a feeling of loss and emptiness hit him with unexpected force. He tried to utter a swift prayer for strength but he couldn't quite find the words. Then he forced himself to walk on. He needed to get home. He needed a drink.

He took a deep breath and fixed his eyes ahead but suddenly he slowed down and felt his mouth go dry. Ahead, just by the arch leading to Singmass Close, he saw two figures embracing. Two women, one middle-aged, one younger. The older woman kissed the younger on the cheek before hurrying off to a waiting car, waving car keys in farewell. Leaving Polly Myers alone standing on the pavement, watching her departure.

Joe paused for a few moments before walking towards her. He didn't want to alarm a lone woman walking home in the dark but, on the other hand, he felt a need to talk to her. As she reached the archway by the Italian restaurant, he called her name and she swung round, her eyes wide with fright. Joe had expected the fear to disappear when she realised that it was him and not some potential rapist or mugger, but if anything she looked more apprehensive as he approached.

Joe smiled to put her at her ease. 'Sorry if I startled you.'

As she gave a small nod of acknowledgement, she shifted from foot to foot, anxious to be away.

'I expect you have to get back to Daisy,' he said.

'No, she's at a friend's. My mother's just taken me out for a pizza. She had to get back.'

'How about a drink?' he asked on impulse. It was late and it probably wasn't wise but, for some reason, he was

122

reluctant to let her go. His heart was pounding like a teenager's on a first date and the feeling wasn't altogether unpleasant.

Polly shook her head. 'I'd better get home. I've got things to do.'

'I'll walk you to your door.'

She said nothing as they passed under the archway and crossed the chilly close. There was no constable on duty now: the powers that be had judged it to be an unproductive use of manpower and had increased patrols instead. But little had changed apart from that: the murder scene was still taped off and the cellophane wrapped around the wilting flowers still twinkled in the weak light of the old street lamps. Polly's house itself was in darkness and once more Joe had the uneasy feeling that he was being watched from the shadows. As Polly unlocked her door he looked round but there was nobody there.

'Thank you,' she said formally as the door swung open.

He knew it was a dismissal and felt a pang of disappointment.

After she'd said goodnight and shut her front door, as though she was eager to be rid of him, Joe stood quite still for a few moments until he saw the lights go on, scolding himself for his folly and telling himself that the resemblance to Kaitlin was only skin deep. He looked up at the window. The doll was still there, watching over the close. If it could have talked, he thought, their job would have been easy. Its sightless glass eyes must have seen who murdered Natalie. But this particular witness wasn't telling.

It took him less that five minutes to reach his flat and as soon as he put his key in the front door, it began to rain. He'd timed it well, he thought as he went through the place switching on the lights. Seeing Polly again and being alone in Singmass Close at night had been a little unsettling and he needed some reminder of the banal world outside. He looked through his CDs but somehow none of the music in his collection appealed just then so he flicked the television to a channel showing an un-demanding police thriller, so removed from real life as to be laughable.

He tolerated the programme maker's inaccuracies for ten minutes before switching on his computer. There was something he wanted to check on. Something that was niggling at the back of his mind.

P. H. Derby was bound to have earned a mention on the Internet in his capacity as an author and it was about time he found out a little more about the man and his writings. Sure enough, he was there on the Eborby House Publications website but he only appeared to have written two books for that particular publisher – *The Children of Singmass Close* and another called *A Walk Around the Walls* about the history of the city walls and Eborby's various medieval gateways.

But when he began to search further, he struck gold. Another small publisher had produced a work by P. H. Derby. It was entitled *Famous Eborby Murders* and, according to the publisher's details, among these famous murderers was a case known as the 'Doll Strangler of Singmass Close'.

P. H. Derby had claimed not to have known about the killings in the 1950s. But he had actually written about them. He'd been lying through his teeth.

When Abigail Emson left the Black Lion at the end of Gallowgate she found that her purse was empty apart from a pound coin and a twenty-pence piece. Hardly enough for a taxi. But then she'd expected the other bar-maid, Katy, to give her a lift home as usual: she couldn't have known that Katy would have missed her shift at the pub because of a migraine.

Abigail looked at her watch before glancing back at the darkened pub. If she'd realised sooner, the landlord would have lent her a tenner but now the doors were locked and bolted and all the lights were out. There was nothing for it but to walk to the bus stop and catch the bus out to the university.

She walked swiftly down Gallowgate, looking nervously over her shoulder. There was a killer about and you couldn't be too careful. She thought the murdered girl had been found somewhere near the little archway just beyond the Italian restaurant. But she couldn't be certain. Everything she knew about the case came from overheard snippets of conversation as she served in the bar. Rumours, half truths and exaggeration . . . the stock in trade of the Black Lion's regulars.

But they must have been wrong about the location. Nobody would be hanging around a murder scene and she could hear a voice quite clearly. A small voice. High-pitched, coming from somewhere beyond the archway.

'Hello. Can you help me? Please help me. I've hurt myself . . .'

Abigail couldn't decide whether the voice belonged to a woman or a child. There was certainly something childlike about it. Pleading. Lisping.

'Please help me.'

Curious, Abigail stepped into the archway and craned her neck to look but the close appeared to be empty. Then she caught a glimpse of a movement by the old Georgian building on the left . . . the building swathed in plastic and scaffolding.

Abigail stepped through the arch. 'Hello,' she said experimentally. 'Anybody there? Are you all right?' But the place was still and silent.

Curious, she called out another soft hello and an answering muffled giggle emboldened her to move forward. The child – if it was a child – was hiding somewhere behind the building. It was dangerous. Kids had been killed on building sites.

'Where are you?' she called, stepping into the shadows, too preoccupied to hear soft footsteps approaching from behind.

Chapter 11

First thing the next morning Joe noticed that Emily looked exhausted. The flesh beneath her eyes looked purple as though she'd been punched. Joe wondered why this was but he didn't ask. She would hardly want to be reminded that she looked rough – one glance in the mirror would have told her already.

But it was Emily herself who gave the explanation while they drove to Christopher Strange's shared student house in Hasledon. Her young daughter, Sarah, had been up half the night complaining of bad dreams; dreams in which her imaginary friend, Grizelda, was in danger from some wicked men. Emily, of course, assured her that as she was a police officer, no bad men would dare come anywhere near Grizelda but this hadn't been enough to reassure her. Sarah's nightmares had seemed real to her and even that morning, she had seemed upset and wouldn't leave Jeff's side. 'If this goes on, I'm going to have to take her to the doctor's,' she said.

Joe had a sudden flash of inspiration. 'Did she see you on TV talking about the murder?'

He saw Emily hesitate for a moment. 'Yes, she did. Jeff let the kids watch it because of the novelty of seeing Mum on the box. Do you think . . .'

'Mum being involved in grisly murders. Could be

misinterpreted. Mum's in danger herself by being connected with something like that. And if she imagines that someone she loves is in danger that might bring out all sorts of insecurities and . . .'

She sighed. 'You could be right. I'll have a talk to her tonight.' She gave him a shy smile. 'Thanks.'

'All part of the service.'

'Any news from Maddy?'

'She called last night. The second interview went well.' He felt the need to change the subject. 'I bumped into Polly Myers last night on the way home.'

He was about to say that he'd walked Polly home but he thought better of it, fearing Emily might make some suggestive comment; a joke at his expense. In the pressure of an investigation CID thrived on dubious humour. It helped to relieve the tension.

'And when I got back I looked up P. H. Derby on the Internet. Remember, he sent me that book he wrote about the children of Singmass Close? Well he told me he hadn't heard of the Doll Strangler murders in the fifties but it turns out he wrote a book on famous Eborby murders . . . including that particular case.'

'Then I think we need to have another word with Mr P. H. Derby. I've known killers draw attention to themselves like that before. . . . as if they couldn't help it.'

'Because deep down they want to be caught?'

'Maybe.' They'd reached Hasledon now where pockets of Victorian property had been divided into flats or shared houses, mostly occupied by Eborby's student population. Christopher Strange lived in one of these houses, a Victorian terrace with a purple front door and filthy windows. Emily got out of the car first, marched up to the front door and pressed the doorbell.

At first there was no answer but Joe found it hard to believe that a house full of students would be empty at eight o'clock on a Wednesday morning. Emily rang the bell again and after a few minutes the door opened slowly and a bleary-eyed young man wearing a T-shirt proclaiming the virtues of a certain brand of lager, stood in the open doorway, blinking at them like a creature more accustomed to darkness than daylight.

Emily held up her warrant card. 'We're looking for Christopher Strange.'

The young man suddenly became alert, as though someone had thrown cold water at his face. 'Bloody hell . . . I mean, er . . . yeah.' He turned and bellowed 'Chris' into the shadowy depths of the house and after a few moments Chris Strange himself appeared.

As he came down the stairs, the first thing Joe noticed about him was how like his father he was. He had the same colouring, similar build – although Vince had filled out with the years – and almost identical mannerisms. Unlike his sleepy house mate, Chris Strange had the wideawake look of the sporty type, something Joe had never been during his time at university. When Joe asked if they could talk inside, he led them to an unexpectedly tidy living room, the only concession to the student stereotype being a brace of empty lager cans sitting on the cheap pine coffee table.

'So what's this about?' he said as he sat down on a low sofa and leaned forward, resting his elbows on his knees.

Emily told him, keeping it simple. And as she spoke, Joe watched Chris's face carefully. He looked wary, as if he was afraid of falling into a trap.

'Where were you last Friday night, Chris?' Emily asked.

The answer came quickly, gabbled almost as if it had been rehearsed. 'I was at home. I went out for a quick drink with an old mate from school and I decided to stay the night at my parents' because it was nearer.'

'What time did you get home?'

'About half eleven. My dad had just got in. He'll tell you.'

'Did you go out again?'

His eyes widened for a split second, then he looked down at his hands.

'Is there anything you want to tell us, Chris?' Joe asked. He hadn't taken his eyes off the student's face.

A flash of panic appeared in Chris's eyes then he hesitated for a few moments before nodding his head. Chris Strange knew something. It was just a matter of coaxing it out of him.

There was a long silence while he gathered his thoughts. Joe waited. He knew he'd get more out of Christopher Strange if he let him make his confession in his own time. Emily was sitting by his side, perfectly still, as though she feared any movement would distract the young man and break the spell.

After a few moments Strange began to speak, his eyes focussed on the ground. 'Look, I didn't want to get involved but . . .'

'Why don't you tell me what happened?' said Joe gently.

'Karen doesn't know. I mean . . .'

'What doesn't Karen know?' Joe asked, trying to sound patient, teasing out the information like a priest in the confessional.

'About me and Nat.'

'You were having a relationship with Natalie Parkes?'

'Mainly physical. And I wasn't the only one, believe me.' He gave a bitter smile. 'Between you and me, she was a bit of a nymphomaniac.'

'Did she ever mention a lad in her year called Brett Bluit? He was at The Devil's Playground on the night she died.'

Strange shrugged. 'She did say some spotty youth used to follow her about sometimes. Don't think he got anywhere. Is that him?'

'Let's get back to you, shall we. Did you see Natalie last Friday night?'

Chris nodded and took a deep breath. 'I'd been out for a quick drink then I went home. But I got fed up. My parents had gone to bed and I remembered Nat said she was going to The Devil's Playground so I thought I might go along. Who knows, I might get lucky.'

'You knew your sister was going?'

'I was hoping she'd have picked someone up and left by the time I got there.'

'Go on.'

'Anyway, I was looking for a parking space near the club when I saw Nat walking down the street. I stopped and we chatted for a bit.'

'She got in the car?'

'Eventually. I asked her if she wanted to go on somewhere else. I didn't particularly want to go into The Devil's Playground if my sister was still there.'

'So what happened?'

'Nat said she was meeting someone. And before you ask, she didn't say who. And I never asked. But she was excited, like she had some big secret. After a few minutes she got out of the car and walked off down the road towards the cathedral.'

'What did you do?'

'I went on to Boodles – saw a couple of mates from uni there. They were off their faces but they'll remember. I can give you their names.'

Joe made a note. But if these mates were as intoxicated as Chris Strange claimed, their estimate of the time he arrived at the club might not be too reliable. He could still have killed Natalie Parkes.

'Did you know she'd lost her necklace in the car?'

Chris shook his head and Joe could see that Emily was watching his face carefully. There were no tell-tale signs

131

that he was lying but, on the other hand, he might just be a good actor.

'Tell me about Natalie.' Emily said. 'What was she like?'

Chris thought for a while. 'Independent. Adventurous. Sexy. Her family background made her tough, I reckon. Her father walked out and went to the States with another woman leaving the mother to bring up her and Will alone. Not that her mother seemed to be much use. She was busy pursuing her own agenda if you ask me . . . series of boyfriends and all that. As soon as Natalie and her brother hit puberty they were on their own.'

This seemed a remarkably mature assessment of the situation and Chris Strange rose a couple of notches in Joe's estimation.

'And your sister, Karen, was her best friend?'

'People like Natalie don't have best friends. Natalie used to tease Karen. She used to say she had a secret and she was making big money from it. It really used to wind Karen up but she still seemed to regard her as some sort of role model. Can't think why.'

'What about Brett Bluit?'

'If that's the spotty youth she used to talk about sometimes, she used to wind him up as well. It amused her to make him think he was in with a chance. Nat could be cruel, you know. She wasn't a particularly nice person.'

'You mentioned the mother had boyfriends. Any chance that any of them were involved with Natalie?'

Chris Strange paused for a few moments, as though he was trying to remember something that might be important. 'Actually there was one . . . just before Thierry. Nat said something happened but she wouldn't say what it was. Just made a joke of it . . . how older men always went for her. It didn't seem to bother her. I wouldn't be surprised if she led him on. She was like that.'

'Anything else you can tell me?'

Chris shook his head. 'Like I said, she was very mysterious about who she was meeting. I had the feeling something was going on . . . something she didn't want me to know about.'

'You realise you'll have to make a formal statement at the station.' He stood up and Chris did likewise.

'No time like the present, eh? My parents don't have to know, do they?'

Joe said nothing. It was probably inevitable that the Stranges would get to know . . . just as they had got to know about where Karen spent the night.

'Ever heard of the Singmass Close Doll Strangler in the nineteen fifties?' Joe asked out of the blue, taking Chris by surprise.

'Only what I've seen in the papers since Nat . . . You don't think it's the same bloke do you? If he's still alive he must be ancient.'

'Ever heard the name Michele Carden?'

Chris shook his head again and the expression in his eyes told Joe that his ignorance wasn't an act.

'Who do you think killed Natalie?'

'No idea. Some nutter maybe?' Chris replied. The trouble was, Joe thought, he was probably right. And sooner or later amongst all the local sex offenders and oddballs that were being interviewed as a matter of routine, they'd come up with a name.

In the meantime Christopher Strange, the last person to admit to seeing Natalie alive, was the best they'd got.

As they drove back to the police station with Strange in the passenger seat, a few spots of rain began to fall.

Michele went about her morning duties with her head bowed and her shoulders hunched, trying to look unobtrusive. If they knew that she'd discovered the body in the freezer she was sure they wouldn't hesitate to kill her.

She kept wondering about the unseen visitor. She knew from the voices she'd heard that it was a man and there was a possibility that he could be dangerous. He might even have killed the girl in the freezer.

She was becoming used to looking after Alice now. Even changing her pads and washing her soiled flesh was nothing more than an ordinary chore. She looked down at her hands. The skin was red and roughened with work and those glossy nails of which she'd once been so proud, were broken and chewed. But she had to work hard. She had to make them like her while she looked for some way out of there.

She'd kept her eyes open for her bag with her mobile phone inside but she'd seen no sign of it. Perhaps if they came to trust her, they'd lower their guard. That was the plan. Looking back, she wondered how she'd been stupid enough to believe Sylvia's story of models and fashion shoots. But we all hear what we want to hear and disregard the rest, she thought philosophically – she'd heard something like that in a song once – a CD that had been one of her dad's favourites.

It was time to give Alice her breakfast and she climbed the stairs with the steaming bowl of porridge and the cooled tea in the white plastic cup with the lid; the type of cup Michele had always associated with babies. She passed Barry on the landing, keeping her eyes lowered, and turned the key to unlock Alice's door.

The old woman was sitting up in bed, her limp body propped up by pillows as she stared ahead with empty eyes. Michele smiled and asked her how she was. It was easier that way, pretending that she was getting a response. And if Sylvia or Barry were to overhear, they would be bound to appreciate the fact that she was making some sort of effort.

After the feeding came the changing. Michele had

134

never had anyone to care about before – her mother hadn't even allowed her a pet, saying it would make a mess in the house – and the feeling that Alice was her responsibility seemed to give her some sort of purpose in that dark, dead house with its unseen resident and its corpse in the freezer.

Once she had assembled everything she needed, she filled a plastic bowl with warm water from the little sink in the corner of the room and pulled the bedclothes back, exposing Alice's scrawny limbs. The old woman's face registered no emotion as Michele took the flannel and soap and began to clean the parchment skin.

When she'd cleaned the small feet carefully, she looked at the old woman and smiled. 'Now how come your big toe's missing, Alice? How did you lose that, eh? An accident was it?' She stared into the old woman's eyes. 'You're a bit of a mystery, aren't you, Alice? Who are you, eh? And who . . .'

The tentative rattle of the door handle turning slowly made Michele fall silent, praying that she hadn't been overheard.

Joe and Emily entered the incident room. There was a lot to tell the team at the morning briefing: Christopher Strange had given his statement and now their priority was to find out who Natalie had planned to meet after he'd dropped her off on the night she died. But before Emily could call everyone together, Sunny Porter came rushing over. He looked rather pleased with himself. Joe knew that look of old – it meant Sunny had discovered something nobody else had.

'I've had someone tracking down everyone involved in the nineteen-fifties murders,' he said. 'Remember the bloke who ran the dolls' hospital – Jervis?'

'What about him? You found him?'

'He's in a nursing home on the outskirts of Whitby. And he had a daughter – name of Bridget.' He paused, as if he were about to announce something momentous. 'The proprietor of that shop, Bridget's Bygones, is a Bridget Jervis. Now there can't be too many of them around . . . not ones who are interested in dolls. And she's vanished into thin air.'

Joe regretted his initial scepticism. Sunny might be an unreconstructed member of the old school but that didn't mean he wasn't sharp.

'And I've traced Peter Crawthwaite, boyfriend of the first victim, Marion Grant. They'd had a row a couple of days before she was killed.'

'Didn't he have an alibi for her murder?' Emily asked.

'Aye, ma'am. He said he were drinking with a bloke who worked with Albert Jervis at the dolls' hospital. Caleb Selly. Selly backed up his story.'

'So where's Crawthwaite now?'

'He lives in one of them almshouses on Boothgate.'

Joe knew the almshouses. He had passed the quaint cottage-like building many times and he'd always been curious to see inside. And now he was keen to speak to someone who had been around when the Doll Strangler was at work. Maybe Peter Crawthwaite would know why the killings had stopped all those years ago . . . and whether the killer had come out of retirement.

'And there's still been no luck with Stallion's mobile,' Sunny said. 'Whoever he is, he's not answering.'

'We need to find him,' said Joe. 'Natalie called him on the night she died.'

'There must be something seriously wrong with a man who calls himself Stallion,' mused Emily. 'And I want to speak to Bridget Jervis. She owns a shop selling dolls like the one left at the murder scene and now she seems to have vanished. If she really is Albert Jervis's daughter . . .'

136

'I'd like to have a closer look at Polly Myers,' Joe said casually.

'Oh aye?' He saw a smile playing on Emily's lips.

Joe felt the blood rushing to his face. Was he that obvious? 'Seriously, boss, I'm sure she knows something. I also want to find out why Philip Derby denied knowing about the nineteen-fifties murders.' He spotted a photograph on Emily's desk of a photogenic girl with glossy dark hair and generous, pouting lips. 'Has that come from missing persons?'

'Mmm. It's Michele Carden. No sign of her yet.'

'She's at the same school as Natalie Parkes. Could there be a connection?'

'They're in different years − don't even know each other. But I'm keeping an open mind.'

'If two girls from the same school go missing, it's usual to assume there's a connection so why not in this case?'

Before Emily could answer the phone on her desk began to ring. She picked it up and Joe sat there watching the expression on her face turn from businesslike efficiency to downright shock. 'Get the scene sealed off. We'll be right over,' she said before replacing the receiver carefully.

Joe watched her. He could tell the news was bad.

'There's been another one, Joe. Same MO. Doll and everything.'

Joe suddenly felt numb. 'Where?'

'About fifty yards from the first one. Behind the old Ragged School. A couple of workmen found her. She was half hidden behind some bins so they didn't see her till . . .'

'And it's the same as the . . .?'

'Looks like he's copying the fifties killings in all their gruesome detail.'

'Who is she? Do we know?'

'A student at the university, name of Abigail Emson.

137

Her student union card was in her bag. We'd better get someone down to the university to get her home details.'

Joe said nothing. He had a sudden vision of the girl's parents going about their usual morning routine, unaware that their lives were about to be shattered. But killers never considered the consequences of their violence, the grief that ripples out to engulf the victim's family and friends. Joe had seen it all too often . . . and had even felt the pain himself.

Emily interrupted his thoughts. 'We'll break the news to the team. Then we'll get down to Singmass Close.'

As Joe walked out into the incident room, he felt stunned, as though someone had hit him . . . hard.

Chapter 12

Emily Thwaite watched as Joe stood by the girl's body, his head bowed. She knew he was praying for her soul and, although she attended church only for weddings, christenings and funerals, this thought gave her a small atom of comfort. At least someone wasn't treating her like a lump of meat. At least someone cared.

Joe looked up. 'She's so young.'

Emily stared at the body lying on the ground half hidden by a row of bins, slumped against the russet brick wall of the old Ragged School, silent now that the workmen had abandoned their posts. Joe was right. The girl did look young lying there as though asleep while Sally Sharpe, the pathologist, went about her business. There were no flirtatious glances towards Joe today, Emily noticed. Sally worked efficiently in funereal silence.

The doll lay next to the body, covered by a sheet of plastic to avoid contamination. The crime scene investigators lived in hope that it would yield some clue but Emily herself wasn't so confident. The last doll had been clean. The killer had been careful to cover his tracks, almost as if he was playing a game with them. This killing was no spur-of-the-moment impulse, no yielding to a frenzied blood lust. This had been planned meticulously. Relished. Enjoyed.

'Strangulation?' Emily asked when Sally looked up.

'Exactly the same as before. Some sort of ligature. Something soft and stretchy. A scarf or a stocking, something like that.'

'Can you give us a time of death?' Emily enquired hopefully.

'Around midnight, give or take an hour.'

'Is that the best you can do?' Emily knew she sounded impatient, but Sarah's nocturnal antics were really beginning to catch up with her.

'Sorry,' Sally said firmly. 'Time of death isn't an exact science, you know. I do my best.' She sat back on her heels. 'The left big toe again. Done with a sharp blade . . . a penknife or something like that.' She looked at the doll in its plastic shroud. 'And he's tried to chop the doll's toe off too . . . but he's not made such a good job of that. It's just broken the porcelain.' She looked at Emily. 'Have you found out where the first doll came from yet?'

'We're working on it,' Emily said with a hint of apology. Putting it into words made her feel inadequate. They had so many leads for Natalie Parkes's murder but all of them seemed frustratingly vague. Bridget Jervis still hadn't been traced – maybe they should make it a priority. And there was Philip Derby . . . but she'd leave him to Joe.

At that moment Sunny appeared round the corner of the building. The fact that he looked so wide awake while she couldn't stop yawning made her feel slightly irritated.

'I've sent someone to check out all the CCTV cameras in the area, ma'am,' Sunny said. 'Mind you, there aren't many if he approached from the cathedral end – and half the ones in Gallowgate aren't bloody working.'

'Mmm,' said Emily. 'Last time was a dead loss.'

Joe spoke for the first time. 'If Christopher Strange was telling the truth, Natalie Parkes had walked off in the direction of the cathedral. The obvious route she would take if she was getting the bus back to her house was down Jamesgate and through Boothgate Bar, then past the theatre to the bus stop outside Museum Gardens. But she seemed to be heading in the opposite direction. I reckon she was on her way somewhere. Somewhere she didn't want her friends or Chris Strange to know about.'

'But that could be irrelevant if our killer's an opportunist,' said Emily, her eyes on the girl's prone body. With her contorted face out of sight, she looked peaceful; as if she was asleep. 'And this second one makes it look more likely that he's choosing his victims at random.'

Emily straightened her back. She was in charge and it was time they got to work. 'Right then. Let's get the good people of Singmass Close interviewed. With any luck someone might have seen something this time. And check out the alibis of everyone we spoke to about the first murder. I want to know where everyone was last night. OK?'

She stared down at the girl's body for a few moments. She wanted to get whoever had cut her hopeful young life short and she'd get him whatever it took . . . this twisted bastard who messed around with dolls and treated living women as if they were disposable playthings.

Polly Myers was frightened. There'd been another death right there in Singmass Close. Too near for comfort.

As soon as she'd finished making a statement to the young constable who'd knocked on her door, Yolanda phoned.

Since the first murder, Daisy had seemed nervous in Singmass Close, huddled in the corner with her dolls, talking to Mary in a whisper. Polly had thought a change of scene would do Daisy good and letting her stay with Yolanda again had seemed like the perfect solution. But Yolanda had told her on the phone that Daisy was missing Mary and this encouragement of Daisy's obsession with her imaginary friend was starting to irritate Polly.

The police were still doing the rounds as Polly left number six and headed for Yolanda's flat above the antique warehouse on Coopergate. Polly had first met Yolanda when she'd visited a psychic fair in search of help when Daisy had acquired Mary, the ragged little girl who seemed so real to her – more real than her friends at school. It was then she'd discovered that Yolanda had gifts denied to all but a special few. Yolanda could speak to the dead.

At first Polly had only intended to ask Yolanda's advice about Mary – just a tentative enquiry, no strings. But Yolanda had known all about Polly's predicament without a word being spoken and she'd claimed that Daisy was in danger. Polly hadn't felt inclined to argue and she'd let Daisy stay at Yolanda's for two nights to see how she settled in. And on the second of those nights Natalie Parkes had been murdered in Singmass Close.

Yolanda's flat was shabby and old-fashioned but it was large with three bedrooms and plenty of room to accommodate a small child. To Polly's relief Daisy had taken to Yolanda, with her long grey hair, her taste for colourful clothes and her gently understanding manner, instantly. And there were enough strange and curious objects around her flat to keep a child with an enquiring mind entertained.

Yolanda had invited Polly to stay too but she hadn't accepted right away, fearing what might happen if he came looking for Daisy and found the house in Singmass Close unoccupied. But with this second murder, Polly had changed her mind: she really needed to get away and she was certain he'd never find them at Yolanda's.

Polly hurried through the crowded streets of Eborby, all the time looking around to make sure she wasn't being followed. And when she finally reached the antiques warehouse she rang the cheap plastic bell beside the door that led up to the flat, feeling a tremendous wave of relief.

Everyone in the Singmass Close area had been interviewed and Joe knew he couldn't put off his return to the police station any longer. Emily had gone ahead of him to wait for word that Abigail's family had been informed and to make arrangements to receive them. He didn't envy her. In his opinion dealing with victims' loved ones was the worst part of the job.

As he walked towards the main road he could hear the builders hammering inside the old Ragged School, having resumed work after the initial shock. He glanced back at Polly's house and noticed that the doll had gone from the window. He hadn't seen her that morning but he knew she'd been spoken to. But she'd seen nothing. There was no excuse for him to go back . . . even if he had the time.

He crossed Gallowgate and walked through Vicars Green, his eyes drawn irresistibly towards the flat where his late colleague Kevin's daughter, Carmel, lived. He hadn't seen Carmel for a while. Perhaps now that she was settled with her boyfriend, he'd convinced himself that she didn't need to see him any more. Or perhaps she reminded him too much of painful times. Maybe he'd give her a call one day. Or maybe he'd let things drift.

He passed the cathedral, thinking that it was about time he had a word with George Merryweather to see what he knew about Singmass Close and the tales of the ghostly children. There was a nagging suspicion in the back of his brain that those stories and the murders, past and present, might be linked somehow because dolls and ghostly children seemed to go together. George was supposed to be the Diocese's expert on such matters so maybe it was worth paying him a visit. And besides, Joe needed to see him again. He valued George's wisdom.

He climbed the cathedral steps to the south door, the entrance used both by worshippers and the never-ending stream of tourists and sightseers, and ran George to ground in an office that looked as though it had just been ransacked by a team of particularly untidy burglars. But Joe knew that was its normal condition.

George was a round man, balding with a benign smile. He cleared a chair of papers and invited Joe to sit. 'How's Maddy?' he asked.

'In London. Job interview.' He paused. He didn't feel inclined to discuss Maddy as there were other, more pressing things on his mind. 'There's been another murder in Singmass Close.'

'How terrible,' said George. He sounded genuinely shocked and bowed his head for a second in prayer.

'What do you know about these hauntings in the close?' Joe asked. 'Is it true or is it just something to give the tourists a cheap thrill?'

George looked up. 'You know there's something in it, don't you? You've sensed something.'

Joe hesitated. Had he sensed something? He'd certainly had a feeling of being watched but that might have been his imagination. 'I don't know, George. There's certainly an odd atmosphere in the place. Is that story about the master of the Ragged School fact or fiction?'

'It's fact all right. The poor man died insane. The good citizens of Eborby used to go and gawp at him chained up in the asylum on Boothgate. That's what passed for entertainment in those days. He ended up scratching his own eyes out, saying the children had done it. He raved on about the children pinching and scratching him . . . even claimed they tried to strangle him.'

'What about the hauntings in the close?'

'People reported seeing and hearing the ghosts of children around the close pretty soon after the event. And there was a resurgence of activity when the old buildings were cleared and the new development built. Ghosts get disturbed by change just like anyone else, I suppose.'

George's words reminded him that Philip Derby had said something similar.

'The Ragged School's being renovated.'

'So I've heard. It's being made into offices, I believe.'

'Do you think there's anything in the stories?'

George shrugged. 'I try to keep an open mind about these things until I'm convinced otherwise.' There was a pause then he looked Joe in the eye. 'As a matter of fact a young woman from Singmass Close came to see me quite recently. Her daughter had started chatting away to a little girl called Mary. An invisible little girl of course.' He smiled. 'I said it could just be an imaginary friend. They're quite common at that age – my nephew had one called Marmaduke. I don't know where he got that from. Mary seems quite mundane by comparison.'

'So what happened?'

'I told her I'd come and visit the child if she was still worried but I didn't hear from her again.'

'When was this?'

'It must be about three weeks ago.'

Joe could feel his heart beating a little faster. 'Was her name Polly Myers?'

'Yes. Do you know her?'

'I've met her,' he said, wondering whether to mention Polly's resemblance to Kaitlin. But he thought better of it. 'Where were the children's bodies buried?'

'In the churchyard of St Andrews, I believe . . . the nearest parish church. I think there's a little memorial to them but I must admit, I haven't actually been there to have a look. There's a common belief that some of the bodies were never found.' He paused. 'I've thought from time to time that I should go and pray there . . . try and put their poor little souls to rest.'

Joe smiled. It was just like George to concern himself with the welfare of ghosts. 'I presume you know about the murders in Singmass Close in the nineteen fifties?'

'Ah, yes. I read about it in the paper. The Doll Strangler. You think he's resumed his nasty little tricks? All I can say is that he's taken his time to get going again.'

'We think it might be a copycat killer. The only trouble is he knows too much. Certain things were kept from the public in the fifties but our killer seems to know all about them.'

'Oh dear.' George rested his chin on his hands. 'You're quite sure the details weren't published?'

'Absolutely sure. We've been through every press report as well as all the true crime books on the subject. This particular thing isn't mentioned.'

'Then your killer might have come out of retirement and struck again. If he was in his late teens then he could be a sprightly septuagenarian now.' He paused. 'Or it might be someone who was involved in the case at the time. A police officer or someone who found one of the bodies. Or the son of someone involved . . . someone whose mother or father told them everything they knew.'

'The details of these particular murders aren't the sort of thing you'd tell your kids as a bedtime story. Are dolls associated with the Singmass Close hauntings?'

'Children have dolls so I suppose that's a connection of sorts. Sorry, Joe, I'm not being much help, am I?'

'On the contrary, George. It's good to talk it over with someone who isn't involved.'

'I'll pray for these girls and their families.'

'Thanks, George,' said Joe softly.

As he took his leave and walked out into the massive

space of the cathedral's nave, he realised that, although he hadn't actually discussed the case with George, everything seemed clearer in his head.

However, he didn't quite know what to make of George's revelation that Polly Myers had consulted him about an imaginary child called Mary. Surely it was unlikely to have anything to do with the murders. Perhaps, he told himself, he was just clutching at any excuse to see Polly again. Perhaps Maddy's extended absence was responsible for this growing obsession. He kept checking to see if he'd missed a call from her on his mobile and each time he found nothing he felt a stab of disappointment. He had only spoken to her last night and she was probably busy . . . as he was.

George's remark about the killer being a sprightly septuagenarian had set him thinking. Peter Crawthwaite, the boyfriend of the first victim back in the 1950s, would be in his early seventies and he lived nearby in the almshouses on Boothgate. He'd been planning to see him but the murder of Abigail Emson had got in the way. Now he wanted to see Crawthwaite sooner rather than later. He wanted to speak to someone who was there back in the 1950s.

Michele was keeping her head down, always on the look out for a potential escape route. But in the meantime she was careful to do as she was told and not ask questions. The girl in the freezer had probably asked questions.

She spooned the soup gently into Alice's mouth. She had seen the empty capsules before, lying on the draining board, but she hadn't realised their significance until that morning. What if Alice's soup was being drugged? What if she wasn't as helpless as she seemed?

As an experiment, Michele had thrown away the soup Sylvia had left on Alice's tray and replaced it with some from the pan on the stove. Her only fear was Sylvia finding out what she'd done. Or the visitor she hadn't yet seen. He was an unknown quantity.

Alice certainly seemed brighter that morning. She managed to lift her head slightly and attempt a smile which made Michele suspect that there might be something in her suspicions that Alice's food had been drugged, just as her own coffee had been when she first arrived.

As she picked up the tray and stood up to leave the room, Alice made a sound, a low grunt as though she was trying to speak. Michele put the tray down and rushed to the side of the bed.

'What is it, Alice? Do you want to tell me something?' she whispered.

'Dolls . . .' The word was unclear but Michele could just about make it out.

There was a sound from outside on the landing. 'Sssh, now Alice. Don't say anything else. I'll come back later. OK?'

Alice's arm went up to grab Michele's sleeve but Michele managed to escape her feeble grasp. 'I'll be back. Keep quiet. OK?'

Michele hurried out of the room, shutting the door carefully behind her and turning the key in the lock as Sylvia had instructed her to do. It wouldn't do to let Alice wander out. Not now she'd started to communicate.

Michele was carrying the tray downstairs when she saw a movement in the hall. A tall, lean man with thinning dark hair was walking towards the living room and she froze, praying he wouldn't look up and see her. She watched as he disappeared through the living-room door. He must be the visitor, she thought. The unseen fifth person.

And something about his face seemed vaguely familiar.

Chapter 13

Emily sounded uncharacteristically subdued when Joe called her to say he was paying Philip Derby another visit. She was still waiting for a call from Greater Manchester Police to tell that Abigail Emson's next of kin had been informed. Even an encounter with Derby seemed preferable to that, Joe thought to himself as he walked to Derby's flat.

He found the author at home and noted the man's smug expression as he answered the door. Joe stepped into the flat, determined to wipe the knowing smile off his face. He was in no mood for pleasantries this time.

'You lied to me, Mr Derby.'

'Philip, please.' He was trying his best to keep up the act of nonchalance but Joe had seen a flicker of panic in his eyes, swiftly suppressed.

'You told me you knew nothing about the Doll Strangler murders in the nineteen fifties?'

'Did I say that?' Derby examined his fingernails, before looking up at him and smiling. 'Look, if you think I killed this Natalie girl, you're barking up the wrong tree entirely.'

'You wrote a book about famous Eborby murders, including the Doll Strangler. You researched all the details. Natalie Parkes's murder was a copycat killing . . . by someone who knows all about the originals.'

The smile stayed fixed on Derby's lips as he shook his head. 'Oh, dear, Inspector, you are clutching at straws. Thousands of people knew about those murders. It was hardly a state secret.'

'So why lie about it?'

The answer was an amused shrug. This man was treating it almost as a joke and Joe had to resist the temptation to punch the smirk off his face or arrest him on the spot. He wasn't sure what for, but he was certain he could think of something.

'Can anybody vouch for your whereabouts in the early hours of last Saturday morning?' he asked formally.

Derby's pale cheeks reddened. 'Yes, as a matter of fact. I was with a friend but I wouldn't want to . . .'

Joe watched him realising that he was actually enjoying the man's embarrassment. 'We'll need a name. And an address. We'll have to check.'

'It could be embarrassing for the friend I was with. You see . . .'

'His name . . . sir?'

'OK.' He took a deep breath. 'It's Ben Cassidy.' He recited an address off Andrewgate . . . around 200 yards from Singmass Close as the crow flies. 'Look, he's a headmaster. If it got out that he . . .'

Benjamin Cassidy. Of course. The head of Hicklethorpe Manor. This case was getting odder by the moment.

'You were at Mr Cassidy's house?'

'Yes,' was the whispered reply.

'What time did you leave?'

Derby swallowed hard. 'About four in the morning.'

'You've known Mr Cassidy long?'

The man's face turned red. 'Not long. And I've not seen him since that night.'

'Where were you last night, Mr Derby? Between eleven, say, and one in the morning.'

'Why?'

'There was another murder last night. Identical to the first.'

Derby's mouth fell open. In Joe's experience it was hard to fake that sort of shock. But not impossible. 'Where were you?'

'I was here. I had a quiet night in reading and listening to music. I went to bed around eleven-thirty. No witnesses, I'm afraid.'

'You didn't go out at all?'

Derby shook his head. A muscle in his eye twitched, making it look as if he was winking. The casual manner was an act. He was on edge. Joe could almost smell his fear.

'When you wrote your book about famous Eborby murders, is there anything you decided to leave out . . . any information about the Doll Strangler murders you got from a police officer who worked on the case, for instance? Something that had been kept from the public at the time?'

'I don't think so.'

Joe looked round the room and noticed, not for the first time, that Derby possessed an LCD TV with a DVD recorder underneath. They squatted there, matt silver and uncompromisingly modern, amongst the old books and shabby antiques like spacecraft descended into a drab 1950s landscape. There was a collection of DVDs too that caught Joe's eye . . . not commercial but home-recorded.

'Do you have any notes you made for the book? Research?'

Derby looked wary and nodded.

'Mind if I have a look?'

It was difficult to read Derby's expression but Joe guessed he was alarmed. He hurried from the room, leaving Joe alone.

When Joe left twenty minutes later, having examined the notes Derby had chosen to show him and found no reference to severed toes, he had a DVD tucked into the inside pocket of his jacket. Technically, he had done the wrong thing, of course. But then there were two young women lying dead in the mortuary of Eborby General and he needed some answers. Fast.

Emily sat with her head bowed. She needed a few moments away from the bustle of the incident room to collect her thoughts. She had just spoken to Greater Manchester Police who had sent someone to break the news to Abigail Emson's parents. An officer had arrived on the doorstep of the unsuspecting couple who'd been preparing for just another ordinary day, unaware that their world was about to be blown apart. What if, in fifteen or so years time, it was one of her own kids? The thought was far too painful to contemplate and she tried to push it from her mind. But it kept returning like a nightmare.

She was glad when Joe entered the office, distracting her from her morbid thoughts. He looked excited, as though he had made some new discovery. She just hoped it was a good one. She needed cheering up.

'I've just seen Philip Derby. You'll never guess who he says he was with on the night of Natalie Parkes's murder.'

'Surprise me,' said Emily with a sigh.

'He claims he was with Natalie's headmaster. Benjamin Cassidy.'

'Does he indeed?' She hadn't liked Cassidy much and somehow she wasn't surprised that his name had come up. Call it a hunch or female intuition – she wasn't sure which.

'So Cassidy's his boyfriend, is he?'

'Well, he didn't go into detail about their exact relationship but . . .'

Before Joe could say more, Jamilla Dal gave a perfunctory knock on the office door and burst in.

'Natalie Parkes's mother's here, sir. She's at the front desk.'

Emily looked at Joe. 'She took her time.' She knew the French police had had trouble tracking her down but she still had an irrational feeling that a mother should have known somehow that she'd lost a daughter in appalling circumstances.

Five minutes later she and Joe were face to face with Tricia Parkes. She recognised one of the men with her as Natalie's brother, Will, who stood by his mother's side protectively. With them was a slim, dark-haired man dressed with casual good taste who hung back slightly behind the pair as though he didn't know quite what to do. This, Joe assumed, was Thierry. And the Frenchman looked around awkwardly as Tricia sobbed theatrically into a disintegrating tissue.

Emily put her arm around the woman and led her firmly but gently into the interview room, hissing to a passing constable that tea was needed. Hot and strong. Two sugars. Will, Thierry and Joe followed, heads bowed like mourners.

Between sobs Tricia told them that she knew nothing about her daughter's love life: Natalie had been entitled to her privacy like everyone else. Emily suspected that this was due to a lack of interest rather than consideration for her daughter's feelings but she said nothing.

However, Tricia did come up with one juicy nugget of information. She thought that Natalie was involved with an older man but she had no solid evidence – just a feeling.

Natalie's room had, of course, already been searched but no clue to any man friend's identity had been found and Stallion still wasn't answering his phone. Even Karen

Strange, the so-called best friend, hadn't known – or had claimed that she hadn't known. The mystery man or men in Natalie Parkes's life was remaining just that – a mystery.

The Doll Strangler sat with a blanket across his knees, his fading eyes squinting to read the local newspaper headlines in the light seeping through the thin, floral curtains. His gnarled hands felt for the glass of water. He had to take his pills. How these doctors loved to keep you alive . . . but that was their job. They saved life as readily as he had taken it.

It had just been on the radio. There'd been another one. She'd been found in the close again, just like before. Just like his girls. He remembered the click, click, click of their high heels on the paving slabs and the children's whispers. 'Here she comes. She's getting nearer.'

This one was called Abigail. It was a pretty name and he knew she would have been pretty like the others. It was the pretty girls who laughed at you. But, after he'd stopped the laughter, they had lain there like dolls. His playthings. It had been so many years ago and now he wanted to see his souvenirs again so badly.

The 1950s had been good years. Everyone full of hope after the War. The girls used to more freedom than they had enjoyed before the days of the War with its ever-present possibility of death. The girls had danced back then – jived and jitterbugged with the soldiers and the Yanks. But they'd never wanted to dance with him so one day he'd decided to stop them dancing altogether. The children nobody else could see had dared him to do it. They had taunted and teased until he had showed them he had the guts to act.

His first attempt at killing had failed miserably and the children had chanted and called him names. But after that, he'd gathered the courage to prove himself and he'd wielded real power for the first time in his life. The power of life and death.

He needed to look at his keepsakes. But it was so difficult to get at them up there in the attic. It needed some thought. Some planning.

He reached out for his frame. If he could manage the stairs and get the ladder down, then he could relive it all again. He could feel the life coursing through his body once more.

But when he heard the key turn in the front door he knew that it was too late now for pleasure. Pleasure would have to wait until another time.

Joe left Emily to deal with Tricia Parkes. He had things to do. And top of his list was checking out Philip Derby's alibi and seeing what was on the DVD he'd taken from his flat.

He'd just sat down when Jenny Ripon came rushing up. Her cheeks were flushed and she looked as if she was bursting to impart some thrilling secret. 'I've been checking out some names, sir. People who've given statements.'

He looked up at her, curious. 'And?'

'Well, according to official records there's no such person as Polly Myers. She even gave false details to the shop where she's been working. Polly Myers doesn't exist.'

Chapter 14

Joe asked Jenny to discover all she could about Polly Myers. He had too much on his plate to do it himself and besides, he felt the matter needed some professional detachment. He'd also called Hicklethorpe Manor School and been told that Benjamin Cassidy was out at a meeting and wouldn't be back till later. Joe felt frustrated that Derby's story couldn't be confirmed but he knew he'd have to be patient.

He opened his drawer and fingered the DVD he'd taken from Derby's flat. The AV room was already occupied by someone examining CCTV footage from the shops on Gallowgate. Besides, he had a mountain of paperwork to catch up on. He closed the drawer and began to sift through his files. But after a couple of minutes he heard Sunny's unmistakable voice.

'There's been a sighting of our escaped prisoner in Scarborough. Someone saw him eating fish and chips on the beach.'

Joe sat back, glad of the distraction. With two murders to deal with, he'd almost forgotten about Gordon Pledge. 'Reliable sighting?'

'Who knows? Uniform's following it up.'

Joe looked down at the pile of witness statements and decided he could do with a short break. And Sunny looked as if he was eager to pass the time of day.

'Pledge killed someone just outside Harrogate, didn't he?'

'Aye. He killed a twelve-year-old girl three years back. Francesca Putney her name was. Got life. Swore he was innocent.'

'Don't they all.' Joe rolled his eyes upwards.

'Oh, Pledge made a big song and dance about it – got himself the best lawyers. Said he was going to appeal but he's not managed it yet. He also reckoned he knew who did it but he had no proof.'

'I presume he let the police in on the secret.'

'Aye. He accused one of his neighbours but the bloke had an alibi and all the evidence pointed to Pledge. They even found the kid's shoe in his shed. He was clutching at bloody straws if you ask me.' Sunny scratched his head.

'I presume uniform have checked out his known associates and his family.'

Sunny grunted. 'That's the first thing they did. Only when they arrived at the parents' address they found they'd done a vanishing act and now there's no bloody sign of 'em. Same goes for Pledge's missus. She buggered off after the trial and now there's no sign of her either.'

Before Joe could say anything the door opened and Emily swept into the incident room, walking through quickly as though she didn't want to talk to anybody. It wasn't like her, Joe thought as he watched her disappearing back. Normally she'd be doing the rounds of the desks checking on what developments there'd been in her absence. Joe stood up and waited a few seconds before following her into her office.

She was on the phone but as soon as he opened the door she put the receiver down and looked up at him. Her face was solemn and there seemed to be a glassy film on her blue eyes . . . as though she was fighting back half-formed tears.

'I've just taken Abigail Emson's parents to see their daughter in the morgue. It was bloody awful.' She sighed. 'I was just trying to ring Jeff to see how the kids are. But there's no answer. He must be out.' She picked up her handbag, rummaged inside then dumped it back on the floor . . . a pointless activity just to give her something to do with her hands. 'Sometimes I wish I still bloody smoked,' she said under her breath.

'You'd only get arrested by the health police,' said Joe as he sat down. 'They're keener on getting a conviction than we are.'

She tried to smile at his weak joke but didn't quite manage it.

Joe reached across the desk and touched her fingers. He knew how she felt: he'd felt like that himself in similar situations – helpless and angry. Emily withdrew her fingers quickly as though she'd had an electric shock and Joe suspected that his impetuous gesture of sympathy had been misinterpreted. He decided to say nothing, to let the incident pass.

'We need to see Polly Myers again and ask her about her real name. Apparently Polly Myers doesn't officially exist.'

Emily frowned. 'What do you mean?'

'Jenny couldn't find anyone of that name in any official records.'

Emily rolled her eyes. 'Are you sure you're not getting a bit obsessed with Polly Myers? She might have just fancied a change of name – or she's changed it to get away from an abusive boyfriend or something. I can hardly see her strangling those women, can you?'

Joe shook his head. 'I just get the feeling she's hiding something. Her neighbours told Jenny that she's gone to stay with a friend for a few days.'

'Not unreasonable in the circumstances,' Emily said. 'Any forwarding address?'

Joe shook his head.

'Like I said, I can't see her as our strangler.'

'But she might know who it is,' Joe observed.

Emily had to acknowledge that he could have a point.

'Any word on Bridget Jervis yet?'

Joe shook his head again. 'You'd think with a shop to run, she'd have been back by now. I wouldn't like to leave my livelihood in the hands of that assistant. She's not much more than a kid.'

Emily checked her watch. 'The Emsons have been booked into a hotel and I said I'd pop round there and see them later. We've got people talking to everyone who was interviewed regarding Natalie Parkes.'

'And we'd better see what Abigail's colleagues at the pub and her university friends have to say for themselves.'

'Already being dealt with,' Emily said. Her natural efficiency was gradually returning.

Joe stood up. 'We need to confirm Philip Derby's alibi with Benjamin Cassidy – that story about them being together at the time of Natalie's murder.'

He saw Emily put her hand up to her forehead.

'You OK, boss?'

Emily straightened her back. 'Just a bit of a headache. I'm fine . . . honestly.' She stood up. 'I'd better go and bring the super up to date.'

Joe watched her as she left the office, walking confidently past the desks of her underlings, stopping for the odd encouraging word. No sign of the tiredness he'd seen a couple of minutes before. But he knew her mind was on the Emsons and what they were going through.

Michele had been told to go to her room and Sylvia had locked the door behind her as she always did now when there were no chores to be done. But Michele suspected that something was going on. She had caught a glimpse of

159

the man now and she couldn't help wondering whether he knew she was there. Or whether he knew about the girl in the freezer.

She turned over the possibilities in her mind as she lay there on the mattress. Was the man potential friend or foe?

When she heard the door being unlocked again she sat up, flattening her back against the headboard. The door opened and for a few moments Sylvia stood silhouetted in the doorway, watching her with those sharp eyes of hers.

'You're to come downstairs,' Sylvia said, an order rather than a request.

Michele obeyed without a murmur. The more she got out of that small attic room, the more likely it was that one day she'd find a possible means of escape.

She followed Sylvia down the stairs and when she reached the hall Barry emerged from the living room, followed by the man Michele had seen in the hall. She saw now that his face was pallid as though he'd spent a lot of time indoors in artificial light. But he looked strong, towering over Michele like a predatory beast.

He turned to Sylvia. 'Well, Mum, I think it's about time you introduced us, don't you?'

The AV room was free at last. But as Joe headed for the door, Emily spotted him and beckoned him into her office.

She looked more strained and weary than she had done earlier. What she needed was to get home early and spend time with Jeff and the children, a bit of family normality. But that was one thing she wouldn't be getting until this killer was caught.

She looked at her watch before she spoke. 'I'm doing a TV appeal with Abigail's parents later, in time for the evening news.' She sighed. 'At least it makes them feel as if they're doing something constructive. I asked Natalie's mother to join us but she refused. Said it was like picking your sores in public.'

Joe could see both points of view. However, Natalie Parkes's mother's apparent indifference to her daughter's death – not to mention her father who was still refusing to budge from his office in the States until the funeral – struck him as cold and heartless, even a little odd.

He sat down, making himself comfortable. 'I'm pretty sure the killings are random, don't you agree?'

Emily pondered the question for a while. 'He targets young women who are walking alone at night so yes, I'd say he's an opportunistic predator.'

'One girl blonde, the other dark – both late teens early twenties.'

'And available. They come to him. Unless he follows them.'

'And then there's the copycat element. Singmass Close . . . where the nineteen-fifties murders took place. And the dolls. Why does he mutilate the feet?'

'He's reliving the Doll Strangler murders in the nine-teen fifties. We're looking for someone who has an obsession with that particular case. Or maybe it is the Doll Strangler himself. He could be a sprightly seventy. Still strong enough to kill.'

'But if that's the case, why did he give up so suddenly after four and why hasn't there been a peep out of him till now?'

'I've got someone checking whether anyone who's been in a mental institution or prison since the fifties has just been released. But there can't be many who'd fit that par-ticular bill.'

Joe thought for a few moments. 'I can't help feeling there's some connection to those stories about the children who died in Singmass Close. Could that have inspired the killer in some way? The dolls . . . children?'

Emily said nothing.

'I want to see everyone who was involved in the original case.'

'Those that are still alive,' Emily muttered.

'We're seeing Albert Jervis in Whitby tomorrow and we can't rule out Peter Crawthwaite. He was the first victim's boyfriend. Mind you, he had an alibi for Marion Grant's murder back in 1956. He was with Jervis's assistant, Caleb Selly.'

'Got an address for Selly?'

'Not yet.'

Emily sighed. 'After all this time he could have died or moved out of the area. It might be a wild goose chase.'

'Look, Emily, if you're busy I could go to Whitby with Jamilla or Sunny.'

'No, Joe, I want to talk to Jervis myself.'

'And we mustn't forget about his daughter, Bridget . . . the doll lady. She still hasn't turned up.'

Emily stood up. She wore an expression of fearful resignation on her face. 'Once more unto the breach . . .' she said, clutching her handbag close to her chest like a shield.

'You'll be fine, boss,' Joe said softly and watched her disappear out of the office door. He didn't envy her. Having to sit there with the grieving parents while the press gave you a good grilling wasn't his idea of a perfect way to spend an afternoon. 'Fancy a drink tonight after work?' he called out when she was halfway out of the door.

She turned round and smiled gratefully. 'It'll have to be a quick one. Jeff's cooking.'

When she'd gone Joe remembered he had Derby's DVD in his inside pocket. It was a long shot but Philip Derby had concealed his knowledge of the Doll Strangler murders.

He smiled at Jamilla Dal as he passed her desk on the way to the small, windowless room that contained the audio visual equipment. In this room, officers pored over hours of CCTV footage and home videos but now, to Joe's relief, it happened to be empty.

It was about time he found out what Philip Derby regarded as entertainment. As he settled down to watch, already considering the best way of returning the disc to Derby's flat without the embarrassment of being discovered, he was willing to bet that he was barking up the wrong tree altogether. It would be something dull and worthy – a recording of some BBC2 documentary perhaps or maybe an opera.

Images began to appear on the screen. There was no sound as the figures moved in silent rhythm. Two men and four young women writhing on what looked like a bed of furs.

Joe recognised the two men. He'd met them both before.

He watched the action on the screen for a while, as a naturalist might observe the mating habits of a group of rare animals. Philip Derby and Benjamin Cassidy certainly looked as if they were enjoying themselves, which was more than could be said for the four girls whose faces were masks of boredom . . . or was it endurance? But Joe's heart began to beat a little faster when he recognised the face of the blonde girl sitting astride Cassidy.

It was a pity Emily had gone out. He would have liked her to be the first to share his discovery. The discovery that Natalie Parkes had been making pornographic films with her headmaster.

Chapter 15

Emily viewed the DVD in silence with a slight smile on her newly painted lips. 'So that's what Derby and Cassidy have been getting up to in their spare time. There's one thing I hate more than a hypocrite and that's a smug hypocrite. No wonder Derby wanted to give us the impression that him and Cassidy were an item.'

'He never actually said they were; he just let us assume. I've rung the school. Cassidy's back from his meeting.'

'Are you ready to go round and tell him his career's in ruins then?' she asked, her smile becoming a wicked grin. 'No, let's send someone to bring him to us. He lied about his relationship with a murder victim. I think that deserves a patrol car sweeping up the drive of his school with all sirens blazing, don't you? Preferably at home time when all the kids and their parents are milling about.'

'I think we can assume that this is the money-making secret that Natalie teased her mates with. Some secret. I can't help wondering why Philip Derby drew attention to himself by sending me that book,' said Joe as he prepared to make the phone call that would bring Cassidy's cosy world tumbling down. 'I suppose it was ego. Pure arrogance. Some people just can't help themselves.'

She knew Joe was right. Derby was just the type who'd enjoy playing dangerous games to relieve the tedium of his life. She saw Joe looking at his watch. With this new development, their trip to Whitby would have to wait. If Albert Jervis was confined to a nursing home, he wasn't likely to make his escape.

An hour later Benjamin Cassidy was sitting in the interview room, bristling like a nervous hedgehog. He blustered a lot, claiming that he knew nothing about the matter, except for the fact that Natalie Parkes and the missing girl, Michele Carden, were both students at his school. What they got up to out of school hours was no concern of his and something over which he had no control.

He was good, Emily had to give him that. If she hadn't seen the DVD with their own eyes, she'd probably have believed him.

Of course, there was the little problem of Joe obtaining the evidence without any sort of search warrant, something she'd rectified swiftly by obtaining one of the precious documents and sending a brace of DCs over to Philip Derby's place to seize the rest of the discs. They would enjoy going through them, Emily thought. It would be an unexpected treat for them . . . something to brighten their day.

Benjamin Cassidy sat on an uncomfortable plastic chair in the windowless interview room, sipping hot liquid from a plastic cup. He was trying to look casual, unconcerned, but the eyes gave him away. Emily knew that he could see his neat little world disintegrating around him.

His solicitor sat by his side, dapper in his pinstriped suit with a white rose in his buttonhole to show he was a patriotic Yorkshireman. Joe had told her that he was acquainted with Harry Lightly – known throughout CID as 'Let 'em off Lightly'. But to Emily, a relative newcomer to Eborby, Let 'em Off was an unknown quantity.

'My client does not deny knowing the girl, Natalie

Parkes,' Lightly began. 'But he can account for his where-abouts on the night of her death and that of the other victim, Abigail Emson. And as far as any other charges are concerned, Natalie Parkes was over eighteen when the alleged liaison took place. There is no case to answer other than a moral one and this is neither the time nor the place.' Lightly sat back in his seat, looking from Joe to Emily with a self-satisfied expression on his face.

Emily took a deep breath. Now she knew how Lightly had earned his nickname. But that wasn't going to stop her. She'd eaten his sort for breakfast in Leeds.

She leaned forward. 'You lied to us, Mr Cassidy. You're finished at Hicklethorpe Manor now, so you might as well tell us everything you know about Natalie Parkes. You did, after all, know her rather intimately.' She glanced at Lightly and gave him a sweet smile. 'And we'll need the names and addresses of those other girls, too.'

Cassidy nodded meekly and the story came pouring out, as if a valve had suddenly been released. Natalie had met Philip Derby in a pub and Derby had got her involved in the 'little parties' as he called them. When Cassidy had recognised her as one of his students, he'd been horrified. But Natalie had found the situation amusing: she'd been a bit of a wild child, he said, always pushing the boundaries.

'You say you were horrified . . . but clearly not too hor-rified to screw her,' Emily observed with studied innocence, enjoying the crimson blush that spread across the man's face.

'We'd had a lot to drink and . . . I was terrified after-wards that she'd tell someone but she never did. She kept it hanging over me like the sword of Damocles.'

'But you still went to the parties,' she said, catching Joe's eye.

'You're not Stallion by any chance?' she heard him ask casually.

When Cassidy's cheeks blushed bright crimson, she knew Joe had hit the jackpot.

'That was Phil's idea. He called it the, er . . . Stallion Club.'

'You were with Derby on the night Natalie died?'

'Yes. There was a small party that night at my flat – just a few select friends. Phil said Natalie would be there – she'd called to confirm the venue. I was rather relieved when she didn't turn up, to tell you the truth. Her presence was becoming a bit of an embarrassment for me, as you can imagine. It put me in a very uncomfortable position.'

'I'm sure it did,' she said, unable to resist a note of sarcasm. If Cassidy was looking for sympathy, he was looking in the wrong place. But at least Cassidy had explained the call to Stallion on the night of Natalie's death. She must have been on her way to his place when she was killed. And the killer either knew where she was going or followed her. And this meant Cassidy and Derby were right back in the frame.

'We tried to call Stallion's number,' she said, watching his face carefully. 'You hung up on us. Then you switched the phone off.'

'I was frightened. I didn't want to get involved,' was the quick reply.

'Was Natalie blackmailing you?' Emily asked, leaning forward. 'Getting rid of a potential blackmailer is a good reason for murder in my book. You must have wanted Natalie Parkes dead. She was an embarrassment. She could have finished you. Admit it.'

Cassidy shook his head vigorously.

'My client's admitting nothing of the sort,' said Lightly. 'He has alibis for both murders so . . .'

'Right,' said Emily, flicking her eyes towards Joe who was sitting by her side listening patiently. Why did he always remind her of a priest taking confession when he listened to suspects' stories? 'We'll need the names and addresses of everyone who was at your flat on the night of Natalie's death. And we'll need all the details of exactly where you were and who you were with on the night of Abigail Emson's murder as well. Everything you tell us will be checked and double-checked.'

Cassidy nodded meekly. And when he looked up, she saw that he was crying.

Joe felt he needed a drink and he didn't really want to drink alone. That was the first step down the slippery slope, as his mother used to say. Emily had hinted earlier on that she wouldn't mind joining him for a quick drink after work, but as eight o'clock came and went, he suspected that she'd probably want to get back to Jeff and the kids. During the investigation, they were seeing precious little of her.

However, he was wrong. It was Emily who suggested a visit to the Cross Keys before heading for their respective homes. She needed to get away from the incident room so that she could think without the distraction of underlings bleating ma'am, ma'am in her ear, needing her permission for something or her signature on some form. Or simply her approval for some little piece of initiative.

As they walked side by side to the pub they hardly spoke. They were both thinking about the day's developments . . . and Cassidy's arrest. Natalie Parkes had harboured darker secrets than your average schoolgirl. When Cassidy had described her as a wild child, he had been spot on.

Emily stopped suddenly when they reached the narrow alleyway leading to the pub. 'I enjoyed seeing that Cassidy wriggling like that. Bloody sex-mad hypocrite,' she said with a hint of venom.

Her glee at Cassidy's fall from grace seemed rather excessive, almost as though it was personal. 'You really don't approve of schools like Hicklethorpe Manor, do you?' he said, watching her face carefully.

'Spot on.'

'When I asked you the other day, you never told me why.'

She looked away. 'If you must know, my parents paid for my sister to go to the best private school in town and I was sent to the local comp.'

Joe guessed that, even after all these years, her sister's preferential treatment still rankled. 'It didn't do you any harm though, did it, boss?'

'How the hell do you know? I might have made Chief Constable by now.'

'So what does your sister do?' he asked, expecting to hear tales of a great and glorious career.

'Oh she went completely off the rails. Got into drugs in a big way and last I heard she was living in some commune in Devon.'

Emily sounded bitter about her sister's fate; sad even. Perhaps it had been the exclusive school that had started her sister on the path of self-destruction. Perhaps she'd made the wrong kind of friends there. But the expression on her face told him that it was something she didn't want to discuss.

Joe let the subject drop. They made their way down the little alley and when they reached the half-timbered pub at the end he held the door open for her as she swept in.

'Do you think Cassidy and Derby are involved in the murders?' Emily said when they were settled at a table in the corner with their drinks. She had ordered a red wine – a large one – and she drank it down thirstily while Joe savoured his pint of Black Sheep.

'Maybe they got bored with their little sex games and

upped the stakes to murder,' he suggested. 'Or maybe Natalie threatened to give away the headmaster's little secret. Maybe they killed her to shut her up.'

'And Abigail?'

'Perhaps that was to throw us off the scent. Derby wrote a book which included a section on the original Doll Strangler murders.'

'But he claims he never knew about the mutilations.'

'Believe him?'

Joe shrugged. 'I'm not sure. I had a look through the notes he made when he was researching his book and I couldn't see any mention of severed toes. But that doesn't mean he didn't find out about them somehow.'

'And what about that Polly Myers? Where does she come into all this? I suppose it is a bit odd that she seems to have changed her name.' She looked him in the eye, a slight smirk on her lips. 'She couldn't be one of the Stallion Club girls, could she?'

Joe felt his cheeks redden. 'I doubt it. She certainly wasn't on the DVD.' At one stage he'd been tempted to tell Emily about her resemblance to Kaitlin, but he'd thought better of it. If Emily knew she might begin to question his objectivity.

'Perhaps you're right and she needs a closer look. Using a false name. Not opening the door to the police after the first murder. And now she's done a runner.'

'Gone to stay with a friend. It's hardly the same thing. You can't blame her for wanting to get away from that place.'

He saw Emily watching him, eyes narrowed. 'Sounds as if you fancy her. You're not letting your loins cloud your judgement, are you?'

'Of course not,' he said too quickly, eager for a change of subject. 'Anyway we'd better think about the case. What else have we got?'

'We're seeing Albert Jervis tomorrow. The matron at

170

the nursing home said not to arrive too early, which suits me fine. Things might have come in overnight. Then we'll have to find his daughter, Bridget. If her shop's the source of the dolls used in the murder . . . All patrols are looking out for her.'

'TV appeal?'

Emily shook her head. 'Not yet. That's a last resort. Anyone else?'

'Chris Strange?'

'Can't really see it myself. And his alibi for Abi Emson's murder has been checked – he was in his student house with all his house mates at the relevant time and the officer who went round was sure they were telling the truth.'

Joe frowned. There was something else. Something they hadn't really given much thought to because of the urgency of the Singmass Close case. 'There's still been no word on this missing girl, Michele Carden.'

'That's hardly surprising. She'll be down in London like your Maddy. That's where she said she was going. The Met are still on the lookout for her but it's a big place.' She drained her glass and sat staring at it for a few moments as though willing it to fill up again by magic. 'That other girl who went missing . . . Leanne Williams. She wanted to be a model too and she was last seen at Eborby Station.'

'It's where the trains to London go from. No mystery there.'

Emily shrugged and Joe knew he was probably right. Two silly girls who, with any luck, would return from the smoke with their tails between their legs, older and hopefully wiser.

'I'd better get home,' said Emily, looking at the clock behind the bar.

Joe stood and picked up the briefcase he'd brought with him. It was heavy; full of files.

'I'm going to go through more of those old files on the nineteen-fifties case tonight. See if there's anything we've missed.'

'Rather you than me. I'm going home to one of Jeff's spag bols – he's not a bad cook when it's the school holidays and he sets his mind to it.'

'Still having to set an extra place for the imaginary friend?'

'At least she doesn't make a mess.' Emily picked up her bag reluctantly.

Joe followed Emily out of the pub, wondering whether he should stop off at Singmass Close on the off chance to see whether Polly had returned home. Perhaps if he asked her straight out about her change of name, she'd tell him. But she'd told a neighbour she'd be away for a few days: he should forget it for now. And yet as he walked home another encounter with Polly seemed more attractive by the moment.

When he passed beneath Canons Bar, however, his mobile rang. And when he answered it, he heard Maddy's voice on the other end.

'She's an old lady and you're bloody drugging her. Your own bloody mother. For God's sake, Mum, what have you been giving her?'

Michele couldn't quite catch the reply from where she stood on the landing but she could just make out the higher pitch of Sylvia's wheedling voice, drifting upwards from the living room.

The man's voice, however, was clear and angry. He was cross with Sylvia, presumably about her treatment of Alice. Michele now knew that he was Barry and Sylvia's son, but she hadn't been told his name and she hadn't seen him since they'd met in the hall. He had kept out of her way, which suited her fine.

She heard his voice again. 'And who's that girl, Michele? Where did she come from?'

Michele stood quite still and listened carefully. If he had to ask the question it meant that he had played no part in what had happened to her and she wondered how Sylvia would explain how she came to be there.

'I need someone to look after Alice and the house. I can't cope on my own,' Sylvia answered, sounding like a petulant child.

'Did you get her from an agency or what? Knowing you, you won't be paying her much.'

As Michele strained to hear the reply she suddenly saw a chink of hope in the darkness. If this man had no idea how she'd been treated, then he might not know about the body in the freezer. He might even be an ally, someone she could confide in. Someone who might even help her get away. But she didn't know whether to take the risk.

'I spent it all on your bloody defence. Every bloody penny.' She heard Sylvia's words come out in a whine.

'That and that bloody car. And the clothes. Got to keep up the image, haven't you, Mum.' Michele could hear the sneering sarcasm in his voice. 'So come on, how did you find that girl?'

Michele couldn't make out the answer. But something told her it wouldn't be honest.

'And what happened to the money from the sale of Gran's house? You and Dad have power of attorney, I take it? Wouldn't do to get your own hands dirty, would it? And it certainly wouldn't do to spend Gran's money on a decent nursing home.'

'I told you.' Sylvia's voice was rising to the point of hysteria. 'Everything we had went on your defence. We got into terrible debt and if it wasn't for your gran's money . . . You've no idea what we've been through. No idea at all.'

The living-room door opened suddenly and Michele

stepped backwards into the shadows. She was carrying the bin containing Alice's used incontinence pads and as she held it to her chest, she caught the pungent whiff of ammonia. But she knew she mustn't move. She mustn't draw attention to the fact that she was there, listening.

The man stood framed in the doorway. Michele couldn't see his face. 'I'm leaving. I need to see my wife,' he said.

'You don't even know where she is.'

'I'll find her.'

'Please, Gordon, listen to me. She didn't want to know you when you were convicted. It's not worth the risk.'

He stepped out into the hall. Sylvia was clinging to his arm. She looked desperate. The desperation of a mother whose son was about to embark on something dangerous.

'She's my wife. I've got to talk to her, explain things. And you still haven't answered my question about Gran. What are you giving her?'

The pair moved to the kitchen and Michele couldn't make out the reply. But she had discovered two important facts. The son, Gordon, knew that Alice was being drugged to keep her compliant. And he didn't seem to have any idea about the girl in the ice.

If Michele could arrange to see him alone, perhaps she could make him aware of some home truths.

Maddy had sounded cheerful on the phone. Positively ebullient and excited for the future. Joe had gritted his teeth and tried to share her enthusiasm. But when the call was ended he felt drained. Keeping up the pretence was a tiring business.

He felt depressed as he strolled slowly back to his flat, forcing himself to think about the case. Natalie Parkes had thought she was clever and had got burned . . . like many people who fly too close to the flames. But was her death a result of risks she took? Or had she just been in the wrong place at the wrong time as Abigail Emson had so obviously been?

Abigail, unlike Natalie, had led a seemingly blameless life. She'd worked hard and had a boyfriend back home. All the people she knew at university said she was a nice, straightforward girl who'd had nothing whatsoever in common with Natalie Parkes. Or maybe Abigail too had a secret life that she'd managed to conceal from everyone who knew her. Joe wasn't counting anything out at this stage.

When he entered his flat he closed the door and stood for a few seconds in the dark, heavy silence before flicking on the light. As he took off his coat and flung it onto the hook, he toyed with the idea of calling Maddy back. But he couldn't face hearing the elation in her voice again as the prospect of triumph opened up ahead of her.

He examined his appearance in the hall mirror. There were dark smudges beneath his eyes and the two grey hairs he'd spotted at his temples that morning seemed to have multiplied during the day. Pressure of work, he supposed. Things would improve if and when they got the killer behind bars. He ran his fingers around the waistband of his trousers. He'd lost weight. If he told Emily, she'd be jealous.

He took a chicken korma from the freezer and shoved it in the microwave before helping himself to a bottle of Theakstons from his well-stocked stash in the sideboard and putting some music on the CD player. He was in no mood for heavy metal tonight. He needed something to feed the soul so he chose a Thomas Tallis mass and sat back with his eyes shut, letting the music engulf him. Kaitlin had sung Renaissance and early music in her university choir and they'd met when she had sung at the church he'd been posted to. From the moment he saw her and heard her singing Tallis's complex harmonies, he'd known that a life of celibacy was out of the question.

Whenever he listened to Kaitlin's music he felt close to her and he concentrated on remembering her every feature, every gesture. But after a while Kaitlin's face became Polly's. So alike but somehow different. Polly wasn't Kaitlin. Kaitlin was dead. He'd never see her again in this life.

He opened his eyes and sat up, breaking the spell. He had work to do. And work would banish the dark thoughts.

At least Maddy's absence allowed him to give the case his full attention. He'd brought some of the files from the 1950s home to read at his leisure and he emptied them out on the coffee table where they sat, emitting the faint odour of musty paper. He poured himself another beer, opened the top file and began to flick through the papers.

He reread statements and reports but he found nothing new.

The name Caleb Selly cropped up regularly. Peter Crawthwaite had given Selly a cast-iron alibi for the first murder and, as far as the next three deaths were concerned, the police could prove nothing against him.

He opened another file, assuming that it would probably be more of the same. But as he read through the papers he realised he hadn't seen them before and he started to feel the thrill of the chase. This was new information. And there was a chance – admittedly a small one – that it could be important.

The report was dated just over a year before the first murder. A young woman had been attacked in Singmass Close on her way home from a friend's house but the CID at the time had seemed rather slow in linking it to the later, more serious crimes.

One dark evening in January 1953, when the nation was looking forward to the coronation of its new Queen, a young married woman had been hurrying home after visiting a friend who lived south of the river. She lived in a terraced house not far from the city walls, on the other side of Andrewgate, and she'd taken a short cut through Singmass Close.

She'd just passed under the arch into the close when her attacker leaped out from the shadows of the medieval chapel and put something around her neck. She'd fought for her life and she'd even managed to scream but eventually she'd passed out and awoke to find an off-duty policeman kneeling by her side. He'd disturbed her attacker and, almost certainly, saved her life. As well as signs of attempted strangulation, her attacker had taken off one of her shoes and had hacked at her big toe until it was almost severed. She was taken to hospital where the toe had to be amputated.

The young woman's attacker had never been found and the attitude in those days was that she should just be grateful to be alive. There was no counselling, no victim support. She'd had to get on with life and bringing up her young daughter.

The music had finished by the time Joe put the file down and he sat in the resulting silence, lost in thought. The woman had been in her early twenties when she was attacked so there was a good chance she'd still be alive.

He had her name and her last address so surely it wouldn't be too difficult to track her down.

As he washed up his dinner plate, her name kept going through his head. Alice Meadows might have seen the murderer. Alice Meadows might hold the key to the whole thing.

Slowly. That was the way to do it. The Doll Strangler heaved his useless body up the stairs, step by step, resting at regular intervals to regain his breath.

Reaching the attic was too much effort so he'd decided

to leave it until he felt stronger. But he knew the diary was hidden in a space underneath the airing cupboard in the spare room. It was a thin exercise book crammed with close writing and graphic, detailed drawings he'd made while the memory was still fresh. They'd wanted him to have central heating put in but he'd said no. He couldn't take the risk of it being found by some curious workman. It was his secret.

In the days of his marriage he had kept the diary and the souvenirs in secret places where he knew she would never look. He knew he should have got rid of them but that would have been like getting rid of beloved children. Those memories were his real, darker self. They were what set him apart from other, more ordinary men.

From time to time over the years he'd taken the diary from its hiding place to read it and experience again that thrill of ultimate power. He didn't do it often, only keeping it as a special treat . . . or when he felt he had to relive the pleasure of destruction.

Slowly he made his way up to the spare room. Thump, thump on the bare staircase. The stairway to ecstasy.

Chapter 16

Early the next morning Joe left his flat to walk to the police station. It had been raining overnight and the grey stone flags were glistening in the weak Yorkshire sun. As he passed Singmass Close he nodded to the unfortunate constable who'd been given the job of guarding the crime scene. Then he retraced his steps and asked him whether he'd seen anybody at number six that morning. But the answer was no. Polly – or whatever her real name was – was still away.

He arrived at the station just as the sun had hidden itself behind the thickening clouds and as he climbed the stairs to the incident room he found himself yawning. He hadn't slept well and, besides, he'd been too excited about last night's discovery to relax. He'd almost rung Emily there and then at eleven at night to tell her about Alice Meadows, but he'd resisted the temptation. There was nothing he could have done till morning anyway.

He found Emily at her desk. She looked settled, as if she'd been there all night. When he opened her office door she looked up. 'You look bloody awful,' were her first words.

Joe slumped down on the chair by her desk. 'I was up reading the files on the nineteen-fifties murders last night.' He leaned forward. 'I discovered that the killer had had a

179

go a year before he murdered Marion Grant. He attacked a young mother in Singmass Close and hacked off her big toe. She survived.'

Emily gave a low whistle. 'Why didn't we find this out before?'

'I don't know if they made the connection back then.'

She muttered something disparaging under her breath. 'Any sign of a doll in the attack?'

Joe shook his head. 'Perhaps he struck on the idea of the dolls later on. The attack on Alice Meadows might have been some kind of rehearsal.'

'Alice Meadows? Any idea if she's still alive?'

'I'm getting the team to trace her. They say old people sometimes remember more about what happened fifty years ago than what they did yesterday.'

Emily gave him a wicked grin. 'Was that an ageist stereotype I heard then? Go and wash your mouth out. Which reminds me, we're seeing Albert Jervis later this morning.' She glanced out of the office window. 'Not a very nice day for a trip to Whitby but beggars can't be choosers.' She grinned again. 'And Weightwatchers can bugger off today. It's ages since I've had Whitby fish and chips and I need the energy.'

Joe left her alone in her office, salivating over the culinary treats awaiting them on the coast. Police work had to have some compensations.

Soon after Emily's morning briefing, Jenny Ripon came up with the news that a widowed woman called Alice Meadows, who was around the right age, lived in a sprawling village that lay between Eborby and Harrogate.

Joe felt a glow of satisfaction. He hadn't expected it to be this easy. Wasting no time, he bagged himself a pool car and drove out alone to the house. It was a Victorian semi, built of mellow old bricks with creeper climbing the walls. But the sight of a skip in the trampled front garden and a demolished for sale sign lying just behind the garden wall gave him the nasty feeling that he'd arrived too late.

The young woman who answered the door told him they'd bought the house from Mrs Meadows around three months ago. Mrs Meadows had had some sort of stroke and had gone to live with her daughter but the new occupiers didn't have a forwarding address for her. It looked as though Joe had hit a dead end.

But Joe wasn't one to give up easily. The neighbour's house looked promising with its green paintwork and fancy net curtains at the windows. It had the look of a house that had been occupied by the same family for years so he tried his luck.

During house-to-house enquiries, Joe had often noticed how the older generation are far more au fait with the lives of those around them than their younger counterparts. And at the house with green paintwork he struck lucky. A retired couple in their late sixties had lived there for thirty years and they seemed all too eager to give chapter and verse on Alice Meadows.

They had known Alice quite well, although she usually kept herself to herself. After her stroke she'd gone to live with her daughter and son-in-law somewhere out in the country on the way to Pickering. An isolated spot, so they'd heard, which had surprised them because Alice's daughter, Sylvia, had been a spoiled girl who'd loved expensive shops and fashion and she'd never been one to get her hands dirty. The harsh judgement was that Sylvia was only looking after her mother to avoid using her money to pay for a nursing home. But when Joe asked for Alice's new address, his luck ran out. Sylvia wasn't one to encourage visits so she hadn't made the effort to let anyone know and Alice hadn't been in any fit state to provide a forwarding address herself.

Joe was about to leave when the lady of the house spoke again.

'I doubt if Sylvia'll welcome a visit from the police, mind. Not after all that trouble with their Gordon.'

'Gordon?'

She looked Joe up and down as though she suspected he was an impostor. 'He killed that little lass. Strangled her. I thought you would have known that, being a policeman.'

Joe sent up a silent prayer of thanks. Miracles happened and this could be one of them. 'Not Gordon Pledge?'

'Aye that's the one. Sylvia married a man called Pledge. Their Gordon's in prison.'

'Not now he isn't. He's escaped. Didn't you hear it on the news?'

'Never watch the news. It's all bad. You're not safe anywhere these days and you coppers do sod all about it,' the woman said with her arms folded.

As yet, no one had managed to trace Gordon Pledge's parents who'd disappeared from their home in Harrogate. But now, with any luck, they might just score a double. Joe gave Alice's former neighbour an apologetic smile and turned to go.

Joe arrived at the incident room just as Emily was returning from a meeting with the Superintendent. She didn't look happy, he thought, but his news was bound to cheer her up.

'Why have you got that smug look on your face?' she asked as soon as he entered her office.

'You know this escaped prisoner, Gordon Pledge?'

'What about him?'

'That woman who was attacked in Singmass Close and survived . . . Alice Meadows. She's his grandmother.'

Emily raised her eyebrows, suddenly alert as though someone had recharged her batteries. 'Small world. Have you found her?'

'She's living with her daughter – Pledge's mother.'

'But we don't know where the parents are. They buggered off somewhere with no forwarding address and probably changed their name to avoid the scandal. Uniform have been trying to trace them since Gordon did a runner.'

'Well, according to the grandmother's neighbour, they moved to an isolated place somewhere between here and Pickering. Shouldn't be too hard to trace.'

'So when we find Alice, we can ask her about what happened back in the fifties and maybe catch her pervert grandson while we're at it?'

'The super's always banging on about efficiency.' This brought a wide smile to Emily's face. 'You ready for Whitby?'

Emily stood up and yawned. Joe guessed that sitting in the centre of the incident room like a controlling spider was starting to get her down. She needed a change of scene.

'Anything new come in on Abigail Emson's private life?' he asked. 'Perhaps some connection with Benjamin Cassidy's sordid little parties?'

So far the latest victim seemed rather too good to be true and Joe was wondering whether anything interesting had come to light. But Emily shook her head. There was nothing new to report. Abigail Emson was an innocent student, making her way home after a shift behind the bar of the Black Lion. No amount of digging had revealed any connection with Cassidy, Philip Derby or Natalie Parkes. And, according to her friends and family, she hadn't been that sort of girl anyway.

'There's still no word of Bridget Jervis,' Joe said as they drove down the A64 towards Malton.

'When we see her dad perhaps he'll know where she is,' Emily replied. But she sounded as if she didn't quite believe it.

'Perhaps,' said Joe softly.

It was a long drive, but the Vale of Pickering glistened in the sunlight, the trees providing an artistic display of autumn golds and coppers. Soon they would shed their leaves and become bare skeletons reaching up to the huge sky. But the onset of winter was something Joe would rather not think about.

He'd always loved Whitby with its ruined abbey glowering on the skyline and its steep winding streets leading down the harbour. But Albert Jervis's nursing home stood on the main road leading into the town.

In Bram Stoker's novel, the undead Count Dracula had landed at Whitby and The Beacons Nursing Home was just the sort of place he'd have chosen to stay on his arrival. Gargoyles leered out from the guttering and the windows echoed the broken arches of the ruined abbey that stood a mile away overlooking the grey North Sea. As the set for a horror film, The Beacons was spot on. But Joe could think of better places to spend your twilight years.

The front door was opened by a fat young woman wearing a cross between a nylon overall and a nurse's uniform, and they were led to a conservatory full of greenery and wicker chairs. At first Joe couldn't see anybody amongst the vegetation but the nurse made straight for the corner where a small, frail, old man was perched on a white wicker chair, his head nodding onto his chest as though he'd just fallen asleep.

The nurse gave him a gentle shake and whispered in his ear. The old man looked up and Joe could see apprehension in his eyes. As though something nasty, that he imagined had gone away years ago, had just returned to haunt him.

Joe stepped forward and introduced himself and Emily before giving the nurse a nod of dismissal. But the young woman seemed reluctant to leave them alone with her charge, as though she feared he might become a victim of police brutality. He caught Emily's eye and she gave a slight shake of the head. If the woman stayed, it would probably do no harm.

They sat down, squeezed together on a small white conservatory sofa with Emily's ample hips taking up most of the room; Joe smiled at the old man to put him at his ease. He glanced at the nurse who was still standing her ground at Jervis's shoulder. She was going nowhere.

'Mr Jervis,' Joe began. 'We've been trying to find your daughter, Bridget.'

The old man looked at Joe, his eyes full of suspicion. 'Oh aye?'

'Do you know where she is?'

The answer was a shake of the head.

'When did you last see her?'

'It was about two weeks ago, wasn't it Albert?' the nurse piped up. 'Remember, she popped in for an hour to see you. Nice surprise for you, it were.'

Albert Jervis's expression suggested that he hadn't considered the surprise to have been particularly pleasing. But he nodded obediently in reply.

Then after a few moments of silence he spoke. 'Aye, it were the Wednesday. Half day closing. She came to see me when she closed the shop. Said she might not be coming for a couple of weeks. She had some'at to do.' Jervis's voice was surprisingly strong, a contrast to his feeble appearance. 'And before you ask, she didn't say what it were. And I didn't ask.'

'Has Bridget got a gentleman friend?' Emily asked.

'She never mentioned owt. But then she might not want me to know.'

'Why's that?'

'We're not close, me and our Bridget. She leads her own life,' he said stoically, staring ahead. Since their arrival Joe had noticed that he hadn't once made eye contact.

'So you've no idea where she is?' asked Emily.

'No. I've no idea.' The answer was final.

Joe glanced up at the nurse who still hadn't shifted from her post. 'You used to live in Eborby, I believe, Mr Jervis. You ran a dolls' hospital in Singmass Close.'

There was no mistaking the wariness that appeared on his thin face. 'Aye.'

Emily caught Joe's eye. It was time for her to take over the questioning. 'Albert, do you remember the murders of four young women in Singmass Close when you were working there? You were questioned at the time. I've seen the statements you gave.'

Albert Jervis stared at her for a while. 'Course I remember, love. They called him the Doll Strangler. They kept on at me, the police. Where were you? What were you doing? Did you know this woman or that woman? I told 'em it were nowt to do wi' me. But they didn't believe me till I were having a drink with a mate of mine who were a special constable when the second murder happened. Then they believed me. Didn't have much choice.'

Joe could hear all the pent-up resentment of years in his voice. The resentment of the innocent man who's hounded for being in the wrong place at the wrong time. Or was he wrong? Was his resentment against the women he'd killed and the police who tried to trap him?'

'We know all about that, Mr Jervis. But we'd like your help. You see, in the last week there have been two more murders in Eborby, almost the same as the ones in the fifties. We think either the same man has struck again. Or maybe someone's copying him.'

186

Jervis snorted. 'Well that ain't much of a surprise, is it? There are all these bloody books and articles these days. What is it they call 'em? True crime? They put ideas in folks' heads if you ask me.'

Emily gave Joe an almost imperceptible nod. It was his turn; the man-to-man approach. 'You see, Mr Jervis, there are certain aspects of the case that weren't made public at the time. And this latest killer seems to know all about them, which makes us think he was around Singmass Close when the original murders took place. Or that he knew someone who was.'

Jervis' eyes suddenly lit up with interest.

'That's why we need your help. Did you know about . . . about any mutilations on the bodies?' He was doing his best to keep it vague. He didn't want the details to be made any more public than they already were.

Jervis shook his head. 'I know they were strangled and that he left dolls by 'em but that's all. And they weren't my dolls, mind. None of them came from my place. I told 'em that at the time. They weren't from my hospital.'

He shut his mouth tight. Either he didn't know about the mutilations or he was an extremely good liar. But the origin of the dolls was a different matter. Joe suspected that he knew exactly where they came from.

'Are you certain they didn't come from your hospital?' Joe looked him in the eye. He saw the pale-grey pupils flicking from side to side as though the man was seeking an escape route.

'Yeah.'

'A hundred per cent certain?' asked Emily.

The old man hesitated, his eyes focused on his liver-spotted hands. 'Well, not a hundred per cent. We had loads of 'em, you see. Hundreds. And I suppose they could have been pinched by someone as soon as they came in and I wouldn't have known.'

'You had an assistant at the time . . . Caleb Selly.'

The man looked up at Joe and frowned, as if he'd just remembered something unpleasant. 'Oh aye. Caleb.'

'Could he have taken the dolls?'

Jervis suddenly looked uncomfortable. 'Suppose he could,' he said slowly. 'But I swear I didn't notice or I would have said something.'

'He was a suspect at the time but he had an alibi. He said he was with a lad called Peter Crawthwaite.'

'Aye, I remember Peter.'

'Peter's girlfriend, Marion Grant, was the first victim.'

'Aye. Right shock it were when she were found like that.'

'What can you tell us about Peter?'

'Nowt much to tell. He were just an ordinary lad. Not that I knew him that well.'

'What about Caleb Selly?'

Jervis thought for a few moments, a frown on his face as though he was reliving uncomfortable memories. 'Caleb were an odd'un . . . funny with women. A lot of mothers used to come to us with their little girls to get their dolls mended but he'd never talk to 'em – it were always up to me. It were like he was scared of 'em. And he always made himself scarce when our Bridget came to see me . . . which she did, being a little lass who liked dolls. He had a big birthmark covering half his face. Might have made him self-conscious . . . I don't know.'

'Why did you give up the dolls' hospital?'

'I sold up in early fifty-eight cos there was talk of re-developing the close. I moved to Harrogate and got a job in a toy shop. Then the wife died and our Bridget left home and never came back . . . story of my life.' He gave Joe a bitter smile.

'That was about the time the murders stopped,' said Joe watching the man's face.

'Aye,' was the only reply. Jervis was giving nothing away.

'What happened to Caleb?' Emily asked.

Joe awaited the answer. Caleb Selly was starting to intrigue him.

'I gave him a reference, like, but I don't know what he did after I'd moved on. Like I say, he weren't much good with the customers. As far as I know he stayed in Eborby.' He raised his hand as though he'd just remembered something. 'And he got married just before I left. Though I'm surprised any woman'd go for him. No accounting for taste, is there. I heard he had a kid and all.'

'A kid?'

'Aye. I think his name was Brian. Or was it Barry? Some'at like that, anyroad. I think I must have heard it from the wife and it went in one ear and out the other, know what I mean?' His eyes met Joe's conspiratorially.

'So let me get this straight,' said Emily. 'Caleb married just before you parted company?'

'Aye, that's right. I didn't know the girl, mind. I remember the wife saying she was a good bit older than him. Probably desperate.'

Joe looked sideways at Emily before saying what he knew was on both their minds. 'So Caleb Selly got married around the time the killings stopped. Do you have any photographs of him?' Joe asked. It was a long shot but it was worth a try.

But their luck was in. 'Aye. I reckon I might have.'

They waited while Jervis made his way back to his room at a snail's pace with the help of his walking frame and the large nurse. After what seemed like an age staring at the plants in the conservatory, the old man returned with a battered photograph album slung in a string bag, which dangled from the walking frame.

When he sat down again he turned the pages of the album until he found the black-and-white photograph he was looking for. A young Albert Jervis was standing proudly surrounded by dolls and – more bizarrely – an array of small disembodied limbs and heads. Standing by him was a tall young man with a small beard, over-large features and a prominent birthmark covering his left cheek. His mouth was slightly open, giving him a blank appearance.

'That's him,' said Jervis, prodding a gnarled finger at the image on the page. 'That's Caleb. But it couldn't have been him, could it? I mean he were with Peter Crawthwaite when the first one were killed.'

'Can we take this picture?' Emily asked sweetly. 'We'll let you have it back.'

Jervis considered the question. 'Aye. Mind you do.'

'And if Bridget gets in touch will you tell her to contact me urgently,' said Joe, placing his card in the old man's hand.

As they stood up to leave Jervis spoke again. 'I were glad to get out of Singmass Close, I'll tell you that for nowt. Some people reckoned it were haunted. Some people said they used to see kiddies, you know – little lads and lasses all in ragged clothes. And people used to say they felt little hands clinging to 'em when they walked through in the dark. Not that I ever saw owt myself, but there was something not right about that place.'

Joe and Emily said nothing. The killer who operated in Singmass Close was very much of this world and not the next. They took their leave and fifteen minutes later, they were eating fish and chips on the quayside, watching the fishing boats chugging into the harbour.

'So what did you think of Albert?' Joe asked after a long period of appreciative, silent consumption of the best fish and chips he had tasted in a long while.

Emily munched on a sliver of crispy batter while she considered the question. 'He'd have had no trouble getting hold of those dolls. But how do we prove anything after all this time? And if he did do the original murders . . .'

'There's no evidence that he did.'

'True. But if he did do the original ones, there's no way he could have killed Natalie Parkes and Abigail Emson.'

'What about Bridget? Why has she gone missing? It looks suspicious, don't you think?'

'Do you see this as a woman's crime, Joe? Cos I don't.'

'She's disappeared. She has access to dolls. And if Jervis is our man in the nineteen fifties, maybe she's only just found out about him being a killer. Maybe it's sent her over the edge and she's reliving her father's crimes.'

'Come on, Joe, we're clutching at straws here.'

Joe looked away, out to sea. He knew Emily was right.

'What about Crawthwaite and Selly?' she asked. 'They gave each other alibis.'

'We've got Crawthwaite's address. I'll pay him a visit when we get back.'

'Good idea. And what about Caleb Selly?'

'Don't you think Jervis was a bit too quick to point the finger?'

'Mmm. Jervis said the dolls didn't come from the dolls' hospital at first. Then he backtracked – said he couldn't be absolutely sure, which isn't what he told the police fifty years back. According to his statements, he swore they were nothing to do with him.'

'So what's the truth?'

'I'm keeping an open mind for now.' She popped the last chip into her mouth. 'Last time the Doll Strangler killed four women. I reckon he's not stopped yet.' She sighed. 'I've asked Jamilla and Jenny to pull out all the stops to find Alice Meadows. And, with any luck, when we find her, we might find Gordon Pledge and all, playing happy families with Grandma.'

'What'll Alice be able to tell us now that she didn't tell the police then?'

'I don't know,' Joe said, knowing that all they could do was hope for a miracle.

Chapter 17

The fish and chips sat heavily on Joe's stomach as he made his way to the almshouses on Boothgate. He'd eaten too quickly, but then he'd been hungry. He blamed it on the sea air.

Each little almshouse, built of red Tudor brick with tiny leaded windows and topped by elaborate chimneys, had its occupant's name printed clearly underneath the doorbell. He pressed Peter Crawthwaite's, wondering how he had come to end up in these picturesque surroundings. It was one of the questions on his list.

When the door opened, he was surprised to see a man in a wheelchair looking up at him. The man looked older than his seventy-three years with a shock of white hair and bright-blue eyes shining out of a deeply lined face, and when he invited Joe in, he manoeuvred the wheelchair expertly into the little lounge.

'So what do you want?' he asked bluntly as Joe sat down.

'I believe your girlfriend, Marion Grant, was murdered in the nineteen fifties.'

Unless Crawthwaite was a remarkably good actor, the shock on his face couldn't have been faked. 'Aye, she was,' he said softly.

'You were questioned at the time?'

'Aye. Course I were. Me and Marion had had words a couple of days before and . . .'

'But you had an alibi for her murder. You were with Caleb Selly.'

Peter Crawthwaite looked away, avoiding Joe's eyes. Suddenly Joe knew he was on to something.

'You weren't telling the truth?' he asked tentatively. He wanted this man to confide in him, not to clam up.

The tactic seemed to work. Crawthwaite leaned forward in his wheelchair. 'Look, between you and me . . . off the record . . . What would happen if I told you I'd lied back then?'

Joe considered the question for a few moments. 'That depends. It was a long time ago. But on the other hand, it was a murder inquiry.'

Crawthwaite looked disappointed and sat back. Joe sensed that he was anxious to get something off his chest, something that had bothered him for decades. And he hoped he hadn't spoiled things with his over-officious words. He tried again.

'I take it you didn't kill Marion?'

Crawthwaite shook his head. 'Course I bloody didn't. I'd never have harmed a hair on Marion's head. It's just that . . .' He hesitated.

'Go on,' said Joe, almost in a whisper.

Crawthwaite looked him in the eye. 'OK. I suppose I'd better tell you. Like I said, I had nothing to do with Marion's murder but I were really worried that I'd be suspected, like. The truth is I had no alibi cos I went home alone and me dad were out so I just panicked. I asked Caleb to say he were with me. Look, I've felt bad about it for years. But I don't know why I should cos I didn't do it.'

Joe took a deep breath. This changed everything. It wasn't only Peter Crawthwaite who had lost an alibi. So had Caleb Selly.

'Do you know where Caleb is now?' Joe tried to keep the urgency out of his voice.

'Could be six feet under for all I know. Not heard of him for years. Not that I particularly wanted to.'

'Ever heard of Alice Meadows?'

Crawthwaite shook his head and Joe stood up. His priorities had suddenly changed.

'Is that all?' Crawthwaite asked, surprised.

'Yes. I think so. Look, thanks for telling me. And I think I can promise you, it won't go any further.'

The old man frowned. 'I heard on the radio the Doll Strangler's at it again.'

'Looks that way.'

'Well I've got a bloody good alibi this time.' He tapped his wheelchair and chuckled. 'Lost both me legs. I were a forty-a-day man.'

'I take it you've given up now?'

'Doctor's orders. Got hooked in the Army.' He tapped the side of his nose. 'That's how I got into this cushy billet . . . old soldier.'

Joe smiled. 'Take care,' he said. But as he closed the door behind him he looked back and saw a look of sheer relief on the old man's face. As though a huge weight had been lifted from his stooped shoulders.

Whenever the opportunity presented itself, Michele had started to replace the dishes Sylvia put out for Alice with food eaten by the rest of the household. When she succeeded she certainly noticed a change in the old lady: Alice became lucid and she could even sit up. And she became upset about the incontinence pads, insisting on using a chamber pot that Michele had to empty discreetly down the lavatory.

But when Alice ate Sylvia's meals, she reverted to helplessness and the certain knowledge that Sylvia was drugging her roused Michele from the lethargy caused by her powerlessness. Now she had Alice to defend from the machinations of her daughter. For the first time in her life Michele felt responsible for someone else. And this had reawakened her desire to fight.

She kept looking out of the window, saying a silent prayer to a God she hadn't believed in since her Sunday School days that help would come. The place was isolated but she clung to that glimmer of hope in the darkness. In the meantime, she had to be on her guard.

Alice's stroke might have dragged down one corner of her mouth and made her slur her speech but she certainly wasn't stupid. She was canny enough to feign sleep when she heard Sylvia or Barry approaching – something they did less and less frequently now that the man they referred to as their son was there. Michele and Alice were left in their own little world . . . which was how Michele liked it.

Michele had seen little of Gordon, the son, and she'd had no opportunity to talk to him alone. From time to time, she toyed with the idea of making an effort to find him and telling him what his mother had done. But she knew that would be a huge risk. Who was to say that he hadn't killed the girl in the freezer himself? Maybe it was only wishful thinking on her part that he wasn't an enemy.

It was almost nine o'clock. Time to settle Alice for the night and lay out the breakfast things before her nightly incarceration. She would put Alice in a fresh incontinence pad and give her her milky drink with the sleeping capsules stirred in to ensure she had a peaceful night. If Alice woke up and disturbed Sylvia it might undo everything she had done. And Michele was terrified of the consequences if her disobedience about Alice's drugs came to light.

Despite everything, she was growing fond of Alice. As she entered her bedroom with the tray, she received a lop-sided smile from the old lady.

'Here's your drink, Alice,' Michele said, trying her best to appear cheerful.

'You come and sit down, dear,' Alice slurred. 'I want to tell you something.'

Michele glanced at the door before placing the tray on the dressing table and perched herself on the edge of the bed. Then Alice beckoned her to come closer and she leaned forward so that the old lady's pale, parchment, face was close to her ear. This was a secret. Something she didn't want the whole world to know.

'I nearly got myself murdered once, you know.'

Michele leaned further forward, wondering what horrifying story this woman was going to tell about her own daughter and her husband. They were certainly capable of anything. The evidence was in the freezer.

'How do you mean?'

'He came up behind me and tried to strangle me . . .'

'Who did?'

'He thought he'd managed it and all. I passed out and woke up in the hospital with me toe missing. They'd had to amputate it. They said it was an accident but I know he'd tried to hack it off . . . take it for a souvenir, like. You should have seen the blood.'

Michele frowned, puzzled. She'd wondered how Alice had come to lose her toe . . . but she hadn't expected the explanation to be so bizarre. Suddenly she wasn't sure whether she believed the old lady. She might be making the whole thing up to add a touch of drama to her limited life.

Alice pursed her dry lips together and continued. 'I wouldn't dance with him, you see. I told him to get lost.'

'Told who? Who are you talking about, Alice?'

But Alice was lost in her own little world. 'Do you think he killed 'em? All strangled, they were. But the papers didn't mention no toes.'

Michele took the old lady's hand and gave it a squeeze. 'Who are you talking about?' she repeated. 'What was his name?'

A crafty expression appeared on Alice's face. 'They said it couldn't possibly be him.'

'Who?'

When Alice said the name, Michele was none the wiser. It wasn't one she recognised.

She walked over to the window and looked out. Why didn't someone come to look for her? What had she done to deserve this . . . apart from having ambitions and dreams?

'So you reckon Peter Crawthwaite's a non-starter?' Emily asked.

'I'd say so. He lied because he panicked. He was suspected of his girlfriend's murder and he was scared stiff, so he asked an acquaintance to say they were together that night.' He paused for effect. 'And that acquaintance was Caleb Selly.'

'Who wasn't suspected because Peter Crawthwaite unwittingly provided him with an alibi as well. We need to find Selly, Joe. As soon as possible.'

'I'm well aware of that.'

As if on cue, Sunny Porter barged into Emily's office with an expression of defeat on his face.

'Can't find Caleb Selly,' he announced. 'No sign.'

'He could be dead,' Emily said bluntly.

'No record of that either, boss.'

'Perhaps he's changed his name,' said Joe quietly. 'If my name was Caleb, I think I'd change it, wouldn't you?'

'You could have a point there,' Sunny conceded. He

leaned forward as though he was about to impart a juicy piece of gossip. 'But I have found a few Sellys in the area and you know you told me that Albert Jervis thought Caleb had a son called Brian? Well there's a Brian Selly living in Abbotsthorpe. We could pay him a visit. See if it's the right one.'

'Good idea,' said Joe. He noticed Emily glancing at her watch. It was getting late and he knew she'd been seeing precious little of her children since the Singmass Close murders began.

Murders. He contemplated the word, hoping – praying – that the killer wouldn't have another go. But there was a constant police presence in Singmass Close now so surely he wouldn't try again. Or maybe he'd just choose another location. That was Joe's greatest fear.

'We'll speak to this Brian Selly first thing tomorrow, eh.'

When Sunny had departed the phone on Emily's desk rang, shattering the calm of the office, set apart like Mount Olympus from the bustle of the main incident room.

She picked up the receiver and listened, rolling her eyes to heaven. 'The super wants to see me,' she sighed when the call was ended. 'He wants another statement to the press, to reassure the public that we're in control.'

Joe swore softly under his breath. 'If you're going to be tied up with the press, I think I might go and have another chat with some of Natalie Parkes's mates: see what they know about her extra-curricular activities. I can't help feeling there could be a link to her murder.'

'That it's one of the Stallion Club, you mean. All the people on that DVD are being traced. But it's not easy because some of them used assumed names.' She smiled. 'I presume Cassidy'll be resigning.'

'I shouldn't think he has much choice. I'll go and see

Karen Strange and then maybe I'll have a word with Brett Bluit. I'll take Jamilla.'

'Wish I was coming with you,' said Emily with a sigh.

Joe wished Emily luck with the super. She'd need it.

The Doll Strangler pushed the newspaper aside.

He hadn't been able to find the diary and at first he'd panicked. Then he told himself that he must have put it up in the attic with the other things and forgotten: his memory wasn't what it was sometimes.

He kept thinking of those souvenirs he'd kept and how he longed to relive those moments of ultimate power; to find a street lamp so that he could see the victim's face as she died. It had been too dark to see back then in Singmass Close, in the shadows behind the Ragged School. And there had been the noises, like mice squeaking with delight . . . and the feel of the cold little fingers on his as he squeezed the life out of her.

He needed to see the diary and his keepsakes but that meant reaching the attic. It was possible. He could do it if he took it slowly. He dragged his useless body up the stairs. His heart was beating fast – too fast – and the blood was pounding in his ears.

At last he reached the top and he could see the door to the attic, closed and mysterious like the entrance to a magic cave.

After pausing to catch his breath, he began to look around for the hook that would bring the ladder down. It was probably in one of the bedrooms. It was just a matter of finding it.

Click, click, click. He could almost hear them again. He could almost smell their fear. He had to find that hook.

Chapter 18

In Joe's opinion his visit to Karen Strange with Jamilla had been a complete waste of time. She'd denied knowing anything about Natalie's activities at the Stallion Club and when they asked about Natalie's relationship with Benjamin Cassidy, the answer had been a terse denial. Natalie had never mentioned anything like that.

Jamilla said afterwards that Natalie must have been an exceptional teenage girl not to confide such a major secret to her supposedly best friend.

Joe pondered this for a while. 'What if she confided in someone else?'

Jamilla looked sceptical. 'Nobody at school admitted knowing about it and I can't see her having a heart to heart with her brother. They hardly seem like a close family,' she added with what sounded like disapproval. Coming from a close-knit family, she found the Parkes clan hard to understand.

'You're right,' Joe conceded. 'Maybe she just kept it to herself. She thought she was above her fellow students – making money out of sex parties with older men.'

He noticed Jamilla give a shudder of disgust. 'That Cassidy should be locked up. Think he's got anything to do with the murders, sir?'

'I don't know. But I'm pretty sure that Abigail Emson

didn't go to any of the Stallion Club parties. She doesn't appear in any of the Derby amateur movies.'

'How can a girl from a wealthy family lower herself like that?'

Joe said nothing. He didn't know the answer.

They had arrived at Brett Bluit's house. But Joe wasn't sure whether they'd learn anything new. It might be another waste of time and effort like the visit to Karen Strange.

Brett's house was a good deal smaller than the homes of his classmates, a small terraced house south of the city centre near Picklegate Bar and the city walls. Brett's mother let them in, saying that her son was working in his room. She was a nervous, birdlike woman in a velour tracksuit with greying hair scraped back into a limp pony tail. It was coming up to six-thirty but there was no sign of a father and no photographs of any man who might fit the bill anywhere on display. The place was quiet and Joe guessed that Brett was an only child. Siblings tended to make a noise.

Mrs Bluit called Brett down and Joe watched his face as he descended the stairs. He looked cool and confident . . . like a young man with nothing to hide. Or a young man who wished to give that impression. He shook Joe's and Jamilla's hands firmly and invited them to sit while his mother bustled out to make a cup of tea.

'Have you made any progress yet?' Brett asked politely. 'I heard about that other girl. It's terrible,' he added with a frown.

'We're following a number of leads,' Joe replied, omitting to mention that so far all their leads had led precisely nowhere.

'I hope you catch him soon. The girls at school are getting jumpy.'

Joe decided a change of subject might be wise. He

noticed a pile of university prospectuses, neatly stacked on the sideboard. 'Which university do you fancy?'

Brett nodded. 'Cambridge . . . natural sciences. Cassidy reckons there should be no problem. He said he'd be surprised if I don't get in.'

This mention of Cassidy gave Joe the perfect opening. 'Did you know that Natalie Parkes had been going to sex parties with Benjamin Cassidy?' He said the words bluntly, intending to shock. They'd trodden carefully with Karen and now he reckoned that coming straight to the point would produce better results.

Brett's face was a picture of amazement. The boy probably didn't realise that his mouth had fallen open and that he was gaping at Joe like a caveman confronted with an aeroplane.

'I take it she didn't mention it to you, then.'

Brett shook his head. 'I'm sure you're wrong.' He spoke as though he suspected Joe of making it up for his own amusement.

'It's not just gossip . . . I've seen the evidence.'

'Surely Cassidy wouldn't be stupid enough to piss in his own back yard. This'll finish him.' His eyes widened. 'What about my reference for Cambridge?' he added in a small, desperate voice.

Joe gave him an apologetic smile. He wasn't sure what a university would make of a reference from a disgraced head teacher. There was a slim chance that they might care. On the other hand, they probably wouldn't. 'I hardly think Mr Cassidy's sex life would be considered relevant to your application,' he said, trying to sound reassuring.

Brett leaned forward, his eyes flickering to and fro. Joe could tell the news had shaken him. 'You think that could have something to do with why Nat was killed?'

Joe ignored the question. 'You were Natalie's friend. She never mentioned . . . ?'

Brett shook his head vigorously. 'She never said any-thing about screwing Cassidy, honest. She never let on.'

'Exactly how friendly were you and Natalie? Did you sleep with her or . . .?'

Brett's cheeks reddened but before he could say any-thing, his mother came in with a tray. She had brought out the best china – cups and saucers of the fussy, floral kind, the sort Joe more readily associated with old ladies. And Brett Bluit's mother couldn't have been more than fifty.

'Thanks, mum,' Brett said and waited politely for her to leave the room, like a chief executive dismissing the tea lady from a confidential meeting. There was definitely something subservient about Mrs Bluit. Almost as though she was overawed by the academically brilliant son she had brought into the world.

Joe thought carefully about how to phrase the next question. 'I expect your mother makes a lot of sacrifices to pay your school fees,' he said, trying to sound casual and hide his curiosity about how Mrs Bluit managed to get her hands on the nine grand a year charged by Hicklethorpe Manor.

'She doesn't. I won a scholarship. I'm a charity case.'

Joe sensed a hint of bitterness behind the words, quickly concealed with a confident smile.

'What did Natalie think about that?'

'She had problems of her own. The poor don't have the monopoly on dysfunctional families, you know. And, boy, were Nat's lot dysfunctional. Have you met the mother?'

Joe glanced at Jamilla and nodded.

'And someone said her dad can't even be arsed to come back from the States. I don't think even my father could top that one,' he added. The bitterness was bubbling nearer the surface now. Brett's father was a painful subject.

'Where is your father?'

'Leeds. He's got himself a new family. I've got two half sisters, can you believe. Not that I'm allowed anywhere near them. He likes to keep his past life separate so I hardly ever see him these days.' He looked away. 'Not that I'm particularly bothered.' The last words were spat out. Brett, so controlled at first, was finally showing his true emotions. And Joe, against all his professional instincts, found himself feeling sorry for him.

'You never answered my question, Brett. Did you sleep with Natalie?'

There was a slight hesitation before Brett shook his head. 'She said she just wanted us to be friends and now you've told me what she was up to with Cassidy, I can see why. Look, I wasn't the only lad in our year to fancy her. With looks like hers there were quite a few queuing up, if you know what I mean. Not that anyone hit the jackpot. She said she preferred older men.'

'But you were still friends?'

'I always thought so. But she kept this thing with Cassidy quiet.' Joe thought that he sounded hurt that she hadn't taken him into her confidence.

He looked the boy in the eye and gave him an encouraging smile. 'Have you been friends since you first went to Hicklethorpe Manor?'

Brett thought for a moment. 'I've known her since the first year but we really started hanging around together when we reached the sixth form.'

'But she never talked to you about any of her relationships?' Joe suspected the answer would be no. If she hadn't confided in Karen Strange, it was unlikely that she'd have shared her secrets with Brett. Unless she enjoyed shocking him . . . tantalising him with details of her sexual adventures.

Brett thought for a few moments then he raised a hand as though he'd just remembered something. 'She said she'd met someone who'd written a book but I don't know if it was true. She used to say things just to impress people. She'd tell you something but when you asked for the details she'd just give you an enigmatic smile and shut up. The Mona Lisa had nothing on Nat. I thought she was making it up half the time, saying she'd gone for rides in sports cars and gone to parties and taken cocaine and all that crap. But she never mentioned Cassidy. You sure you got that right?'

The boy was looking more confident now. 'I'm afraid so. If you can remember any details about those parties she talked about – names or places – that'd be very useful.'

But Brett shook his head. 'Sorry, like I said she kept it vague. I thought she was making half of it up so I didn't pay that much attention.'

'Did you like Natalie?'

'Suppose so,' was the quick reply.

'What about Karen?' It was the first time Jamilla had spoken and Brett studied her with interest before answering.

'What did she say?'

Joe's eyes met Jamilla's. They weren't falling for that one. 'You tell me what you think she said.'

He watched as Brett gave an enigmatic smile and shook his head. 'Nat thought Karen was immature. She called her a silly kid.'

Joe nodded. His mental picture of the dead girl seemed to be coming into clearer focus. The secretive fantasist who couldn't resist boasting about the parties she went to and the money she made, but who'd still been too embarrassed about what she actually got up to with their headmaster to mention it to her closest friends. Perhaps Cassidy had pressured her into it. Perhaps she hadn't been the willing participant he'd claimed she'd been. He suddenly felt desperately sorry for Natalie

Parkes: behind the brash, sophisticated exterior he guessed there'd been an insecure, attention-seeking young girl. An easy victim.

He decided to change the subject. 'How well do you know Michele Carden?'

'I don't know her but I heard she'd gone missing; everyone at school's talking about it, but I can't say I've ever had anything to do with her. She's a couple of years below us and . . .' He frowned. 'You don't think she's been murdered too, do you?'

'We're keeping an open mind. You do know there's been a second murder in Singmass Close where Natalie was found? Girl called Abigail Emson. She was a student at the university.'

'I heard,' he said quietly. 'Maybe she was involved with old Cassidy too. Could that be the link?' His eyes lit up and Joe suspected that secretly he was rather enjoying the situation.

'Like I said, we're keeping an open mind.' Joe produced his card. 'If you remember anything . . . anything at all . . . call me.'

Brett took the card and studied it. 'Plantagenet, eh,' he said with a grin. 'Should I bow or what?'

'If you do happen to remember anything, a phone call to my mobile will do,' Joe answered. There were times when he wished his name was Smith.

Emily had had a bad afternoon. First of all the super's insistence that it was more important to reassure the trembling public than to busy themselves trying to apprehend the killer had irritated her. She needed his support and his approval of her overtime budget, not another press conference.

And the hour she'd just spent with Abigail Emson's family bringing them up to date with developments confirmed her belief that she was in the right. The killer who had targeted the young student when she'd been on her way home from her bar job had to be caught before he deprived another family of their daughter.

She'd just telephoned Jeff to tell him she'd be late again and remind him that he had to drop Matthew off at Cubs, then take Daniel to his swimming lesson while Sarah's friend's mother took her to ballet. There were times when organising the family required the strategic ability of an army general. Compared to that, Emily thought to herself, running a full-scale murder inquiry seemed relatively straightforward.

Grabbing a precious spare moment to herself, she studied the names written on the white board that filled one wall of the incident room. The two victims and all the names that had cropped up during the investigation.

Then there was the name of the escaped murderer, Gordon Pledge. Alice – Gordon Pledge's grandmother – had been the victim of the Doll Strangler's first murder attempt and the current murders had started soon after Pledge's escape. He could easily have guessed at the Doll Strangler's MO from seeing Alice's injuries. Gordon Pledge was right up there in the frame. He'd killed once – strangled a child – and they said that murder was easier the second time around.

Of course, Emily had to acknowledge that the killer might not be on their list. The team was still trying to trace all the officers who worked on the original case in the 1950s – anyone who might know about the unpublished details.

She was deep in thought when a voice made her jump. She turned to see Jenny Ripon waving frantically, trying to catch her attention.

'Ma'am, there's a lady down in Reception.' She paused

for effect. 'She's heard we've been looking for her and she wants to talk to someone.'

Emily took a deep breath, wishing Jenny would come to the point. 'Who does?'

'It's Bridget Jervis. She's back.'

Chapter 19

Joe returned from his visit to Brett Bluit at seven-thirty, just as Emily was making her way down to the interview room. As soon as he heard about Bridget's reappearance, he couldn't resist seeing the woman for himself.

He sat beside Emily looking at Bridget Jervis. She was a big woman with hips that would send the health police reaching for their calorie counters. And it seemed to Joe that she had spent so much of her life with dolls that she had begun to resemble one. She had a small, rosebud mouth, a pretty turned-up nose and bright-blue eyes; in spite of the fact that she had passed her half century, her skin was clear and unlined.

'You know why we've been looking for you?' Emily said.

'Something about my dolls. Simone, my assistant, said you'd spoken to her a couple of times.' She looked at Joe accusingly. 'You scared the bloody life out of her. You know that?'

Joe shifted in his seat. There was something vaguely alarming about being scolded by a fearsome oversized doll.

'We need to know whether any of the dolls in your shop are missing.'

She shook her head. 'I took a look at the stock today as

soon as I got back. Simone's fairly reliable but record keeping isn't really her thing, if you know what I mean.'

Emily had brought down the evidence bags containing the two dolls left by the bodies of Natalie Parkes and Abigail Emson. She put them on the table in front of her and pushed them over towards Bridget whose eyes lit up with recognition.

'This one's Perault Freres – French, about eighteen ninety-six. And this one's German – Hoffmann.' She began to examine the dolls closely and when she noticed the feet she frowned. 'They're both damaged in the same way.' She looked up at Emily. 'Is that significant?'

Emily didn't answer.

'Do you recognise them?' Joe asked.

Bridget shook her head. 'No. I'm sure these haven't been through my shop.'

'How can you be so sure?' asked Emily sharply.

'I just know.' She paused and gave Joe a shy half smile. 'I love my dolls. They're like my children, I suppose. And I don't recognise these two.'

Joe and Emily looked at each other. It certainly sounded as if Bridget was telling the truth.

'Where have you been, by the way?' Joe asked.

Bridget began to wind a strand of hair around her fingers and her lips turned upwards in another coy smile. 'If you must know I was with a man. I met him on the Internet and we spent a few days at a hotel in Scarborough.' One look at her face told Joe that the sojourn in Scarborough had been a successful one.

'And you didn't think to tell your assistant where you were?'

'I told her I was going away for a while and to look after the shop. That's all she needed to know. I don't like all and sundry knowing my business.'

Joe nodded. 'Did your, er . . . gentleman friend take an

211

interest in the dolls you stock or . . .' It was a long shot but it was worth asking. Some malevolent person could have befriended Bridget over the Internet because of her tenuous connection with the old murders. Unlikely but possible.

'Dolls?' She snorted. 'Do me a favour. He's a lorry driver.'

'We went up to Whitby to have a chat with your father,' said Joe thinking a change of subject was probably advisable. 'He told us about a man who used to work for him . . . a Caleb Selly.' He watched her face for a reaction to the name . . . some sign of recognition. And he wasn't disappointed.

She leaned forward. 'I remember Caleb Selly. He worked for Dad for a few years.'

Something in the way she said it made Joe suspect that there was more to tell.

'Selly – or Mr Selly as I called him back then – never used to talk to me – but I could see him watching me. He had this birthmark covering his cheek – I remember that all right. Dad never said anything but I think I sensed there was something not quite right. I remember him saying to come to him if Selly said anything to me. I didn't really know what he meant then but . . .'

'Your dad thought he might have been a paedophile?' This was something Jervis hadn't mentioned. And Joe wondered why. He looked at Emily and saw that she was listening intently.

'Well they never used that word in those days but . . .'

'Strange that your dad gave him the job then. He must have come into contact with children at the dolls' hospital.'

'You've got to remember this was the fifties. It was a different world and people weren't as aware of things like that. If Selly was good at his job and my dad was always on the premises anyway, I guess he thought he couldn't do any harm. And besides, I don't think he had any evidence that Selly was a pervert. Just a gut feeling. And you can't sack someone who's perfectly good at their job because you feel uncomfortable about leaving them alone with your daughter, can you?'

'And were you ever alone with him?' Emily asked.

Bridget nodded. 'Just the once.'

'And?'

Bridget shook her head. 'Nothing. He never said a word . . . just kept looking at me and smiling, all nervous like. I thought he was creepy but there's no way I can accuse him of anything improper. Look, you don't think he killed those girls, do you? Because if you do, I can tell you you're wrong. He isn't capable.'

Joe saw Emily lean forward, like a cat who'd spotted a bird. 'What do you mean?' she asked. Joe could tell she was trying to sound casual.

'I saw him a while ago. It must have been in the school holidays because it was the day this woman came in with her two obnoxious brats who kept trying to lift my dolls' skirts to look at their knickers. The woman had just gone when I left Simone to hold the fort and ran across the road to get a sandwich. I remember I was feeling pretty stressed with the foul kids and I thought I'd treat myself to a cake while I was at it.'

'Go on,' Joe prompted, wishing she'd get to the point. It was almost nine now and he was hungry. And besides, he'd promised to call Maddy.

'I was just about to cross the road when this car pulled up on the double yellow lines. A man got out and then helped this old bloke out of the back. He had one of those metal frames and I could tell he was having problems walking so I didn't say anything about the double yellow lines. The younger man helped him out and they went

213

into the dentist's surgery next door to my shop.' She paused to take a breath. 'I had a good look at the old man and I'm certain it was Caleb Selly. I saw the birthmark on his cheek. He wouldn't have recognised me of course, cos I was only about eight when he last saw me.'

'So you didn't speak to him?'

She shook her head.

Joe said nothing for a while. From what Bridget had said it looked as if Caleb Selly was still in Eborby. And Caleb Selly was top of Joe's list of people to interview.

Brian Selly had left work early because he had to make sure the old man was OK. He was his father, after all.

Brian Selly's father had hated his middle name Caleb, and yet that was what everybody had called him until his marriage. But from that time on he'd been known by his first name, Edward – a new man.

The old man seemed so frail now . . . quite unlike the father Brian had known in his youth. His father had been a big man but he'd never been a bully. He hadn't been one of those men he'd seen around the rougher pubs of Eborby who were quick with their fists and always liked to come off best. His father had been a quiet, brooding, watchful presence.

Edward had started life under the thumb of his mother – Brian remembered his grandmother as a formidable Yorkshirewoman with a sharp tongue and unshakeable opinions. Then he'd married another strong woman. Brian's mother had called the shots in their house while Brian and his father just went along with it. It had always been difficult to know what Edward thought of the situation: father and son had never had the sort of relationship that included sharing confidences.

During his teens, Brian had come to suspect that his father had some hidden life away from his wife's domestic

214

tyranny. Secret drinking, perhaps, although he had never found any evidence. Or betting. Or even a mistress . . . although his father always seemed rather gauche with the opposite sex. After a while Brian had dismissed the idea as rubbish. But even now he still had the feeling that there were certain hidden things in his father's life that must never be mentioned.

They had never been particularly close but, since his mother's death ten years before, Brian felt obliged to visit his father regularly, just to keep in touch and see that he was coping.

When he arrived, opening the door with his own key, he found his father in the living room, slumped in his armchair with a shabby blanket over his knees. Brian noticed that there was a brown stain down the front of Edward's shirt and felt a pang of filial guilt.

The old man looked up at him with watery blue eyes. They had once been a bright, cornflower blue but the colour had faded with the years. The birthmark on his right cheek stood out a vivid red in contrast. 'What you doing here? Bugger off home. I know you want to.' The voice was weak but the eyes held a determination that surprised Brian.

'You need more help, Dad. I'm going to get onto Social Services . . . see if the home help can do more hours.'

'Stupid bitch doesn't do owt. Flicks a duster round for show and that's your lot. Them kids were better. At least they painted the bloody bedrooms.'

The ingratitude annoyed Brian. He knew the home help did her best, and if he would accept extra help, it would take some of the burden off his shoulders. As for the kids, that had been a one-off . . . some community project. However, he had to hand it to them, he'd called in while they were painting and they'd certainly been working hard. And that pair of girls had been easy on the eye

215

with their crop tops revealing the pale flesh of their bare midriffs.

One of those young decorators had been that girl who'd got herself murdered. Natalie Parkes. She'd worn a paint-splattered shirt, which kept falling open to reveal a low-cut T-shirt, and her blonde hair had been scraped back in a ponytail.

The other girl on the project had faded from Brian Selly's mind . . . totally unmemorable. But Natalie Parkes wasn't the sort of girl you'd forget very easily.

Chapter 20

The previous evening Sunny Porter had contacted the dentist whose surgery stood next door to Bridget's shop and the man confirmed that he had treated an elderly NHS patient by the name of Selly – he wasn't a regular but he remembered him particularly because he had a disfiguring birthmark on his cheek. He'd seen him a couple of months ago – although he couldn't tell them the exact date of the appointment, or the patient's first name or address, without consulting his records at his surgery. However, the old man's son, Brian Selly, had been a patient of his for a long time and he knew that he lived somewhere in Abbotsthorpe.

Sunny hadn't needed any more details. The knowledge that Caleb Selly was alive and still living in Eborby had been enough to satisfy Emily Thwaite.

Emily looked tired as she drove out to Brian Selly's address with Joe. It was half-seven in the morning so they'd be sure to find him in. Abbotsthorpe lay 3 miles south of Eborby city centre, sandwiched between suburbia and open farm land.

As they pulled into Selly's road she yawned.

'Everything OK, boss?' Joe asked.

'I had another bad night last night, that's all,' she said quickly. 'It's just starting to catch up with me.'

'How's your Sarah?'

A smile appeared on her lips, softening her face which up until then had worn a hard, businesslike expression. She looked rather gratified that he'd taken the trouble to ask about her daughter. A lot wouldn't have bothered. 'She was the reason for the bad night. I'm going to take her to the doctor's, Joe. This thing with bloody Grizelda's getting beyond a joke. We thought her having an imaginary friend was quite cute at first but now it's beginning to get to me, and Jeff too, especially now Grizelda appears to have developed insomnia. It's as if she's obsessed.' She suddenly realised she was saying too much. This was working time. 'Looks like this is it.'

Selly's house was semi-detached, built in the 1930s for the respectable lower middle class. In more prosperous times it had sprouted a kitchen extension and acquired gleaming plastic windows. There was a brand-new black Mercedes saloon in the drive – Bridget Jervis had said the car Caleb Selly got out of was a black saloon, but she hadn't been sure of the make.

Joe reached for the doorbell and pressed it long and hard. After a couple of minutes the door opened to reveal a large middle-aged man with a fine beer gut and dressed in his working suit, ready for the day ahead. Joe held up his ID and Emily did likewise.

'Brian Selly?' The answer was a wary nod. 'We'd like a word regarding the murders of Natalie Parkes and Abigail Emson. May we come in?'

There was no mistaking the worry on the man's face. Joe caught Emily's eye. Perhaps this was the lead they'd been waiting for.

As they entered a neat living room a plump woman in a dressing gown appeared in the doorway looking more curious than concerned. When Brian Selly told her it was OK, nothing to worry about, to Emily's surprise, she retreated to the kitchen. Joe knew there was no way the DCI herself would ever have been so obliging but Mrs Selly's acquiescence would make life easier for them. And it told them something about the couple's relationship.

'Mr Selly,' Joe began. 'Are you the son of Caleb Selly who used to work at a dolls' hospital in Singmass Close in the nineteen fifties?'

Brian Selly looked wary. 'My dad's called Edward Selly.' He paused, as if making a decision. 'His middle name's Caleb but he uses Edward. I don't know where he worked in the fifties. That was before I was born.'

'Has he ever mentioned the dolls' hospital? Or his boss . . . a man called Albert Jervis?'

He shook his head but the wariness was unmistakable. The subject of his father obviously made this man uncomfortable. And Joe wondered why.

'Do you see much of your father?' Joe asked innocently.

'Not much.' Something about the way he said it told Joe and Emily that he was lying.

'He's a hard man to find. Why the change of name?'

'He's not changed his name.'

'He used to be known as Caleb.'

Brian shrugged. 'He hates the name Caleb. Maybe people used to call him that to wind him up.'

'A couple of months ago you took your father to the dentist.'

The man's eyebrows shot up, as though he was surprised that his domestic arrangements were of such interest to the police. 'He asked me for a lift. He can't get about much these days.'

Emily glanced at Joe. She'd take over. She looked into Selly's eyes. 'We need your father's address,' she said in a voice that suggested that Brian Selly didn't have much choice in the matter.

There was a short period of silence while Selly

considered his options. But he realised he didn't have any. He recited an address on the Drifton Estate and Joe wrote it down carefully in his notebook.

'Look, I don't want him upset. He's an old man. He's not well.'

'We only want to ask him a few questions,' said Emily firmly. 'Can you tell us where you were around one o'clock last Saturday morning?'

Brian Selly began to drum his fingers on the side of his chair, a nervous habit. 'I was in A and E with Craig, my son. He'd fallen out of bed and banged his head so I thought I'd better get him checked out. Waiting three hours I was. Disgusting the state of the Health Service.'

'And around midnight on Tuesday. Where were you then?'

'In bed. Some of us have to get up in the morning, you know.'

'Have you ever met Natalie Parkes or Abigail Emson?'

The man's mouth opened and closed like a fish. Then he shook his head.

But Emily and Joe knew that he was lying. He'd known one or both of the girls all right. There was even a chance that he might have killed them.

'I didn't like Brian Selly,' Joe pronounced as he bit into his tuna mayonnaise sandwich.

'Unfortunately we can't arrest everyone we don't like,' was Emily's reply. She sounded as if her mind was elsewhere – with Sarah probably. She was worried about her daughter but only during their increasingly rare breaks from the investigation did she allow herself to let down her guard and show it.

Joe looked round. They'd decided to grab some lunch at the Black Lion on Gallowgate – the pub where Abi Emson had been employed as a barmaid for two evenings each week. It was a pleasant pub – comfortable and old-fashioned with dark oak panelling, plush red upholstery and a richly patterned red carpet, all slightly shabby, which added to the homely atmosphere. It was hardly a dive. Abigail Emson should have been safe here. But of course what happened outside the pub, in the narrow night-time streets after closing time, was a different matter.

'Think we should bring him in for questioning?' Emily asked.

'He has a good alibi for the first murder.'

'That still has to be checked out. His alibi for the second is shaky to say the least.'

'If you're innocent you don't expect to have to account for your movements.'

'I still think Brian Selly was hiding something,' she said absentmindedly. 'But it hardly sounds as if old Caleb's in a fit state nowadays to go round murdering and mutilating women. Mind you, it's always possible that his son's carrying on the family tradition.'

Joe nodded. Emily could well be right. Perhaps the old man had confessed what he'd done and the son had felt the urge to try it out for himself.

Joe's mobile rang and he had a sudden notion that it could be Maddy ringing with momentous news . . . like she'd been offered the job. But when he took the phone from his pocket, his heart racing, he saw that it was the police station. After a short conversation he looked up at Emily with a triumphant smile.

'They've found the Pledges. Place called Windy Hill Farm about two miles south of Pickering. A search warrant's being organised.'

Emily sat back, a satisfied expression on her face. 'Good. Hopefully we'll pick Gordon up and Alice will provide us with the name of the Doll Strangler. Don't you think it's odd that the first murder took place the night after Gordon Pledge's escape?'

'The thought had occurred to me.' Joe drained his half pint of shandy. He yearned for a pint of Black Sheep but he knew he'd be driving. Perhaps a visit to Windy Hill Farm would solve all their problems.

He hadn't been able to find the hook for the attic. That son of his must have put it somewhere. Hidden it from him. But he wasn't going to give up.

He shuffled along the landing, trying to ignore the pain welling in his chest, tightening like a band of steel . . . like the stocking had tightened around their slender necks. The stairs swam before his eyes as if they were bobbing on a rough and treacherous sea.

If he could just see his souvenirs once more . . . relive that time when he'd been all powerful. But the shabby hallway around him was fading in and out of focus and he felt ice cold. His legs began to buckle beneath him and he suddenly felt afraid.

Laughter. They were laughing. The children had come back to torment him. Or was it those women with their doll faces and their dirty looks?

'Please,' he uttered as he sank to his knees. 'Please help me.'

But as he collapsed to the floor, scratching at the threadbare carpet, the children became one again with the shadows and he knew that the last enemy was in the house. And his name was death.

Chapter 21

Emily stared out of the window as they passed the white horse carved into the hillside, a landmark visible from miles around. 'The Pledges certainly chose somewhere out of the way,' she said after a short silence. 'No neighbours to gossip about you out here. What did uniform say?'

'According to the letting agent, Windy Hill Farm is rented by a Mr and Mrs Barry Palmer. They fit the description we have of the Pledges and they said they wanted three bedrooms because Mrs Palmer's elderly mother was going to live with them. A couple of patrol cars are meeting up with us there to search the premises.

'We're here. This is it.' Emily had spotted a battered wooden sign that told them they had reached their destination. Windy Hill Farm. Once they had turned onto the rough track it seemed a long time before they caught sight of the house, which looked rather dilapidated with a large, overgrown garden separated from the surrounding fields by a tall hedge. If the Pledges had chosen the place to escape from the public gaze, the pointing fingers and the wagging tongues, when their son had been convicted of strangling twelve-year-old Francesca Putney, they had certainly made the right choice, Joe thought. And they had been using a false name – Palmer – which had made them doubly difficult to find.

'There's a car parked outside,' Emily said as Joe steered down the rough track way. 'Big posh model. Where did they get the money for that, I wonder? They must have spent a bloody fortune on their precious son's defence lawyer. Mind you, from what I've heard our Sylvia has always liked to keep up appearances.'

'There was talk of an appeal, wasn't there?'

'Escaping won't help his case.'

Joe brought the car to a halt and switched off the ignition. 'He claimed he went for a walk and saw the neighbour, Jones, talking to the little girl just before she disappeared. Trouble is, nobody else saw him . . . and he had no witnesses to the little walk he said he took. It was raining so the place was deserted.'

'You have to admit, all the evidence was circumstantial.'

Joe didn't answer. He climbed out of the car and walked towards the front door. He lifted the knocker and banged it down. It must have sounded like thunder inside the house – but that was the intention.

The front door was opened by a thin, hard-faced woman. She looked elegant in beige slacks and a v-necked pink cashmere jumper with a silk scarf artfully tied at the neck.

'Sylvia Pledge?'

At first the woman's eyes widened in panic but when she saw their warrant cards she nodded grudgingly, her expression giving nothing away. She had no idea where her son, Gordon, was, she said, but as far as she was concerned, he'd told her he was innocent and she believed him. If she'd thought for one moment that he'd killed the little girl, she would have disowned him. A mother could forgive most things but not that.

Sylvia Pledge was convincing, as was her husband Barry, when they stated that they hadn't seen Gordon since they'd visited him at Wakefield two months ago. If he was on the run, they said, this was the last place he'd come because it was the first place the police would look. Barry let Sylvia do the talking and Joe suspected that in the Pledge household, it was always her who called the tune.

'We haven't actually come about your Gordon. But some officers will be here shortly to search the place,' said Emily, sneaking a look at her watch. Uniform were taking their time. 'I believe your mother lives with you. Her name's Alice Meadows.'

Sylvia's face registered shock, swiftly concealed. 'Yes, but you can't see her. She's bedridden. She had a stroke and she's not up to receiving visitors.'

Joe suspected they were going to have a fight on their hands. But he wasn't going to give up easily. 'We need to speak to her,' he said. 'We promise not to upset her.'

Sylvia folded her arms defensively. 'You'll be lucky. She can't speak. I told you, she had a stroke. A bad one.'

Emily stepped forward. 'We'd like to see for ourselves.'

Joe could tell Sylvia was making a decision. 'I'll have to check how she is. Like I said, I don't want her upset.' She nodded towards a door to their left. 'You can wait in there.'

They were shown into a little sitting room while Sylvia and Barry disappeared upstairs. There was a photo album on the table by the sofa and Joe couldn't resist picking it up and flicking through the pages out of casual curiosity. But then he suddenly froze, his eyes fixed on the open page.

When he looked up he saw Emily staring at him. 'What's the matter, Joe? What's up?'

He felt his hand shaking slightly as he handed Emily the album. The resemblance to Kaitlin still had the power to shock, even when it was on photographic paper. 'That's Polly Myers from Singmass Close.'

Kaitlin – or rather Polly – was standing next to Gordon

Pledge whose image was familiar from a thousand TV reports. He was wearing a suit with a carnation in the buttonhole and she wore a long white gown and was carrying a bouquet.

Emily opened her mouth to speak but before she could say anything the door opened. Joe hurriedly replaced the album. His heart was pounding and he took a deep breath, willing himself to stay calm, professional. He tried to go over the implications of this new discovery in his head. No wonder Polly had been avoiding the police.

Sylvia Pledge stood on the threshold, barring the way out. 'Alice is asleep. I'm not going to have her disturbed. You'll have to come back another time.'

Joe knew Emily wasn't going to take no for an answer. 'We need to talk to her about something that happened to her in the nineteen fifties. It's very important.'

Sylvia smirked. 'The nineteen fifties? She doesn't even know what day it is. She won't be able to tell you anything. This is police harassment and I'll have no hesitation in making a complaint. I also know a journalist who'll be very interested to know you've been coming here to harass an old lady.'

The Emily Joe knew didn't like being ordered about and she probably regarded Sylvia's threats as a personal challenge. 'It really is very important,' she said reasonably. 'I must insist on seeing her. It could be a matter of life and death.'

Sylvia Pledge appeared to be considering the matter. In the face of Emily's determination, she probably knew she had little choice but she was making them sweat.

Joe picked up the photograph album and pointed to Polly's photograph. 'Is this Gordon's wife?'

Sylvia scowled. 'You've no right to look at that. It's private.'

'I'm sorry. But now I've seen it, you might as well answer the question.'

Sylvia gave him another scowl. 'It's Paula . . . or Polly as she calls herself. And before you ask, I've no idea where she is. She buggered off with the baby when our Gordon was arrested. Said she couldn't face being married to a man who'd murder a kid and we haven't seen her since. She had no loyalty, that girl. Our Gordon was far too good for her.' She pressed her lips together as if that was all she was prepared to say about her errant daughter-in-law.

Joe stared at the picture. The new revelation explained a lot. No wonder Polly had been on her guard. No wonder she'd left the close. Singmass Close was hardly a good place to lie low at the moment.

'Could Gordon have gone looking for her?' Emily asked. 'Surely he'd want to see his child.'

'I doubt it. Now if that's all, I'm busy. I have to look after my mother, you know. And I suggest that you obtain a search warrant if you want to do any more prying.'

Joe cut her off. 'We've got one.' Suddenly he heard the sound of sirens outside. The cavalry, in the form of two patrol cars, had arrived. 'Our uniformed colleagues will be searching the premises but, like the chief inspector said, we really do need to talk to Alice now. It's important.'

With the arrival of the patrol cars, Sylvia seemed to recognise defeat. 'OK. But don't tire her,' she said ungraciously and led the way upstairs. She progressed slowly, taking one step at a time as though her joints were stiff. Or perhaps to give somebody up there a chance to hide. Barry was hovering in the hall and Joe noted the look he gave his wife as she passed. These two were definitely concealing something. And that something could well be Gordon Pledge.

There was a loud knock on the front door.

'I suggest you answer that, Mr Pledge,' said Emily. 'And

don't forget about the search warrant. They'll need to see everything.'

Barry obeyed without a word and when they reached the landing Sylvia stopped at the end door. Joe saw there was a key in the lock.

'This is Mother's room' Sylvia said in a whisper. 'We have to keep it locked in case she wanders.'

'I thought she'd had a stroke,' said Joe sharply.

'She still tries to get out of bed,' Sylvia replied. 'I worry about her trying to get down the stairs and falling.'

Sylvia craned her neck nervously to see what was happening downstairs. Half a dozen uniformed officers were swarming around the hall, starting their quest to recapture Gordon Pledge.

But Joe and Emily had other preoccupations. 'After you, Mrs Pledge,' Emily said pointedly.

Faced with Emily's determination, Sylvia unlocked the door and entered the room. Joe and Emily followed her in and the first thing Joe noticed was the row of dolls on the shelf above the bed, staring down at the old woman who lay there, her bony arms resting on the floral duvet that was pulled up to her chin. Her cloud of pale grey hair was thin, revealing the scalp beneath, and her flesh was the colour of parchment. Joe glanced at Sylvia. She looked annoyed. Perhaps because her claims that Alice was asleep had been proved wrong. The old lady's watery blue eyes were wide open and watchful.

The dolls watched impassively as Emily stepped forward, smiling and perched herself on the edge of the bed. 'Hello, Alice. My name's Emily and I'm with the police. This is Joe.'

Joe smiled and gave the old woman a little wave.

'There's nothing to worry about,' Emily continued. 'We'd just like to ask you a few questions about something that happened a long time ago. Is that all right?'

228

The old woman's eyes flickered towards Sylvia, as though seeking approval.

'I'm sure Alice won't mind if you leave us alone, Mrs Pledge,' said Emily. 'And you'll be wanting to make sure our officers aren't doing any damage,' she added, making the words sound like a thinly veiled threat. 'We'll call you when we're ready.'

Joe watched as Sylvia opened her mouth to protest then shut it again, unable to think of a valid excuse for staying that wouldn't arouse suspicion. She addressed her mother. 'Is that all right, Mum?' She sounded as though she hoped the answer would be no . . . that her mother would become distressed and beg her to stay.

But Alice gave a barely discernible nod and Joe noticed something that looked like defiance in the old woman's eyes. One look at the expression on Sylvia's face told him that this wasn't meant to happen. Sylvia had lost control of the situation and now he and Emily held the balance of power. Emily sat on the edge of the bed and gave Alice a reassuring smile as Sylvia hovered in the doorway, uncertain what to do next. But Joe made her mind up for her, shutting the door gently on her, leaving her outside on the landing.

When he returned to the bedside, Emily had already begun to question Alice gently, chatting about the old days when she used to live in Singmass Close. The old woman's eyes had lost their glassy look. She was interested . . . alive. Reliving her youth.

Joe could tell from the thin, birdlike hand clutching at Emily's sleeve that she was anxious to communicate something. As Emily seemed to have established a rapport with Alice, he left her to it.

Because of her stroke, Alice's speech was slurred and it must have taken some effort to tell her story. But it emerged slowly and Joe knew from watching the old woman's face that it had been something she'd been longing to share with someone who'd understand.

She'd been walking home one night and someone came up behind her and slipped something around her neck. Next thing she remembered was waking up in Eborby General Hospital, her foot heavily bandaged and her throat so sore that she couldn't speak. It was a couple of days before she was told that she had lost a toe. This was in the days when doctors tended to keep information to themselves.

Alice had no longer felt safe in Singmass Close so as soon as she was well, she and her husband had moved out to the suburbs. Then, a year later, the Doll Strangler claimed his first victim, but the police never came to question her. It was almost as if they'd forgotten about her. And for some reason best known to herself, she'd never tried to contact them to point out the similarities.

'Have you any idea who attacked you?' Joe asked quietly. As soon as the words had left his lips he realised it was a stupid question. If she'd had any suspicions, she would surely have told with the police at the time. So he was surprised when she spoke again. 'I told the lass . . . the lass who looks after me. I told her.'

'You mean you do know who attacked you?' Emily said. She was trying to keep her questioning gentle and calm but Joe could sense her suppressed excitement.

'Aye. I saw him when I went there with our Sylvia.'

'Went where?'

'The dolls' hospital. He were there. He smelled of this cheap scent and the man who tried to kill me smelled the same. And his hands. I saw them when he had that stocking. And I saw those same hands fixing a doll. They were all warty and I'd felt the warts all rough on me skin. I'm sure it were him. I'd been at a dance and he'd asked me for a waltz and I said no. Maybe I were a bit cruel in them

230

days . . . maybe I told him I wouldn't fancy dancing with the likes of him. He wasn't pleased but I never thought owt about it until . . .'

'So why didn't you tell the police who you thought it was?'

She pressed her lips together. 'Well I'd not got any real proof, had I? And my Harry said I should just forget about it . . . not get involved. He said I'd be up there in court and they might lock me up for telling lies. He never liked the police much did Harry.'

Joe caught Emily's eye. 'So you kept quiet because your husband said so . . . even when you heard about the murders?' Joe said, trying to keep the disapproval out of his voice. They needed to get at the truth here and antagonising Alice wasn't the way to do it. He stood looking down at her. Her cheeks were pink now, as though the life blood was flowing back into her.

'Aye. That's right. My Harry knew him, you see. Drank with him sometimes. He said I was a lying bitch.'

'So who attacked you, Alice? What was his name?' Joe glanced up at the dolls who seemed to be leaning forward on their shelf, listening intently, waiting for the answer just as he was.

Alice closed her eyes and for a few moments Joe thought she'd lapsed into unconsciousness. He saw disappointment on Emily's face. Just when they were so near.

Then suddenly the watery blue eyes snapped open. 'I never told no one . . . not until my little lass asked me and I told her. But I couldn't swear it were him, like. Not in a court of law.'

'Why don't you tell us who you think it was, Alice?' Emily said, giving her hand a gentle squeeze. 'It might make sure no more girls get hurt.'

Alice hesitated then she beckoned Emily to come closer with a claw-like finger. Emily leaned over until she could feel the old woman's hot breath on her cheek. Joe stood behind, straining to hear.

He couldn't quite make out the name Alice had spoken so softly. But he saw Emily straighten herself up, a satisfied smile on her lips. 'You've done the right thing, Alice,' he heard her say. 'Thanks.'

Her eyes met Joe's. 'It's about time we made a move.' She turned back to Alice and smiled. 'We might want to speak to you again, Alice. Is that all right?'

Alice nodded although Joe could see that the effort tired her. 'Aye. You come when my little lass is here. She looks after me, you know. She's a good lass.'

Joe wouldn't have thought of Sylvia Pledge as a little lass . . . but mothers look at their children through different eyes.

'Well, who was it?' he whispered as they left the room.

When she mouthed the name he smiled. At last it looked as if they were getting somewhere.

Chapter 22

Polly was frightened. That was why she'd changed her name. And that was why she was staying in Yolanda's flat above the antique warehouse, sleeping on the spare bed with the broken springs.

Before she'd met Yolanda she'd visited a clergyman at the cathedral – Canon Merryweather, whose job it was to deal with anything of a supernatural nature. She usually avoided churches and she didn't know why she'd sought his help but it had seemed a good idea at the time. Or perhaps she'd just been desperate and didn't know where to turn.

George Merryweather had been kind and he'd listened patiently, even offering to visit her house if she was still worried. But after she'd met Yolanda she hadn't contacted George again. Yolanda disapproved of clergymen and organised religion and Yolanda's disapproval had been so strong that Polly hadn't had the heart to argue with her.

Polly sat there watching Daisy play with her dolls, going over things in her mind. She'd married a man who'd turned out to be a child killer. At first she hadn't believed Gordon capable of murder but then the evidence against him had stacked up like weights on old-fashioned scales until they'd tipped one way to the inevitable confirmation of his guilt. For a while she'd not been able to come to terms with it but, little by little, she had had to accept the truth. Her life with Gordon had been a lie and he had deceived her.

She'd remembered his parents' odd ways and his mother's almost pathological obsession with status and money. She dressed like an assistant at a high-class cosmetics counter, spending a fortune on clothes and manicures, and somehow she'd managed to coax Polly and Gordon into doing most of her household chores while her ineffectual husband simpered in the background. Sylvia Pledge used people and there had even been times when Polly had been a little afraid of her. But perhaps the Pledges had known all along that Gordon was a potential pervert or killer. Perhaps living with that burden had made them strange and set them apart from the rest of humanity.

After Gordon's conviction Polly had changed her name and rented the house in Singmass Close, determined that she would have no more contact with her husband or his family. He'd murdered a child. He was the lowest of the low. And she suppressed those minuscule doubts about his guilt that rose to the surface from time to time like bubbles in a stagnant pond. Gordon was a murderer and his escape seemed to confirm it more than ever.

Daisy never asked about her father these days. He had just become a dim memory – not as real to her as Mary. Mary had appeared soon after the move to Singmass Close – in Daisy's mind if not in the flesh. At first Polly assumed that Mary was an imaginary friend made up by a lonely, confused child. Daisy talked about Mary as though she was real and she even insisted on leaving food for Mary because she was hungry. The food was never touched, of course. Imaginary friends don't eat.

But there were times when Polly herself thought she glimpsed a little girl in a dirty white dress with matted hair out of the corner of her eye, and sometimes she'd been sure she felt the light touch of a little hand in hers. But she must have been imagining things. It was probably the stress of her situation.

Yolanda, however, was convinced that Mary was real. The children of Singmass Close, she said, had been seen often over the years. Poor little souls wandering about the area of the close, seeking the human comfort they hadn't experienced in life. The city's ghost tours stopped there and sometimes one of the tourists would feel a small hand in theirs. Or someone would discover the shape of a child on a photograph taken there. And an archaeologist digging there in preparation for the new development had felt a small hand tapping her shoulder as she worked away with her trowel . . . and had found red finger marks on her flesh that evening when she undressed. The children couldn't hurt them, Yolanda said. They might be mischievous like earthly children but they meant no harm. And Polly had dismissed all this until the murders started . . . and the dolls had been left by the bodies.

The thing that really frightened Polly was the fact that the first girl had died shortly after Gordon's escape. She had a dreadful feeling that it had been some sort of message to her; that prison had twisted Gordon's mind making him kill again in that horrific way. If she'd gone to stay with her mother he might have come looking for her there so she was grateful to Yolanda for offering them a refuge where Gordon would never think to look.

The local papers were full of the Doll Strangler murders in the 1950s. Four women had died back then and it looked as if someone was copying the original killer. Gordon had been in prison. High security. What if he had shared a cell at some stage with that killer – now elderly of course – who had reminisced about his past crimes? What if Gordon had acquired the taste for death when he'd murdered Francesca Putney? What if he had killed the girls in Singmass Close? Polly kept turning these questions over in her mind. In a moment of panic she'd toyed with the idea of getting in touch with Joe Plantagenet and asking for police protection. But she knew the wives of child murderers shouldn't trust the police. She would have to deal with it on her own.

She looked down at Daisy who was still playing on the floor with her dolls. The child looked up with solemn eyes. 'I want to go home, Mummy. I want to see Mary. Mary's scared because she saw the lady fall over.'

Polly's heart started to pound. 'What lady?'

'The murder lady. Mary saw her. She told me.'

'Did she, dear,' said Yolanda who was reading quietly in the corner.

Polly's head began to ache. Mary again. Would they never escape from Mary? Perhaps staying with Yolanda had been a mistake. She only encouraged Daisy's obsession.

Yolanda turned her smile on Polly as if she could read her mind. 'You should tell the police what Mary saw, Polly. Until you do, you're both in danger.'

Polly stared at the woman. Yolanda treated Daisy's fantasies as the truth. 'I don't want Daisy involved,' she heard herself saying. 'It's better this way. Honestly. If we just keep our heads down we'll be fine. Look, Yolanda, I left my mobile at the shop. I've got to go out. And I'll tell them I won't be in for a while. You don't mind looking after Daisy, do you?'

'Of course not,' Yolanda replied. 'But take care, won't you. He's out there. And he's waiting.'

Polly's heart began to pound. 'There'll be lots of people around. Gordon wouldn't dare to do anything in the street, surely.'

Yolanda shook her head, a sympathetic smile playing on her lips.

'Not Gordon, dear. The danger doesn't come from Gordon.'

Gordon Pledge knew the perfect hiding place in case of emergencies. As soon as he'd heard the police arrive he'd moved aside the three loose boards behind the cupboard in the attic room where Michele slept. Behind the boards was a hidden space about 6 feet square; probably some sort of storage area, forgotten over the years.

He'd removed the boards and then replaced them carefully as soon as he was inside. And once he'd made himself comfortable there, he was almost tempted to stay, to creep out in the night and surprise Michele as she slept – he was, after all, a frustrated man, starved of female company. In prison, he'd been treated as a nonce – a child killer. The lowest among the low. But he hadn't deserved it and there was no way he was going to become a rapist now – he'd met enough of them inside and even being near them made him feel dirty. Michele would be safe – unless she was willing, of course, that would be different. Perhaps he'd try his luck if he ever got a chance.

He wondered where his mother had found her; the stunning, willowy girl who was willing to endure domestic slavery for her keep and possibly a bit of pocket money. He guessed she was a drug addict or something because she looked spaced out most of the time and he'd noticed the way his mother locked her in at night. Sylvia had done some stupid things in her time but taking on a girl like that to avoid using his grandmother's money to pay for a care home must take the cake. Anyway, a girl like Michele was hardly likely to stay there indefinitely. She would disappear into the wide blue yonder one day leaving his parents with Alice on their hands. And God knows what would happen then.

But his mother's domestic arrangements weren't really his problem. He had plans of his own.

Once he'd heard the police drive away, Gordon had found his mother in his grandmother's room, giving the old woman a drink, and when he'd entered, she'd looked up guiltily as Alice lolled back on the pillows.

'What's going on, Mum? What did the police say? Did they find anything I'd left round? Did they say they'd be coming back?'

Sylvia looked up and scowled. 'I think you're safe. The two detectives just wanted to talk to your gran. Spent a long time with her, they did.' Gordon saw her look down at the old woman with distaste. 'God knows what she told 'em.'

He came up to the bed and took his grandmother's hand. 'Hi, Gran. You all right?' He smiled at her but she closed her eyes as though she hadn't seen. Gordon felt a prick of sadness. He'd always been fond of his gran and he didn't like to see her like this. He looked up at his mother. 'Where's Michele?'

'Outside somewhere,' she answered, avoiding his gaze.

'I just hope you're paying her well.'

Sylvia looked away.

'Is she on something? She looks really out of it sometimes and she always looks scared stiff when you're around. Where did you say you found her? Which agency was it?'

'I told you before, it's none of your business,' Sylvia answered quickly.

He looked down at Alice. Her eyes were closed now, as though she was in a deep sleep. 'I'm moving on,' he said.

'Where are you going?'

Gordon hesitated. He supposed his mother was owed some sort of explanation, as long as he wasn't too specific. 'I'm going to try and find him.'

'Who?'

'The man who should be serving life instead of me. I met someone inside who knows him. He said he's drinking heavily; falling to pieces. So I reckon with a bit of persuasion, he'll admit what he did and clear my name.'

Sylvia looked at him, exasperated. 'Prison's given you too much time to think. And what are you going to do about Polly . . . and your daughter? What about Daisy?'

He looked down at the old lady on the bed, now unconscious and snoring softly. 'Polly's my problem, not yours,' he said, clenching his fists.

He swept out of the room, ignoring his mother's pleas to come back and talk. And not to do anything stupid.

It was almost eight-thirty when Emily Thwaite swept into the incident room like a ship in full sail with Joe following in her wake. It had been a long day but discovering the identity of Alice's attacker had lifted their spirits.

'Caleb Selly's our man,' Emily announced triumphantly as everyone stopped whatever they were doing and turned to look at her. 'We've just spoken to a woman he attacked in the nineteen fifties. Apparently he took offence when she refused to dance with him. He attempted to strangle her and he took a knife to her foot – she lost a toe. We need to talk to him as soon as possible.'

Joe looked round the room and saw that several mouths had fallen open. Such a positive identification was a rare and precious thing, even if the case was over fifty years old.

Joe felt his heart beating a little faster. All along he'd suspected that Polly knew something about the Singmass Close murders but now it seemed likely that she'd been concealing something altogether different. Perhaps he was losing his touch.

But he couldn't dismiss the possibility that, if Pledge

had discovered Polly's new address, he might have come looking for her. But had Gordon Pledge really killed two women in the vicinity of his wife's house, perhaps as an awful warning? He could certainly have learned about the Doll Strangler's methods from his grandmother, even down to the amputation of the toe.

The sound of Emily's voice interrupted his thoughts. 'So if Pledge's ex-wife lives in Singmass Close, it means that he has a connection with our case and he's still high on our list of suspects. We need to find him.' She looked at her watch. 'I suggest we get ourselves an early night. It'll be a big day tomorrow. We'll call on Caleb Selly first thing. Seven in the morning suit you, Joe?'

Joe didn't answer. He heard Emily give a deep sigh as she swung her handbag over her shoulder and looked at him expectantly. 'What do you reckon to Gordon Pledge as our killer?'

He thought for a few moments. 'I suppose it's a possibility. But, like you said, we need to find him first. If we're seeing Caleb first thing, what about Brian Selly?'

'We'll send someone along to bring him in while we're seeing his dad. I don't know about you but I need to catch up on some sleep and remind my kids what I look like. Caleb and Brian aren't going anywhere within the next few hours and they certainly won't be expecting the knock on the door first thing.'

Emily was interrupted by the sound of someone clearing their throat politely behind her. A young DC had come to impart the news that one of Abigail Emson's fellow students had rung in while they were out. He wanted a word with the person in charge of the case. Something was worrying him but he wasn't sure whether it was important.

'Got the address?' Joe saw Emily's eyes light up with the excitement of the chase. She looked at Joe. 'If he's a student he won't be tucked up in bed yet. We can pay him a visit on our way home, eh, Joe.'

Joe's shoulder began to ache a little but he nodded bravely. At least it would delay his return to his empty flat.

Half an hour later they reached Hasledon and parked outside a large Victorian house a couple of streets away from Christopher Strange's place. Like Christopher's, the house bore the tell-tale signs of student occupation. The weed-filled front garden, the unwashed windows decorated with garish stickers. They could see a light shining in the front-room window. Someone was in.

A fair-haired young man answered the door. He'd been expecting them and, for once, someone looked happy to see the police. He introduced himself as Harry Wilde and invited them in.

Joe sat beside Emily on the saggy sofa and watched as she moved to put her bag on the beer-sticky coffee table but hugged it on her knee when she thought better of it. 'You want to tell us something about Abigail Emson?' he said.

Wilde shuffled his large feet, encased in boat-like trainers. 'I was really gutted when I found out what happened to her. She was really nice. Sweet, you know. Never had a bad word to say about anyone.'

'You liked her?' Joe asked, watching the young man carefully.

'Yeah. But we were just friends. She had a boyfriend back home.'

'So what do you want to tell us?'

Wilde thought for a few moments. 'It might not be important.'

'Why don't you tell us and let us decide for ourselves?' Emily said, sneaking a surreptitious glance at her watch.

Wilde took a deep breath. 'It was just that for our group work she contacted this author who'd written a book on

241

wartime Eborby. It was published by a small press specialising in local interest books so it was easy to get in touch with the author. She went to see him and interviewed him about his research. When she came back she said he'd been very helpful . . . but then he kept ringing her. He said these friends of his had parties. In the end she had to be quite firm.'

'Did he give up?'

'Well, this was only about three weeks ago and last time I saw her she didn't mention it . . . so I presumed he hadn't been giving her any more hassle. That was the trouble with Abi . . . she could be too nice.'

'What was the author's name?' Joe asked.

Wilde sighed with frustration. 'I can't remember. Oh, hang on. I think it might have been something to do with horse racing.'

'Derby? Philip Derby?'

Harry Wilde looked surprised, as though Joe had just done a particularly amazing conjuring trick. 'That's it. How did you know?'

'He's psychic,' said Emily, standing up.

It looked as if Philip Derby had just been added to their visiting list.

As soon as the police had arrived at Windy Hill Farm, a drowsy Michele had been bundled into the boot of the car parked round the back of the house. As her head had started to spin, she realised that she shouldn't had drunk the orange juice Sylvia had given her as soon as the car had been spotted coming up the drive. The juice had been doped, of course, she knew that now and felt stupid. It could have been her chance to catch the visitors' attention and she'd blown it without thinking. Because she felt thirsty.

She'd slept like the dead for what seemed like hours and now she'd awoken, cramped and dry-mouthed in the stuffy darkness of the car boot. She had no idea how long she'd been there. But she could hear the sound of birdsong outside, the joyous clamour of the dawn chorus, and she wondered whether she'd been there all night.

She hadn't expected the car to start and the movement and the smell of the exhaust fumes made her feel sick. Her head ached and her mouth felt like sandpaper as she wondered where she was being taken.

She didn't even know who was driving the car. Was it Barry? Or Sylvia herself? There was always a chance it could be the son called Gordon. But whoever it was was taking her somewhere. Possibly to kill her . . . like they'd killed the girl in the freezer.

The car had been driving fast for a while – travelling down some motorway perhaps. Then it had stopped and she'd heard the door slam. Then, after the slammed door, there had been silence and she'd drifted into unconsciousness again.

When she awoke again she could make out the faint rumble of distant traffic. But there was no sound of human voices – no chance of rescue. She breathed in deeply. She was hot now in that metal prison and she could feel sweat pouring down her face. The boot was stuffy as though the air was running out. Perhaps that's how they intended to kill her. Suffocation left no marks.

She closed her eyes in the darkness and prayed. Then she heard footsteps and the car door opening and they were off again.

Joe rose early the next morning after a restless night. He climbed out of bed, wolfed down some cereal and made himself a strong coffee to wake him up.

He felt rather down as he walked to work through the empty streets. There was a low mist over the city, giving everywhere a monochrome look, like a 1950s photograph.

He arrived in the incident room a couple of minutes before Emily and watched her march in with a determined look on her face before following her into her office.

'Ready to pay Caleb a visit?' he asked.

'Too right. We're going to crack this today,' she said with a confidence Joe found he couldn't share. Then she grinned at him. 'Positive thinking, Joe. I want both Sellys, dad and lad, and I want Philip Derby. He knew Abigail as well as Natalie so he's right back on our list.' She shuffled some papers on her desk.

'There's still no sign of Gordon Pledge. And we don't know where the wife's gone.'

'Perhaps they're together. Perhaps the estrangement was all an act.'

Before Joe could answer Sunny entered the office after a perfunctory knock. He looked as though he had news to impart.

'You know those DVDs we found doing the search of Derby's flat? Well, I've just been looking through the last ones.'

'That's true dedication to duty, facing that sort of thing at this hour in the morning,' Emily said with a twinkle in her eye.

Sunny's face turned red. 'Natalie Parkes is on some of them and I've found some new faces . . . I'm trying to get an ID on them.'

Joe caught Emily's eye. Natalie's killer could have got to know her through Derby's parties and arranged to meet her on the night she died. Every lead had to be followed. Joe and Emily followed Sunny into the cramped AV room where he'd been viewing the DVDs.

'Hope all this hasn't corrupted your morals,' Joe quipped as Sunny set the disc running.

'Not so you'd notice,' Sunny replied, shooting Emily a

coy look. Back at the time of the first Doll Strangler murders in the 1950s, a policewoman wouldn't have been expected to view material like this. But the world had changed and Joe saw that Emily Thwaite looked quite unconcerned as the bodies writhed on the screen ... Benjamin Cassidy's naked form amongst them.

'I hear Cassidy's resigned,' said Joe, tilting his head to get a better view of the action.

'Doesn't surprise me,' said Emily. 'I bet the PTA would pay good money to see this. Hey up. Who's that ... just joined in the fray?'

Sunny pressed the pause button and they all leaned forward. Then Joe saw a wide smile spread across Emily's face. 'I think we've got ourselves another suspect, gentlemen,' she said as Brian Selly's naked body flickered, frozen for posterity on the screen. 'What's the betting he's followed in his daddy's footsteps. I want him brought in now.'

Chapter 23

With this new development Joe and Emily reasoned that their visit to Caleb could wait until they'd spoken to his son, Brian and to Philip Derby. After all, Caleb wouldn't be going anywhere for a while.

Half an hour later Sunny Porter had run a half-dressed Derby to ground at his flat above the bookshop and brought him in, protesting.

But Joe decided to keep him waiting. A period of uncertainty would soften him up and he wanted him in a co-operative frame of mind when he asked him about his harassment of Abigail Emson. Abigail had contacted him about her university work and Natalie had attended the parties. Derby had known both victims. And that made him a suspect.

While Derby was being brought in someone had been sent to Abbotsthorpe to fetch Brian Selly – Derby and Cassidy's co-star in their nasty little movie productions. Selly looked nervous as he was led into the interview room and his fingers kept moving towards his lips as though he was smoking an imaginary cigarette. But as the police station was a no smoking area, he had to make do with a cup of tea from the machine.

Joe and Emily were waiting for Selly, Emily's fingers lingering impatiently over the tape machine. He sat down opposite them, feigning indifference but failing. They could see the anxiety in his eyes. So far he had refused the services of a solicitor but Joe suspected that would soon change.

'Do you know why you're here, Mr Selly?' Joe asked, breaking the uncomfortable silence.

'No idea. I presume it's something to do with why you came to the house before. But I don't know anything. Honest.'

Emily smiled sweetly. She was usually at her most dangerous, Joe thought, when she smiled like that.

'You didn't tell us that you knew one of the women murdered in Singmass Close – name of Natalie Parkes.' She tilted her head to one side and gave him another disarming smile.

Selly swallowed hard. 'I didn't know her. Never saw her in my life. What makes you think I knew her?'

Joe had kept the still photograph from Philip Derby's DVD face down in front of him on the table. He turned it over slowly and pushed it under Selly's nose. 'You and Natalie Parkes. Looks as though you knew her pretty well. Intimately, I'd say.' He looked at Emily and she nodded in agreement. 'Ever drunk in the Black Lion?'

'I go in there from time to time. Not a crime is it?'

Joe presented him with a second photograph. A smiling Abigail Emson in happier days. 'This girl worked as a barmaid at the Black Lion. Recognise her?'

Selly stared at the picture and nodded. 'I think I've seen her. But I've never talked to her. She was just a girl behind the bar. Look, I've got an alibi for the time of the first murder. I was at the hospital.'

Joe leaned forward. 'We're checking it out.'

'I knew you would,' the man said defiantly. 'That's why I'm telling you the truth. And that second murder, the barmaid, I was home with my wife. She'll vouch for me.'

He sat back, arms folded, looking smug.

There was nothing else for it. Unless they could disprove Brian Selly's alibi and find something incriminating at his home, they had no reason to keep him there so, with some regret, Joe told him he was free to go but they might need another word with him. He was about to say 'Don't leave town' when Emily spoke the words instead.

'Don't leave town, Mr Selly. We'll need to speak to you again. And we need to see your father.' She looked at her watch. 'He'll be at home, I take it. And we'd like to conduct a search of your house. Do we have your permission or do we have to get a warrant?'

Selly considered the question for a while. 'You can get a bloody warrant. But you won't find anything, I can tell you that for nothing.'

Selly wasn't going to make life easy for them. Now they would have to track down a magistrate to obtain a search warrant, which would take up more valuable time. However, in the meantime they could see what Philip Derby had to say for himself.

When Selly had gone, Derby was brought in. Unlike Selly, he had elected to bring his solicitor, a seedy-looking man in a shiny suit with a large beer gut. Like Selly, he denied everything. This was getting tedious.

Yes, he'd known Natalie from the parties. He'd made no secret of that. And yes, he'd helped Abigail with her work. He'd invited her to the parties but she'd never accepted the invitation. Perhaps, with hindsight, that was a good thing, he said. She looked as though she might be a bit of a prude. But pretty. Abigail Emson had been very attractive. And he'd tried his best to help her.

In the end Joe had had enough of Derby's oily protests. One man's helpfulness is another man's lecherous stalking. And he knew from her fellow student, Harry Wilde, how Abigail had interpreted the author's attentions.

They had nothing on Derby so they let him go for now. They would always reel him in again if necessary. Joe noticed that Emily had lost her initial bounciness and there were dark rings beneath her eyes.

'You OK, boss?' he asked as soon as they were alone.

Emily shrugged. 'Jeff's been having more trouble with our Sarah while I've been working these late nights. She's stopped eating now because she says Grizelda's told her not to. It's just attention seeking, I know that. Maybe when we've got this case sewn up . . .' She didn't finish the sentence. Her guilt was almost palpable. Sarah wanted her mummy but Mummy was too busy chasing after bad men to spend any time with her.

He left Emily's office, intending to see what progress had been made with the warrant to search Brian Selly's premises. As he entered the incident room his mobile bleeped. It was a text message from Maddy telling him what time she expected to be back the next day. And to say that she had something she wanted to discuss with him.

Emily wasn't the only one with problems.

Gordon Pledge had set off just before dawn in the car he'd taken from his parents' place. He'd wanted to arrive early to make sure Jones was in. He needed to see Harley Jones. He needed to make him tell the truth.

Only a close neighbour could have planted the dead child's shoe in his garden shed; someone who knew Gordon's movements and knew how to get into the garden. And Jones had been used to walking in whenever he wanted. Gordon hadn't liked that, not with Polly and Daisy about. Jones had given him the creeps sometimes, staring at Polly like that.

Francesca's murder had shocked the whole neighbourhood. But Gordon hadn't voiced his suspicions about

Jones at first, thinking that Francesca – that forward little madam over the road – must have been the victim of some random killer. People you know, people you pass the time of day with, couldn't possibly be capable of murdering a child. But Jones had been sly when he'd pushed all the blame onto Gordon.

Jones had told the police that he had seen Gordon talking to Francesca. It was a pack of lies of course. He had never said two words to the silly girl in all the time he'd lived in Almond Crescent.

But by the time he realised what Jones was up to, it was too late. Jones's carefully engineered evidence against him stood up and eventually even Polly had come to believe the lies.

During those long days locked in a narrow cell, Gordon had pieced the whole thing together. But all his efforts to lodge an appeal had failed because of a lack of new evidence, and the only hope he'd clung to was what he'd heard on the prison grapevine – that Jones was now a reclusive drinker who might be vulnerable enough to make a confession and tell the world how he had killed Francesca and lied to throw suspicion on his innocent neighbour.

He'd sat in the car for a while going over and over what he was going to say. He'd prepared it all in his head and when he'd knocked on Jones's door and there'd been no answer he'd felt numb with disappointment. But even though Jones hadn't answered the door he wouldn't give up.

He climbed back into the driver's seat. It was a cold day; too cold to hang about outside and there was a chance that some neighbours might look out of their windows and recognise him. The car at least gave him cover.

He looked round the crescent with its small semi-detached houses behind their neat front gardens, some of them paved over to give extra off-road parking. This was where he and Polly had brought Daisy home to from hospital. Number five had been their first home together and they had been happy there for a while. Until the bomb of Francesca Putney's murder had been dropped in their midst, shattering their lives.

As he closed the car door he suddenly heard a noise. A scratching, shuffling sound. He listened for a few seconds and heard it again. It was coming from somewhere behind him. Something was moving in the car. But there was nothing in the back so perhaps it was in the boot. He listened for a while, wondering what to do. Then he made a decision.

After looking around to make sure nobody was watching from any of the windows around the crescent, he got out and walked to the back of the car, keys at the ready. Then he unlocked the boot and stood back, as though he expected a wild animal to spring out. But as the lid lifted slowly, he saw a face looking up at him, terrified.

'Michele. What the hell . . .'

'Don't hurt me . . . please,' she whispered, her eyes wide with fear as she cowered there like a wounded beast.

When Joe next saw Emily she was clutching a search warrant triumphantly like an archaeologist showing off some rare and precious find. Brian Selly's place was about to be searched thoroughly, torn apart.

They took some uniformed officers along with them. In Emily's opinion there was nothing like the sight of a couple of patrol cars screeching to a halt outside your front door to engender co-operation. Selly's alibis had been checked and the one for Natalie Parkes's death wasn't as watertight as it first appeared. Brian Selly had indeed been at A and E in Eborby General that night with his son, Craig, but, according to the hospital's records,

251

Craig had been seen and treated by midnight. He'd been dealt with quickly to clear capacity for the expected influx of Friday-night drunks. And as for the second alibi, that he was having a cosy evening in with his wife, it was hardly worth the trouble of writing down on the statement sheet.

Alice had named Brian's father as her attacker and Caleb's alibi for Marion Grant's murder, provided by Peter Crawthwaite, had now been blown to pieces. Alice had claimed that he'd mutilated her foot because she'd refused to dance with him. Had this rejection been the last straw in a life spent enduring mockery and revulsion? Had it really sent him over the edge and made him a killer? Joe knew that people had killed for less – for a few coins or a hostile stare.

Caleb Selly was the prime suspect for the Doll Strangler murders in the 1950s and now they needed evidence to link his son with the recent deaths. But Caleb, Emily observed, had been living with his secret since the 1950s, so he'd keep for another few hours. His son, Brian, on the other hand, was far more likely to do a runner or claim another victim. Joe couldn't argue with her logic. But a small voice somewhere inside him was still telling him that she was wrong.

When they arrived in Abbotsthorpe, Brian Selly and his wife stood there side by side, saying little, the wife on the verge of tears. There was no sign of young Craig: perhaps he was up and about already and had gone to see friends. Or perhaps he was one of those children who could sleep through an earthquake and he was having a lie-in.

Emily's plump face looked smug as she waved her precious search warrant in front of Selly's nose. When the team set to work Joe stayed with the Sellys while Emily hurried upstairs to supervise the search.

Joe couldn't help wondering whether Mrs Selly had any inkling of her husband's sexual tastes. Brian Selly was the type you'd pass in the street without a second look, but he shared an interest in sex parties and young girls with Benjamin Cassidy and Philip Derby. Brian Selly had a dark side that his wife probably knew nothing about. And seeing the tears trickling down Mrs Selly's face, he didn't feel inclined to enlighten her.

He had been sitting in silence with the Sellys for ten minutes when a boy joined them: he was about nine years old and he'd been frightened by the policemen who'd barged into his room and woken him up.

Joe was trying to think of something to say when Emily burst into the room. From her expression he knew that something had been found. Brian Selly hid his face in his hands while his wife put a protective arm around her son.

'Mr Selly. I'd like a word,' said Emily in a voice that didn't invite any argument.

Selly stood up and Joe followed him out into the hall where a burly uniformed sergeant was holding two dolls at arm's length as though he didn't wish to be associated with them. They were Victorian dolls in dirty white smocks with painted porcelain faces and matted curls, remarkably similar to the ones that had been discovered beside the bodies of Natalie Parkes and Abigail Emson.

'Where did you get these, Mr Selly?' Emily asked.

Selly's eyes flickered from right to left, as though he were seeking an escape route. 'They came from me dad's place. He used to have a job mending the things.' He paused and Joe could almost hear his brain ticking. 'The wife took 'em. That's right. She fancied having a couple on display then she changed her mind.' Mrs Selly nodded vigorously while her husband looked from Emily to Joe, pleading with them to believe him.

Joe could predict Emily's next words. They were ones he'd used himself many times.

'Brian Selly, I'm arresting you on suspicion of murdering

253

Natalie Parkes and Abigail Emson. You do not have to say anything . . .'

'I didn't do it,' Selly shouted in the direction of the lounge as he was led away. But either his wife and son hadn't heard them or they had chosen not to witness the spectacle of his arrest. They stayed on their sofa quite still, cuddling together for comfort as the tears began to fall.

Chapter 24

Gordon Pledge put out his hand to help Michele out of the boot of his mother's car. 'You OK?' he asked.

Michele was still cowering there, too frightened to speak.

'Look, I'm not going to hurt you.' He held up his hands, as if to prove he wasn't intending to touch her. After what he'd been through, the last thing he wanted was a false accusation of sexual assault on his hands . . . and this girl's eyes were wild. She could do or say anything and he just hoped she wouldn't ruin the moment he'd been anticipating for months. The moment when he'd confront Harley Jones.

But Michele just lay there quite still with her mouth tight shut, suspicion clouding her face.

Gordon tried again. 'I've got to see someone but after that I'll give you a lift anywhere you want to go.' He hesitated. 'OK?'

There was no answer. The girl was obviously traumatised and again he wondered how she had come to be looking after Alice. And how she had ended up in the car boot.

'OK. You wait for me in the car if you want. I won't lock it. You can walk away any time you like.'

The girl shifted, a glimmer of hope in her bloodshot

eyes. When he'd first met her he'd thought she might have been on drugs, or maybe a little slow, and he wished he'd pressed his parents for some honest answers. But now all he knew was that he had to get rid of her somehow. This business with Jones was too important to allow this strange girl to get in the way. His freedom was at stake.

As he helped her out of the boot he felt her body shaking. She looked so thin, like a fragile flamingo, all legs. He opened the passenger door and as she climbed in he uttered more reassuring words. Where the hell had his parents found a specimen like this? It was just like them to employ some junky straight out of rehab to look after Alice if she came cheap. The cheaper the better for them.

Once the girl was safely in the car, he turned his attention to Jones's house. He knew the layout of these houses only too well – the claustrophobic dark hallway with the narrow stairs; the through lounge and the kitchen across the back of the house with a back door leading to the small square of garden. He walked round the side of the house, his heart pounding in his chest. In the noisy isolation of his prison cell the image of his final confrontation with Jones had been magnified to epic proportions. This was going to be the climax. This would give him back his freedom.

He reached Jones's kitchen window and he stood there, staring in. He could see the man inside, sitting at the breakfast bar. Jones wasn't tall but he was overweight with a gut that spilled over his ill-fitting jeans. At almost sixty Jones should have known better than to wear a T-shirt with a risqué logo on it. He looked haggard, like a man with a great weight on his shoulders, and many years older than when they'd last met.

Suddenly Jones looked up and when he caught sight of Gordon his eyes widened in terror. The two men stared at each other for what seemed to Gordon like an age before

Jones shuffled to the back door and undid the lock. His face was ashen, like a man who had seen his own death and, for a split second, Gordon almost felt pity for him.

'When I heard you were out, I knew it wouldn't be long,' Jones whispered as Gordon stepped inside. Gordon opened his mouth to speak but Jones carried on. 'The wife guessed after I asked her to give me an alibi. She buggered off after the trial so I've been on my own with it . . . with that girl's ghost since . . .'

'So you'll tell the police what really happened?' Gordon hadn't expected it to be this easy. But, looking at Jones now, he knew that living with what he'd done had destroyed him. He hadn't gone to prison but, somehow, Jones had come off worst.

Jones grasped the material of Gordon's shirt. 'She said she'd tell everyone I tried to touch her. She kept on and on and in the end I just put my hands around her neck and squeezed.' He spoke vehemently, his face so close that Gordon could smell onions on his breath.

'You should have heard the filth she was coming out with. I just wanted her to stop. I'm not a pervert. I'd never have . . . She said if I didn't give her money she'd tell everyone I . . .'

Gordon took a step away, wondering why it was that all the bitter hatred he had felt in prison was melting away, only to be replaced by a sort of pity. 'Why me?' he asked in a whisper. 'What had I ever done to you?'

Jones shook his head, avoiding Gordon's eyes. 'It was nothing personal. You were just there and I was shit scared.'

Gordon saw tears streaming down Jones's face and he was torn between a desire to punch him and put a comforting hand on his shoulder.

'I'm sorry,' Jones sobbed as he sank to his knees, as though he was begging Gordon's forgiveness.

'You're going to tell the police.'

Harley Jones nodded meekly and a shudder went through his body.

Jones made no protest as Gordon picked up the telephone fixed to the wall nearby and dialled nine nine nine.

After the call was made, Gordon couldn't bring himself to stay there any longer with his betrayer. The police would sort out the mess from now on. That's what they were paid for. He walked out without another word, leaving Jones weeping pathetically on the hard, cold, kitchen floor.

When he returned to the car, Michele was still sitting in the passenger seat. Somehow he'd expected her to flee back into the underworld he'd imagined she came from. No questions asked, no explanations given.

'The police are coming,' he said to her gently. 'Do you want to wait or what?'

Michele nodded. And when the police turned up fifteen minutes later, they found Gordon Pledge sitting in his mother's four by four with a young woman, both staring ahead and not exchanging a word. And inside the house they found the body of Harley Jones hanging from the banisters.

'We need to see Caleb,' Joe said as they arrived back in the CID office. 'This whole thing revolves around him, I know it.'

'OK,' Emily replied. 'We'll let Brian Selly contemplate the error of his ways for a while. I've not had much to do with the Drifton Estate so far. I suppose it'll do me good to get to know more of my patch.'

'Can't do any harm,' Joe said. It was mainly uniform, the drug squad and CID's lower echelons who dealt with the relatively petty crime that dogged the Drifton Estate.

Caleb Selly's address was easy to find. Farley Rise was a

cul de sac of small, shabby council houses with scrubby front gardens and a generally uncared-for look. This was the Eborby the tourists didn't see.

The curtains of Selly's house were drawn over and as Joe pressed the doorbell, Emily went from window to window looking for a gap in the grubby, unlined drapes so that she could get a glimpse inside, but she had no luck. Joe pushed the doorbell three more times and heard the harsh jangling echoing inside.

'According to Brian, he never goes out,' said Joe.

'You believe him?'

Joe wasn't sure what to believe. It was always possible the Caleb Selly was now fitter than he'd been when Bridget Jervis had seen him and was capable of making his way to Singmass Close to re-enact the murders of his youth. But, on the other hand, according to Brian, he was physically frail and never left the house. Joe was impatient to find out which was true.

He lifted the letter box and looked inside at the hall. A couple of letters were lying on the floor – brightly coloured junk mail. And Joe was sure he could hear a faint sound coming from somewhere inside the house. Very low pitched and barely audible. A low buzzing like distant machinery. He let the letter box drop with a clatter and stood back, taking a deep breath, feeling the tingle of nerves in his fingers. It was a sound he'd heard before.

He told Emily to stand away from the door but she put a warning hand on his arm. 'You can cut out all that macho crap. The super's not going to be delighted if we go round smashing doors down.'

Joe ignored her and took a run for the door. It looked flimsy but the lock held and as he prepared to have another go, he felt Emily grab his wrist. 'Steady on, this needs a woman's touch,' she said, delving into her bag and drawing out a set of skeleton keys.

Joe stood aside, feeling a little foolish. He'd almost forgotten Emily's hidden talent. Passing the time of day with the burglars of Leeds had some uses. A minute later they were inside the house and Joe knew that his fears were about to be realised.

The buzzing seemed to come from the top of the stairs. Emily put the silk scarf she was wearing up to her nose, exchanging the scent of death for the sweet fragrance of Chanel. Joe knew what they were about to find and as he climbed the stairs slowly, almost catching his foot on the frayed carpet, he could hear Emily's footsteps behind him and drew some reassurance from the thought that he wasn't alone.

The old man lay on the landing, a look of desperation in his staring eyes, as though he was clutching at something just out of reach. He wore an ancient checked dressing gown, rough as an old horse blanket, and his head was twisted at an unnatural angle. Out of habit, Joe bowed his head and said a swift prayer for his soul. When he opened his eyes he saw that Emily was walking slowly round the body, shooing away the gathering flies with her hand.

Keeping his eyes on the corpse, Joe took his mobile phone from his pocket. 'It doesn't look suspicious to me but we'd better call the team out.'

'That Sally Sharpe'll be demanding overtime.' She smirked at Joe. 'But once she knows you're here, she'll turn up all the quicker.'

Joe felt his cheeks burning but he said nothing.

'We'd better tell Brian Selly his dad's dead and all. What's your money on then? Natural causes?'

Joe studied the corpse for a few seconds. 'There's nothing to suggest otherwise.' He leaned over and whispered in her ear. 'How about a little look round before the circus arrives?'

Emily's eyes met his and her face wrinkled up in a mischievous smile. 'Well he's in no fit state to ask us for a search warrant, is he? Come on. We'd better not be too long.'

Joe looked down at the body. Lying there dead, Caleb Selly looked frail and harmless. A shrunken old man robbed of all his muscle and aggression by anno domini. But once he had been young . . . and powerful. Once he had attacked Alice Meadows. And, if Joe was right, he had killed four women in cold blood way back in the 1950s.

Emily interrupted Joe's thoughts. 'Now we're here we might as well begin upstairs.'

The bathroom obviously hadn't been touched since the house was built but the two small bedrooms had had a fairly recent coat of magnolia paint. Perhaps Brian Selly had done some decorating for his father. But on the other hand, Joe thought, he had moaned enough about taking the old man to the dentist's so he couldn't imagine him making the effort to decorate his house.

In the bedrooms they made a quick search of the wardrobes and drawers. But there was no sign of any antique dolls – or anything else suspicious, come to that – and Joe felt a little disappointed. Perhaps Brian Selly had lied about getting those dolls from his father's house. Or perhaps Caleb Selly kept the things elsewhere.

They sidled round the body on the landing and made their way downstairs. In the claustrophobic living room Joe began to make a fruitless search of a massive dark wood sideboard while Emily concentrated on a plywood chest of drawers in the corner.

After five minutes he heard Emily say his name and, from the excitement in her voice, he knew she'd struck gold. 'Listen to this. This is to confirm that the students named below have been assigned to help decorate your

261

property as part of Hicklethorpe Manor School's Community Action programme. I feel it is vital that Hicklethorpe Manor students develop social awareness and contribute to the needs of the elderly and disabled in the local community and each year I pay a personal visit to those people who benefit in order to discuss the programme and any special requirements they may have. Please do not hesitate to contact me if you have any questions. Yours sincerely, Benjamin Cassidy, Headmaster.' She turned to Joe with a grin on her face. 'There were three students in all. There was an Andrew Young. And two girls. Guess what their names were.'

'Go on, surprise me.'

'Natalie Parkes and Karen Strange.'

Joe gave a low whistle. 'So Benjamin Cassidy must have come here to discuss the programme like the letter says.' He let the idea sink in for a while. 'He must have actually met Caleb Selly. Trouble is, there don't seem to be any dolls on the premises.'

'Perhaps those two we found at Brian Selly's house were the only ones left. Apart from the ones he left by the bodies of Natalie Parkes and Abigail Emson.'

'You still think Brian Selly did it?'

Joe watched Emily's expression as she considered the question. 'If his dad was really the original killer, perhaps he made some sort of confession to his son. Perhaps Brian had been fantasising about it for a while. Then Natalie presented herself; he knew her from the parties. And Abigail worked at the pub he drank in and she had a lonely walk home on her own past Singmass Close. Maybe he targeted both of them.'

Joe followed Emily's logic but he had a nagging suspicion that the letter she'd just found from Benjamin Cassidy was important somehow. Suddenly he heard the sound of a police car siren. It was nearby, probably outside in the street. Their impromptu search was over and from now on things would have to be done by the book. His eyes met Emily's and she winked at him.

'We'll make a more detailed search once they've dealt with the body,' he said. He knew Emily was as keen as he was to delve into the murky waters of Caleb Selly's private life.

Joe's mobile phone began to ring and after a short conversation he turned to Emily. 'Gordon Pledge has just been picked up. And guess who he was with. The missing girl, Michele Carden.'

Emily smiled. 'Well isn't life full of surprises?' she said as the police cars screeched to a halt outside in the street.

The killer had become used to the handwriting in the yellowed exercise book: an old person's hand, flourishing yet neat.

Old Caleb had killed four women back in the 1950s. And a year before the first death, he had made an abortive attempt to kill a girl called Alice who'd refused to dance with him. He had hacked off Alice's toe to ensure she'd never dance again but she had survived. That was before Caleb had hit on the idea of the dolls. It was the dolls that had brought him luck and made him invincible.

The killer didn't understand the bits Caleb wrote about the children; how they'd taunted him, daring him to kill, calling him names. He'd written that the children wanted vengeance and they'd used him as their instrument. The killer wondered who these children were. Had they been the local kids who'd lived on the close back then? Hardly. These children hadn't been ordinary. The way Caleb wrote about them, they sounded evil. But perhaps they'd just been in Caleb's head . . . part of his grisly fantasies.

But the little girl who'd been watching at the window of six Singmass Close was real enough and she must have seen everything on the night he'd killed Natalie. He'd looked up and he'd seen her face staring at him, pale as the moon. As far as the killer knew, she hadn't reported what she'd seen to the police yet. Perhaps her mother hadn't believed her or she hadn't wanted her to become involved. But nobody could rely on the silence of an unpredictable child for ever so she had to be dealt with. The great taboo had to be broken. And when it was, the nosy kid's silence would be of the permanent kind.

The killer closed Caleb's diary and then hid it in its special hiding place. The place where nobody ever looked. More than anything the killer needed to feel the power coursing through his veins again as the victim realised that death was inevitable.

Power like that was addictive. It made you feel alive.

Chapter 25

Michele Carden was home at last in the heart of her loving family. Or at least that was what Emily had been told by Jamilla, although she detected a note of cynicism behind her words. According to Jamilla, Michele's mother, rather than flinging her arms around her daughter in relief, had begun to scold her for going off without telling her and disrupting two important business meetings.

As soon as Emily got a whiff of this new development, she'd joined Jamilla at the Cardens' house, leaving Joe to supervise the search of Caleb Selly's premises. Michele had poured out the whole story to Jamilla over tea and biscuits in their top-of-the-range kitchen. How she had been tricked by Sylvia Pledge – who'd called herself Palmer – into believing she was about to be signed up for a modelling agency; how she'd been persuaded to stay with elaborate promises before being drugged and kept there against her will to do the housework and look after Sylvia's bedridden mother, Alice.

Then Michele revealed something far more disturbing, as though she was keeping the best till last. She had found the body of a young girl of around her own age in a freezer in the lean-to off the kitchen. Once she'd made this discovery, she'd become terrified of what the Pledges might do if she tried to escape.

And besides, she added gruffly, by then she'd become quite concerned about Alice. Sylvia had kept Alice drugged but, whenever possible, Michele had exchanged the drugged food for the food eaten by the rest of the household so that she was able to get some sense out of the old lady.

Emily noticed how Michele's eyes softened when she spoke of Alice and she let the girl continue with her story. She had learned secrets from Alice; terrible things that had happened to her many years ago. When she was young, a man had tried to strangle her and had chopped off her toe.

'Where were you when we came to the farmhouse and searched the place?' Emily asked, curious.

'I saw you arrive and I was planning to attract your attention somehow. But Sylvia pushed me into the car boot and shut it. She must have put something in my drink because I slept for ages. I think I must have been there all night and when the car started I thought they were taking me somewhere to kill me.' She shuddered dramatically.

She told Emily and Jamilla how she'd been terrified when Gordon had opened the boot, but he'd told her that she was free to go if she wanted. Then he'd called the police and all hell broke loose. Things had happened that she didn't understand. She'd even heard that a man had been found hanged. She looked at them keenly, hoping they'd fill her in on the things she didn't know about. But Emily said nothing. The details could wait.

Emily knew that the Pledges were now in custody and Social Services had taken charge of Alice. Police had swarmed all over the farmhouse and had found the girl's body in the freezer. Sylvia Pledge had told the officers that the dead girl had worked for her and that she'd fallen down the cellar steps and died accidentally. Even though the girl's death hadn't been their fault, Sylvia said self-righteously, they'd panicked and hid the body from the authorities, knowing the police would jump to the wrong conclusion: just look what had happened to their Gordon.

Emily wasn't sure whether to believe her story, but no doubt the truth would come out when Sally Sharpe conducted the post-mortem. In the meantime Sylvia and Barry were being charged with false imprisonment and concealing a death . . . which was plenty to be going on with.

The discovery of Michele Carden, safe and well, and Gordon Pledge's rearrest had been a temporary distraction from the investigations at Caleb Selly's house. When Emily returned from the Cardens' at four o'clock Joe met her in Caleb Selly's small front garden.

Joe saw her glance at her watch as she walked up the path. 'Jeff's promised to make me steak and chips when I get in,' she said wistfully.

'At least the Gordon Pledge business has been cleared up,' he said, a sudden vision of Polly flashing across his brain. He wondered if she'd be reconciled with Gordon if and when his innocence was confirmed. But he told himself firmly that it was none of his business. 'What have the Pledges got to say for themselves?' he asked Emily. 'What made them hold that girl prisoner?'

Emily shrugged. 'They say they were desperate for help in the house and they'd run out of money to pay anyone because they'd spent all their cash on Gordon's defence. Apparently Sylvia couldn't stand the thought of her inheritance from Alice going down the drain paying for a nursing home.'

'Didn't stop her driving round in that flash car and going around all dolled up.'

'She likes the good things in life does our Sylvia. Apparently she tricked Michele into working there – said she could offer her modelling work. Then she was drugged and locked up so she couldn't escape. It all got out of hand.'

'Oh, Sylvia'll find some way to justify it to herself.'

'She must be mad,' Emily said with a sigh.

'The capacity of human beings to fool themselves that what they're doing isn't wrong never ceases to amaze me,' said Joe quietly.

Emily smiled. 'We're getting a bit philosophical, aren't we?'

As Joe led the way into Caleb Selly's house he noticed that the weak sunlight had lured the neighbours from the comfort of their sofas. Kids in fake designer sportswear were haring up and down the street on bikes while their mothers, tattooed arms folded, were leaning on gates, chatting as they enjoyed the excitement. They stopped and stared like curious cattle as the uniformed officer on duty lifted the crime scene tape to admit Joe and Emily to the house.

Joe knew that three DCs under the supervision of Sunny Porter had just completed a search of the premises and when Sunny came out into the hall to greet them he wore an expression of suppressed excitement, like a child who is in possession of some wonderful secret.

'Well,' said Joe. 'What have you found?'

'You're not going to believe this.'

'Try us,' said Emily.

Sunny produced a plastic box from behind his back. 'We found this in the attic. Four silk stockings – or at least Forensic reckon they're silk. And these wrapped in tissue paper.' He wrinkled his nose as he held out the open box for them to examine. 'Look like big toes if you ask me.'

Joe saw that Emily had taken a step back, distancing herself from whatever the box contained. He steeled himself and put on a pair of plastic gloves before taking the box from Sunny. Sure enough, there were four objects inside which could have been either thumbs or big toes.

'Oh bloody hell, take it away,' said Emily. 'Give it to Forensics . . . they like that sort of thing.'

But Joe was staring at the things in the box, fascinated. The objects rather reminded him of some obscure pickled vegetable you might find in an exclusive delicatessen. 'I think they've been pickled,' he said. 'Some kind of alcohol by the smell. Find anything else?'

Sunny nodded enthusiastically. 'You should see the attic. Loads of them horrible dolls . . . all staring down with their beady glass eyes.' He looked at Emily. 'There's a loft ladder, ma'am. Not too hard to get up there.'

'Thanks a lot,' she muttered under her breath. 'You go and have a look will you, Joe.'

Joe followed Sunny up the stairs, leaving Emily in the hall. He climbed the loft ladder and when he reached the top he looked around the attic. Sunny was right. There were about twenty dolls up there, sitting in rows on metal shelving.

'He must have collected them,' shouted Sunny who had stayed on the landing. 'Probably pinched them from the dolls' hospital while that Jervis wasn't looking.'

Joe made his way down the ladder. 'Probably,' he agreed as he joined Sunny on terra firma. He saw that Emily had come up the stairs and was standing beside Sunny, awaiting the verdict.

'There's just one thing that's a bit worrying,' said Joe.

'And what's that?'

'Well, they're sitting in rows on the shelves but it looks as if some are missing. It's pretty dusty up there and you can see where they've been. They've been moved recently.'

Emily looked at him, worried. 'How many?'

'As far as I can see there are six missing. Someone's trying to outdo the Doll Strangler.'

Joe turned to Sunny. 'I think we need to see Brian Selly again. Now.'

Polly heard it on the radio. Child killer Gordon Pledge had been rearrested near his old home. Another man was found dead at the scene.

It was almost as if they were talking in code. What man? And how did he die? Had Gordon killed again?

'Mummy. I want to go home. Mary's lonely – I know she is.'

Daisy was sitting on the floor, looking up at her with reproachful eyes. Mary again. She bit back the impatient remark that was forming on her lips.

She was getting sick of Yolanda's flat – and a little tired of Yolanda if the truth were known. And Gordon was safely behind bars again so there was no chance he could come and find them now.

'OK, love. We'll go back.'

She saw Daisy's face light up with a blissful smile.

The cathedral's bells were ringing out for Evensong as Philip Derby picked up the phone. He'd been on edge since he'd had the call from Brian Selly to say that the police had searched his house but now his hands were shaking. It would only be a matter of time before they came back and searched his place more thoroughly. The police had taken some of his DVDs but they had been the tame ones taken at the parties. There were others that he kept well hidden . . . and they were the ones he didn't particularly want the police to see. He was reluctant to destroy them so he'd have to find somewhere safe to keep them, somewhere they wouldn't think to look, until the fuss died down.

He held the phone to his ear while it rang out at the other end. He needed to speak to Ben Cassidy. Needed to extricate himself from this sorry mess.

'Ben, is that you?' he asked when he heard a voice on the other end of the line.

'Who else would it be? What do you want, Philip?' He sounded wary, as if Derby was the last person he wanted to speak to at that moment.

'Brian Selly's been arrested . . . for killing Natalie.'

For a few seconds Cassidy said nothing. Then 'They've got nothing on us, Philip. They know about the parties but that's all. They don't have to know how far things went and they can't prove a thing if we just stay calm.'

'They might start digging.'

'You're panicking, Philip,' said Cassidy, his voice rising a pitch. Derby knew he was starting to lose his cool. 'I'm not panicking. I've lost my job and my reputation because of that silly little bitch but I'm not panicking.'

There was a long pause. Then Derby spoke again, putting into words the question that was gnawing at his mind. 'Did you kill her, Ben? Did she go too far and . . .?'

Philip Derby suddenly heard the dialling tone. Benjamin Cassidy had rung off.

As the box containing the stockings and preserved body parts was placed in front of him, Brian Selly gave it a casual glance and shook his head.

'We have evidence that your father killed four women back in the nineteen fifties, Brian.' Joe sat back and waited for a reaction.

'No comment.' Selly leaned back and stared into Joe's eyes, challenging him to a duel of wills.

'There's a collection of antique dolls in his attic. Did you ever go up there?'

'No.'

'You said the dolls at your house belonged to your father. You must have got them from the attic.'

'They were in the dining room. I took 'em from the dining room.'

'And you've never seen this box before?'

Selly shook his head. 'I've just lost my father and you're just sitting there accusing him of being a killer. It's not right.'

'Neither is killing innocent women,' Joe snapped. He glanced at Sunny Porter who was sitting by his side, looking as though he was dying for a smoke. Emily had gone upstairs to bring the super up to date with developments, muttering something about steak and chips. Joe too realised that he was hungry. But then that was his own fault. He'd volunteered to interview Selly but now he was beginning to regret it. The man wasn't talking and, although they had plenty of evidence against the father, the evidence against the son was purely circumstantial – nothing that would stand up in court.

Jack the Ripper had had a double event . . . so why shouldn't it happen in modern-day Eborby? Two for the price of one.

It was getting dark and the archway leading into Singmass Close from Andrewgate was in deep shadow. The woman who always wore black as though she was in perpetual mourning had just returned to number six with her brat in tow – and the killer had watched as she opened the front door. She'd been smiling and she looked relieved, happy.

But that would soon change.

Chapter 26

The next morning Emily arrived in the office, remark- ably cheerful, in spite of the fact that Brian Selly, her chief suspect, had been released on bail because they hadn't enough evidence to charge him. But when Joe went to see her just before the morning briefing, he discovered the reason for her good mood.

'This has just come in,' she said, handing him a sheet of paper, her eyes twinkling. 'Fingerprints found at Caleb Selly's loft. Spot the interesting names?'

Joe smiled as he read the list. 'Caleb Selly was there of course. And Brian Selly. Philip Derby's prints were there too. And Benjamin Cassidy's.'

'Brian Selly claimed he'd never been up there. And what the hell were Philip Derby and Benjamin Cassidy doing up in Caleb Selly's loft?'

'Collecting dolls to leave next to the bodies of their victims?' Joe suggested, half flippantly. 'It says here there were also some unidentified prints.'

'Could be anyone. Some plumber or builder who's done some work up there maybe.'

'It'll be interesting to see what Derby and Cassidy have got to say for themselves. I take it Gordon Pledge is out of the frame for this.'

He saw Emily nod. 'He didn't even know his estranged

wife was renting a house in Singmass Close – wasn't even sure where it was. There's absolutely no evidence that he ever knew Caleb Selly. And as it looks like he didn't kill Francesca Putney . . .' She didn't finish the sentence. Gordon Pledge could probably be struck from their list. She looked up at Joe. He could see the frustration in her eyes. 'Oh Joe, this should be so straightforward now we've discovered the source of the dolls. But we keep going round in bloody circles like flaming flies around a light bulb. If we could just nail Brian Selly . . .'

Joe sat down and considered the matter for a few moments. 'I want to know about Derby and Cassidy's involvement.'

Emily stood up. 'It's about time Selly suffered a bit more police harassment, don't you think?'

Joe felt uncomfortable. If Emily pushed things too far with Selly, it could be counter-productive.

'Isn't your Maddy back today?'

Joe looked at her, surprised at the sudden change of subject. 'Late afternoon.' When he'd called her briefly the night before just to confirm her plans, she hadn't mentioned the job in London and neither had he. Although it had been suspended between them like a rotting cadaver dangling on the end of a noose.

Emily gave him her version of a sympathetic smile, so quick he might have missed it if he hadn't been looking at her. 'I've got to see the super . . . report on our progress. Why don't you go and have another word with Selly?' She grinned. 'And if we're lucky, he might even want you to hear his confession.'

Joe forced himself to smile even though he'd heard Emily's joke many times before.

Half an hour later Joe found himself in Abbotsthorpe, parked in front of Brian Selly's house. Selly's car wasn't there so he assumed that, as his father had just died, there would be arrangements to make: funeral directors and paperwork. But when he called at the house, the mousy Mrs Selly said that Brian had gone to work. Saturday was his busiest day. He hadn't been close to his father so he saw no point in taking time off and wasting his precious holiday entitlement. Joe tried not to show his surprise, asking instead for the address of Brian's work and promising to be discretion itself. Brian Selly's colleagues wouldn't even know the police had called.

Brian Selly was manager of a car showroom – the Mercedes place on the Tadcaster Road, which explained the shiny new black saloon he drove. Joe parked outside the showroom, experiencing a prickle of envy as he ran his eyes over the gleaming lumps of expensive metal on the forecourt. He gave his name to the receptionist but left out his rank. He wanted to gain Selly's confidence and catch him off his guard.

He found Selly sitting in his office, smart in red tie and shirt sleeves, his suit jacket flung casually over the back of his chair.

He looked up at Joe and scowled. 'Look, I've told you everything I know. And if you weren't so bloody incompetent you'd know I'm telling the truth.'

'I won't keep you long – promise.'

Joe's attitude took the wind out of Selly's sails, which was the intention. It's hard to argue with someone who's being calm, reasonable and apologetic. He sat back. 'Go on then.'

'In your statement you said you had never been up in your father's attic.'

'Well . . . er . . . I didn't say I'd never been up there. I just didn't make a habit of it.'

Joe decided not to comment on this change of direction. 'We found a number of fingerprints up there.

Actually I think you know the people from your . . . er . . . parties. Philip Derby?' He tilted his head to one side expectantly and waited for an explanation.

Brian Selly suddenly came over all co-operative. 'I asked him if he could come and have a look at some of dad's old books. He bought the lot for fifty quid.'

'They were in the attic?'

'That's right. Like I said, he went up there to have a look at them and he bought the lot.'

'And what about Benjamin Cassidy?'

Selly snorted. 'The headmaster.' An unpleasant smirk spread across his face.

'He visited your father?'

'Yeah . . . something about his kids doing decorating for old folk.'

'Why did he go up into the attic?'

Brian Selly frowned and shook his head. 'Search me.'

An hour later Joe Plantagenet was standing on the threshold of Benjamin Cassidy's flat. It was a spacious apartment, occupying the entire ground floor of an elegant Georgian house; a home fit for the headmaster of a prestigious school, an upright pillar of the community. But maybe now Cassidy's furtive sexual tastes had been exposed he'd probably choose to move on.

Joe could say one thing for Cassidy, he was putting on a brave face. From his manner nobody would ever guess at his disgrace. He had all the front of a professional politician caught with one hand in the till and the other up his mistress's skirt. He gave Joe a businesslike smile but didn't invite him in until Joe asked if they could talk indoors. He wasn't going to be kept on the doorstep like a naughty schoolboy.

When they were in the drawing room Cassidy sat on the sofa, his fingers arched and an expression of polite expectation on his face. He still looked every inch the headmaster even though he'd now been forced to resign. Perhaps, Joe thought, he'd never be able to break the habit.

'I'll come straight to the point,' Joe began. 'We have reason to believe a man called Edward Caleb Selly killed four women in the Singmass Close area in the nineteen fifties. You know his son – Brian Selly.'

Cassidy looked wary. 'I don't see what this has to do with me?'

'You also knew Edward Caleb Selly. You wrote to him.'

'I don't think so.'

Joe produced the clear plastic folder containing the letter and passed it to him. He noticed the relief on the man's face as he scanned it.

'My secretary wrote these letters. I just signed them. I can't possibly remember everyone we contacted as part of the community project.'

'The letter clearly states that you visit the old people involved in the project.' Cassidy spread his hands as though conceding Joe the point. 'And you must remember Caleb Selly. You went up into his loft. And before you deny it, we found your fingerprints up there. Along with his collection of antique dolls. Some of those dolls were taken, Mr Cassidy.' Another pause for effect. Joe was starting to enjoy this. 'And those dolls were found next to the two girls killed in Singmass Close. We found other items on the premises as well. Stockings that had been used to strangle the victims . . . and body parts.'

The last words made Cassidy turn pale. He leaned forward, the nonchalant manner suddenly gone. 'Look, Inspector, I'd hardly have allowed my students to decorate his house if I'd known he was some sort of serial killer. We do have a strict child protection policy in place at Hicklethorpe Manor.'

'And you've always taken your responsibility for your students so seriously, haven't you, Mr Cassidy? Especially the female ones.' Joe knew this last remark was wicked, but sometimes temptation is hard to resist.

Cassidy's face turned beetroot red and he blustered for a few seconds. Then he took a deep breath. 'Natalie Parkes was over eighteen and she was hardly an innocent victim, I assure you.' He leaned further forward, man to man. 'In fact I'd say that she took the lead . . . if you see what I mean.'

Joe ignored the remark. 'Tell me about the community project. Was there any particular reason why Natalie and Karen Strange were assigned to Selly's house?'

'They were friends. We tried to keep friends together. There was a boy there too. Andrew Young.'

'I'd like to talk to him.'

Cassidy gave a bitter smile. 'You're asking the wrong person, Inspector. I'm no longer in charge at Hicklethorpe Manor. You'll have to ask my deputy. Sorry, I mean the acting head . . . Mrs Walton. But I'm sure there'll be no problem. The boy's over eighteen.'

Just like Natalie, Joe thought as he took his leave. But he said nothing. Cassidy had begun to pay for his stupidity. And things could only get worse. However, Joe found it impossible to feel sorry for him.

The killer turned the pages of the exercise book he'd found in the house, covered with Caleb Selly's neat, almost childish handwriting.

Marion never suspected a thing. She even smiled when she told me to get lost. I had the stocking in my pocket and I could feel it, soft and slippery in my fingers. I waited until she'd turned away. I couldn't do it if she was facing me, looking into my eyes. I felt this power welling up inside me

*just like I'd felt when Alice started to walk away from me.
How I'd wanted to dance with Alice. How I'd wanted to
kiss her and feel her little breasts but she wasn't having any
of it. I had the stockings I'd bought for her in my pocket –
real silk – but she told me to stuff them. She was a married
woman, she said. And there was no way she'd ever fancy a
man who was pig ugly and played with bloody dolls for a
living anyroad.*

*When she started to walk away the children began
laughing and giggling. 'She doesn't like you, Caleb. She
thinks you're pig ugly. You play with dolls, Caleb.' Giggle,
giggle. How I wanted to kill them – to shut their stupid
mouths.*

*I felt this fury inside and before I knew it, I'd taken the
stocking out of my pocket. I ran after her and saw that she
was smirking like them – like the kids. She told me to take a
running jump but I put the stocking round her neck and
squeezed. When she fell to the ground I thought she were
dead and I felt so glad, like I'd got rid of their voices out of
my head. Like they'd seen what I could do and now they'd
leave me alone.*

*Then I saw that her shoe had come off and I could see
her bare foot. It were so perfect . . . like one of those
sculptures in the art gallery. All pale and perfect. She'd loved
dancing but she'd never dance with me . . . never. And that
one time I asked her she'd just laughed at me. I don't know
why I took my knife from my pocket and cut off her big toe
but it felt right. She'd never dance with me so I made sure
she'd never dance again. I'd worked in a butcher's once and I
knew how to cut between the bones so it was easy. She'd
never bloody dance again. Never.*

Caleb had written it all down. His thoughts. His feelings.
Everything he'd done. And the killer had read it through
so many times. It had started when Alice Meadows had

279

rejected his advances. Alice had survived somehow. But with the others he'd made sure he'd done the job properly.

It was time to arrange things, to send the e-mail. 'From Dead Dolls. Double Event Tonight'.

Chapter 27

Jamilla had received her orders from Joe. She was to go to Bacombe and have another word with Karen Strange. It was Saturday so she'd probably find her in.

It was Karen herself who answered the door. Jamilla thought she looked nervous. But then a week ago her best friend had been murdered and that would be enough to shake anybody.

Jamilla smiled to put the girl at her ease. 'Don't worry, Karen. It's just routine. I'd like to talk about the community work you did back in the summer. You did some decorating for the elderly on the Drifton Estate, I believe?'

Karen nodded.

'You decorated the house of a man called Selly.'

Karen wrinkled her nose. 'I remember. The place bloody stank.'

'You were with Natalie and a boy called Andrew Young.'

'That's right.'

'Did any of you go up into the attic?'

'Andy did, I think. He was looking for something we could use as dust sheets.'

'Did Andrew say he'd seen anything unusual in the attic?' Jamilla watched the girl's face. She'd been surprised and rather appalled when she'd heard about the dolls in the attic. She'd always loved dolls when she was small but since she'd been involved in this case, she'd begun to regard her former playthings as slightly sinister. The association with violent, perverted death had ruined their innocence for ever.

Karen shrugged. 'He said he'd seen some dolls up there. He said they were antiques . . . probably worth a bit. He said the old bloke probably didn't realise how much they'd fetch.'

'Anything else you can tell me?'

Karen shook her head.

'It was bloody hard work, specially when Andrew made himself scarce. Said he had a stomach bug. Left me and Nat to it.'

'How did you cope on your own?'

Karen gave Jamilla a withering look. 'Most of the work had been done by then. It wasn't a problem.'

'You didn't ask your brother to help? If he was at a loose end and . . .'

Karen's eyes widened for a second. 'No. I told you. We did it on our own . . . me and Nat.'

'Did Mr Cassidy call in?'

She rolled her eyes. 'Yeah. He liked to suck up to the old codgers . . . get his face in the local paper. Saint Benjamin. If only they knew.' She shook her head, a smirk spreading across her face. 'I still can't get over Natalie and those parties. I mean, she kept it all so quiet. And with Cassidy.' She wrinkled her nose with disgust. 'Screwing bloody Cassidy.' She glanced at the clock. 'Look, is that all? I've got revision to do.'

Jamilla knew when she was being dismissed. And she knew she wasn't likely to get anything useful out of Karen Strange just at that moment.

So once she was outside the house, she took out her mobile phone and made a call to Inspector Plantagenet.

But she wished she hadn't bothered when he gave her more work to do. He wanted her to visit two old ladies who lived in Caleb Selly's street. At least there, she thought, she'd probably be offered a cup of tea.

Confessing to Joe Plantagenet that she'd lied to him and that she was, in fact, Gordon Pledge's estranged wife had taken courage. But Polly had felt the need to call him, to find out what she could about Gordon and ask him about the man who'd been found dead at the scene of his arrest.

She had been surprised that he already knew about her deception. And he also said that he'd been looking for her, which gave her a small glow of satisfaction. She'd explained that she'd needed to get away, that she hadn't felt safe while Gordon was at large. Joe had seemed to understand.

The little house in Singmass Close had never seemed like home to her. Perhaps it was because it was rented. Or perhaps it was because it had a strange atmosphere. She hadn't believed in ghosts until she'd lived there but now her mind was open to all sorts of possibilities. Or it could be all Yolanda's talk of the supernatural that was making her over-imaginative.

Now that Gordon had been rearrested she felt she could relax, although Joe Plantagenet had told her that he had been given leave to appeal against his conviction. The man found dead at the scene had apparently committed suicide. Gordon hadn't killed him and she felt more relieved at this news than she'd expected. She found herself hoping that Joe would make the effort to keep in touch. He was different. He had understood and hadn't threatened her with punishment for lying. Perhaps it had been a mistake not to tell him the truth about Gordon from the beginning.

She watched as Daisy played on the floor in front of her

dolls' house, keeping up a constant narrative, asking Mary questions and listening carefully to answers only she could hear.

She walked over to the front window and stared out at Singmass Close through the thin layer of muslin. The flowers still lay where those girls had died. For a while she'd feared that Gordon might have killed them; that he had found out where she lived and done it in front of her house as some sort of awful, twisted warning. She'd reasoned that if Gordon had killed Francesca, he was capable of killing again, especially after spending time in prison in the company of other killers, fuelling each others' violent fantasies. They say prison changes people.

With hindsight she should have known from the beginning that Gordon hadn't killed the girls in the close. Daisy insisted that Mary had seen the first one die and she hadn't said that it was Daisy's daddy who killed her. Perhaps she should have believed Daisy's little ghost.

It had begun to rain on the dying flowers. On Monday Polly would return to work and Daisy would start school again after half term. On Monday things would be back to normal.

As for Gordon, Polly would treat herself to a bottle of wine that evening and contemplate the problem.

Caleb Selly's neighbours, Vera and Doris, had taken a liking to Jamilla, offering tea, asking her about her family and her job and telling her all about their grandchildren, illustrating their revelations with photographs.

Of course they remembered those kids from Hicklethorpe Manor who'd done that decorating for them. Not that some of the kids looked too delighted about it: positively sullen some of them were. Doris was surprised that Mr Selly had accepted their help, being rather a recluse and very odd with that big birthmark on his cheek. They were sorry he was dead, of course, but he'd kept himself to himself, never saying a word to any of the neighbours from one year to the next. Jamilla hadn't mentioned Selly's murderous past. The ladies would read about it soon enough in the tabloids – all the details the police knew and probably a few more besides from the journalists' fertile imagination.

Eventually Jamilla steered the conversation round to the students who had come to do their decorating. Vera and Doris said they were a couple of stuck-up little madams who hardly said a word to the old folk and spent a lot of time complaining. But the other one was all right . . . positively chatty compared to the madams and very appreciative of Vera's fruit cake. And that headmaster, Mr Cassidy, had called in a couple of times – such a nice man.

When Jamilla returned to the police station, her stomach filled with tea and fruit cake served in the traditional local manner with a slice of Wensleydale cheese, she made straight for Joe's office. He was closeted in there with Emily and they looked up as she came in.

'Well,' Joe said as soon as she crossed the threshold. 'How did you get on?'

'Very well,' she said. 'The girls and Cassidy weren't the only ones who visited Caleb Selly's house during the community project. Someone stepped in to help finish the decorating.'

'Go on,' said Emily. 'Who was it?'

Jamilla felt rather pleased with herself as she said the name and saw the look of excitement on the DCI's face.

Emily stood up. 'We'd better get over there,' she said with more than a hint of urgency.

Jamilla watched as she swept out of the office with Joe following close behind, and felt a warm glow of job satisfaction.

*

When Joe and Emily reached Brett Bluit's house there was nobody at home and Emily was almost tempted to kick the door in frustration. This was the best lead they'd had in ages. But she controlled her destructive urges.

'How about breaking in?' she said, giving the door a gentle push.

'Without a search warrant?' Joe's eyes met hers in mutual understanding. 'I think in view of what Jamilla's just told us, we'd be neglecting our duty to the public if we didn't take a little look.' He grinned. 'Have you still got those skeleton keys in that handbag of yours?'

Emily hesitated. She had never been one for doing things strictly by the book – that was how she had managed such a good clear-up rate back in Leeds. But this was rather blatant even by her standards. And Joe was egging her on.

She fished the keys from the depths of her bag and they walked round to the back of the house. She jiggled the key in the lock and the back door swung open. 'Some people never learn about security,' Emily observed with a wink. When they reached the bedroom they found the computer switched on. Emily put her hand on the mouse and clicked until the e-mails appeared.

'Bloody hell, Joe,' she whispered. 'Dead Dolls. This is it.'

She felt Joe's hand on her shoulder and she took a deep calming breath. When she looked down at her hands she saw they were shaking. They were in the killer's room. Reading the killer's e-mails.

'Who's it addressed to?'

'Someone calling themselves Alice.' Emily clicked on the message. 'Witness elimination tonight. Double event. Caleb.' She looked up at Joe. 'What witness? Someone who lives in Singmass Close?'

'It must be.'

'This Alice can't be Alice Meadows. There's no way she could . . .'

'Hardly. She wouldn't know one end of a computer from another. Anyway, she's safe in a nursing home and Selly's dead.' He thought for a moment. 'This means our friend knows all the details of Caleb's crimes, including the first unsuccessful attack on Alice Meadows. And he's not working alone. That's something we never considered till now.'

Emily sighed. 'Perhaps we should have, Joe. They've been running rings round us.'

They began to search the room, opening drawers and cupboards, then shutting them carefully. It wasn't long before Joe found a large wooden box on top of the wardrobe. He took it down and Emily held her breath while he opened it. Inside were four dolls lying squashed up to each other, their dresses crushed and their hair matted. Next to them was a silk stocking, stretched out of shape. And next to that was a smaller box – a plastic ice-cream tub with some kind of liquid inside. He didn't bother opening it. He knew what it contained.

Emily leaned forward and picked up an old exercise book that lay on top of the dolls. She began to flick through it, stopping to read at the last page.

'Caleb wrote it all down,' she whispered. 'Brett must have found this in his house along with the dolls when he was helping with the decorating. He's copied the lot . . . can't even think up an original idea.'

'He's got something planned for tonight.' Joe sounded worried.

'He'll be picked up well before then,' Emily said with confidence.

After making sure everything was exactly as they found it, they sneaked out, locking the door behind them.

Chapter 28

'It's a joke,' said Sunny Porter. 'It's a bloody joke. It must be.'

Joe shook his head. There were times when Sunny got on his nerves and this was one of them.

'You mean we've got to stop up half the night? Bloody great.'

Joe turned away. Brett hadn't returned home and there was no sign of him in any of his usual haunts. He was out there somewhere and so was his accomplice. And nobody had any idea where he'd got to.

'We've no choice, Sunny. Unless he turns up in the meantime, we'll have to stake out Singmass Close. That's where it'll happen and I intend to be there waiting for them.'

'You're sure?' Sunny sounded doubtful.

'I've seen his e-mails. It's planned for tonight.' He looked at Sunny and regretted his sharpness. Sunny was exhausted by a week of eighteen-hour days . . . as they all were.

Half an hour earlier Maddy had called to ask if he'd be able to meet her from the station. He'd been at his most apologetic as he'd told her he was tied up with the case. She'd put the phone down without a word. But there was nothing he could do about it so he tried to put her out of his mind.

He looked round and saw that Jamilla was standing near his desk looking concerned. 'How did you and DCI Thwaite come by this information, sir?'

It was a good question but one he wished Jamilla hadn't asked. 'A tip-off,' he said quickly, hoping she'd be satisfied with the vague answer.

Sunny stomped away, no doubt to call his wife to tell her he'd be home late, and Jamilla gave Joe a shy smile. 'I don't fancy being round that close in the dark. It gives me the creeps.'

Jamilla was right. There was something about Singmass Close that made him uncomfortable. But perhaps it was just the place's association with murder. 'Don't worry, we'll get them tonight,' Joe said with a confidence he didn't feel and Jamilla gave him a wan smile in return.

The killers had to be put out of action tonight. They couldn't be allowed to kill again.

Polly knelt by Daisy's bed and watched her daughter as she slept, listening to her breathing, suddenly overwhelmed by a feeling of deep love as she put out a hand to stroke her hair. Daisy shifted slightly at her touch and hugged her doll, closer to her. Polly took a last look at the sleeping child in the bed and tiptoed out of the room.

She'd already checked the house was secure and now she undressed slowly, examining her naked reflection in the dressing-table mirror. It was hard to judge these things, but she was sure that she was still desirable; the way that policeman – DI Plantagenet – had looked at her told her that. He had made her feel human again. Not just like the wife of a murderer trying to hide herself and her child from the world.

She slipped into her pyjamas and went to the window, peeping out between the curtains at the close below. There were still lights in some windows – her elderly neighbours sometimes kept late hours. It was no longer raining and the cellophane on the dying shrine flowers shifted in the gentle breeze, catching the light from the old-fashioned street lamps, glistening like diamonds on the grey pavement.

Polly climbed into bed and turned out the bedside light. Then, as she closed her eyes and drifted off to sleep she imagined she heard a faint rustle on the landing. Mary's rustle.

How she wished that child would go away.

Only the chiming of the cathedral clock broke the pall of silence that had fallen over Singmass Close. As Joe had passed beneath the archway leading from one world to another, he had heard the sound of drunken singing – students on their way home from an evening of curry and karaoke at one of the pubs down Gallowgate. But then everything had been quiet and it felt as if the city had fallen into a deep sleep.

Once in Singmass Close, he stuck to the shadows, positioning himself in the darkness underneath the scaffolding that surrounded the old Ragged School, not far from the spot where Abigail Emson had died. From there he had a good view of the close and he could just see that number six was in darkness. He presumed Polly had returned there for good. Perhaps when this business was over – when they'd flushed out the killer – he'd make contact again just to make sure she was all right.

He heard footsteps, soft and furtive, and he flattened himself against the wall. But when a shadowy figure emerged from the archway, he saw that it was Emily. She was clutching her handbag close to her body and when Joe stepped out of the gloom she jumped.

'Bloody hell, Joe, you nearly frightened the life out of me,' she whispered, her hand to her chest as though to still her pounding heart.

'Everyone's been on standby since sunset.' Joe looked round. The officers keeping watch on the close were keeping well hidden.

'Any sign of activity?'

Joe shook his head. 'Quiet as the grave,' he said, immediately regretting his words. Talking of graves might be tempting fate.

'I take it we've got people posted round the back?'

Joe was suddenly assailed by doubts. What if the killer had changed his plans? What if he'd guessed the police were onto him? What if he'd made plans to strike somewhere else in the city since Joe and Emily had read that incriminating e-mail?

He looked at his watch. Five to midnight and there wasn't a movement in the close.

Emily suddenly put out her hand and clutched his arm. 'Did you hear that?'

Joe shook his head. He hadn't heard a thing.

'It was like a muffled scream.' Joe saw Emily freeze, listening, like a native tracker in some forest, listening for distant wild beasts. 'There it is again. Where's it coming from?'

'He can't have got in without being seen. No way.'

'Unless he walks through walls.'

Joe felt the blood draining from his face. 'He – or they – might have got in there early this afternoon, before we ever arrived.' He was cross with himself for not considering this possibility earlier. He cursed his stupidity and one look at Emily's face told him that she was thinking the same. 'We assumed he'd go back home for the dolls but . . .'

There it was again. A plaintive cry. Joe stepped out of the shadows to get a better view of the close. Then there was a sudden bang, as though someone had knocked a dustbin over. The sound came from behind the houses

291

that backed onto the old chapel. Joe and Emily edged forward. If they were right, they might just be in time to save someone's life.

Then Emily gave Joe a nudge as a ginger tom cat prowled across the flagstones as if it owned the place. They looked at each other and smiled, suddenly relaxing after the tension.

For ten minutes they listened to the sounds of the sleepy city: distant traffic, an ambulance siren shattering the night-time peace as it made for the hospital; more amorous cats; a snatch of drunken shouting from outside one of Gallowgate's many pubs. But Singmass Close was silent. Until they heard a thud, like something being kicked against a wall, followed by a muffled cry.

Suddenly the front door of number seven opened to reveal a small figure. An elderly lady in hairnet and quilted dressing gown. She looked up and down the close then at the house next door.

Joe began to run towards her, Emily puffing behind him. The woman looked alarmed and was about to close the door when he held up his warrant card. When she saw it, the door opened wide.

'I heard a noise from next door,' the woman said, suddenly garrulous. 'Like there's a fight going on. I heard she was married to that escaped murderer so I thought . . .'

Joe's heart began to pound. Word had got round fast. But whoever Polly was fighting with, it wasn't her husband Gordon. As far as he knew, she was in there alone with little Daisy. He fumbled for his radio. 'Number six. Break the door down if necessary but get in there now.'

Suddenly the close was alive with police officers, all making for number six. Sunny Porter was first at the door, playing the hero to little effect. It was Jamilla Dal, accompanied by a couple of uniformed constables, who got in there first by breaking a window in the back door and turning the key in the lock.

Joe and Emily dashed round to the side of the house to join her and the broken glass crunched beneath their feet as they stumbled into the kitchen. Joe signalled everyone to keep back. Going in mob-handed could be a mistake in a delicate situation. And this one could be very delicate indeed.

He crept forward. There it was again, the noise, like a muffled scream, cut off suddenly.

'I'm going up,' he whispered to Emily before climbing the stairs, two at a time. When he found himself on the landing all the bedrooms were in darkness. But when he heard a thud coming from the one on his right, he barged at the door and fumbled for the light switch.

A tall figure was standing behind Polly, tightening the silk stocking around her neck. Polly had both hands round the stocking and was putting up a spirited fight. As soon as the light snapped on, the distracted killer lost his grip and Polly collapsed to the floor, coughing and spluttering.

Brett Bluit turned and looked straight at Joe and smiled.

'It's over, Brett,' said Joe softly, taking a step forward.

Joe wasn't prepared for the speed with which the boy turned and ran at the bedroom window, flinging himself at the glass and passing straight through it like something out of an action movie, before landing spreadcagled on the stone flags below.

Chapter 29

Emily rushed to the broken window with its jagged shards of glass protruding like a frame. 'Pity there was no double glazing – the bastard would have bounced off,' she said as she stared down at the limp body below, now the focus of attention of a dozen police officers, all milling about like sheep awaiting guidance. She shouted down to them to call an ambulance. However, the consensus of opinion was that Brett Bluit was dead.

'Oh bloody hell,' she whispered. 'He's just a kid.'

Joe bowed his head in silent prayer for a second. Then he knelt down by Polly who was half sitting, half lying on the floor, too shocked to speak, and put his arm around her, holding her thin, shaking body close to his, feeling the warmth of her skin through her pyjamas. He shouted to the young policewoman hovering by the door to fetch a drink – something stronger than tea.

'We should get her to hospital – she's in shock,' he said to Emily.

'Never mind that now,' Emily said, giving him an impatient nudge. 'What about this double event? Where's the person he sent the e-mail to?'

Joe's eyes widened for a second. 'Make sure Polly's OK, will you? I'm going to check on the kid.'

As he walked out onto the landing there was an

ominous silence. A thick, heavy quiet as though he were being watched by some unseen presence. Whether this presence was benign or malevolent, he couldn't tell, but it was definitely there.

The door to the bathroom stood open, revealing the sink inside, so the only other door must belong to Daisy's room. Joe grasped the handle and pushed it open quietly, not wanting to wake Daisy up and frighten her if she'd slept through the commotion.

But when the door opened his heart skipped a beat. A figure was silhouetted against thin curtains that glowed golden from the street lamp outside. It stood quite still, as though straining to hear what was happening in the rest of the house, a stocking stretched between its hands.

The figure turned and Joe saw that it was female but he still couldn't make out the face. 'Don't come any closer or I'll kill her,' she said in a hoarse whisper.

'It's over. Brett's dead.' Joe could see that the child in the bed was lying quite still. Either Daisy was fast asleep or he was too late.

He held out his hand. 'Come away from her. Come on.'

The girl by the bed shook her head vigorously. 'No way. You're lying.' She lowered the stocking and picked up a pillow that was lying by the side of the bed. She held it suspended above Daisy's head.

As the pillow began to descend, Joe stepped forward and grabbed Karen Strange by the arm. She began to swear, hissing beneath her breath like a viper. She was struggling and kicking out like a captive untamed beast and as Joe tightened his grip on her he felt a sudden pain in his hand. She'd bitten him, sunk her teeth into his flesh.

He managed to pinion her arms by her side and push her out onto the landing where she collapsed to the floor. She crouched there looking up at him, breathless and defiant as if she was about to spring at him like a wild cat.

Emily had just appeared on the landing and she grabbed the struggling Karen by the arm, calling for assistance while Joe rushed back into Daisy's room. He dashed over to the bed and touched the child's cheek, terrified of what he might discover. But when she stirred, he sent up a prayer of thanks. Daisy was alive and fast asleep, oblivious to the dramatic events happening around her.

Emily had handed Karen over to a constable to be taken to a waiting police car and now Emily was standing on the landing, breath held, unsure whether the news would be dreadful or welcome.

'She's OK,' Joe said in a whisper. 'She slept through it.' Before he knew it Emily's arms were around him, holding him close in that moment of precious relief.

They parted awkwardly, slightly embarrassed, and made their way downstairs, passing the doctor who had just arrived to pronounce Karen's accomplice dead and to check whether Polly needed medical attention.

As they stepped outside into the close Karen was being led away. Joe knew that he ought to wait until she was in the interview room with her solicitor present and all the tapes running, but he couldn't resist asking the question. 'Why, Karen? Why did you do it?'

Karen Strange was about to climb into the back of the car when she froze and looked Joe in the eye, a smile of triumph on her face. 'Because we weren't like all those little people with their little lives. We were someone. When you're dead, they'll remember us . . . write books about us. We made history.'

Joe found her words so appalling that he couldn't think of anything to say in reply.

Emily picked up a note that had been waiting for her on her desk. 'Harley Jones left a full confession – scribbled it down before he hanged himself. Gordon Pledge's conviction's going to be quashed.' She looked Joe in the eye. 'Just in time to go and comfort his wife and daughter.'

Joe didn't reply. It was none of his business now.

'No doubt there were plenty of film crews outside the prison eager to highlight the police's gross incompetence.' Emily buried her face in her hands. Joe knew she was exhausted. So was he.

Emily looked up. 'We'll start questioning Karen Strange first thing and I've got to go with Mrs Bluit to identify her son.' She glanced at her watch. 'Two in the morning. Good job Jeff's a tolerant man.'

'Do you want me to come with you to see Mrs Bluit?'

Emily looked at him gratefully. 'Yes please. I mean, telling someone their only son's dead is bad enough . . . but having to tell her he's also a wannabe serial killer . . .'

Joe gave her a sympathetic smile. 'I never considered Brett Bluit as a serious suspect, not till Caleb Selly's neighbours told Jamilla that he'd replaced that boy, Andy, on the decorating team. Then I started to wonder why Karen had kept so quiet about it.'

Emily shook her head in disbelief. 'I still can't understand what made them do it.'

'I believe they call it folie à deux. A psychologist would be able to give you chapter and verse.'

'No doubt.' She hesitated. 'Karen actually said killing was fun,' she said with disgust.

Joe sighed. 'Wonder if she'll still think that after her first ten years inside.'

Emily stood up. It was time to face Brett Bluit's mother.

Joe didn't arrive home until four in the morning. With everything that had happened, he'd pushed Maddy's return to Eborby to the back of his mind.

He was glad that she had decided to go straight back to her own house rather than waiting for him at his flat. He needed time to think. As he lay there in the darkness longing for sleep to come, he kept seeing Mrs Bluit's anguished face. It would have been easier if she had cried and wailed her grief, but instead she just stared ahead with wide, empty eyes and didn't utter a word. It was as though something in her had died. Emily had seemed to understand. She was a mother herself.

Mrs Bluit had had no idea what Brett had been up to. She had had no idea what he'd kept in his room because she hadn't been allowed in there for a couple of years. Brett was so clever, she kept repeating like a mantra. All the sacrifices she'd made to keep him at Hicklethorpe Manor – taking two cleaning jobs as well as her job at the supermarket – had been worth it because his teachers said he had a good chance of getting into Cambridge.

Perhaps Brett had been embarrassed by a mother who cleaned and worked at a supermarket checkout to pay for him to stay there while his classmates' mothers drove expensive cars. Perhaps he'd felt it set him apart somehow. Or was he just making excuses for the boy? Perhaps Brett Bluit had just been plain old-fashioned evil. Joe knew there was a lot of evil about – more than people imagined.

He lay awake till six then dropped into a fitful sleep until the alarm clock woke him at eight. He stumbled from his bed and made a strong coffee. He needed to see Maddy so he dressed quickly and walked the short distance to her small terraced house in a pretty street near Canons Bar.

He found her already up and dressed in jeans and baggy sweater. She looked pleased with herself and a little excited. As he sat down on her saggy leather sofa and accepted a cup of coffee, he felt reluctant to ask the inevitable question. But he couldn't avoid it for ever.

'Well?' he heard himself saying. 'Tell us about London.'

She played with a stray auburn curl for a few seconds

298

and took a sip of coffee before answering. 'I never thought I stood a chance. I mean the British Museum . . . you can't get much better than that, can you?'

Joe caught the passion in her voice and he knew what was coming. 'They've offered you the job?'

She looked at him for a few moments and he could see a flicker of uncertainty in her eyes. Suddenly he felt a glimmer of hope. She'd decided to stay in Eborby. But her next words made his heart lurch. 'It's a chance that only comes along once in a lifetime. There's a good train service from Eborby . . . only takes a couple of hours,' she said with what sounded like desperation. 'You can come down and see me most weeks.'

Joe put his hand on hers. 'Course I can.'

'And I'll be back quite often. I mean you're here and all my friends and . . .'

He took a deep breath. He hadn't known how he was going to feel when the news finally came and the depth of his emotion surprised him. He had taken Maddy for granted while he clung desperately to Kaitlin's memory. Perhaps this was his punishment.

'Congratulations anyway,' he said, although the words stuck in his throat. He took her in his arms and kissed her but after a few seconds she pulled away, a preoccupied half smile on her face.

'What about you?' she said suddenly. 'What's been happening with these murders in Singmass Close? The papers have been full of it.' Joe could tell that her mind was taken up with the new London job and that she was only asking out of politeness. How was your day? He gave her an edited account of the previous night but he didn't feel like going into detail. Maybe in a few days' time, he could face talking about it. In the meantime Mrs Bluit's pale face haunted him.

'What's the matter,' she asked, looking into his eyes.

'Well, it's just struck me that you're actually leaving.'

She turned her head away. 'Well, it was you who didn't want commitment.'

He opened his mouth to speak but no words came out. She was right, of course. It was his own fault.

'I'd better go,' he said and as he stood up he felt that he'd suddenly changed from lover to visitor; a subtle alteration but undoubtedly there.

He said goodbye to Maddy with a tentative kiss and made his way to the police station, trying to put her departure for London out of his mind. He'd have to face the reality of the situation soon but, in the meantime, he just felt like burying his head, ostrich style.

He walked down Gallowgate, past Singmass Close, now cordoned off with police tape after the events of the previous night. After showing his ID to the constable on duty he made his way to number six where another constable guarded the door. The Forensic team were still there examining the broken window glass scattered all over the stone flags, some of it stained with Brett Bluit's blood, but Joe avoided looking in their direction.

The constable on duty told him that Polly had gone to stay with her mother. There was nobody in the house. But as Joe glanced up, he was certain that he caught a glimpse of a pale face at the window. Either the constable was mistaken or his eyes were playing tricks.

He left the close and made for the police station. He hadn't realised until that moment of disappointment how much he had wanted to see Polly, to make sure she was alright.

When he reached the incident room Emily gave him a beaming grin as she told him it was her birthday – but not to tell the team because she didn't want a fuss. Jeff was arranging a babysitter so they could go out for a meal that evening so clearing up the case had come just at the right time. Joe was about to say it hadn't come at the right time for Abigail Emson but he bit back his words. It was good to see the DCI in such a cheerful mood. Over the past days she'd been under a lot of strain.

'Gordon Pledge is being released this morning. It's been on the news. There was a lot of bleating about how mistakes were made in the original investigation.'

'Just be thankful it wasn't our case.' He hesitated. 'I haven't heard the news this morning. I take it they reported what happened last night.'

'They just said an incident occurred in Singmass Close in which an eighteen-year-old man was killed and a woman arrested.' She pulled a face. 'I'm giving a press conference later this morning. Then all hell will no doubt break loose but I'll leave that to the press office till tomorrow.'

She picked up a sheet of paper and waved it in the air. 'We've got a positive ID on the dead girl at the Pledge's place. It's Leanne Williams all right. And the post-mortem appears to confirm the Pledges' account of how she died. But I'm keeping an open mind. Mind you, even if it was accidental, Sylvia Pledge is hardly blameless. She kidnapped her and forced her to work as a domestic slave. And she was drugged – that could have contributed to what happened. The CPS should throw the bloody book at her.'

'Presumably, Gordon didn't know what his mother was up to?'

'Do you believe that?'

'I think so. After all, he was in prison while most of it was going on. What about Alice?'

'Settled in the nursing home. She keeps asking when her little Michele's coming to see her.'

'So nobody's had the heart to enlighten her?'

Emily pulled a face. 'She probably wouldn't understand

301

if they did.' She paused. 'Apparently, Michele Carden's been saying she wants to see Alice. Looks like she became quite fond of the old girl in spite of everything. Funny how things work out.' She looked at her watch. 'Karen Strange is waiting in the interview room with her solicitor. You ready?'

Joe nodded, suddenly impatient to discover what had made a schoolgirl turn into a heartless murderer.

Karen leaned forward, her eyes shining, as though she was reliving some enjoyable party or concert. 'When we were painting the old man's place, Brett was having a nose around and he found this box in the attic.' She gave a small giggle. 'I thought they were fingers but Brett said they were toes.'

Joe glanced at the tape turning in the machine. Even the solicitor in the Paul Smith suit sitting by her side couldn't control the eager flow, although he kept warning her that she was saying too much. But Joe and Emily wanted her to continue . . . to let it all gush out.

'And you came across the diary?' Emily asked.

Karen nodded, a smirk on her lips. 'Yeah. It was hidden in the airing cupboard. We read it while we were eating our lunch – me, Brett and Nat. Nat said it was gross . . . the old boy had been a bloody serial killer.' Another giggle. 'Brett said he wondered what it would be like to kill someone and I said why don't we try it . . . just to see how it felt.'

'I really must warn you, Miss Strange . . .' the solicitor said firmly.

Karen raised her hand as if to brush him away like an annoying insect. 'No, I'm going to tell them. They want to know and I'm going to tell them.'

Joe glanced at Emily and saw that she was staring at the girl with fascinated horror.

'It was all in the diary . . . about the dolls and cutting off the toes and all that.'

'So you pinched some of the dolls?' Joe asked, trying to keep any emotion out of his voice.

Karen's smirk widened. 'Yeah. Then we had to decide who we were going to kill.'

'Go on,' Emily prompted gently. 'Why did you decide on Natalie? She was your friend, wasn't she?'

The lawyer turned to interrupt again but when Karen ignored him he slumped back in his seat. He'd done his best.

Karen snorted. 'She was a pain. She used to keep on about how she was earning a fortune and how she knew secrets about people . . . even about Cassidy. She thought she was so fucking great. I really hated her.'

'But you copied her,' Emily said. 'You even used to buy the same clothes.'

Karen looked away. 'Don't know what you mean.'

'I think a little part of you admired her. I think you wanted to be like her.'

'Fuck off.' She pushed her chair back hard and it scraped loudly on the interview room floor.

As Karen's solicitor put a warning hand on her arm, Joe and Emily looked at each other. Emily had hit a raw nerve. The identical handbag had been bought by Karen to emulate Natalie, not the other way round. Karen had been the subservient one. The dog that had turned on its mistress.

'What about Brett?'

'What about him?'

'What did he think of Natalie?'

Karen hesitated for a few moments. 'He really hated her. He asked her out once but she just laughed at him. She called him a loser.'

'But he hung round with her.'

Karen shrugged.

'What about the murders?' Joe asked quietly.

Karen giggled. 'That doll bit got you really confused, didn't it?'

'So it was all planned? Brett brought the doll to the club so you could kill Natalie that night?'

Karen grinned. 'He had it in his rucksack – left it behind one of the bins near Bluebell City till we were ready.' She gave another giggle. 'We reckoned you'd just think Caleb was up to his old tricks again. It was so funny . . .' She began to laugh then suddenly she clamped her hand to her mouth. But when she withdrew it, the amused smirk was still there.

Joe saw the solicitor give her a look of distaste. 'I think my client's had enough for now,' he suggested hopefully. The interview hadn't exactly been going Karen's way, Joe thought. He could almost read the solicitor's mind – if he could only have another firmer word with her, advise her how to answer and how to conduct herself, he might be able to limit the damage already done.

But Karen was having none of it. She ignored the man by her side and carried on talking. 'It was amazing. I can't begin to describe how it felt, deciding whether someone lives or dies. Watching someone walking down the street and thinking "she's going to die tonight". It's fantastic. I can't explain . . .'

'Why don't you try?' said Joe.

Karen's eyes darted between Joe and Emily, a ghost of a smirk still visible on her lips. 'You wouldn't understand.'

'Make us,' said Emily, barely able to hide her disapproval.

Karen thought for a few moments. 'It was like being high on something. You have this power over life and death and when anyone puts you down you think to yourself you don't know who you're dealing with. You're like

God. You decide who lives and who dies.' Her eyes were shining again. Joe had seen people like this high on drugs but never high on the ultimate power over life and death.

He opened his mouth to speak but thought better of it.

It was Emily who brought the proceedings back to the mundane. 'I'm a bit puzzled about the handbags,' she said. 'Did they really get mixed up at the club?'

Karen shook her head. 'No, it was when we . . .' She gave another small giggle. 'I dropped my bag and Nat must have landed on top of it. I picked hers up by mistake. The stupid bitch had seen mine and bought one just like it. Always copying me, she was.' Karen's eyes flickered from side to side. Joe knew that she was still deluding herself.

'Natalie thought you were her friend.'

Karen leaned forward and put her face close to Emily's. 'Friends don't put you down all the time. Friends tell each other secrets. Why didn't she tell me she was screwing Cassidy . . . and my own brother.' She sat back and shook her head. 'She was just a stupid cow.'

'How did you persuade Natalie to go to Singmass Close?'

'That was easy. I told her the place was supposed to be haunted and I said it'd be a laugh to walk back that way. I dared her. Me and Brett followed her but when I saw her talking to Chris in Mum's car I thought we'd have to call it off and do it another time. But then Chris drove off and . . .' Her eyes glowed with relish at the memory.

'What about the man you spent the night with?'

'I joined him afterwards back in The Devil's Playground, didn't I? Then we went back to his room.' She smirked. 'I tell you, I was ready for it. It was good. Best ever.'

There was a long silence, then Joe spoke. 'What about Abigail Emson?' he asked. 'What had she done to offend you?' He was finding it hard to keep the anger out of his voice.

Karen shrugged casually . . . maddeningly. 'We were waiting for the right person to come along . . . and she did. I called out to her and the silly cow had to come and see who it was. It was her own fault. That's all.'

'That's all?' Emily's voice was raised an octave. 'That's all. She had family and friends. People loved her and you just snuffed her life out on a whim.'

Joe put his hand on her arm. The last thing he wanted was for Emily to give the lawyer any reason to complain about the way the interview was being handled.

'And what about last night? Why did you and Brett want to kill Polly Pledge and her little girl?'

'Polly Pledge . . . is that her name?' She gave a little giggle. 'Polly Pledge, Polly Pledge,' she repeated as though she found the sound of the name amusing.

'Why did you try to kill her?'

The giggles stopped. 'We saw the kid looking out of the window on the night we killed Nat. Staring right at us, she was. When the police had gone we called at the house but there was no answer. I think they'd gone away. Then when we saw a light on in her house again we knew they'd come back and we couldn't take the chance of the kid saying something or identifying us, could we? And if we killed one, we'd have to kill both of them. Makes sense, doesn't it?' She said the words in a matter-of-fact voice that chilled Joe's blood. 'Brett broke in with a credit card in the afternoon while they were out. We hid in the coat cupboard under the stairs and waited for them to go to sleep.' Another giggle. 'We peed in the umbrella stand. It was so funny.'

She began to laugh again. Joe looked at Emily and guessed that she was fighting the impulse to slap the girl's face. Instead she spoke, loudly and clearly. 'Daisy Pledge, the little girl you tried to kill, wasn't at home on the night you killed Natalie. She was staying with her mother's friend. So you couldn't have seen a little girl looking out of that window, could you? There was a doll in the window but . . .'

Karen stopped laughing. 'You're a bloody liar. It wasn't a doll I saw. It was a little girl. All sort of pale she was . . . wearing white. She was there watching us . . . real as you are.'

'You must have been seeing things,' Emily said. 'Like I said, Daisy wasn't there that night.'

'Perhaps you saw a ghost,' Joe said with a smile, his eyes focussed on hers.

Karen Strange uttered an obscenity and leapt up, sending her chair flying. 'You saying I'm mad? I'm not fucking mad,' she screamed, clawing at Emily's face.

Joe pressed the panic strip and the alarm began to sound as he pulled the furious girl off the DCI.

'What do you reckon, Joe, is Karen Strange mad or bad?' Emily asked, sipping from a large mug of coffee, bought from a coffee shop nearby. The stuff from the machine was virtually undrinkable . . . and they were celebrating.

Joe had pondered the question since they'd interviewed her. Emily still bore the scars of battle in the form of a cluster of red raw scratches on her face, patched up by the doctor and now expertly covered with make-up. 'If I had to put money on it, I'd say bad,' he said. 'But I could be wrong.'

Emily put her hand up to her face and winced. 'Wonder what made Brett do it. He was brainy. He was bound for Cambridge.'

'But that wasn't what he wanted, was it? He wanted to keep up socially and sexually. And Karen was always in Natalie's shadow – the duller friend. That can really hurt at that age. Resentment and powerlessness can be a lethal mixture sometimes.'

She smiled. 'Ever thought of taking up psychology as a career? Funny about Karen swearing they'd seen the kid at the window.'

Joe hesitated. If he mentioned the ghostly children of Singmass Close she might think he needed psychological help himself. 'It's something that can't really be explained,' he said, hedging his bets. He paused. 'Has your Sarah still got this imaginary friend?'

Emily smiled. 'Grizelda? She suddenly seems to have faded into the background, thank God. Yesterday our Sarah went back to school after half term and she made a new friend – a little girl who's just moved into the area. She's called Kayleigh and so far Sarah thinks the sun shines out of her backside so . . . To tell you the truth, I reckon Sarah was probably lonely. When you think about it, she's not been at that school here very long. We'd taken her out of her old school in Leeds when we moved up here and . . . It takes time to make friends, doesn't it?'

'Problem solved then,' he said.

She gave him a weary smile. She looked exhausted. 'I keep forgetting to ask you about Maddy. How . . .?'

'She's taking the London job.'

He saw Emily open her mouth to say something but she thought better of it. Then, after a few seconds, she gave a forced smile. 'Hey, this doesn't mean you'll be applying for a transfer, does it?'

Joe shook his head and when he looked up at the DCI he thought he saw relief on her face. But it could have been his imagination.

Emily stood up. 'Look, why don't we both go home,' she said. 'Make a fresh start in the morning.'

Joe didn't argue.

Chapter 30

A month later

'You must miss Maddy.' Canon George Merryweather handed Joe a mug of strong coffee. The mug was chipped. But then George never noticed things like that.

They sat in George's office next to the cathedral chapterhouse and to Joe its homely chaos seemed strangely comforting.

'She'd given the move a lot of thought. It was too good a chance to miss. She called me yesterday. Everything's going well.'

George gave a small nod and waited for Joe to carry on.

'If she hadn't gone she'd always have wondered whether she'd done the right thing.'

'That's very true.' George took a sip of coffee then he looked Joe in the eye. 'I was talking to someone who knows you yesterday. She asked to be remembered to you.'

'Who?'

'Polly Pledge. She moved out of Singmass Close a couple of weeks ago. Her husband's just been released from prison.'

Joe nodded, wondering what was coming.

'Do you remember me telling you that she consulted me a while ago? Her daughter acquired an imaginary friend when she rented that house in Singmass Close?' He smiled. 'She said you were a bit of a hero, Joe. Said you saved her life.'

Joe gave a modest shrug. 'Me and a few dozen others.' He paused. 'Mary – the imaginary friend's name was Mary.'

'That's right. And there's an interesting little addendum to the story. Did you read in the local paper about a plumber finding the mummified remains of a child during the renovation of the old Ragged School? He'd been drilling through a part of the cellar ceiling and lo and behold a little skeleton tumbled down onto the cobbles in front of him. Gave the poor chap the fright of his life.'

'As a matter of fact we were called in – had to make sure the body was old . . . not our concern.'

George smiled. 'Of course.' He leaned forward, as though he was about to share a secret. 'I was called upon to give the poor child a Christian burial. And funnily enough it was on the day the body was buried that Mary disappeared. Polly popped in to tell me that Daisy suddenly announced that Mary had gone – at precisely the time of the funeral.'

'How is Polly?' Joe tried to make the question sound casual. But he saw that George was watching him intently, almost as though he'd guessed.

'She looked well. And she said she's seen her husband again. She says things are still awkward and he's still angry with her for not trusting him but . . . Perhaps in time there'll be some sort of reconciliation, who knows.' George thought for a few moments before he spoke again. 'I was shown an old exercise book that was found near the body of that child in the Ragged School. The child it belonged to had practised her name. Mary. She'd copied it over and over again in her best handwriting.'

'Mary was a common name in those days,' said Joe.

George didn't answer. He drank his coffee. It was all over. And one of the little ghosts of Singmass Close could now rest in peace.

When Joe walked home past the arch that led to Singmass Close, he couldn't resist making a detour to take a quick look. The rain had long since washed away Brett Bluit's blood and number six stood empty, a 'to let' sign outside.

He had seen enough. As he turned to make his way back to his empty flat, he thought he saw a movement just out of his line of vision; the impression of a ragged boy with a filthy face in the corner of his retina. A boy who'd been watching him with Brett Bluit's cold blue eyes.

He hurried on past the Ragged School and back onto Gallowgate. Too much solitude fed the imagination.

Don't miss Kate Ellis's
DI Wesley Peterson novels

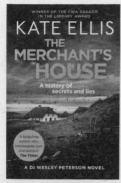
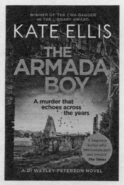

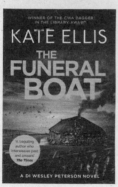
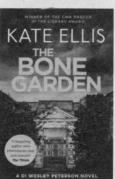

For a full list of the novels and to find out more
visit Kate Ellis online at:

www.kateellis.co.uk
@KateEllisAuthor

Discover Kate Ellis's mysteries in the
Albert Lincoln trilogy

To find out more visit Kate Ellis online at:

www.kateellis.co.uk
@KateEllisAuthor